ALTERIO'S MOTIVE

A NOVEL

DAVID CULBERSON

CALUMET EDITIONS

Minneapolis

CALUMET EDITIONS

Minneapolis

SECOND EDITION December 2022
ALTERIO'S MOTIVE Copyright © 2016 by David Culberson.
All rights reserved.

This is a work of fiction. Names, characters, places and incidents either are the product of the author's imagination or are used fictiously. Any resemblance to actual persons living or dead, events, or locales are entirely coincidental.

10 9 8 7 6 5 4 3 2

ISBN: 978-1-960250-07-0

To Brown Dog

Acknowledgements

Thanks to all who helped me with this effort at Calumet Editions and special thanks to Amy, Jordan, Mike and Jeff, who are always available to read and critique clunky first drafts.

About the Author

David Culberson grew up in small town middle America. After a higher education in a warmer climate, he spent much of the next three decades living and mixing with the cultures of the Caribbean, Mexico and Lake Superior, where he pioneered sustainable development and built several low-impact resort properties. He keeps a U.S. home on Lake Superior.

ALTERIO'S MOTIVE

A NOVEL

DAVID CULBERSON

Prologue

Fernando Munoz, better known as El Simpatico, liked feeding people to the sharks.

He currently stood on the lower stern deck of his one-hundred-and-ten-foot fishing yacht with a cup of coffee and an excited expression. He looked past the stern and into the pre-dawn horizon to see if he could see the mainland of Cuba. He couldn't be sure. It was still too dark.

They were a few kilometers from shore, drifting slowly with a northeast current over the deepest part of the San Antonio reef. The lightening eastern sky was evidence that the sun would show itself in the next twenty minutes or so.

Perfect time for feeding, he thought. The nighttime fish were going back into hiding, and the daytime fish were coming out to start their search for food. Sharks knew this too. Sunrise and sunset were the best times for them to find a meal.

"Turn the lights on," El Simpatico shouted.

The faint sound of a generator deep in the hold competed with the sound of the light surf sloshing against the hull and dive platform. Floodlights from the upper deck and bridge shown brightly onto the sea on all sides of the boat. The blood from a barrel of chum his crew had dumped into the water from the dive platform twenty minutes earlier drifted with the yacht and lingered in a milky cloud around the stern, the larger chunks of fish heads and animal parts having sunk or been eaten by the predators and scavengers that were attracted by the blood trail. Dorsal fins occasionally broke the surface as they swam back and forth in the cloudy murk, the floodlights reflecting off the watery, grey-brown skin.

"Atlantic sharpnose and a few blacktips," El Simpatico said, to nobody in particular. "They're all small."

He waited.

A few minutes later, he spotted a much larger shape gliding through the translucent water a few feet below the surface. He knew from its length what kind of shark it was. No other Caribbean shark grew to twenty feet or more.

"A tiger shark. A big one. It's about time."

El Simpatico had become an expert on shark behavior. He had been feeding them for years. He found it difficult to bring sharks near humans without chum in the water and something thrashing around in the middle of the chum. He had discovered that sharks were free-loaders, attracted to anything that can't fight back, thus representing an easy meal—like a wounded fish. They tend to shy away from humans, large animals that don't usually swim away. This is because humans, out of their element underwater and with limited peripheral vision because of dive masks, don't see the sharks until they are close and right in front of them. Then, most swim like hell to get out of the water. But humans are not a normal food source for sharks. They're too bony. Sharks like a big bite of meat, like the side of a yellow fin tuna. Sometimes, if a diver or swimmer doesn't see it coming, a shark will take a test bite to see if they are about to get a mouthful of meat. After they crunch down on a few of the hundreds of bones found in a human body, they let go and move on to look for a better meal. By that time, though, it's usually too late for the human.

El Simpatico watched the sharks a moment longer, hoping to see the tiger again. He turned toward the man who stood a couple of steps behind him. "Bring him, Joacho."

Joaquin walked to the doorway of the main cabin and shouted, "Vamos. Rapido."

Joaquin's two main henchmen, Raton and Nacho, came onto the deck leading a short, rotund man who wore nothing but dirty boxer shorts. His hands were bound behind his back with plastic ties and a rag was stuffed into his mouth. His legs were hobbled with a short nylon rope so that he could shuffle his feet just enough to walk. Raton and Nacho insisted on this after struggling to carry the fat man from their van to the yacht a few hours earlier.

When the fat man saw El Simpatico, his swollen eyes widened and a muffled scream came from behind the rag. He fell to his knees.

Perfect, El Simpatico thought. He smiled and said, "There is a lot of flesh on this man. All we need to do now is to make him thrash like a wounded tuna."

"He's heavy," Raton grunted, as he and Nacho tried to get the man to his feet.

"El Gordo. What the fuck kind of name is that?" Joacho said with a sneer and reached down to help his companeros lift the fat man.

El Simpatico enjoyed the fat man's terror. He walked up to the man, who stood a head shorter and said, "El Gordo... Joacho is right. What kind of name is that? It makes people in our profession look silly."

El Gordo fell to his knees again. His shoulders slumped as he sobbed behind the rag.

"Get him up."

Joacho and his two men hefted el Gordo up again.

"You weren't long for our profession, anyway, *el Gordo.* You should have stayed in Guadalajara as... what were you? A third-rate thug? Somebody's errand boy? Instead, you came to my territory to try to squeeze into my profits. And you thought I wouldn't find out? Que chingadera."

El Gordo shook his head violently back and forth, begging—pleading with his eyes. But he had little fight left in him. Raton and Nacho had seen to that during the four-hour boat ride to his final destination.

El Simpatico heard a splash behind him and saw el Gordo's terrified gaze move from him to the splash. He turned to see what the fat man saw. A large tailfin swished through the brightly lit water behind the boat. El Simpatico smiled and looked at Joaquin. "Cut him before you push him in, Joacho."

Joaquin took his folding pocket knife from his pants pocket and reached for El Gordo's left ear.

"Joacho. What are you doing? I don't want blood on my deck."

Joaquin nodded to the men holding el Gordo and motioned toward the dive platform. The fat man struggled against the two men, his eyes darting frantically from the water to El Simpatico and back.

When all four men were on the platform, a small shark surfaced and rolled back into the murk, splashing water onto the men's legs. El Simpatico smiled. Raton and Nacho leaned back toward the deck, their eyes as wide as el Gordo's.

"Hold him still," Joacho shouted.

He reached up and pulled el Gordo's right ear away from his head and cut it off. Blood ran down the fat man's face and dripped onto the platform, through the slats, and into the water. Joaquin threw the ear into the water, and it was snatched up immediately by a three-foot shark. El Gordo's muffled screams increased. He jerked harder. Joaquin stepped to his left and cut el Gordo's left ear off and threw it into the murk. It sank a couple of inches before a second, slightly larger shark disappeared with it. More blood dripped into the water below the platform.

Joaquin shouted, "Listo?" to the two henchmen. They nodded. Joaquin knelt and cut the nylon rope that hobbled el Gordo's legs. He stood and removed the rag from el Gordo's mouth. The screams were deafening. El Gordo slumped, held upright by Raton and Nacho.

El Simpatico sipped his coffee.

Joacho quickly cut the plastic ties around el Gordo's fat wrists and kicked him into the water. He momentarily sank and then re-surfaced, trying desperately to reach the platform. Raton and Nacho had jumped back onto the deck and laughed at the fat man bobbing and thrashing in the water. At first, all of the sharks swam away— but only a few feet. A four-footer was the first to return and bump el Gordo. He reached for the platform but couldn't hold on. El Simpatico reached down to the side of the deck, pulled a gaffing hook from the gunwale, and handed it to Joaquin. Another shark bumped el Gordo and he reached for the platform again. Joaquin shoved him away with the gaffing hook. Raton and Nacho laughed.

El Simpatico was getting bored. Where was the tiger shark?

El Gordo's head went underwater and resurfaced like a fishing bobber. The head went under and surfaced a second and a third time. Something was tugging at his leg. El Gordo screamed even louder, and the murky water turned brighter red. He continued to thrash and kick toward the platform. El Simpatico could see that el Gordo's right leg was missing below the knee. He turned and shouted into the main cabin for another coffee. The captain's mate came immediately with a fresh cup.

El Simpatico turned back to the feeding frenzy in time to see a blacktip shark bite into el Gordo's shoulder. It shook and twisted and was able to tear away a grapefruit-sized chunk of flesh and disappear into the cloudy water with its prize.

El Gordo was losing consciousness and was drifting from the platform to the edge of the light. El Simpatico was disappointed. He was ready to tell the captain to start the engines and back up to retrieve Gordo's body. Maybe he could be revived and tossed in again. Then he saw the dorsal fin of the tiger swim through the light toward what was left of el Gordo. The tiger moved close and slowly swam by the fat man. Four meters later it arched its large back, lowered its pectoral fins, turned around, and exploded into el Gordo's body. It was over in a moment. A final swish of its massive tail and the shark was gone—with el Gordo.

Joaquin laughed and stepped onto the deck. Raton and Nacho were silent. El Simpatico knew that these two violent men were accustomed to man-on-man death. They didn't seem to appreciate a graceful death by nature.

El Simpatico threw what was left of his coffee over the side and shouted, "Vamanos!"

The floodlights shut down and the engines kicked in seconds later. The yacht took a westerly bearing back to its homeport—Cancun. The sun had risen enough so that the clear outline of the western edge of Cuba could be seen. Joaquin stepped up to El Simpatico and pointed to the northeast.

"Cuban patrol boat, Jefe."

"Don't worry, Joacho. It will let us pass."

El Simpatico, thanks to his generous cash handouts, could freely navigate in and out of Cuba and its territorial waters. His yacht was well-known to the authorities. The patrol boat got within a hundred meters and turned around. El Simpatico smiled. *It is good to have so much power*, he thought.

"Joacho. Tell the captain to push the throttles to full. I want to be back in Cancun in five hours."

"Si, Jefe," Joaquin said, and started to walk toward the ladder on the port side of the lower deck that led to the bridge.

"And call the pilot. I want the helicopter ready when we get there."

"Jefe?"

"We have a meeting mid-afternoon with my good friend, the president."

"He is at his beach house?"

"Yes. And he wants to introduce me to a young man who he thinks we can do business with."

Joaquin hesitated and said, "Jefe, we know the people we can do business with. Why would the president think that he knows more than us?"

"This is a different kind of business, Joacho."

Joaquin waited.

"It is a possible land deal. You will see. Just get us there today."

"Si, Jefe," Joaquin said and left El Simpatico to watch the sun rising over Cuba and the wake left behind by the two-hundred-ton yacht.

Chapter 1

Alterio Delgado knew that his driver was frightened.

"Just keep going," he said. "Don't stop."

The driver had taken his foot off the gas and the SUV jolted slightly.

"No, no, no. Don't stop. They'll stop the van behind us. Don't worry."

Juan, a short, stocky Mayan, originally from a village near the Yucatan city of Madre, drove the beat-up SUV as fast as he dared on the narrow, sandy road. He could do little to avoid the myriad of bumps and holes in the road. His eyes were on the checkpoint and the soldiers a half kilometer ahead. Alterio knew they would be there. They always were. He knew they had weapons and would want the vehicle to stop. With difficulty, he turned in his seat and looked for the van that had been following fifty meters behind. He thought he spotted it through the dust and sand kicked up by his vehicle. He turned back to face forward and kept himself from bouncing against the door or hitting his head on the roof of the SUV by holding white-knuckled onto the worn plastic handle carved into the dash.

"Pedro's still behind us, right?"

Juan glanced into the rearview mirror.

"Si."

Alterio turned around again. He couldn't see much through the dust trail behind the SUV.

"Dry season. Damn. This road is rough. But we wouldn't be able to make the trip in rainy season. Are you sure he's back there?"

"Si."

"He's got the cooler, not to mention the dive gear and the putas."
Alterio turned around to look again.

The SUV had almost reached the soldiers. Alterio glanced right
and then left and silently cursed. There was no way to avoid them.
The road, if you could call it a road, was enveloped on either side by
thick, low-canopy jungle. To their right was a wall of impenetrable
vegetation. To their left, through several man-made cuts in the jungle, was an occasional glimpse of the Caribbean Sea and a few beachfront vacation homes sprinkled along the remote coast. Alterio saw
glimpses of a large, partially-built mansion. He recognized the grey,
concrete monstrosity. It had belonged to an infamous cartel leader.
All construction activity had ceased before any finishings, including
windows and doors, had been applied. The cartel leader was dead—
killed by his rival, *El Simpatico*, a few years earlier in Cancun.

Alterio looked ahead at the soldiers manning the checkpoint.
Military checkpoints are a pain in the ass. *Why is there always one on
this road?* But Alterio knew the answer.

He knew that several years earlier the dead cartel leader had
made a deal with his friend, the then governor, to acquire the land,
which was strange because it wasn't the governor's land to sell. It
wasn't anybody's land. The land had no title. It was ejido land—ag-
ricultural land confiscated by the government from wealthy land-
owners after the Mexican Revolution. The land was to be used by the
indigenous farmers and fishermen who had been employed by the
wealthy landowners until they lost their jobs when the government
took over.

Alterio wasn't sure who currently owned the land that the dead
cartel leader's partially-built mansion stood on, but after the death of
the cartel leader, and to demonstrate to the people that he was doing
his part in the war against drugs, Mexico's president demanded that
the governor place a small military roadblock on the sandy patch of
road in front of it. *Not that it accomplished much*, thought Alterio. The
cartels never used this bumpy stretch of nothingness to move drugs.
The Yucatan was too far away from the more direct route to the US
through the meat of the country where they shared a border.

"Keep going. Speed up. They won't shoot."

Alterio had guessed, hoped, that the soldiers were bored, maybe asleep. They would be surprised to see a vehicle, let alone two vehicles at the same time pass their palapa lean-to. Only one soldier stood guard. He motioned for the SUV to stop. The other three roused from their supine positions and were getting to their feet. None of them hurried. Alterio was relieved to see that none were prepared to fire rifles into his vehicle. He ducked anyway as they sped past the checkpoint and leaned forward enough to see their reflection in the mirror attached to the passenger door. All of the soldiers stood looking and held H&K G3 semi-automatic battle rifles. But their attention switched to the van that followed closely behind the SUV.

Alterio could hardly afford to be stopped and searched by a bunch of soldiers who weren't even from the Yucatan. Soldiers who manned checkpoints throughout the Yucatan were always from Mexico. He didn't trust any Mexican not from the Yucatan. He wasn't worried about running the roadblock and going to jail—he had far too many influential friends who would keep him out of jail, no matter what crime he might commit. He was worried that the soldiers would find the plastic bag full of cash and drugs he had stashed in a large cooler in the back of the van. He turned in his seat, looked around the interior of his cramped SUV, and wished there was room for the cooler to ride with him. He looked through the back window, through the dust and to the van. If it was stopped and the soldiers checked inside the cooler, they would happily confiscate the bag for their personal use and send the van on its way. They might even deem the Mayan driver a kidnapper and rescue one or two of the young putas for personal interrogation before sending them on foot back the way they had come. Alterio would lose his party favors and the money needed to keep the prostitutes alert and ready for the next three days. And his host, the president, would be disappointed.

Mexico's president kept his Caribbean home a couple of hundred kilometers south of Cancun. He loved his time at his remote Caribbean house and usually visited it without his wife. He relied on friends, or family members of friends, like Alterio, to subtly provide local entertainment and whatever else he requested. He had called Alterio a week earlier to tell him that he planned to spend one last hard-partying and diving weekend there before he was to leave office and would appreciate Alterio's ability to supply *provisions*.

"I told you they wouldn't shoot, no?" Alterio said.

He turned his head and leaned forward to look into the outside mirror again and saw his reflection, and relief.

"Si, but they stopped Pedro and his van."

"The soldiers will let them go after they get a good look at the putas, who'll give them a show."

"Should we stop and wait?"

"No. There's nothing between us and the village. No place to hide if we have to. Keep going."

"Si," Juan said, keeping his eyes on the bumpy road.

Alterio continued to hold on to the plastic handle as the SUV bounced down the bumpy road until it ended an hour later at the small fishing village of Punta Eek.

The village consisted of a few dozen thatched and metal-roofed wood and concrete shacks, one tier deep on either side of the sandy road. Behind the shacks on the right was a large, turquoise lagoon edged with thick mangrove. Behind the shacks on the left were the sugary, white sand beach and the blue water of the Caribbean. There wasn't enough land to build any more structures, and there weren't enough people to fill them if they could.

Juan parked the SUV near one of the shacks, which he claimed belonged to a cousin. Alterio had no idea how long the soldiers would keep Pedro and the van. He got out of the SUV to stretch. He stood in the hot sun and watched fishermen land their boats on the beach, where they started to offload the morning's catch of lobster and fish. Watching it made Alterio hungry, and hunger was his second favorite feeling. Satiated was his favorite.

Alterio told Juan to check on his cousins, especially the testy wife of the mayor, and walked across the sandy road to a shack that consisted of a palapa roof and one wall. Behind the wall were a smaller shack and an outdoor food prep area. Of the two restaurants in the village, Alterio preferred this one. He knew that the lady who owned it would have the best ceviche in the village. Her husband was the president of the ejido and had his pick of fish and lobster each day when the fisherman returned with their catch. The three white, plastic tables under the palapa were empty. Red and white checkered plastic tablecloths were held in place with conch shells and salt shakers. The sea breeze threatened to blow the checkered plastic from the tables and into the mangroves a few meters away on the edge of the lagoon. The mangroves were already littered with napkins and beer bottles and less recognizable old trash.

Alterio chose the table farthest from the road and eased his large frame into one of the plastic chairs, shifting the chair legs and his weight from side to side and front to back until they settled to an uneven conclusion in the soft sand. A small, clear plastic bag filled with water had been tied to a thin log that served as a roof rafter and hung a meter over the center of the table. It swayed lightly in the breeze. A thin, young waiter hustled out and placed his hands on either side of the table, using his barely noticeable weight to make the table as level as possible. Alterio leaned his body to the right and pulled his cell phone from his left pants pocket. There was no reception. He placed the phone on the table.

"Dame un ceviche mixto. Grande. Y una cerveza."

The waiter would probably have preferred to go through the normal routine of asking the customer what he would like to drink first. But Alterio didn't do normal well. The waiter nodded and disappeared behind the concrete wall that held up one side of the palapa roof. Two narrow tree trunks, which looked as though they had just been taken from the jungle, acted as posts and held up the palapa roof on the other side. Alterio leaned back in his chair to peek behind the wall where the waiter had gone. He saw a heavy Mayan woman chopping onions and tomatoes on a thick wooden table. The table was well used. Next to the table was a large black mangrove, which offered the woman just a little shade. Behind the black mangrove were red mangroves and then the blue-green water of the lagoon. Flies swarmed around the woman and the shiny fish that lay flat on the table. More flies swarmed over the fish guts and discarded scraps of food lying on the ground below the table.

The village was practically empty. Alterio saw no tourists. The only tourists who stumbled into this village were fly fishermen and young backpackers, and this was not the season for either. A few children played a hundred meters or so down the beach. A couple of village women walked by and paid no attention to Alterio. Most of the men had returned from the sea and congregated in a large concrete building fifty meters up the beach. Alterio laughed to himself as he stared at it. The building was a community center, the government's lone contribution to the little village. It was a poorly designed concrete building painted god-awful lime green and burgundy that took up space on an otherwise lovely beach. Hurricanes had destroyed most of the doors and windows and half of the roof. The men were huddled in the shade under the remaining half and were busy with loud conversation and beer.

The waiter returned immediately with a bottle of Sol and a plate of sliced limes. Alterio took a long drink from the bottle and set it on the table. His thoughts drifted to the military checkpoint, the unfinished mansion, and El Simpatico. He was known as the Teflon cartel leader. Everybody seemed to know who he was and what he did, but he was never arrested and never indicted. He moved freely around the country while government officials could prove nothing about his sordid activities. Alterio had seen photos in the newspapers of El Simpatico with famous people—actors, businessmen, and politicians. Tall and dashing, with a shock of white hair, most would think that he charmed his way into power. He didn't. He was brutal. He specialized in human trafficking, which was just as deadly or maybe a deadlier business than drug trafficking. Alterio had heard that El Simpatico's lieutenant, Joacho, was a psychopathic maniac who killed just as easily as he breathed.

The Yucatan was a small place with an even smaller wealthy elite, and because of the family Alterio married into, he could navigate in and out of it effortlessly. Alterio was glad that he had, so far, not met El Simpatico, who socialized with many of the same people and was known to be close to Mexico's president. Alterio shuddered at the thought that he might be with the president at his palapa now.

The waiter brought Alterio's order. He ate the ceviche quickly. He guessed that the fish was grouper. The shrimp was good. He liked the conch, but he left a few octopus arms on the plate and looked around for the waiter. He didn't see him. He turned toward the opening in the palapa where the heavy Mayan lady still chopped vegetables and fish.

"Joven!"

The waiter scrambled through the opening and up to Alterio's table.

Alterio thought he might enjoy another plate, this time conch ceviche, and a beer. Before he could order, he heard a car enter the village and turned to see Pedro park next to the SUV.

"Un momento," Alterio said, and pushed his plastic chair back in the sand and walked over to the van.

"What took you so long?" Alterio asked Pedro.

"They had big guns pointed at me."

"The bullets were probably fake."

"I didn't want to find out. Those soldiers were very young. And they were angry that you didn't stop."

Alterio looked into the van to make sure none of the putas or other cargo had been taken by the soldiers. He smiled and asked, "So what happened?"

"After I stopped, the soldiers split up and surrounded the van. They didn't say anything. They just stared at me. Then one of them pointed down the road and asked if I knew who was in the SUV that didn't stop. One of the putas in the back giggled. I don't think the soldiers knew they were back there at first. But they lost interest in me when they peeked into the windows in the back and saw all of the lipstick and tits."

Alterio opened the large cooler that Juan had taken out of the van. The plastic bag was still there. Alterio's smile widened.

Pedro continued, "Two of the putas lowered their tops and showed some nipple. The soldiers weren't angry anymore. At that point I knew that we were going to be okay. The soldiers encouraged the putas to show more."

"Did they?"

"A lot more. The soldiers lowered their guns and just looked at the putas with wide eyes. I figured that was a good time to leave. So I drove away. The soldiers didn't do anything."

"Claro. Wait here for the lanchas." Alterio returned to the restaurant. He sat at the same table and pulled out his cell phone. Still no reception. Flies circled Alterio's plate and landed on the octopus legs; he shooed them away. *So much for the water-filled plastic bag, Alterio* thought.*Mayans. Just because they invented the concept of zero they think they know everything*

Alterio looked around. "Joven. Joven."

The waiter appeared from behind the wall where he had gone earlier and bounced toward Alterio's table.

"Mas ceviche. Caracol y camaron. Y una cerveza."

"Si," the waiter said and disappeared.

Alterio heard the sliding side door of the van open and watched as the four putas stepped out into the hot sun. The tall one was the most attractive. She probably had some Spanish genes buried somewhere in her Mayan ancestry. She caught Alterio looking at her from the restaurant. The two youngest were very pretty Mayans and certainly under twenty years old. Any older and they would lose their waists and develop a boxy figure, like their older sister, the last one out of the van. Juan had told Alterio that she had insisted on coming along. Maybe the president likes the boxy shape of an older Mayan woman. Who knows? The other three would satisfy him for sure. They all wore slinky dark dresses and carried their heels. It looked like they shopped at the same clothing store. Alterio could smell the perfume as it drifted toward his table with the ocean breeze.

The waiter returned with two plates of ceviche ten minutes later. Alterio enjoyed the conch first. He saw Juan walking down the sandy road toward the SUV across the road. Alterio motioned him to the table. Juan explained that he had finished his obligatory salutations to his cousins and a few other villagers he knew. Alterio told Juan to sit and have a beer. He watched with amusement as his driver shifted from side to side until he rested his butt on the plastic seat.

"Joven!" Alterio shouted, "Una cerveza para, mi amigo! Con limon!"

The waiter quickly brought a beer and a plate of sliced limes and set them in front of Juan.

"Have you paid for the lanchas?" Alterio asked Juan.

"Si, my cousin will have two boats for us on the beach in a few minutes," Juan replied, nodding across the road where the captain of the first lancha forced the bow of his narrow boat onto the beach with a twist of the throttle of the outboard motor on the stern. In one motion, he shut the motor off and grabbed it by a handhold on the back of the plastic housing and lifted the lower unit out of the shallow water so the prop wouldn't gouge the sandy bottom. A few minutes later, one of the fishermen, whom Alterio had watched unload his catch of lobster earlier, maneuvered his lancha next to the first and lifted his motor out of the water as the bow slid up onto the beach. The two lanchas were just like every other lancha in the village, or any other village in Mexico. They were the same boat design he'd seen in other third-world countries. In some places they were called pangas. Here they were called lanchas—mono-hulled fiberglass boats about six or seven meters long, less than two meters wide, and powered by a small outboard motor.

"Couldn't you get us lanchas with tops?"

"No. They are all on the lagoon side of the village. They're for tourists to go up the canals and look at crocodiles and birds. These are fishing boats. They go faster with no canvas tops."

Alterio squinted at the sparkling sea and started to protest but knew it was useless.

"Claro. Have you talked to all of your cousins?"

"Si."

"Even the mayor's wife?"

"Si."

"What is the mayor doing?"

"The mayor is in Cancun. He'll be back in a couple of days. We can see him then. His wife told me that he will stop in Playa del Carmen to check on the permits for your land. She wanted to know how you became the owner. I told her that I didn't know."

"Good. It's better that nobody knows. Besides, I'm not the legal owner. You are."

"She claims that you stole the land."

"She should accuse you of stealing the land then."

Juan smiled but didn't seem too happy.

Alterio was always careful to put someone else's name on the title of land that he acquired through convoluted transactions. All of the transactions he was involved with were clouded with ambiguities and as much legal grey areas as he could convince the notarios to accept. On paper, anyway, he owned nothing. The comfort he got from that was deniability.

Alterio noticed some commotion across the street. Two local ladies were complaining to Pedro that the putas were not welcome in the village. The men in the community center and the fishermen still tending to their boats on the beach had stopped talking to each other and watched the putas. The putas shouted back at the two local ladies in Mayan. Though Alterio had Juan pick them up in Playa, he knew now that they were from small villages in the Yucatan.

"You better get the putas out of here," Alterio said to Juan.

Juan hustled across the street and said something to Pedro. Pedro led the putas down to the lanchas. Juan told the two village women to go home.

Alterio stood and left some pesos on the table. He took one last bite of ceviche and walked toward the boats, opening the passenger door of the SUV to grab his Tulane baseball cap on the way. At the edge of the surf, Alterio put his cap on, took his shoes and socks off, and rolled up the legs of his dress pants. He stood and watched the four putas wade through the gentle surf in their slinky outfits. The tallest puta turned and smiled at Alterio. They carried their black heels in one hand and hiked up their dresses with the other as they made their way to one of the lanchas. The captain smiled and lifted each over the side and into the boat, grabbing more ass than needed to accomplish the task. Pedro placed the dive gear and large cooler into the other boat. He took the women's overnight bags from the van and tossed them one at a time to the still smiling captain of the lancha that would carry the women. Both Pedro and the captain tried to impress the women with their effortless tosses and catches.

"Date prisa!" Alterio shouted.

The women sat on the two benches in the center of the lancha. They turned back and forth and talked simultaneously, oblivious to their spread legs and bunched up dresses as they gesticulated. Pedro and the captain stole glances and were further rewarded when one of the excited prostitutes fell back onto the bottom of the lancha when jostled a little too hard by her friend. All four laughed. A few nearby fishermen stopped what they were doing and watched.

Alterio looked at Juan and said, "You and Pedro ride with the women."

He wanted to be with the cash and the dive gear. He could care less about the young women wearing slinky dresses and too much makeup. They were noisy and Alterio needed to think. He waded to the other lancha and dropped his shoes and socks into the bottom of the fiberglass hull. He grabbed the side of the boat with both hands and lifted his left leg as far as he could toward the side rail. With the captain pulling on Alterio's belt from inside the lancha, he rolled over the side and into the boat.

Once settled on the wooden bench in the center, Alterio shouted, "Vamonos!"

Within minutes, the two lanchas filled with dive gear, putas, money, and drugs were in deeper water and heading south. Alterio turned back and watched the village shrink as they left the calm water and the protection of the world's second largest barrier reef and started across the choppy waters at the mouth of *el Bahia de la Ascencion*. He looked up, squinted at the sun, and turned to face the wind, removing his baseball cap before it was blown off. He silently cursed and wished that he could get to where he needed to go by car. He braced himself for the twenty-kilometer ride that would take him to his ultimate destination—a small spit of jungle and sand on the other side of the bay. On it was a luxury fly-fishing resort, and next to the resort was the president's beachfront palapa.

The trip across the bay would have impressed tourists. The lanchas passed a series of small islands that were proclaimed bird sanctuaries by the federal government. Scores of species of birds took off and landed on the mangrove branches and small beaches. Tourists would have wondered what kind of birds they were. Alterio wondered how he could get ownership of the islands and sell them. He thought homes or condos would look good surrounded by a bird sanctuary. All he would have to do was remove the mangroves and maybe bring in some more sand.

Forty-five minutes later, the lanchas approached the beach in front of the president's palapa. The house had been built so close to the beach that one could almost jump into the sea from the canti-levered upper deck. Behind the palapa was an expansive lawn that was part of an unearthed and partially re-built small Mayan ruin. The lawn served as a heliport for the president. Alterio glimpsed the

large, white presidential helicopter. A smaller, sleek-black helicopter sat next to it. He looked up to the second story deck. The president
stood with both hands on the wooden rail, watching the boats arrive.

There was no dock. The captains drove their lanchas onto the
beach. Alterio wished he was in better shape so he could jump from
the bow directly onto the sand, especially with the president watching. Instead, he would have to climb over the side of the lancha and
wade to shore. He was glad the seas were calm.

Chapter 2

El Simpatico, Fernando to the president, had been sitting with his longtime friend for over an hour. He pretended to be interested in the president's story, but as was his habit, he was thinking instead of ways to kill him. He always had a plan to kill everyone he met. The sound of outboard motors in the distance pulled him from a satisfying reverie wherein the president screamed in the red water as sharks tore pieces from his thrashing body.

"That must be our guest, Fernando," the president said with a smile. "He's bringing some local talent. You'll like them. Alterio is good at picking the prettiest women."

"I'm sure he is, Carlos, but I will not be staying long enough to enjoy them."

The president stood and walked to the rail for a closer look.

El Simpatico remained in his comfortable seat in the shade under a thatched awning. He reached for the ice water in a clear glass tumbler that had been placed on the low table in front of him by one of the president's servants a few minutes earlier. He could see just fine between the vertical balustrades of the rail. The captains of two lanchas steered the bows up onto the beach. One boat carried an overweight, barrel-chested man dressed in creased slacks and a pin-striped dress shirt who stood on the bow, seemingly contemplating jumping down to the sand. He wore a ball cap, a gorro, on his mop of black hair, rolled up trousers, and held dress shoes in his right hand. The other lancha was full. Besides the captain, there were two Mayan men. One was short and stocky, the other just short. Four young prostitutes, wearing skimpy dresses, stood in the center of the boat. The two Mayans jumped over the side of their boat and were struggling to lift a large cooler and dive tanks from the boat with the fat man still standing on the bow. They carried them onto the beach and returned to the other boat to help the prostitutes over the side.

The president glanced back at El Simpatico and nodded toward the women. He smiled when the women hiked their skirts up around their waists and waited their turn to be lifted over the side of the lancha and into the knee-deep water, where they chirped and giggled and waded the short distance through the surf onto the beach. They carried their heels. The two Mayan men carried their floral patterned overnight bags and placed them on the cooler. They let the women sort out whose bag belonged to whom.

The big man with the gorro stepped off the bow and back onto the deck of the boat and bellied over the side into shallow surf. He stumbled to shore. His pants had not been rolled up high enough and sea-water dripped onto the sand around his feet. El Simpatico heard him order the two Mayans to take the cooler and the putas to the guest house next door. He then ordered the captains to take the boats back to the fishing resort they had passed just up the beach until he called for them.

"That's Alterio," the president told El Simpatico, motioning for the barrel-chested man to join them on the deck. "He's the one I've been telling you about. You'll see."

Yes, I will see, El Simpatico thought and continued to size up the fat man with the handsome face. He thought it strange that he made the long trip across the bay with four putas and rode alone in a boat with only the captain as company. *Maybe he's mariposa.* It didn't matter. If this man that the president spoke so highly of was as talented and half as corrupt as the president had said, he could possibly represent a gold mine, and the fat man would probably never know it. Maybe, some day, he would need to kill this fat man. He would think of a creative way to do it and watch as Joacho carried it out. Maybe he'd have another mariposa tie him up and bite his dick off, then feed him to the sharks—still alive and bleeding from his dickless crotch. That would be interesting.

In what seemed like an afterthought, the president looked at Fernando and said, "Alterio might need a little comforting after he meets you. Please do your best to be nice to him. And for God's sake, don't introduce him to Joaquin just yet."

El Simpatico smiled. He sat back and watched the activity on the beach.

The president turned back to Alterio, who was making his way up the beach to the stairway that led to the deck. He shouted, "I saw your picture in the newspaper again." He continued to smile and watch the prostitutes walk under his deck to a path that led to the guesthouse.

One of the short Mayans struggled with the dive tanks and gear. The other dragged the heavy cooler behind him through the sand. Alterio temporarily disappeared when he reached the palapa. El Simpatico could feel the building shake with each step Alterio took on the exterior stairway that led to the deck. His head and its thick mop of black hair came into view through the rail as he came closer to the top of the stairway. He'd taken his hat off. Alterio paused for a moment at the top of the stairs to catch his breath. He puffed and said, "I guess they ran out of important people to interview."

"What did the article call you? 'NAFTA Boy'?" the president asked with a laugh.

"I guess that is better than 'fat boy,'" Alterio said. He smiled and playfully rubbed his large stomach. "That name has stuck with me since a magazine interview many years ago, during the NAFTA thing. I had just opened my retail stores."

El Simpatico took a closer look at Alterio. He took pride in his ability to size people up quickly—and rarely misjudged. He could tell that there was some Mayan blood mixed with his Spanish features, though barely noticeable, and he doubted that the fat man would admit it. He could also see that behind Alterio's charm and sparkling eyes was greed and ambition. Perfect.

"Excuse me, Mr. President. Just a moment please." Alterio shouted down to Juan, who stood in the sand below the deck. "Tell the women to rest. Set up the tanks. We may dive yet this afternoon."

Alterio turned back toward the president and said, "I'm sorry. I need to be sure that everything is ready for you."

"That's fine, my young friend. Let's talk for a while. How is your wife?"

"Very good, Mr. President. Thank you for asking."

"Please allow me to introduce my friend, Fernando Muñoz. We grew up together in Guadalajara."

Fernando offered a genuine smile and stood to greet Alterio. He knew what was to come in the next moment. He leaned in close and softly said, "Mucho gusto." There was recognition in Alterio's eyes. He took Alterio's hand, gave him a mild hug, and stood back to shake his hand again—the Yucatecan way, just as the president had done a moment earlier. Only this time Alterio said nothing. Fernando was used to it. It was just one of the many pleasures he enjoyed as *El Simpatico*.

The president slapped Alterio's shoulder and shouted for his servant to bring ice water for Fernando and a shot of tequila for himself and Alterio.

"Please sit," the president said, motioning toward the empty chair opposite the sofa where El Simpatico settled once again. "I'm happy that you have arrived when you did. I've thought about introducing you two for a while now," the president said and nodded toward Fernando. "Fernando has many business ventures in Mexico, and he's always looking for new opportunities. A young entrepreneur, especially one as successful as you, Alterio, might benefit from Fernando's financing ability and contacts."

El Simpatico nodded toward Alterio and watched him sweat. He then turned his head toward one of the two large openings that led into the spacious interior of the palapa and called out something Alterio didn't catch. A medium-height, wiry man wearing a white dress shirt, dark slacks, and a smirk came through the opening. He looked at Alterio like a lion looks at its dead prey, wondering where exactly in its soft underbelly it would tear its teeth into first.

"Joaquin. Please tell the pilot to be ready in one hour."

The president looked at Fernando, clearly displeased that he had brought Joacho in so soon.

Fernando smiled.

Joaquin retreated into the palapa without taking his eyes from Alterio. Alterio's eyes darted from Joaquin to the floor and back again, until Joaquin disappeared from his view.

Fernando looked at Alterio and said, "I understand that you own several successful hardware stores."

"Uh, yes. Just a few."

"But I understand they are a financial success, no?"

"They do all right."

"Just all right? I heard that you have revolutionized the way we do business here in the Yucatan... that your stores are like the stores we see in the US."

"Thank you. But there is talk that one or two of the large US stores want to set up franchises here in Mexico. It could be difficult for me."

"Fernando, don't let Alterio's charm and boyish looks fool you. He is as smart and as ambitious as anybody I've met. And he has a talent for understanding how business really gets done here in the Yucatan." The president placed his hand on Alterio's forearm. "Isn't that right, Alterio?"

"Thank you, but I think that you are too generous with your praise."

Joaquin walked back out onto the deck. He stared at Alterio. When Joaquin blinked, his eyelids slowly closed and opened—reptilian eyes. El Simpatico smiled at Alterio and then turned his attention back to Joaquin.

"Excuse me, Jefe. The pilot will be ready. He needs to know where we are going."

"Thank you, Joacho. I'll let him know after we're in the air."

"But, Jefe..."

"That's all, Joacho."

Joaquin sneered at Alterio before disappearing back into the palapa.

El Simpatico turned to Alterio again and said, "I'm sure that your businesses will compete well with other stores, if they choose to enter this market."

"Yes. Thank you El... Señor Muñoz."

"*Fernando* will be fine, Alterio. We are equals here," El Simpatico replied, staring at Alterio with a frozen smile.

Alterio had no reply. He wasn't comfortable in the presense of El Simpatico and struggled to maintain his composure.

The president snapped his fingers and a servant appeared from the palapa's interior. "Dos cervazas, por favor. We'll change to beer. Is beer okay with you, Alterio?"

Alterio glanced at his untouched tequila and said, "Yes, that would be fine, thank you."

The president looked at Fernando's glass and told the servant, "Y un vaso mas de agua."

The servant went to get the drinks.

The president sat back in his chair and looked out across the sea. He said, "In a couple of weeks I'll be retired from politics."

"Are you looking forward to that?" Alterio asked.

"I will miss the excursions, especially to this house... and the diving... and the girls." He laughed.

"But you can still enjoy these things, no?" Alterio asked and glanced at El Simpatico.

El Simpatico smiled and gave a questioning look toward the president, acting as though he was interested in this conversation. He didn't give a damn. This president would be gone in a few weeks, and he'd already made inroads with the president-elect.

"It will be harder. I don't know if I will even stay in Mexico. With the corruption rumors, especially surrounding my brother..." The president sighed. "Let's just enjoy this weekend. It is great diving weather and the girls look beautiful."

"But... I could still bring women and dive gear..."

The servant brought a tray with two bottles of Sol and cold mugs. He placed a mug in front of each man and poured as much beer into them as they could take without foam spilling over the top. He set the half empty bottles of beer next to each mug and then placed an ice-filled glass of water in front of Fernando.

"My young friend, you do not understand the complexities of a man on a pedestal. I am afraid that after I leave the office of the presidency, I will not be able to move around this country in the secrecy needed to maintain this lifestyle that I enjoy so much," the president said as he looked ponderously at the light surf breaking on the beach. "And my wife," he continued, "she is always looking for ways to catch me in the middle of one of my little infidelities. I have reasonable protection from her snooping as long as I am president. But afterward..." The words faded as he looked down at the floor. After a moment he laughed and held his mug up. "Salud."

"Salud," Fernando replied.

"Salud," Alterio said.

Alterio fidgeted.

The president leaned back in his chair. "You seem hesitant, my friend. Do you have something else to ask?"

"I have been hearing rumors. I just bought a lot of Christmas inventory from the US for my stores, and I have taken a big risk by doing so. If the peso falls... well... is our economy in good shape?" Alterio asked.

The president smiled at Alterio. "You have done very well for yourself, especially at such a young age. I am confident that I will be leaving the country in very good economic shape. You will do fine. Your stores will thrive." The president took a drink from his mug.

Alterio smiled and said, "Just one more thing."

The whining sound of a jet engine helicopter starting up drifted from the lawn out back, through the palapa, and to the deck.

"Yes?"

"I have been thinking about getting out of the retail business. And—"

"But you just got into it, and I just told you that the peso will remain strong," the president interrupted.

"Yes, but I'm worried about the large retail chains moving in. And I've been thinking for a long time about either going into politics or becoming a developer," Alterio said.

The president glanced at Fernando. Fernando smiled and gave the president a slight nod.

The president leaned back in his cushioned chair and said, "You know, politics in Mexico are complicated. I think you would be good at the political game. But it is a dangerous game." The president took a long drink from his mug and said, "But development... ah, there is an interesting opportunity. Besides the growth we expect here along the Caribbean coast, I think there will be much opportunity with ejido land. Some time ago we offered to privatize all of the ejido land and give the local ejiditarios the title to the land. They can sell it legally or lease it, or form partnerships to develop the land."

Alterio seemed to ponder this and, after a long moment, asked, "This land is free for them? It's a gift?"

"Yes. That's what Fernando and I were just talking about."

The president glanced at Fernando. Fernando turned to Alterio and asked, "Do you know about real estate?"

"My family owns a lot of land. I've been involved with some of their transactions."

"Some of the parcels are quite large and have wonderful beaches. A smart developer could get control of this land and build a large resort area," Fernando said, taking a drink from his tumbler. He watched Alterio and knew that he was already thinking about all of the land he could control. "This... opportunity... is interesting. But for me... I don't know. I know little about real estate." El Simpatico shrugged and said, "I would need a partner in such ventures. Somebody to find and secure the land."

The president interrupted and said, "What my friend, Fernando, is saying is that he doesn't usually dabble in real estate. A man of his reputation... well, let's just say that he doesn't have time to find land deals that work for him."

El Simpatico smiled, looked at his watch, and said, "It seems like a young man's game, something that maybe you would be good at. Perhaps the next time we meet you will be a wealthy land developer."

Alterio swallowed hard and seemed to fumble for a response. He said, "Perhaps. Thank you." His eyes darted from El Simpatico's to the floor.

El Simpatico smiled and relished the fat man's discomfort. He winked at the president. The seed had been planted.

The president looked toward the guest house and said, "I'll tell you more about ejido land opportunities later. Fernando needs to leave in a few minutes, and we have to attend to the pretty guests you brought."

Alterio sat up on the edge of his chair and asked, "But just one more thing about ejido land...?"

"We have all weekend." The president smiled, leaned forward, and patted Alterio's knee. "Let's have some fun first. Are you going to join the party this time, Alterio?"

"But…"

"Alterio, you never partake in the fun part of our visits. You leave the women alone and only drink when I offer you something. You should relax. Life is short. Enjoy the good things in life."

"But… how much ejido land has been privatized?"

The president looked at Alterio and Fernando and eased back into the chair. He said, "Not much. The locals who live on the land are peasants—farmers and fishermen with little education. They don't understand the concept of individual title. All of the ejidos initially rejected our offer to do all of the legal and surveying work so that they could get titles from the Reforma Agraria. We have convinced a few entrepreneurs to step in and try to convince the ejidos to work with them to get titles to the land. It is important to the government that this land becomes private land. It will be more economically advantageous for them and for us. And the laws are clear—the titles must first go to the ejiditarios."

"Have any of the entrepreneurs been successful?"

"A few. But there is a lot of ejido land left to privatize. Almost half of Mexico was once ejido land. Not many people know that."

"But this must be expensive and take a lot of time?"

"Yes, it does take time. The land must be sub-divided and the legal work—well, my friend, this is Mexico. The legal paperwork is forever. The right people must always be taken care of… You know what I mean," the president said, with a slight shrug.

Alterio smiled.

"You would be very good navigating your way through the bureaucracy. And you could use your charm to get the ejiditarios to cooperate with you."

El Simpatico looked at his watch again. As far as he was concerned his business was done here. The seed had been planted.

The president looked toward the guest house—again.

"But, one more thing. How does the entrepreneur get paid?" Alterio persisted.

"With land, Alterio. The ejidos will have a lot of land. You can demand some of it as payment for your efforts. You could become wealthy, particularly if you choose to work with the ejidos who have land with beachfront, or an island. And if you need money for all of the legal and surveying work needed, you could ask Fernando to be your partner."

Joaquin walked onto the deck and nodded to Fernando.

El Simpatico stood.

Alterio fidgeted and looked at the president.

"Claro. Just one more thing."

But the president was no longer paying attention to Alterio.

The sound of a helicopter reverberated throughout the palapa. What started as a low, chopping rumble quickly turned into the full-fledged sound of the blades of a helicopter—close by. It wasn't the sound of a jet engine. It was a larger aircraft. And it had the president's complete attention.

"Mierda. It's my wife. She has the second presidential helicopter this weekend. She told me she was going to Cabo. Shit! You need to hide the girls!" the president shouted to Alterio.

El Simpatico laughed all the way to his waiting helicopter, passing Mexico's first lady on the way. She paid no attention to him.

Alterio scrambled to get the girls off the island before the president's wife found them. He failed.

Three weeks later the president was out of office. A short while after that he was divorced and had moved to Ireland.

Chapter 3

Arlan O'Brien walked up three brick steps to a revolving door he had passed through scores of times in the past couple of years. He unbuttoned his jacket and pushed at the heavy door, which was sluggish from the collection of dead leaves. The door picked up momentum as Arlan shuffled forward in the pie-shaped space between wood and glass panels and, with a slight hop, he was inside. He looked around the 1800s-style, wood-trimmed room, typical to the Washington, DC area. He saw that most of the booths around its perimeter were empty.

Good, he thought. A quick gaze at the two bartenders serving drinks from inside the rectangular bar in the middle of the room and the empty bar stools in the far corner showed him all that he needed to know.

"Hey, Arlan, what's up?" Bruce asked. He'd already placed a beer on the bar in front of Arlan's stool.

Arlan thanked Bruce, sat down, and squeezed the lemon wedge into his mug of light beer. It was early in the evening, the best time for him to come in for a couple beers before the place filled up with a younger, noisier crowd.

This bar was one of many establishments located in historic Old Town Alexandria. It happened to be within staggering distance of his rented flounder just a couple of blocks away and offered him an occasional refuge from loneliness after his recent divorce and move back to the US from the Caribbean.

Not only did Bruce allow Arlan an unofficially reserved seat, he knew most of the patrons. Bruce let Arlan know which of the pretty ladies were available and which ones to stay away from—even if they were available. Arlan only challenged his vast knowledge once. She was beautiful and fun, and she stole his credit cards while he slept. From then on, Bruce's judgment ruled.

"Hey, I got this guy coming in who travels to a lot of weird places, just like you. He owns an adventure travel business. You two probably have shared a lot of similar experiences—wrestled alligators, fought off herds of Kodiak bears, ran with pirates... that kind of thing," Bruce said with a smile. "He's an interesting guy and knows of some of your real estate developments in the Caribbean. He says that he's visited some of them."

"That was my last life. I live here now."

Bruce shrugged. "Maybe he's got a new adventure for you. He told me that he was working on a land deal in Mexico someplace. That's when your name came up. Anyway, you should listen to what he's got to say. I'd hate to lose your business, but you've been moping around here too long."

"Mexico? To hell with that place."

"Bullshit. You'd give your left nut to be back there."

"The Caribbean, maybe. But not Mexico."

"Yeah, right," Bruce said with a smirk.

Arlan hadn't ever fooled Bruce. Arlan's recent divorce and the fact that the once charming little island that was his home for fifteen years now resembled a chock-full Monopoly game that had been allowed to play way too long, brought him back to the US a few years ago; but he longed to be back in the Caribbean. It was on his mind daily, as it was right this moment.

Three thirty-something women entered and sat at the bar opposite Arlan. Their giddy interaction and big smiles at Bruce indicated that they were probably regulars—at least on weekends. Bruce gave them a head nod, grabbed three beer mugs from the freezer below the bar, and headed to the tap closest to their side of the bar. One of them sneaked a glance in Arlan's direction.

Cute, but not tonight honey.

Arlan's thoughts went to Captain Jay, who, once upon a time, was his circumstantial friend and mentor, but not in the conventional way; circumstantial because they lived in the same small community in the Virgin Islands at the same time; nonconventional because Captain Jay was the unofficial king of the island. It was his show. And he took it upon himself to mentor Arlan the first day he jumped off the ferry and into paradise. Captain Jay was a lovable, larger than life, modern-day pirate. Generous to a fault. And reckless. Dangerously reckless. Captain Jay had tested Arlan by fire, almost getting him killed several times. But Captain Jay's tutelage, if you could call it that, gave Arlan the confidence to learn how to survive, even thrive, on the island. In a few short years of the early eighties, as the world was quickly changing and when the Caribbean was being discovered by the modern, affluent traveler, characters like Captain Jay found that they had worn out their welcome.

Partially because of this new immigration, but mostly because of a few more nefarious events, Captain Jay had imploded, barely escaping death on his way down. Arlan hadn't seen him in years. The last Arlan had heard, Captain Jay was somewhere in Belize.

Arlan's thoughts were interrupted by a slight brush against his shoulder.

"Sorry. I was trying to hang my jacket on this hook. I know it's here somewhere," the newcomer said and leaned forward on the edge of the stool, his left hand blindly searching for the hook along the underside of the wooden bar top.

Bruce came over with a mug of beer and placed it in front of the man who rubbed his hand back and forth along the underside of the bar, still searching for a coat hook.

He looked at Arlan and said, "This is the guy I was telling you about. Arlan, meet Greg."

Greg hung his jacket on the unseen hook and adjusted his weight back onto the stool.

"Thanks, Bruce." He turned to Arlan and offered his hand.

"Nice to meet you."

"Same."

"Bruce told me about you and said that you'd probably be here tonight. I've stayed at some of the places you developed in the Caribbean," Greg said.

"That was a long time ago."

"I was in your part of the Caribbean just a month ago, after the hurricane. Most houses lost their roofs, or worse. All of your projects were still standing. They didn't seem to have *any* damage."

"I had a few good people around me. They were more responsible for those buildings still having their roofs than I. Hell, I didn't know what I was doing when I built those places. I was way too young to know much about anything."

Arlan looked at his beer and said to nobody in particular, "I still don't know much about anything."

"Well, you did something right. The places you developed are architecturally way better than anything else I saw. They survived the hurricane intact, and they seemed to be the most popular places I visited. I'm not talking about popular with the everyday tourist. I'm talking about the tourists who seem to know their way around. The ones who respect the local culture. The ones who want authenticity. You provided it."

Arlan shrugged and turned toward his beer. "I guess so."

Greg talked about many of the places he took paying guests and his favorite places to visit. All were physically demanding and not found on the normal tourist brochure.

"You've traveled a lot," Arlan said.

"And you haven't?"

"Yeah, but my favorite place in the world has always been the Caribbean, and I never saw a good reason to venture much farther for any length of time."

"I have a trip planned to the Yucatan in a couple of weeks. Ever been?"

"Yeah."

"Ever been to the Sian Ka'an or kayaked down the Mayan built canals?"

"No. I was pretty busy with a land deal that went south."

"There are canals carved out by the Mayans a couple of thousand years ago. They're crystal-clear fresh water with a slight current. They start just south of Tulum and flow through a series of estuaries on their way to the Caribbean. It takes an entire day to reach the sea. And that's paddling hard," Greg explained. "The canals are filled with big tarpon and an occasional crocodile swimming below you. At the end of the canals is Punta Eek, a little village sandwiched between the Caribbean and the *Bahia de la Ascencion*. Great little fishing village."

Greg took a drink and said, "I've got a little kayaking business near Tulum. I rent a house on the beach and run tours from it. But an investor friend and I have been looking at some land near the rental home. We want to buy it and build a small hotel. Neither of us knows how to go about that. This is the kind of thing you do, right?"

"Kind of."

"How much would you charge us to take a look at the land and give us some design ideas?"

"I don't know if that's something I'd be interested in."

Bruce came back and took away their empty mugs. He brought two fresh beers, leaned over the bar toward Arlan and said, "I heard that. It's bullshit. You're the only person in this bar who doesn't know that you're begging for an opportunity to go to Mexico or the Caribbean or wherever it is that you swim with sharks and run with pirates."

Arlan shrugged and took a drink. "Is this a job offer?" he asked Greg.

"Well, yeah. We're working on a tight budget, and I thought that maybe you wouldn't charge as much if I could offer some adventure along with a trip to Mexico."

Bruce gave a thumbs-up to Arlan and turned to take drink orders from a couple that had just arrived.

"While we're there we could pick up a couple of spearguns from my buddy who watches my business and kayak out to the barrier reef and spear some dinner. It would be a good time. I'll show you around and introduce some locals."

"Thanks, but I don't need any introductions."

Two attractive women came in and sat next to Greg. Greg smiled at Arlan and turned his attention to the ladies.

Arlan thought about the offer—and Mexico. Unfortunately, he already knew a lot of the locals in that part of Mexico. Not too many years earlier he had gone to Mexico's Caribbean coast at the urging of a wealthy conservationist who wanted to buy a large tract of land a few kilometers south of Cancun. It was in the path of a development boom, and he wanted to save it from being turned into a mass of hotel rooms and swimming pools. The land consisted of several kilometers of beach and hundreds of hectares of mangrove and savannah. Arlan's job was to create a low-density development model that would preserve the beaches and leave the mangroves intact.

Greg leaned toward Arlan and said, "Nice, but a little stuck up."

"What's that?" Arlan asked, refocusing on the present.

"The women," Greg whispered and nodded to his left.

"Oh."

"What about Mexico? What do you think?"

Arlan took a long swallow. "It's not my favorite place."

Greg frowned.

"The place is corrupt—top to bottom. Just another pirate's paradise. Shake hands with some of those characters down there and you better start counting your fingers."

"Jesus. I guess you really like Mexico."

"I like a lot of the people. The culture is interesting—ancient Mayan, colonial, and modern. But there's a good reason why it's still the third world."

Arlan hadn't noticed that Bruce had returned with a bar towel over his shoulder and two more beers.

Arlan struggled to focus on the fresh mugs of beer on the bar in front of him and said, "Shit. I guess we have to drink these."

"As if that's a chore?" Bruce replied. "Sounds like you need it."

"Sounds like he doesn't like Mexico," Greg said.

"No. It's not like that." Arlan already felt a little more than a buzz from too many beers. Just enough to let loose the diatribe that had been festering for a couple of years.

"Look. Same as you, I've been around. But I've never experienced the depth of corruption that I ran up against in Mexico." Arlan thought for a moment and added, "The corruption in Belize might be worse, more overt anyway. Belizean politicians think small... but it's all the same. Why do you think all of that land and beaches up and down the Caribbean coast of Mexico and Belize are fucked up beyond recognition?"

"Belize?" Greg asked. "A friendly place. It doesn't look so fucked up to me."

Arlan took a drink and smiled. "Yeah? You should look a little deeper. I had lunch once with a group of Mexican businessmen and politicians in Chetumal. Do you know where that is?"

"Of course."

"So I asked these guys if they ever did any business with Belize. It's right across the border. All of the Mexicans at the table laughed or snickered. I asked what was so funny. One of the Mexicans said that Belize is too corrupt, that they could never do business with Belizeans." Arlan took a long drink and set his mug back on the bar. "Can you imagine that? Mexicans calling Belizeans corrupt?"

Greg laughed.

"Don't laugh. They were right."

They each took a drink from their mugs. Arlan had stayed too long. It was getting hard to hear himself talk.

"What about buying land in Mexico? I've heard that most of the land is communal and Americans can't get title, something like that."

Arlan looked at Greg. He saw a nice guy who was about to make a big mistake and lose a lot of money. He needed help. Fucking Mexico. He finished his beer and let loose.

"Americans can get title if the land *has* title. If the land is within thirty-one miles of the coastline, they have to own it through a Mexican entity, like a bank trust or a Mexican corporation. In theory, the system works. The problem has been, though, that too many Americans buy land that they are told has title, but it really doesn't. And, even if it does, titles are easy to steal in Mexico."

"You know this firsthand?"

Bruce came over with two beers and looked around the bar. He must have been satisfied that everybody's drink was in good shape. He put his elbows on the bar, crossed his forearms, and joined the conversation.

"Yep. I know… firsthand."

"You've been burned?" Bruce asked.

"I haven't, but an investor friend of mine was. I was in the middle of it."

Arlan turned to Greg and said, "The communal land you mentioned is called ejido land. You'd better hope that the land you're looking at is not ejido. If it is, stay away from it."

"I've heard of it, and people have tried to explain the concept to me... but I just don't get it."

"The government created ejido land after it took it from the wealthy hacienda owners many decades ago. They proclaimed the land as *the people's land* and let the employees who used to work for the wealthy land owners live on it, farm it, whatever. But it wasn't their land. It belonged to nobody. Before long, agriculture production shrank to nothing. Most of the land sat idle, and after a few decades it turned back to jungle, sprinkled with a few subsistence farms. That didn't keep the locals from illegally selling some of it though, particularly beachfront land. Some parcels were sold—to different buyers at the same time."

"What?"

"I'm not kidding. During the seventies and eighties, when tourists discovered Mexico, many fell in love with the place and, after a few visits, asked around about buying land or a beach palapa. Unscrupulous locals showed the tourists some land they claimed that they owned, presented accompanying paperwork that looked official, and quoted prices that were too good to pass up. Many foreigners bought the cheap land and built vacation palapas, or purchased land with existing palapas. The new buyers visited their palapas a few times a year. Sometimes other buyers who bought the same palapa showed up at the same time. Fights broke out. Often the police were called, and they routinely kicked foreign buyers out of the palapas. Attorneys representing the locals who illegally sold the land to the foreigners produced legitimate paperwork from a federal government agency, Reforma Agraria, declaring that only members of the local ejido, ejiditarios, could use the land where the palapa stood. Because the deals were never recorded properly, the ejiditarios didn't have to return the buyer's money. 'Thank you for our new home,' the ejiditarios would say as the foreigners left the country."

They both laughed.

"Anyway, around the same time as the NAFTA agreement was signed, the Mexican government determined that the ejidos were economically unproductive and that all ejido land needed to become private land, to be put on the real estate tax rolls. As additional incentive, the government declared that the ejiditarios will receive title to the land they lived on—free, a gift from the government to the downtrodden peasants of the many ejidos around the country. So a lot of land in the Yucatan has been or is being privatized, not by the government, but by wealthy businessmen who pay for the surveying and mountains of legal work in return for some of the land. The process is a mess. All of the bad apples have risen to the top. Land has been extorted, stolen, and extorted again."

"Who's extorting it? The attorneys?"

"Yeah, and the ejiditarios—all of them."

"Is that what happened to your friend?" Bruce asked.

"Something like that. My friend, Mike, spent decades diving off that coast and the barrier reef, all the way down to Honduras. After witnessing the damage to the barrier reef from construction and aquaculture run-off and trash, even suntan lotion—hell, anybody who has been diving in any ocean for any ten-year period is appalled by its degradation—he decided to use some of his wealth to try to save as much of the reef as possible from further destruction. He negotiated to buy a sizeable piece of land from the local ejido, who had taken the offer to privatize. He hired attorneys and researched the laws that governed the land. He thought the laws were fair and would be enforced, if needed."

"Let me guess..." Greg said, smiling.

"Mike thought he had good legal representation in Mexico. So he paid the asking price and signed a contract with the ejido. The ejido was waiting for clear title for the land from Reforma Agraria. All of the paperwork was in place. The contract mandated that the ejido give my friend the title once they received it. Mike hired me to help him design and develop a small resort on the land... something that would showcase the natural environment."

"The ejido never got the title?" Greg asked.

"Oh, sure they did. It took time but the ejido finally received title from the federal government—the title they were legally obligated to hand over to my friend. I went down to place the title in the public registry in the name of my friend's Mexican corporation he had set up. But the ejido wouldn't give the title to me. I was told by the attorneys for the ejido that my friend must pay for the land first. I showed him the contract signed by my friend and the accompanying receipt that showed that he had already paid for the land. It did no good. They told me to talk to the ejiditarios. I went to talk to the ejiditarios. They told me the same thing. They also mentioned that they thought my project was too small and that they could be hired to clear the mangroves so that we could build more hotel rooms."

Arlan took another sip of beer. He looked across the bar where Bruce had gone to tend to a couple of more thirty-something buddies who had just come in and sat down. They laughed at something Bruce said and searched for the hooks below the bar.

"What happened to the land?" Greg asked.

"I went to talk to the politicians, some of the governor's representatives. They told me that I needed to deal directly with the ejido. They suggested that my friend should pay the ejido more money. They then told me that, in return for a lot or two, the governor would see to it that my project gets permitted with twice the density allowed."

Greg let out a *humph* and took a long drink from his mug.

Arlan paused and looked at Greg. "Sorry. I didn't mean to rant. I've had too much beer, and the Mexico thing is still a bit too fresh. As Twain said, 'Humor is tragedy plus time.' I guess not enough time has passed."

"No problem. How did it end?"

Bruce brought two more beers. He set them down on the bar and asked, "Hey, Arlan, did you tell Greg about the lopsided house you live in? What is it called? A Fish? You still trying to bang your landlady?"

Arlan raised his palm toward Bruce and took a drink.

Greg looked at Arlan.

Arlan laughed and said, "Another story."

"Okay. How about after you've told me how the land deal ended?"

"How about not?"

"Oh, it's one of those, eh?"

Arlan took a drink and offered Greg a tight smile. He continued with the Mexico story.

"I returned to the US to discuss the problem with Mike. While trying to decide what to do, we received word that the ejido had sold the land again to a Spanish developer for a lot more money. He planned to build a large, all-inclusive resort. My friend hired an international law firm to review the contract he had signed with the ejido. They told him that the contract was well crafted and that he would prevail in court if he chose to fight it—but that it was Mexico. It would take ten to fifteen years. They suggested that he make a deal with the ejido."

Bruce returned and eyeballed Arlan and Greg's half empty mugs.

"There was nothing my friend could do about it. He didn't want to spend another peso in that corrupt place. He walked away. The Spanish developer built his resort. The coast lost more natural habitat. Mangroves were decimated. The beach shrank as sand disappeared into the sea. The turtle population declined. And more of the barrier reef died because of unfiltered runoff from construction activity and land clearing."

"Who cares about the turtles?" Bruce asked, and laughed.

"Hell, you wouldn't know a sea turtle from a bowling ball," Arlan said to Bruce. "You've never been past the Potomac River."

"Hey." Bruce held his hands up in mock protest. "While you two chase crocodiles and try to save the world, I'm busy every night with the pretty young ladies in here. I mean, with you guys gone, who's going to do it?"

By now the booths were full, and the drinkers were two to three deep at the bar.

"You live in a fish?" Greg asked.

"A flounder."

Bruce said, "Yeah, and his landlady is hot. Older, but still hot. He brought her in here once. I thought it was Arlan's older sister—or mother."

"Funny. She's not hot. She's bright and engaging. And I'm not chasing her."

"Bullshit."

Greg turned to Arlan and asked, "What the hell is a flounder?"

"It's a building."

"Come on. I'm curious."

Arlan erased Fiona from his mind, turned to Greg, and said, "A flounder is an architectural term unique to Old Town. In the mid-

1700s, when Alexandria was founded, city lots were offered to plantation owners or anybody else who they wanted as residents at very low prices. The offer came with a stipulation to stop speculators—a home had to be built on the lot within two years. Plantation owners were happy living on their plantations and didn't particularly want to move to the new city with its crowded tobacco and slave ports. So, many of them, in order to buy and keep their inexpensive city lot, hastily built one or two-story, shed-roofed buildings with windows and doors on all but one side of the structure. This apparently gave the buildings the look of a 'flounder.' The side of the flounder with no windows or doors would be the side that the eventual, much larger, home would be attached to when built later. In a few cases, a larger home was never built and, to this day, you can see free-standing flounders in Old Town. Though historically attractive, they have an unsettling incomplete feel to them—kind of like a twelve bar blues song that finishes on the eleventh bar."

Greg laughed. "I get it. I think I saw a couple of those things this morning on my run."

Arlan looked around. The cacophony of loud drinkers was too much. The bar was too crowded. He'd stayed too long. And he was starting to think about Fiona too much.

Greg looked at Arlan and asked, "So, did you bang her?"

"What?"

"Your landlady. Like Bruce said."

"No. She doesn't seem to be interested in me," Arlan said and turned toward his beer.

Greg shrugged and finished his beer. Arlan did the same.

"Hey, it's been good to talk with you, but I need to go. I've got your number and will let you know in a couple of days if I can help you with your project in Mexico. Don't hold your breath though. As you can tell, it's not my favorite place."

"I'm not asking you to buy land or to develop a project. I'm just looking for some advice on a land investment."

"If it's ejido land, stay away from it."

"I'll find out about that. But I'm telling you that kayaking those canals is a blast."

"I'll think about it."

Arlan looked over at Bruce and made the universal sign for 'check please' by scribbling in the air with an imaginary pen.

"I'm leaving," Arlan shouted to Bruce.

"The usual," Bruce said.

Arlan smiled and placed a twenty on the bar for the beers and another twenty for Bruce. The tab was always twenty dollars—whether he had one beer or ten. He always left Bruce a twenty-dollar tip on top. Arlan figured that in the long run Bruce came out ahead. But it didn't matter. Bruce made the place feel like home.

Arlan shook Greg's hand, nodded to Bruce, and then half-staggered out of the bar to make his way the short distance to his rented flounder on Duke Street. It was late. Other than a car trying to find a parking spot and a little dog barking through slightly parted curtains at the window of one of the old townhomes he passed, he was alone. It was getting colder. He stumbled up a cobblestone road and thought about the offer to visit the warm Yucatan again.

Why would I want to go back there? Arlan thought. Maybe I could check out Greg's land and head farther south to Belize and try to find Captain Jay. Arlan stubbed his toe on a cobblestone and stepped over to the sidewalk. He shivered in the cold and buttoned the top of his jacket. A trip to warm weather would be nice. A block later another dog barked and growled at him through a closed window with heavy curtains that the little dog had somehow pushed aside.

Arlan stopped on the sidewalk just outside the two-hundred-year-old, red brick, federal-style home that was attached to his flounder. He noticed that he had a slight list to the left. No, it was to the right, and then to the left again. He tried to right it and found himself falling forward. A half step later he found his balance.

"Shit, here I am floundering in front of my flounder. What the fuck am I doing here?"

Arlan laughed, stood back, and took in the entire front facade of the house. The shed-roofed, two-story flounder shared a common wall with the main house along the second story. To get to the courtyard behind the house, and the entrance to his flounder, he had to navigate through a thirty-foot-long brick archway about three feet wide that ran between the flounder and the main house. He peered into the dark passageway. The only light was a pale porch light that shone in the distant courtyard on the other side of the passage. The brick that it had been built of had crumbled over time. The once smooth surface had deteriorated into dirty walls busy with sharp edges. Some nights the long, dark tunnel with the faint light at the other end looked to Arlan like an abyss—an open mouth filled with rows of small sharp teeth, waiting for a meal.

"Okay. This is my night to make it through this archway without banging into the wall... and those damn sharp edges."

He glanced at the historic plaque on the front of the main house and remembered the first time he had seen it. He was separated from his wife and needed a place to stay that was close to his ex-house and his children. There had been a small *For Rent* sign tucked into the upper corner of one of the windows. He was rollerblading through the streets of Old Town and had stopped and studied the old house. He thought that it could be perfect. He called the next day and made an appointment to visit. That's when he met Fiona. She and her sister owned the historic home and the flounder attached to it, along with a wonderful brick-walled garden filled with rose bushes and large trees, many as old as the home. Fiona's sister lived in the main house, and Fiona lived in Mexico but was up for an extended visit, which she said she did at least once a year.

Arlan moved in a week later. Fiona endlessly tweaked in her garden before she returned to her home in the Yucatan two months later. Whenever he spotted her digging a hole to plant a sapling or pruning a rose bush, he made some kind of excuse to be outside of the flounder. Sometimes he offered to help, and other times he pretended to be going out, but he always stopped to talk. Over a few weeks, they had built a bond. He told her of his experience in Mexico—the corruption, ejido land and confusing titles, the politicians, and his friend's lost investment. She told Arlan that his experience was typical and that she'd seen the same thing happen time and time again during her years living in Mexico.

He listened to her talk about her passions, which included anything equestrian and preserving the environment. She was active in the Yucatan with both. They learned that they both had focused on habitat preservation most of their adult lives. But they had polar opposite methods of achieving it. Arlan was a developer—a tree-hugging developer, but still a developer. Fiona was a fierce and very influential conservationist and no stranger to rolling her sleeves up and fighting tooth and nail for her favorite cause—saving the turtles and birds of the Yucatan. What kept their discussions interesting was that she was a realist and seemed to respect Arlan's development philosophy.

Arlan found himself attracted to Fiona—for a lot of reasons. Their conversations were effortless and full of interesting opinions and ideas. Arlan was frustrated that Fiona wouldn't respond to his obvious flirting, but he was careful not to try to push it too far. He still had some baggage from his recent divorce to sort out, and Fiona was his landlady. He didn't want to blow that connection. She *did* invite him to visit her the next time he was in Mexico. Maybe it was perfunctory politeness on her part. Maybe it wasn't. Arlan had yet to visit.

A large, noisy street cleaner lumbered by and shook Arlan back to the present. He started down the arched passageway that led to his flounder.

Just one more reason to meet Greg in the Yucatan in two weeks, he thought as he scraped his right shoulder against the wall.

"Ouch. Shit. That hurt."

Chapter 4

Alterio drove through a crowded residential neighborhood on the north side of Madre and parked in the driveway of the headquarters of Las Ambientalistas. The largest environmental activist group in the region had been co-founded by Fiona Anderson two decades earlier. The organization was set up to protect all wildlife habitat in the region, but Alterio knew that Fiona's passion was saving the sea turtles and the beaches where they nested, which included the entire Yucatan Peninsula and the few islands offshore.

Alterio stepped out of his old, beat up, but air conditioned, SUV and closed the door. His breath shortened as he sucked in the humid air. He walked away from his vehicle and hoped that nobody saw him get out of it. He needed a new SUV, something more fitting for his new profession as a developer—and soon-to-be-wealthy developer. The first bead of sweat ran down his forehead as he walked through the open entrance and into a small reception area.

A receptionist looked up and said, "Hola, Don Alterio. Como estas?"

"Buenas tardes. Muy bien, gracias," Alterio answered.

The receptionist told Alterio that Fiona was a few minutes late and that he could wait in the conference room. She nodded toward the hallway behind her desk. Alterio knew his way around. He'd been using his father-in-law's prominence and friendship with Fiona to get as close to her organization as he could. He walked down the short hall and through the open door of the conference room. He smiled at the irony. It was he who was always late. But he dared not be late for this meeting. He needed to control Fiona and her group but had found early on that he couldn't do it through charm and bribes—his preferred methods. Fiona was a typical gringa... and serious about punctuality.

The conference room was more like a war room. There was nothing modern or comfortable about it. It was not the type of conference room Alterio, or any other Mexican, would have in their offices. Maps and charts littered the rectangular table in the center of the room. A variety of plastic and folding metal chairs were spread unevenly around the table and around the room's perimeter. The walls were covered with large maps and charts. Most were marked with black and red scribbled notes. The largest map depicted the most crucial turtle nesting areas on the twenty-kilometer stretch of beach on the seaward side of Isla X'lak. Alterio looked at the map closely. A legend at the bottom showed light to dark burgundy squares that matched the one-hundred-meter blocks of colors along the beach. The darker the color, the more concentrated the nests. There wasn't an area on the island's beaches that wasn't colored, most with dark burgundy. Alterio knew that this would be an issue. He would need to find a clever way around it.

Alterio sighed. His shirt was wet under the armpits, and a growing wet spot formed where the shirt stuck to his body at the top of his formidable belly. More sweat ran down his face. He could hear cars and buses through the open windows as they passed by on the busy city streets just a few steps beyond the tall masonry wall that surrounded the house. Exhaust fumes permeated the room.

He turned his attention to the easel in one corner. On it were layers of large hardboard charts. He leafed through them and saw that all were busy with hand drawings, arrows, and writing. It seemed to be a presentation that addressed the bird habitat throughout the Yucatan Peninsula and the paths the birds took to get to their northern seasonal destinations in the US and Canada.

Hello, Alterio," Fiona said, surprising Alterio, who stepped away from the easel and toward the entrance to the conference room.

Fiona walked into the room with a lady she introduced as Maria, the new director.

"Very good to meet you, Maria." Alterio lightly shook her hand.

He turned to Fiona and gave her a warm hug, which she returned.

"It is very good of you to meet with me. Don Francisco sends his best."

Fiona turned to Maria and explained that Don Francisco was Alterio's father-in-law and that she and Francisco had known each other for years. Maria nodded and smiled. She said that she knew of Don Francisco. Everybody in the Yucatan knew of him.

"How is Don Francisco? Is he recovering?"

"Yes, thank you. He is doing well and hopes to be riding again in a couple of months. He is already walking with just the aid of a cane."

"You should remind him to stick with jumping competitions. What in the world was he thinking when he decided to learn to bullfight—on horseback?" Fiona asked.

"It was something he saw while in Spain on his last visit. He thought it would be safer than bullfighting on foot," Alterio said with a laugh.

"Well, a broken femur is nothing to be taken lightly."

Alterio smiled and waited to be invited to sit. Fiona and Maria remained standing near the entrance to the room. Neither spoke. had asked for the meeting.

"I would like to talk to you about Las Amientalistas."

"Yes?" Fiona asked.

Alterio glanced at the table and chairs. Fiona didn't ask him to sit.

"I... Don Francisco and I, would like to contribute to your organization."

Fiona smiled and looked at the floor.

"It is good that Don Francisco is interested in our group," Fiona finally said.

"Yes. And along with our contribution I would like to be actively involved with your organization, if possible."

"Don Francisco has not told me about this," Fiona said.

"He has been busy with his injury, but he told me to come to talk to you about it."

"But why do you and your father-in-law want to do this?"

"We feel that what you are doing is important, and we want to help."

After a long pause, Fiona said, "Alterio, you have been helping ejidos gain title to their land, most of which represents valuable wildlife habitat. A lot of it is on the coast. It seems that whenever the land is privatized all of the vegetation is cut and burned. We are losing hundreds, thousands of hectares of valuable habitat for our birds and the jaguars." She paused. "Your business activities conflict with our environmental goals, Alterio."

"But the locals always clear the vegetation from the lots they receive when their ejido is privatized. It is how they delineate their land."

"They're not the ones driving the bulldozers clearing mangroves to make way for the new hotels and resorts."

Alterio laughed to himself. Fiona was wrong. The locals were not driving the bulldozers that cleared the way for beachfront resorts, but they using their machetes to cut and burn the interior jungles as fast as he and his competitors could help them get clear title to the land.

"Yes, I know. But I want to help change that."

"How is that, Alterio?"

"By helping you and your organization."

Fiona turned her head and sighed. She seemed to gather her thoughts and said, "I have heard that you are working with the ejido to privatize Isla X'lak. You know that we value that island so much that we are lobbying the federal government, including the president, to declare the land outside the village a federal preserve."

"Yes. But that will be difficult. The locals will fight it. If you don't get the federal government and the president to declare the island a preserve, it will be sub-divided and sold to speculators and developers."

Fiona shook her head and said, "Why not just leave the island alone?"

Alterio fidgeted for a moment, then said, "I have competitors and they've had greater success than I at privatizing ejido land, especially along the Caribbean coast. And they don't care what happens to the land after they get their share. Two of them have already been to X'lak to try to make a deal with the ejido, but they would rather deal with me."

Silence. More sweat ran down Alterio's face. He wiped the side of his face with his sleeve.

He added, "I want to create a destination for five-star boutique hotels. Not like Cancun."

Silence.

"Have you seen the Four Seasons in Bali or on Bora-Bora?"

"I know of them."

"That is what I want for the island. Nothing like Cancun. And I want to showcase the Mayan culture. And I will work with you and your organization to help preserve the beaches where the turtles live. I am a great fan of turtles."

"Alterio, the turtles don't live on the beaches."

"I'm sorry. I meant to say, where they nest." He pointed to the chart on the wall.

"Alterio, neither you nor your father-in-law are developers. Why do you want to put hotels on Isla X'lak?"

"Oh, but we are bringing in a partner. A very successful developer."

"Who?"

Alterio smiled and said, "He is from Spain."

"A Spanish developer. My lord, Alterio, look what they've already done to the Maya Riviera."

"No. This one is different. You will see. I'll bring him to visit after we close the deal."

After an awkward silence Fiona said, "I'm not happy about the thought of any development on Isla X'lak outside the village. It is far too valuable as a wildlife sanctuary. I'm certainly not happy about a Spanish developer having anything to do with it."

"But we can work with you. Maybe your organization can help us design ways to protect the turtles and birds."

"That would best be accomplished by leaving the island alone."

The receptionist entered the conference room and whispered something to Maria, who looked at her watch and then to Fiona.

Fiona said, "Alterio, I have another meeting in a few minutes, but let me offer this. I have a friend in the US who specializes in sustainable development. He's committed to land preservation and has been able to develop environmentally sensitive land in ways that protect its wildlife. But he's very selective about which projects and who he works with." Fiona paused and added, "As you say, we may or may not get the federal government to agree to make X'lak a preserve. But I can assure you that we will try our best. The next best thing would be a truly low-impact, educational tourism development on the least fragile parts of the island, if those exist. I would feel more comfortable if my friend was involved."

"That would be very good. Can you introduce me to him?"

"Let me ask him if he would be interested first. He worked in Mexico before and didn't have a good experience. I don't know if he'll come back."

"But this could be a very good project for him."

"We'll see. In the meantime, you said that Don Francisco wants to support our organization?"

"Yes. We would like to participate in your group."

"We need expertise and funding, Alterio. I don't think that you or your father-in-law have the expertise to help us."

"Yes. But we can donate money to your cause. And we know a lot of influential people."

"So do we, Alterio. But not all of them care about the environment. But we'll welcome any financial support you can offer. You can contact our office through the receptionist and set up an appointment with Maria to talk about that."

"We will pledge two hundred thousand pesos."

Fiona and Maria looked at each other. Alterio didn't know if they were angry or surprised.

"The first year," he said.

Fiona looked at her watch and said, "That is a generous offer, but you know that we will never support any development of X'lak or anywhere else, regardless of your donations. That's not the way we work."

"Claro. But just one more thing. If your friend helps us create a suspendable development plan you would support that, right?"

"*Sustainable*, Alterio. Your English is not quite perfect. You need to learn these terms before you offer something you don't understand."

"Yes. I'm sorry."

Before Fiona had a chance to say anything else, Alterio said, "I will tell Don Francisco about our meeting today. He will be very pleased."

"Okay, Alterio. Please go over the details with Maria. I have another meeting I need to attend."

"Thank you very much, Fiona." He turned to Maria and said, "It was very nice to meet you, Maria. I'll contact you very soon."

Fiona and Alterio hugged and he walked to his car. Fiona was always difficult. He hoped that her gringo friend was easier. Alterio got into his SUV and started it up. He waited for the AC to cool the interior before he backed out of the driveway. By the time he got to the first stop sign, he had decided that he would only tell Don Francisco if he actually needed to come up with money, though he couldn't imagine why that would ever be necessary.

Chapter 5

El Simpatico and Joaquin sat under a large umbrella at a poolside table that belonged to one of Cancun's most luxurious hotels. Other than their security team and a hotel wait staff, they were alone in the late morning humidity.

"Jefe, why can't we sit inside? Look at the sea. There are no waves. Look at the palm trees. The fronds do not move." He removed utensils from atop a white cloth napkin that had been folded into a crinkled shape and was supposed to resemble a swan or a flower and wiped sweat from his forehead.

"Security suggested it. It's the safe move. You know that," El Simpatico told his lieutenant.

A young waiter approached their table. His eyes glanced at the three large men who wore suits and sunglasses and stood a comfortable distance from the table, but close enough to take action required to protect their boss.

El Simpatico, perturbed with the interruption, said, "Vuelve en un momento."

At *his* houses the waiters were trained not to interrupt. If this wasn't a public place he would have slapped the little shit, and if he protested he'd have him shot. Maybe he would then have this little shit cut up into small pieces. The chum supply he used to attract sharks was getting low. He kept the chum in six, fifty-five-gallon oil drums in a warehouse near his yacht. Two were empty and the others were filled with rotted fish and animal parts. Human parts would be just as tasty to shark.

El Simpatico watched the waiter scurry past two other men who stood in the shadows of nearby bushes. Raton and Nacho didn't wear suits, and they weren't particularly large, but they were menacing. Their matching, light-blue Guayabera shirts didn't conceal the large handguns stuffed in the fronts of their dress slacks. El Simpatico smiled when he saw that the waiter had moved away a lot faster than he had approached.

"It's better out here. You complain too much, Joacho."

"Can we at least get something cold to drink?"

"Fine," he said, and snapped his fingers in the direction the waiter had disappeared.

The waiter returned and they ordered mimosas.

"We are here so you can give me an update on Isla X'lak."

Joaquin smiled and said, "The island will be privatized. We screwed up by backing La Vaca. He couldn't get along with the ejiditarios. They kicked him off the island. They like Alterio and will give him the contract to privatize the land. He understands the game and knows who to pay, though I think he pays too much."

"That's your opinion?"

"Yes."

El Simpatico grunted. "I don't want opinions, Joacho. Opinions are grey areas. We eliminate grey areas. We survive because our world is black and white."

The waiter returned with two mimosas. Both had small toothpick umbrellas placed in them.

"What more have you learned of that fat fuck, Alterio? He seems to have lucked into this ejido deal."

Joaquin smiled. "His name is Alterio Delgado. He married into a wealthy family but didn't go into his in-law's business. But he has the father-in-law's support. They're partners in the effort to privatize X'lak."

"Does he know about us?"

"No. Well, other than our short introduction at your friend's palapa, he just knows we exist. He doesn't know that we are behind this deal, and he knows nothing of what we have planned."

"And how is it that you know he will be the one to get the contract to privatize Isla X'lak?"

"Through one of the advisors closest to the new president. He grew up with the governor of this state. The governor is very close to Alterio. Alterio tells him everything. We know everything that the governor knows. That's how we found out that Alterio was trying to get the contract to privatize the island."

"Can Alterio get this thing done before the ejido kicks him off of the island too?"

"So far he has the locals in his pocket. He's smart that way."

"Can he be controlled?"

"Easy. As you say, he is a greedy fat fuck. He wants the same thing we want—the next Cancun. He's promised it to the ejido and to the governor."

"Have we made Alterio an offer?"

"Yes, through our construction company in Mexico City. That was a smart move on your part to set up a construction company. It's a perfect front. It is now the third largest in the country and only the new CEO and the CFO know that own it, and they can be trusted."

"Nobody can be trusted, Joacho. How much did they offer?"

"Sixty million US dollars—for fifty percent of the island."

El Simpatico thought about that for a moment.

"How much land does the hotel zone of Cancun have?"

"Less than one thousand hectares. We will have fifty percent of four-thousand hectares on Isla X'lak to develop."

"I want to control the entire island. After we make our deal with Alterio, and when the time is right, we'll take it all."

"Absolutamente."

El Simpatico thought for a moment and asked, "Has anybody else made Alterio an offer?"

"We think a Spaniard might. But it is unlikely that he will offer more than us. The island is not worth more, no matter how many hotels and resorts he can cram onto it. The infrastructure costs alone will be tremendous."

"Isn't that what we want, Joacho—to launder our money?"

"Si, Jefe."

"Then we will have clean money to invest in other opportunities around the world."

"Si, Jefe."

"I don't like that there are other possible offers out there. Can we get to the Spaniard?"

"Almost impossible. He is a billionaire and is well protected. And he is rarely in Mexico."

"All right, but stay close to the situation. Use our contacts."

"Jefe, I am more concerned with effort to have the island declared a federal preserve."

"That will never happen, but I will remind my friend, the president, to keep it in check."

El Simpatico looked around and took a drink of his mimosa.

"Jefe, maybe we need to bring Alterio in and explain to him how important this is to us. I could break his arm, or cut off a finger..."

"No, Joacho. Not yet." El Simpatico looked into the eyes of Joaquin and said, "I've known you since you were a baby. Your father was the best lieutenant I ever had, except maybe for you. Your father was skilled at killing our enemies. You have more than skill... you have a passion for it." El Simpatico took another drink and said, "I want you to be more than a killer. I have put you in charge of this critically important operation for a reason. Nothing, I mean, *nothing*, can lead back to us. The Yucatecan family must never know that we are their partners. The government, other than the president, can never know we are involved. Success depends on nobody knowing that we plan to launder millions, maybe billions, by building another Cancun." He paused and then said, "We've built a few hotels and resorts in the past—but an entire destination? It is an opportunity like this that is precisely why we set up our construction company. Do you think I ever wanted to be in the construction business? We're lucky that Alterio's group is about to get the contract to privatize this particular island and that they're searching for a partner with a lot of money."

El Simpatico paused when the waiter approached and asked if they needed anything else. He made the mistake of looking at Joacho's reptilian eyes. El Simpatico smiled and watched the waiter squirm before he sent him away. He almost fell into the pool when he tried to avoid a large security guard who had stepped out from behind a hibiscus bush.

Joacho gave El Simpatico an impatient look.

"Joacho, we could force our way in and pay off everybody need-ed to permit and develop the entire island, but a destination known, even rumored, to have been built and controlled by a drug cartel would not attract very many tourists... Entiendes?"

"Si, Jefe."

"You'll manipulate this situation. You will *not* force it. You *will* remain in the background. And, unlike your normal style, I don't want to see bodies strewn about. I don't want to *hear* about bodies strewn about. We will do this deal quietly—until I say different."

"Si, Jefe."

Chapter 6

Alterio drove to Don Francisco's offices for a scheduled update on the Isla X'lak situation. He thought about his visit with Fiona the day before. He wondered why all gringos were so damn direct. It was a rude disposition. He could only hope that Fiona and his father-in-law didn't speak for a while. He needed time.

Alterio parked his SUV on a quiet street next to a tall, yellow masonry wall that took up an entire block. Large trees lined the sidewalk near the middle of the block. All of the parking spaces shaded by the trees were already taken. Damn. The interior of his SUV would reach one hundred and twenty degrees or more in about two minutes as soon as he turned the engine off. He put the gum and lip balm he kept in his ashtray into his pocket and walked toward the wooden gate in the middle of the long wall.

Alterio marveled at his father-in-law's compound. He wanted one just like it. Completely walled in from the city streets on all four sides, the hacienda that Don Francisco had built in a residential neighborhood in Madre took up an entire city block. The walls were painted with a yellow pigment mixed with calcium, giving them a textured classic patina. Within the walls were two large buildings. One was his private residence. The other housed several offices for the staff, a large conference room with its own kitchen and staff for formal meetings and a small conference room where Altrerio normally met with his father-in-law. On the grounds of the hacienda between the two structures was a small stable and paddock that allowed Don Francisco to bring three or four of his one hundred horses from his larger hacienda in the country to the city to show or to ride.

Alterio stood outside the gate and pressed the button on the intercom. He was immediately buzzed in and escorted to a small conference room. His father-in-law, Don Fernando, and his personal attorney, Pepe, were seated in two of the four cushioned chairs around a round glass table in the middle of the room, situated adjacent to Don Francisco's office. They didn't seem pleased to see him.

Alterio made no effort to acknowledge that he was late. They were used to it. They didn't greet him with the customary handshake and hug and said nothing as Alterio sat down heavily on one of the chairs. The furniture on the perimeter of the small conference room and the artwork on the walls were clearly high quality Yucatecan and indicative of the furnishings throughout the hacienda. None of it stood out. It all fit as though it had been there forever.

Francisco's secretary entered with a glass filled with ice and Coca-Cola and placed it in front of Alterio. Moisture ran down the sides and spread onto the glass-topped table. He turned toward the open door and a desk where Francisco's secretary sat. "Could I have a napkin,?"

Francisco looked up from a document he had been reading and asked, "Alterio, what is the status with Isla X'lak?"

As usual, when by themselves or among friends or family, Alterio used the more reverential form of addressing Don Francisco. "Tio, we have most of the one hundred and fifty ejiditarios on our side. The colonel is ready to call for the assembly where they can award us the contract to privatize their land."

"I guess that's good. You've had Julio and Flaco living with them for over a year. We have spent a fortune on TVs, golf carts, and boats that you have given the ejiditarios. We have even paid for medical bills and two funerals. When does it stop?"

"I had to pay for those things. We need for the ejiditarios to like us and trust us. So far, I have been able to keep our competitors away. But I think that one of them, Chalo, has bought a few of the ejiditarios. He is paying them to vote against us. I've convinced the colonel to call for the vote in a few days, before Chalo can buy more ejiditarios."

"Is the colonel still the president of the ejido?"

"Yes, and he is firmly on our side. We've paid him well. But he only has three months left as president. We need to keep the money coming in until we get the contract and maybe a while after that."

"The contract seems to change all of the time," Pepe said. "Every week you bring in a different version. Has it changed again?"

"A little. We have a new subdivision plan that the ejiditarios will accept, according to the colonel. Everybody in the village will receive title to the homes. The ejido as a group will have some common land near the village to sell, if they want to."

"And what about the rest of the island? The important part?"

"We have divided fifteen of the twenty-five kilometers of the beach into equal-sized lots. Each ejiditario has agreed to receive one lot, which will be placed into a trust. The trust will keep the lots out of the hands of our competitors until our partnership can buy them. We'll receive eight kilometers of beach on the east side of the island as payment for our efforts to privatize the island. We'll subdivide the remaining two kilometers and use the lots to pay off some of our friends."

"Are you sure that the federal government will support this subdivision?" asked Pepe.

"The government must approve it if it is done properly and all of the documents are filed correctly. But even if we are missing a document or two, we will have no problem—I've promised the governor seven lots."

"Why would we be missing a document or two?" Pepe asked.

"Pepe, the ejido privatization process is still new, and there are many, many documents that must be signed and filed. There are mistakes made all of the time. That is one reason I have temporary power of attorney from Tio—the one you fought so much. He doesn't have time to review all of the necessary papers that we need. Jose and I are doing all of that."

Pepe questioned everything. Damn lawyers. He didn't understand that Alterio needed to be off-leash in order to be successful. He required money to wine and dine and supply prostitutes or drugs when needed. And he needed the full power of his partnership with Don Francisco to make promises in order to get things done.

When Pepe didn't respond, Alterio added, "The governor's henchmen have ways to funnel a couple of the lots to the federal authorities in Chetumal. The colonel has been promised an extra lot, and we still have several lots left over to give to judges or whoever else we may need until we have secured the land and have permits for development."

"And these lots will come out of the two kilometers?"

"Yes. We are able to subdivide the two kilometers into twenty large lots."

Don Francisco seemed satisfied. Pepe sneered. Don Francisco had years of experience in a business culture that was steeped in corruption, but he didn't approve of it. Alterio thrived on the knowledge that his country's economy was grounded in corruption. Nothing moved forward without bribes. And it took real talent to know *how much* and *to whom*. Alterio had talent. Neither Don Francisco nor Pepe were aware of the extent of Alterio's bribes and promises.

"What's the price of the lots in the trust?" Pepe asked.

"We will negotiate with each ejiditario individually."

"How much more money will we need?" Don Francisco asked.

"Besides what you've already put into it, we might need as much as thirty million dollars, maybe more."

Don Francisco and Pepe looked at each other.

"I have put far too much cash into this deal. We need a partner. How is your search going?"

"Tio, that's why we need more money. We have flown more than fifty wealthy investors from all over the world to X'lak. The broker's attorneys have supplied each potential investor with the legal package. We have many more interested investors who want to visit the island. Helicopters and hotel rooms are expensive."

"You keep telling us that," Pepe said.

Don Francisco nodded and said, "And you insist on entertaining in the most expensive restaurants, flying first class, and staying in five-star hotels."

"Has anybody made an offer?" asked Pepe.

"We have a very good offer from a Spanish developer."

"Is that the only one?"

"A construction group from Mexico City has made an offer. But it is far less than that of the Spaniard."

Don Francisco said, "Alterio, I'm tired of being the only person putting money into this. Make the deal with the Spaniard. Quit screwing around with helicopter rides and expensive restaurants."

With that, Don Francisco stood up and left the room.

Chapter 7

Arlan slouched on his futon, one of four pieces of furniture that fit into the bottom floor of his two-floor flounder. His legs rested on a coffee table between two stacks of books that were always on the table. The small, built-in bookcase below the splintered trim of the windowsill on the opposite side of the room was full. He had a Spanish dictionary in his lap but wasn't sure why he was boning up on the language. It could have something to do with his meeting Greg the week before and his request to have Arlan look at some land in the Yucatan Peninsula. More likely, it was what Bruce had said about him floundering around Alexandria, Virginia, wishing he were back in the Caribbean. Bruce actually said 'moping,' but floundering seemed more appropriate to Arlan as he looked around. He set the book on the coffee table and walked the three steps to his half-sized refrigerator that sat next to the bookcase.

He was thirsty.

"Ugh. Bud Light. Who would drink that crap?"

Then he remembered that a friend had brought the six-pack over a few nights earlier. He looked at his watch and decided that it wasn't too late to visit Bruce. His bar would be open for another three hours. He opened the door to the courtyard and the cold breeze hit him.

"Damn."

He grabbed his jacket from a hook on the back of the heavy door as his phone rang. It was Fiona. He closed the door and returned his jacket to the hook. The beer could wait.

"Are you in Old Town?" Arlan asked, a little hopefully.

"No. I'm in Madre. I wanted to call to check on the flounder."

"Oh." Arlan paused and said, "It's fine. I like living in it."

"That's very good to hear. I wouldn't like it much if Joan had to find another tenant. It was a long time until you came along."

Arlan paused and said, "You know, an interesting thing happened last week. I met a guy who owns an adventure travel business, and he wants me to meet him in the Yucatan next week to look at some land that he and a partner are thinking of buying. And maybe kayak the Mayan canals south of Tulum."

"Are you going to do it?" Fiona asked.

"I don't know. I'm not too interested in doing any business in Mexico again, but I like the idea of kayaking the canals. I might also go to Belize to look up an old friend. It's close. Maybe I could kill two birds."

"Let's not talk about killing birds," Fiona said. "But that's interesting, and maybe fortuitous. How about three birds while you're at it?"

"Explain."

"I have something I would like to discuss with you. I, we, could use your expertise and help."

"Where?"

Fiona paused and said, "In Mexico... but don't say anything yet. Let me explain. A prominent family here in Madre is working with an ejido to help them privatize their land on an island near Cancun. The island is very important to us. It's one of the most important ecosystems in the region, maybe in this hemisphere. We're trying to have most of the island declared a federal protected preserve, a biosphere."

"You know I'd help you any way I can. But I'm a developer. I can't develop preservation land... And you know what I think of Mexican politicians and ejido land."

"The island has miles of virgin beachfront and jungle habitat. And the beaches are the most important turtle nesting areas in the Atlantic and Gulf of Mexico, particularly for the hawksbill turtle. I know the family that will probably be helping the island's ejido privatize the land. I'm close friends with the family patriarch. I would like to ask you to help them with their development plans for the island."

"But I thought you want the island to be a protected biosphere." Arlan said.

"Yes, we do. But that may not be possible politically. We don't want the land to be developed into another Cancun or Maya Riviera. I know that you think there are better ways to develop land... ways that preserve the environment. We've talked about it. I've seen your projects..."

Fiona paused and then said, "I'm sorry. You probably don't have time to listen to all of this now—over the phone. I can explain all about the island when you come to visit. You were planning to visit me in Madre when you come to kayak next week, right?"

Arlan smiled and said nothing.

Fiona said, "You'll need to decide, but when you come we'll play tennis and I'll introduce you to some friends who work with our foundation. They are also alarmed at the rate of the habitat destruction here on the peninsula."

Arlan thanked Fiona for the call, told her he needed some time to think about looking at work in Mexico again, and hung up. He knew immediately the decision had been made for him, and it had nothing to do with an island or Fiona's friends.

Arlan grabbed his jacket and searched the pockets for Bruce's business card—the card he stuffed into his pocket a week ago—the card with Greg's number on the back.

Chapter 8

Alterio, Don Francisco, Pepe, two attorneys, the colonel, and the governor's brother flew first-class to Madrid. It was a celebration. Alterio bought seven of the fully reclining first class seats on the Boeing 767 flight—with Don Francisco's money.

All of the details of the agreement between the Spanish developer and the partnership of Alterio and Don Francisco had been worked out and the agreement was to be ratified in the Spaniard's castle in Spain. Pepe argued that the document needed to be notarized and filed in Mexico and that the signing should take place in Madre or Cancun. Alterio solved the problem by bringing his notario, Jose, and his individualized notario stamp along. It didn't help Pepe's protests that the Spaniard agreed to pay ninety million dollars for a fifty percent ownership position in the corporation that Alterio and his attorney had set up to buy and own four thousand hectares and world-class beach on Isla X'lak.

Don Francisco wasn't happy that the ejido's attorney, Chino, the colonel, and the governor's brother tagged along.

"These guys are worthless," Don Francisco told Alterio. "Chino is a loudmouth. Does he even have a law degree? The governor's brother is a puppet, and the colonel is embarrassingly unsophisticated... they all are."

Alterio insisted that they were all needed to further their political clout, which they would need when they presented a project for the island. He didn't know if that was true, but he *did* know that they would send glowing reports about their trip to Spain, giving

Alterio more independence from Don Francisco and more control over their partnership in the eyes of the ejiditarios and the governor.

Alterio and his entourage were met at the Adolfo Suarez Madrid-Barajas Airport by a heavy-set man who held a sign with Alterio's name on it. He introduced himself as their driver, Jose Maria. He walked with them to retrieve their baggage and led them to a luxury van parked illegally just outside the doors of the baggage claim area. Jose Maria handed a security guard a wad of cash and, with the guard's help, loaded the Mexicans' bags into the back of the van. When the last bag was in the van, the driver thanked the security guard and explained to Alterio that they would be driving south to the Andalucía region of Spain. Alterio knew that their host, Roberto Jacinto, was a multi-billionaire developer who lived in a Moorish-built castle near Granada and, according to Jose Maria, wanted his guests to see his beautiful country—more than they could see from a jet. They were to take the scenic route. Alterio looked at Pepe and Don Francisco and shrugged. They couldn't refuse—not if they wanted to collect Roberto's money during this trip.

Alterio offered the front passenger seat to Don Francisco, who declined and climbed in the side door and sat in the seat behind the driver. Alterio took the front seat and watched everybody else climb in and settle into the three rows of seats behind him. The *scenic* route turned out to be a lengthy tour through the southern part of Spain so that Alterio could see many of the properties Roberto had developed.

From the airport they headed south, skirting the west side of Madrid and passing several dense townhome and commercial projects developed by Roberto, according to Jose Maria. The city and its suburbs gave way to hilly countryside and scores of small towns. Roberto's projects were easy to recognize as Jose Maria drove past them. They were identical. Roberto must have had only one architect on his staff. Every one of Roberto's projects was built with the same materials and colors and shared a simplistic, modern design that caused them to look ridiculously out of place, particularly in historic neighborhoods where most of them were built. Alterio could imagine what historic structures were razed so that Roberto could build and sell these ugly ones.

Five hours later, the van drove under a large green sign that indicated Granada was to the left. Alterio could see the snow-capped
mountains of the Sierra Nevada beyond the city to the east. He expected Jose Maria to take the left exit to Granada and to wherever
Roberto's castle was located. Instead, Jose Maria stayed on the main
road and drove west and south to the Mediterranean coast. Alterio
started to protest.

"You need to see Roberto's resort developments on the coast,"
Jose Maria said. "They are even more beautiful than the properties
you've seen so far. We can stop for lunch there."

Pepe, who sat behind Alterio, tapped his shoulder and whispered in English, "This is the kind of tour you take your potential
investors on. All of this driving is making me sick."

Alterio turned and whispered, "Sit back and act like you enjoy
it. We'll be multi-millionaires in a couple of days." He glanced to the
back of the van and saw that the colonel, the governor's brother, and
the ejido's attorney were all asleep, which could have had a lot to do
with the large amount of scotch and whisky they drank on the red-
eye flight to Spain.

Two hours later, after miles of sun-baked hills and winding
roads, they reached Marbella, where Jose Maria turned off of the
main road and took a coastal road that passed scores of wall-to-wall
resort developments. There was no land left along the coastline to
develop. Roberto needed another country to develop, and Alterio
knew that Mexico was a good fit—the same language and sufficient-
ly corrupt politicians who could be paid to look the other way while
he turned mangroves and beaches into all-inclusive hotels. None of
this bothered Alterio. Roberto probably knew he'd agreed to pay too
much for a fifty percent share that Alterio offered for beachfront
land on X'lak, but it was a way for the Spaniard to get his foot in the
door and have local partners with political juice that could help him
with future projects in Mexico.

Several kilometers and a hundred resorts later, Jose Maria
turned the van around and announced that they would be stopping
for lunch and then returning to Granada and Roberto's estate. Alterio turned in his seat to see how the rest of the group was doing. Pepe
and Don Francisco appeared to be pissed off, obviously tired of the

tour. The three in the back row were still sleeping. The colonel's head rested on the governor's brother's shoulder, and a line of drool ran from the colonel's mouth to the brother's shirt sleeve. Even Alterio was tired. He slumped in his seat and closed his eyes.

All were relieved two and a half hours later when the van turned onto a winding road that gave them a clear view of a hill with a large, medieval castle on top of it. They had reached their destination.

There was still enough daylight to see the manicured gardens and pastureland that surrounded the castle as they approached it. There were a few dozen horses and a stone stable to the left of the castle. Don Francisco, who owned eight thousand head of various breeds of beef cattle in the Yucatan, commented that the cattle he could see on the right side of the winding road were Andalusian cattle, the ancestors of the Texas Longhorns. Pepe saw grape vines on a small section of land near the horses and wondered out loud what kind of grapes Roberto grew and if he had a winery nearby.

Jose Maria stopped the van at the massive castle entrance comprised of Moorish arches and tiled porticos. Two servants had come down the entrance steps and opened the doors of the van. Everybody exited the van and looked around while Jose Maria started to remove the bags from the rear of the van and hand them to two servants who carried them into the castle. Within a minute, Roberto came out to greet his guests and led them into the cavernous entry hall. A series of smaller Moorish arches than those Alterio saw on the exterior sat on top of ornate columns. They held up a vaulted tile ceiling that was at least ten meters high and stretched thirty meters or more to the back of the entry. To the right was a six-meter-wide stairway that led down; to the left an identical stairway led up. Roberto told the servants to take the bags to the rooms upstairs.

"You will all have your own rooms, if that suits you," Roberto told the group.

Nobody answered for a moment, still taking in the overall scale of the interior of Roberto's castle. Finally, Alterio said, "Yes. Thank you, Roberto. This place is very... large."

Roberto laughed and gave them a truncated tour of the castle before leading them up to their rooms. There was nothing about Roberto that wasn't ostentatious, from his loud and overbearing personality to the ornate furniture and appointments throughout the castle where Alterio and his entourage were to be spending the next three days. As they were about to learn, Roberto had planned the next three day's events down to the hour.

During the days, he took his guests to many of his nearby real estate developments, which were simply more of the same over-crowded projects they had seen with Jose Maria. He also took them to many of the regional attractions—mostly other castles. In the evenings, Roberto entertained in the library and, after several drinks, would then lead the group to the large formal dining room for dinner where he had gourmet food and fine wines served and he dominated the conversations.

The dinners started late and lasted for hours, which pleased the Mexicans. The first night, between his development and business diatribes, Roberto pointed out various pieces of art and historic artifacts he had placed around the huge room. During the second night's dinner, Alterio feigned interest at his host's non-stop stories and occasionally nodded his head and asked a question—when he remembered the topic. Pepe seemed bored and was quiet except when Roberto pointed out his prize possession—two lances that hung above the fireplace, which was large enough to stand up in.

"Those are original," Roberto bragged.

Pepe was the only person at the table who seemed to be interested.

"I'll bet nobody in this room can guess what they are," Roberto said with a smug smile. After a long silence, Alterio thought somebody should say something.

"They're spears," Alterio answered.

"Not spears. They're lances. And not just any lances," Roberto said. "They were Caesar's. They are priceless."

"They are hastas," Pepe said and took a drink of wine. He added, "This wine is quite good. It's not Spanish."

Roberto's smugness evaporated. "You don't look like the warrior type. How would you know about a legendary Roman lance that killed so many?"

Pepe said, "I don't know how effective they would have been in battle, or if they were ever used in battle. Under Roman law, they were symbols of ownership. One was always present whenever a court held its session and whenever there was a land sale."

For once, Roberto shut up. Alterio leaned into him and said, "Pepe is just showing off. He used to teach Roman law at a Mexico City university."

The colonel and the governor's brother were not willing or able to contribute to any of the dinner conversations. They seemed in awe of their surroundings. The ejido attorney, Chino, was oblivious to his surroundings. Alterio hoped that he would keep his mouth shut. He didn't.

"The mayor is my sister," Chino blurted from the far end of the dining table.

Nobody responded.

With a confused look, Roberto finally asked, "Mayor of what?"

"The mayor of Isla X'lak."

Alterio gulped wine.

"I can get a lot of things done for you on the island... for just a small fee," Chino said and lifted his glass. "Salud."

Nobody toasted.

"You will need men to cut the mangrove. I can supply them. My cousin is the island's largest builder. He built the new ejido office."

The colonel had his wine glass up to his mouth and snorted. Globs of wine landed on the table. "Yes, and it blew away in the storm last year. And it was a small storm."

Roberto looked at Alterio, who shrugged and smiled. Roberto looked down at the far end of the table at Chino and asked, "Who are you again?"

"I am Chino, the attorney for the ejido on Isla X'lak."

"I see. It must be difficult work."

"Yes. It's very difficult. But I know how to get things done. My sister is the mayor."

"And from what school did you get your degree?" Roberto asked.

Chino's smile disappeared. He glanced at the colonel and looked down at his plate.

Alterio decided it was time to change the direction of the conversation and asked Roberto about a hotel development on the Costa del Sol. Five minutes later he regretted asking. And the night went on... but at least Chino was shut down.

The next day was spent playing golf on Roberto's private course. The night before the contract was to be signed at a celebratory brunch, Alterio decided it was time to be... Alterio. Dinner was to start at ten. Alterio thought that was too early. He took a nap. When he awoke he looked at his watch. It showed eleven. He shrugged and took a shower.

Thirty minutes later, Alterio walked down the stairs and stood at the entrance to the dining room. He could see that everybody was seated around the dinner table in the same seat that they had sat in the previous two nights. The seat to the left of Roberto was occupied by Don Francisco. The seat to Roberto's right, the seat that should have been occupied by Alterio, was empty. The Mexicans were used to Alterio and his complete disregard for punctuality. They drank the excellent wine that continued to flow. No wine glass sat more than half empty for more than a minute before a servant quietly appeared with more wine. Alterio heard Roberto's voice above all others. He had just asked about Alterio and where he was.

Alterio made his way to the table. Roberto stood. His anger dissipated—at least on the outside. The two shook hands, hugged, and then shook hands once more—the typical Yucatecan greeting and one that Roberto had learned during his last visit to Mexico.

"I'm sorry I am late."

"No problem. The jetlag, no doubt. Please sit. Enjoy some wine. Dinner will be served shortly."

Roberto continued to speak of his projects and real estate and his favorite subject—Roberto.

Alterio was distracted. He was close to inking the partnership deal for Isla X'lak with a developer and wasn't ready for the negotiations to end. To Alterio, negotiating meant living large. He wasn't sure that actually going to work and developing the island would be as much fun.

Roberto finally noticed Alterio's lack of engagement and asked, "Are you feeling well, my friend?"

"I have been thinking about our deal," Alterio said, loudly enough that everybody around the table could hear.

The conversation stopped.

All eyes focused on Alterio. He looked down into his lap for a moment, then raised his head and looked straight at Roberto with the most innocent expression he could muster and said, "The price," he said quietly. "The price needs to be higher."

Alterio glanced at Don Francisco and Pepe. He hadn't told them he was going to change the price. He looked at Roberto, whose mouth opened slightly.

"The price for the fifty percent of our partnership should be one hundred million dollars," Alterio said.

Don Francisco lowered his gaze and shook his head. Alterio didn't care. One hundred million simply sounded better. It was a more round number.

Roberto stared for a long time at Alterio, his smile long gone.

"What? You can't do that."

Alterio looked at Roberto with a tight smile.

Roberto stood, leaned down toward Alterio, and shouted, "Pendejo! Chingate!"

Alterio rocked back in his seat. He glanced around the table and looked for support. The colonel, the governor's brother, and Chino looked at each other and then for the nearest exit. Francisco offered a tight smile, as though he had been expecting this. Pepe and Jose said nothing.

Roberto stomped out of the room without looking back.

Alterio shrugged and said, "He'll come around and pay our price. He wants it too much."

Alterio finished his wine and looked around for the head servant, who was standing behind him, also looking for an exit.

"When will the food be served?" Alterio asked, and smiled at his countrymen.

Don Francisco stood and said, "I think it is time for us to go back to our rooms and pack, before Roberto sends in those large security guards we saw around the perimeter of this place." He looked directly at Alterio and said sternly, "You better place a call to the Mexico City construction company as soon as we return. And you better hope that they are still interested."

The Mexicans flew back to Cancun the next day. During the flight, Alterio reassured them that Roberto would come around. "He wants it too badly," he told them repeatedly.

Chapter 9

A comforting wall of heat hit Arlan as he exited the air-conditioned terminal. He ducked his head under a 'Bienvenido a Cancun' banner and saw Greg immediately. He stood out next to a group of Yucatecan men who wore starched white shirts and dark dress pants. He was taller than the rest of the group and was the only one not holding a cardboard sign with an American surname on it or shouting 'Taxi' at the passing tourists.

"You driving taxis now? Where's your sign?"

"Si, senor," Greg answered with his best Mexican accent. "Your limousine waits in the parking lot."

"The parking lot? No door to door service?"

"But there are no doors where we are going," Greg said, and then added, "Señor."

Arlan followed Greg to a beat-up burgundy VW Bug.

"First class transportation," Arlan said with a smile and tossed his bag in the back. A plume of dust mushroomed from the seat.

"It belongs to a friend of mine. He's German, so don't make fun of his car when you meet him. He's a little strange that way. We're going to stay at his hotel in Playa before heading south to the land I want you to see and the canals."

The drive to Playa del Carmen took less than an hour. The road was new and improved—four lanes of well-paved highway. The drivers were bad. Cars in the left lane moved dangerously fast, causing slower drivers to move to the right, narrowly missing local pedestrians on the far right of the paved road, skirting thorny tropical bushes that grew where the pavement stopped. Some rode rusty bicycles with wooden carts on the fronts, the carts full of fruit or women and children. Others walked, many with fruit baskets on their heads.

Except for more lanes, it was as Arlan remembered it from his last trip to the area a few years earlier. What was with Mayans and driving? The wheel was a relatively new concept in the more than two-thousand-year-old culture. Before automobiles and bicycles there was no need for the wheel. Mayans walked. There were no animals in the Yucatan's ancient history large enough to pull a cart—except maybe a jaguar, which would have been interesting. What was exasperating was that he knew the Mayans to be extraordinarily friendly people—until they were behind the wheel of a car. Maybe it takes time to get acquainted with the wheel, especially a steering wheel. Arlan laughed at the irony.

"Something funny?" Greg asked.

"Yeah. This whole fucking place."

"Relax. Roll with it."

"Right. I forgot. I'm here to help you out with some land. It's just that the place brings back a lot of memories—not good ones."

The beat-up VW clunked along in the right lane. It was too slow to be a threat to the pedestrians to the right. They could hear it coming and got out of the way. Arlan sat back, astonished at the amount of development since his last visit, just a couple of years earlier.

"Are you having fun yet?" Greg asked Arlan.

"No. Are we there yet?"

"Come on, enjoy the scenery."

"What scenery?" Arlan asked, pointing to the median strip in the new highway. "Progress?"

Large palm trees had been planted in the median strip of the four lane highway, propped up with temporary cables and wooden braces. Dump trucks lined up to dump their loads of broken limestone and sand next to the palms. Laborers struggled to spread and level the mix around the trees. They passed a small section of median that was apparently finished. Grass had been planted and somehow grew on top of the limestone and sand that had been spread around a dozen or so trees.

"The place is growing pretty fast," Greg said with a smile.

"That's what I've heard. But growth isn't necessarily progress. Look over there," Arlan said, pointing to the right.

They passed several commercial-type structures built from concrete blocks and metal windows that had been erected where there was once mangrove. The buildings that were finished, or close to it, displayed signs that read 'Furniture' or 'Building Materials' in Spanish.

Greg said, "So? People need furniture for their new condos."

Arlan slumped in his seat and shook his head. He pointed to their left and asked, "And what are those?"

The ocean side of the road was lined with large, out of place walls with gated entrances to hotels and all-inclusive resorts that had names with no significance in the Mayan language, just a couple of short syllables thrown together—just like Cancun.

"The names don't even make any sense."

"They're Mayan," Greg said.

"Are you sure? When was the last time you spoke Mayan?"

"They sound Mayan. Maybe they're nice places," Greg said.

"They might be. But that's not what I'm talking about."

Arlan watched a couple of scrawny dogs with short brown hair venture out onto the highway. Their ribs showed and one had a noticeable limp from a previous injury. Greg swerved the VW to avoid hitting them. The dogs didn't seem frightened. They simply leaned into the roadside brush as the VW passed, as though they had done it a thousand times before. Arlan turned around and saw them lope out onto the median strip, making it just before a line of fast moving taxi shuttles passed them.

"What are you talking about then?" Greg asked.

"A beach runs along this entire coast, all the way to Belize. It's narrow and bordered on the inland side by a large beach dune. At least there used to be a dune. Where it's been destroyed I'd hate to see the cost to replenish the beach or see the damage from the back surge of any major storm. Further inland are mangrove forests and savannahs. In most spots, they stretch beyond the main highway that runs parallel with the coast—the highway that we're on. Look on either side of the road."

Greg looked left and right and then at Arlan and said, "And?"

Arlan looked at Greg and said, "You, better than most, should understand the importance of mangroves. Without their ability to filter nutrients and runoff from the mainland, the reef out there that you make your living from will die."

Arlan pointed to the gates and walls that lined the highway on the ocean side.

"Every one of these hotels that we've passed was built by clearing the mangrove forests—just like Henry Flagler did in South Florida in the late 1800s."

"I thought you were a developer. Don't you build things?"

"Yeah, and I know when land shouldn't be abused too. There doesn't need to be development everywhere. Some places are better off left alone. Where valuable habitat is left alone, the property around it is more valuable." Arlan paused and then said, "Space, meaning open areas, the new luxury. People pay extra just to be near it. And I'm not talking about man-made golf courses. I'm talking about nature."

"People need someplace to live," Greg said.

"That's what cities are for."

"What? Everybody should live in a city?"

"Yeah, that's what I think. Or in rural areas. Suburban sprawl is a waste of resources. Suburbs cut off wildlife corridors. They have no sense of community. They create far too much traffic, and they promote voodoo ecology with their lawns that die each winter and are fertilized back to life each spring, with the fertilizer runoff destoying nearby waterways and tributaries. Eventually the quality of life for anybody living in or near suburbia suffers."

"Okay, okay. I didn't expect a lecture."

"Well, you asked. But, while a lot of major cities are seeing urban revivals, suburbs will become the next slums in the US. It's already happening in some parts of the country."

Greg drove for a while and said, "I guess I'd have to agree with you, especially about the coral reefs. I've been diving on this reef for years. The coral up here on this part of the reef is mostly dead. There are a lot fewer fish. Sometimes we don't see any larger than a wrasse or a red hind. I wonder if the people responsible for these resorts or the corporate execs who invest in them ever snorkel the reefs or visit the jungles. I wonder if they even know that the way they're developing is destroying the beaches and the reef—the things that attracted them here in the first place."

"Of course not. And if you tell the CEOs about it they'll say, 'We answer to our shareholders.' In most cases, the shareholders are oblivious to where their retirement funds are invested. They just want a high performance portfolio so they can continue to travel to areas just like this, where they spend their entire vacation with their fat asses parked on poolside lounge chairs looking out at the sea and sleep in air conditioned rooms with ubiquitous interiors that could be found in any resort anywhere in the world. They couldn't care less what was or who was displaced in order to build the resort and have no clue what damage continues to be done to the mangroves and the beaches."

Greg smiled and said, "Out of sight, out of mind."

Arlan continued, "By the time the coral reefs are dead and the beaches eroded, the portfolios will have moved on to prey elsewhere—wherever there is promise of more short-term profits."

"Jesus, Arlan. This stuff pisses you off, doesn't it."

"I guess so." Arlan slumped in his seat and said, "I'll shut up."

"Good, because we've reached Playa."

Arlan sat back up to see what had changed since his last visit. They entered the outskirts of Playa and continued to drive through at least a half dozen more stoplights and past hundreds more buildings that weren't there during his last visit. He rode in silence and took it all in. Then he said under his breath, "This place has really changed."

Near the center of Playa del Carmen, and a half block from the beach, Greg pulled into a parking space in front of a small, funky hotel. On either side were new glossy hotels. It looked familiar. Arlan had probably walked past it during previous visits. It had definitely been built before Playa became a 'destination.'

Arlan followed Greg into a small office about two meters from the road. It took a moment for Arlan's eyes to adjust from the intense sunlight outside. He heard Greg say, "Alemayan. Como estas?"

"Hola, my gringo friend. Don't call me Alemayan," a blond-haired man sitting behind the desk said. His accent reminded Arlan of Arnold Schwarzenegger. Actually, it reminded him of a *Saturday Night Live* skit.

Greg introduced Arlan to Peter.

"Nice to meet you, Peter. What's with *Alemayan*?" Arlan asked.

"I am German, which is Aleman in espanol."

"And?"

Greg interrupted, "Peter thinks that his German roots allow him to run his hotel with perfection."

"Look around. It perfection," Peter said.

Arlan looked back at the beat-up VW they arrived in and another one parked next to it and up at the crooked marquee that hung precipitously above the entrance to the hotel by a rusted chain. He reminded himself not to walk under it when... if... he checked into a room inside. The whole place needed to be painted. The one window in the office was cracked, and the chair Peter sat in was missing an arm.

Greg said, "Because Peter's busy perfecting his hotel, and because apparently nobody in Playa is good enough to last more than a week as an employee, he ends up doing everything himself. He has no time for German punctuality."

Peter feigned indignation and said loudly, "My friends call me Peter, not Alemayan. And I am never late. And these people I hire always steal from me." He paused and asked, "And now, after that introduction, you want rooms from me, Greg?"

Greg smiled. Peter grabbed two room keys from a box on his desk.

"Are you here to wrestle with crocodiles and stare down sharks, or are you going to act like a normal tourist this time?" Peter asked Greg, looking to Arlan with a grin.

These two seemed to know each other well, and Arlan listened to their banter for a while. After a few minutes he decided to let the two of them catch up. He stepped out of the office and sat in a plastic chair, one of two that were haphazardly placed at a small plastic table a few feet from the office entrance. Arlan leaned forward and placed his elbows on the table, the weight causing the table to drop an inch on his side.

Arlan could hear the steady rhythm of the mild surf and the cacophony of beach-goers that he knew were just on the other side of the buildings across the street. He breathed in deeply just to feel the warm, heavy Caribbean air—until the exhaust fumes entered his lungs.

A couple of scooters sped by. Their drivers' faces and those of the passengers on the back were hidden behind helmets with face shields. But there were more pedestrians than scooters or cars on the road. It was late in the afternoon and a transition time for the streets of Playa. People who wore beach attire and carried sandy towels were leaving the beaches late. They mixed with people who had already showered and dressed for up-coming nighttime activities on Fifth Avenue.

Arlan and Greg tossed their bags into the rooms shown to them by Peter and started to walk toward Fifth Avenue. Before they left, Peter told them that he would take a night off and join them later for dinner. He wanted to catch up with Greg on his adventures since his last visit.

"It's still light. Let's walk over to the Blue Parrot Beach Bar for a beer first," Greg said to Arlan.

"Fine with me. I'm just a tourist today," Arlan said, and they walked a few meters to a short path that led to the beach and the Blue Parrot bar. It took less than two minutes.

"What the hell happened to the beach?" Arlan asked Greg. He walked to the water's edge and looked up and down the beach at the fronts of many of the older hotels in Playa. "The sea is right up to the pools and hotel rooms. There's no room for beach chairs."

"Look north. See that long pier?"

"I see it. It's empty. It wasn't there the last time I was here."

"It was built by the government to accommodate cruise ships. But large cruise ships can't get inside the barrier reef."

"The last time I was here there was a wide beach."

"Well, not anymore. Let's have a beer and then walk up to Fifth Avenue."

They spent the next couple of hours walking up and back down the length of Fifth Avenue to see the numerous new stores and bars that had opened. Some of the shops were just boxy spaces filled with trinkets, and some had marble floors and fancy display cases. Some of the shops sold local crafts and many more were internationally known chains. A few of the bars and restaurants were small holes-in-the-wall with plastic chairs and tables. Others were built by more creative designers who left some of the original jungle and limestone formations to intertwine throughout the interiors. Several of the bars had live bands playing and some had boxed music, but all of them had tables and chairs that spilled out onto the avenue. The chain restaurants had their corporate design stamped inside and out.

Greg and Arlan decided to sit at an outside table on a busy corner of Fifth Avenue. They waited for Peter and watched the mass of tourists sauntering by. Some of the tourists were drunk, and many drank as they walked. Some walked with a purpose. Most of them just bumped into other slower moving tourists in front of them, mesmerized by the plethora of restaurants, bars, and shops available every few steps. Greg was astounded at how many beautiful women walked by. Arlan agreed.

As the night wore on, more tourists packed into the avenue—groups, couples, and some who walked alone. At times, so many tourists tried to pass through the busy intersection that the pedestrian traffic came to a brief, sweaty halt in front of their table.

This was a different Playa—still interesting, but no longer fresh.

Arlan reflected on the Playa del Carmen he had visited several times in the past. His first visit was in the eighties. There were no stoplights coming into town. There was no town. Playa was a fishing village with a plaza and a ferry boat service to the island of Cozumel, eighteen kilometers to the east. The village was on the beach a kilometer east of the north-south road that ran from Cancun to Tulum, which, at the time, had two lanes from Cancun to Playa and then turned into one lane from Playa to Tulum. There was a lot to like about the laid back atmosphere and remote beach and the more adventurous tourists had started to discover Playa.

Arlan's next visit was in the late nineties. Playa, by happenstance, was on its way to international tourism glory, with Fifth Avenue as the foundation that allowed Playa to grow into one of the most unique experiences in the world. It wasn't planned by a bunch of government consultants who, had they been given the chance, would have turned Playa into a seventies-style mass of clunky concrete buildings and parking lots. Playa's popularity took everybody by surprise, which allowed it to grow organically.

Within a couple of years, Playa del Carmen found itself the not-so-secret mecca for the world's cool people. But none knew precisely why. Its identity then was that it had identity, certainly not one that could be accurately described. The experience was so unique that Playa del Carmen couldn't be labeled as any single type of tourist destination. To Arlan, and to everybody he met there at that moment, Playa was in a perfect place.

During the day, everybody was at the beach. At night, Fifth Avenue ruled. Fifth Avenue was finally allowed to shut down to any vehicular traffic, except morning delivery trucks, as it filled with curious tourists, mostly from Mexico, South America, and Europe. Most Americans stayed close to Cancun until a hotel opened between the beach and Fifth Avenue and promoted itself as a perfect place for US corporate retreats. Then, among the scruffy circus of Europeans, backpackers, beautiful women from South America, a few Mexican nationals, and even fewer American adventure travelers, clean-cut American families strolled down Fifth Avenue, taking it all in with confused but happy expressions.

Everybody who walked the street looked out of place, yet nobody looked out of place. There was a comfort level in the wonderment of it all.

But the phenomenon was big, and it had a mind and momentum of its own, controlled only by its unbelievable success in attracting an unlikely cross-section of the world's demographics without even trying. It kept growing.

Arlan sat and enjoyed the show, but he could see that the party was ending. The corporate chains had arrived in Playa and squeezed the last bit of charm out of it. The tourists who walked by didn't know it. And the local business owners wouldn't admit it.

"Alemayan has arrived," Greg said loud enough for Peter to hear as he approached the table and to bring Arlan back to the present. Peter sat at the table with a 'humph'—one and a half hours later than he said he'd be there.

"Who's running the hotel? Won't it fall down without you?" Greg asked Peter.

"Very funny, my gringo friend," Peter responded, not smiling.

A waiter came over and took Peter's drink order. He asked if they would be eating and said that he would return with menus.

"I understand you've been in Playa a long time," Arlan said to Peter.

"Yes. When I built my hotel it was the only building on the block. I was surrounded by jungle."

"It's a different kind of jungle now, eh?" Arlan asked. "I've been here several times but not for a few years. I'm pretty sure that I've walked by your hotel before." Arlan took a drink and said, "This place has really grown—quickly."

"It's the fastest growing city in this hemisphere."

Arlan wondered where that information came from and if it was true. He didn't know of anybody keeping records like that. How would they go about it? It seemed a pretty subjective science. But it was precisely those kinds of statements that provided the hype needed to fuel the fire.

"Maybe that's not a good thing," Arlan said to Peter.

"What are you saying?" Peter asked. "Growth is a bad thing?"

"It can be."

Peter's drink came and he gulped half of it in one sip.

Greg said, "Arlan is a developer."

"He doesn't talk like one," Peter replied.

"Well, he's not a typical developer. And you might want to listen to what he says. He knows a lot about resort development and environmental destruction."

Peter laughed and asked, "Aren't those the same thing?" He took another long drink and asked, "Arlan, why do you think growth is bad?"

Arlan smiled and thought of Arnold Schwarzenegger again. He said, "I didn't exactly say that. But I can see that Playa has grown too much, too fast. And I can see problems."

"What kind of problems? Look around at all of the happy tourists," Peter said and pointed to a group of Japanese tourists who had stopped walking in the middle of Fifth Avenue and tried to take photos. They were jostled by a passing group of loud Italian men who wore plaid fedora hats, bright-colored shorts, and loafers over their black socks.

"Playa was at a good place in its evolutionary cycle a few years ago. Maybe it was the perfect place in its life as a tourist destination. I don't see the same crowd here now," Arlan said.

"And what is this evolutionary cycle?" Peter asked.

"It's the lifetime of a place," Arlan answered.

"My English is not so good. What does that mean?"

"Every place has personality. Places are living, breathing, complicated mixes of geology, buildings, people, flora, fauna, and attitude. And every place on earth is in constant change. They're either evolving or devolving."

"So Playa is like an animal?" Peter asked.

"Kind of. Listen, places have a beginning—a birth. Most started out simply as a good place to settle because they offered natural protection or an abundance of resources. This was the stage. In most cases, this stage began hundreds, or even thousands of years ago."

Greg and Peter watched four well-dressed women walk by. Arlan stopped and asked, "Are you listening?"

Peter and Greg nodded, their eyes still on the women.

Greg said, "We're listening."

"Okay. If the place survives and if the resources are sustainable, it grows. Families multiply, new settlers stumble in. Their families grow. Services and organization are needed. This ushers in the *pioneering* stage.

"Once the pioneers have learned how to tap into the natural and human resources and have secured a semblance of organization and government, the first few variations of *pre-development* stages might be introduced, which leads to a *full-development* stage."

"What is the development stage?" Peter asked.

A drunken beggar stumbled up to the table next to theirs where a young American couple was dining. Arlan could smell him from ten feet away. He mumbled something in Spanish to the young couple and held out his hand. The couple didn't ignore him but didn't acknowledge him either. After a minute he stumbled past their table and started to harass an older tourist couple a few tables down. They sent him on his way. Peter paid no attention.

"The development stage starts when a place grows beyond its original physical boundary capacity and needs to spread out. Some call it growth. Others call it suburbs. In either case, additional infrastructure is built, allowing more people to arrive. And the natural resources start to suffer."

"And that is the stage that you think Playa is in, Arlan?"

Arlan said, "No, Peter. I think Playa is well beyond that. People come, infrastructure is needed and built. More people come. More infrastructure is needed. More is built. The cycles eventually stop, depending on available remaining sustainable resources. If the cycle doesn't stop, and when the available resources are spread too thin, an *over-development stage* begins. This stage is easily confirmed when the quality of life for everybody in the community, not just the service sector, which, by this point, has already been suffering a very low quality of life, declines."

Competing mariachi bands struck up songs outside restaurants on either side of them. One group wore traditional white, sequined outfits and large, white sombreros. The other group wore the same outfit in black. Their annoyingly loud music selections clashed. None of the tourists offered them money.

"Where did these bands come from? Mariachi isn't even a Yucatecan tradition," Arlan shouted.

Peter shouted back, "They came from Cancun. The hurricane that blew through Cancun last year put them out of business. So they all crowd into Playa."

The beggar returned and stumbled into the trumpet player of the white outfitted band. The trumpet player smiled politely and shoved the beggar farther up the avenue.

"Peter, I'd say that Playa is in the over-development stage and on the brink of something worse."

"What would that be?"

"The *implosion stage.* The collapse of any sustainable growth and an exodus of inhabitants, those who can afford to leave."

Peter smirked. Arlan could tell that he wasn't buying into this.

Peter asked, "What then?"

"After a significant amount of time has passed, and if anything remains in the area that is worth saving, a re-birth or renewal might take place—the *re-building stage*. But, even if it does, the new place is never the same as the old one."

Greg's phone chirped. He answered it. With a serious look, he stood and walked into the street to talk.

"But all of this evolution takes time, no?" asked Peter.

"It depends. Like I said, some places have been in the pioneering stage for hundreds or even thousands of years. Some have been enjoying the development stage for hundreds of years, with a few missteps toward implosion, but recover to survive a few more missteps, until one step takes it over the edge. Yet, there are other places that were, or are, doomed from the beginning. They build up and die very quickly, most of the time because their growth was based on a naïve or dishonest assessment of their sustainability."

"And how do you know all of these things, Arlan?"

"Peter, look around. Twenty years ago you were a pioneer here."

Arlan pointed to a T.G.I. Friday's restaurant a block down the avenue and asked, "How many corporate restaurant and retail chains have set up shop in the past two years?"

"A lot," Peter answered.

"Rents are astronomically high, aren't they?" Arlan stated, more than asked.

Peter didn't answer. Instead, he looked toward the T.G.I. Friday's and then ordered more drinks.

"How many restaurants does Playa need? How many start up and go under within a few months?"

Peter's eyes registered that Arlan was onto something. He said, "Rents are high. Restaurants open and close every day."

"Greg and I walked up and down Fifth Avenue before we sat down. I saw scores of international real estate broker franchises offering to sell the thousands of condos and homes being offered by developers. Most of these condos and homes aren't built yet. They were depicted as 'coming soon' on site plans hung in the windows of the brokers' offices. I can't see how Playa can sustain this kind of growth. It probably reached equilibrium several thousand condos ago."

The waiter brought three more drinks.

"And what other places have died because they grew too fast?" Peter asked.

"There are examples of dead or dying places all over the world and throughout history, one right here in the Yucatan—Chichen Itza. There are plenty of other ancient examples... cities such as Machu Picchu, Tikal, Great Zimbabwe, Mesa Verde."

"But nobody knows why those places died."

"There are modern examples—present day Detroit, East St. Louis, or New York City of the seventies."

"But those are different than Playa," Peter said.

"Not really. Look at the once bustling mining towns of the American west that are now ghost towns. Parts of the Costa del Sol on Spain's Mediterranean coast were over-built to the point of complete failure. Hotels and resorts were abandoned, requiring the government to step in and raze the empty buildings, removing the eyesores and creating more open space in an attempt to lure tourists back.

"Look at Haiti. Long before the earthquake, the mountains were denuded of trees, cut by locals to make charcoal. The lack of soil stability sent millions of tons of loose sediment down the slopes and into the sea, which turned an ugly brown color and destroyed the coral reefs and the sea life... and tourism."

Arlan stopped and took a drink. Maybe he should stop talking. Just as Greg returned, a waiter appeared and asked if they were ready to order food.

"Necesito mass tiempo," Greg said and the waiter disappeared.

"Problem?" Arlan asked Greg.

"I need to go to Cancun tomorrow. My partner is flying in with his family for a short vacation. He's thinking about pulling the plug on our business deal down here." He looked at Arlan and said, "I'm going to have to cancel our trip south. I'll still pay for the room. With Peter offering a discount it won't cost me much."

Peter protested, "I'm not offering a discount."

Arlan said, "That's too bad, Greg. Do you think you can turn him around? Should I wait here for a day or two to see what happens?"

"I don't know. He's fickle, and I've been through this with him before. I wouldn't bank on this thing moving forward. Sorry that I brought you down here for nothing."

Arlan should have been more disappointed, but he wasn't. He'd been through so many deals in the Caribbean, many of them failures because they never got off the ground. He was used to it. People tend to become emotionally involved with the idea of an investment in the tropics while they're there, but once they return to their real world they tend to focus on the day-to-day grind and lose interest in putting money in paradise. He shrugged it off, knowing that he would find other things to do.

"I'll need the VW, if that's okay," Greg said to Peter.

"No problem. It will cost the same price as before."

"I don't even get a discount on the VW? It barely runs," Greg said with a laugh.

"I don't think you will get a discount. Your friend Arlan is telling me that Playa is doomed. I'll need all of the money I can get."

"Wow," Greg said and pointed to a group of four ladies who sashayed down the avenue. "Look at the two in front."

Peter laughed. "So, you now like men who dress like women, my gringo friend?"

"What? Are you kidding?" He looked at them again. "There's no way," Greg said. "Are you sure?"

The transvestites waved to Peter. He waved back and shouted, "Hola, muchachas. Como es el negocio esta noche?"

One of them answered in a husky voice, "Toto bien, Peter. Esta guapo hombres ocupados?"

"Posible mañana," Peter answered, and they continued down the avenue.

"I can't believe that those are men. You know them?" asked Greg.

"If I wasn't here to protect you, you would end up with a dick in your ass, Greg. I should charge more money for the room and the car."

Arlan watched the exchange. The two in the front *were* good. He couldn't see any sign that they were males.

Greg finished his beer and looked around for the waiter. "You ready for another round?" he asked Peter and Arlan.

"Sure."

Greg looked at Arlan. "Why do you think Playa is doomed?"

"I didn't say it was doomed. I was just pointing out obvious changes and growth problems that could lead to its collapse. It's just my opinion."

Peter asked, "What other problems do you see?"

"I used the baño earlier. A sign in there read, 'No paper in toilet.'"
"So."
"You have a sewage collection problem in Playa?"
Peter didn't say anything.
"And all of the construction and the promises of more condos and homes?" Arlan asked.
"What about it?"
"Where do all of the workers come from?" Arlan asked Peter.
"I don't know. I think Chiapas and Cuba."
"And where do they live?"
"The construction laborers live in cardboard boxes and under metal roofing material on the construction sites," Peter answered. "But a lot of the workers live across the highway."
"In barrios?" Arlan asked.
Peter took a drink and looked at a menu that lay on the table. Both Peter and Greg seemed contemplative.
Another beggar passed by, followed by another loud group of Americans. Behind them was a large group of Italians. The language didn't give their country of origin away... their goofy attire did. The women had sagging boobs that hung out of skimpy bathing suit cover-ups and fat men still wore Speedos they had worn earlier on the beach. Three very attractive women in long, sequined dresses walked by. They were more hurried than the rest of the tourists.
Greg said, "I've heard that the cartels have moved into Playa and are shaking down business owners."
"They don't bother me," Peter stated, with more bravado than confidence.
Arlan said, "I hate to be a doomsayer, Peter, but the pioneers, the interesting characters and the eccentric tourists... those who put places like this on the map, are disappearing. They're being pushed out. It looks to me like they are being replaced by over-dressed, wannabe interesting people and under-dressed homeless people."
The waiter returned and took their food order. Peter struggled with the preparation of the fish of the day, which was served whole. After a lengthy discussion, the waiter agreed to remove the head and tail and give Peter a filet. He then left the table with an exasperated smile.

Peter turned his attention back to Arlan. "So, we are doomed to be taken over by normal tourists? Do you have any more predictions for us, Arlan?"

Arlan smiled and shook his head. He turned to Greg and said, "I hope you can work things out with your partner. Like I said, I'll be around for a few days if you do. Let me know what happens."

"What are you going to do?" Greg asked Arlan.

"I think I'll head down to Belize to look up an old friend."

Another group of attractive ladies walked by, flirting with their eyes and giggling amongst themselves. They stopped in front of a shop across the street. Arlan guessed they were transvestites. He made the mistake of smiling at them. They giggled and gave him coy looks.

Arlan ignored them and asked Peter, "What's the easiest way to get to Belize from here?"

"Drive or take a bus. But the bus stops at the border, and you'll have to find a ride to Corozal, where you can fly to Belize City. It's easier to drive."

"Can you suggest a car rental agency?" Arlan asked.

"I have another VW you can rent."

"Do you mean that beat up black one parked in front of your hotel?"

"It is a German-made car, Arlan."

"I think that one was made in Mexico."

Peter smiled and said, "Not all Volkswagens are made in Mexico."

"Well, I would like to take your German car, made in Mexico, to Belize."

"Why do you want to go to Belize, Arlan?"

"As I said, I want to look up an old friend."

"How long are you going to need my German car?"

"I'll be back in less than a week."

The group of transvestites from across the street approached their table. Greg rolled his eyes and said, "I think I can tell with this group."

Peter said something to the transvestites that Arlan couldn't make out.

The transvestites swaggered away, giggling a little louder, which must have taken one of them out of character because the voice register of one of the giggles was quite low.

Greg said, "Wow. There are a lot of transvestites in Playa."

With a big smile, Peter turned to Arlan and said, "Maybe we are not so doomed after all."

Chapter 10

It was almost impossible for Arlan to keep Peter's VW on the road. After witnessing three serious accidents, five recently squashed dogs, several unrecognizable masses of meat and fur in the road, and passing through two military checkpoints, Arlan arrived at the Mexico-Belize border.

Arlan continued toward Belize City and reflected on how much this part of the world, especially Mexico's Caribbean coast, had changed since he first started to visit the area more than twenty years earlier. The innocence and naiveté of the people he had enjoyed during his past trips had given way to a faster-paced experience where everybody hustled. Tourism had become entrenched, some of it the result of growth from genuine curiosity of the natural environments and cultures in the region; more of it was the result of contrived development sponsored by greed, arrogance, and stupidity.

What was clear during his first visit to the area a couple of decades earlier was that, other than Cancun, this entire area, from south of Cancun and into Belize, was a primitive paradise, an honest place that accepted what it was and didn't pretend that it was anything else. It was an authentic experience for travelers to the area, and their word of mouth brought adventurous tourists who were tired of the typical experience that offered nothing to stimulate their curiosity. But there was little tourism infrastructure in place—roads were bad, there were few hotels and restaurants, and there were no organized tours.

The few developers who stepped in to meet the new tourism demand knew only how to cater to a mass tourism market. They envisioned large hotels, golf courses, and shopping centers. What they built had changed the area forever. Their developments promoted two things, the two easiest to promote: the beaches and the hotel rooms—not the wildlife or the barrier reef or the historic culture of the area. The type of tourist they attracted came and went, proclaiming, 'It was a great place to visit. We got drunk and went to the beach. We met a nice couple from Kansas City. We all got drunk together and learned how to say *beer* in Mexican.'

As the number of tourists increased, a growing number of them wanted to see local wildlife. So developers carved water parks from the mangroves, and dolphins were brought in and trained so tourists could swim with and pet them. A couple of crocodile farms went in on the mainland and on the island of Cozumel. Arlan had heard about an Asian tiger in a cage at one of the large, all-inclusive resorts south of Cancun.

Mexico's Caribbean coast grew into the *Riviera Maya*, which had been anointed the *new destination*. With that, buildings, people, and tourist activities that had no earthly business trying to fit into the local vernacular arrived—over-scaled hotels, fake sixteenth-century pirate ship cocktail cruises, Polynesian Kon Tiki boat tours and, of course, the omnipresent local hotel grounds keepers made to dress in a fashion deemed by the hotel management to appropriately signify that the guests had arrived to a nineteenth-century Mexican village.

Once entrenched, the better-funded hotel and resort developments, the big guys, rode the wave of market studies from any one of the major hospitality accounting firms that could tell a developer everything that had happened in the resort development world for the past twenty-five years, but could not tell the developer anything about what the market would demand tomorrow. So the developers made it up. The hotels with less funding, the majority, simply rode the coattails of the big guys, copying, as best they could, everything they saw the big guys do, assuming that the big guys knew what they were doing.

What had been created was the quintessential model of booming mass tourism. The ingredients needed were: a major airlift, Cancun Airport; a government that could, and would, supply needed tourist infrastructure—power, sewer, water, and roads; local politicians who didn't care about the environment or where the growing number of workers would live; and developers who thought like the politicians.

It was evening by the time Arlan reached Belize City. He drove the VW past the open sewage ditches and the dilapidated Victorian homes mixed with newer, ugly concrete structures with small aluminum jalousie windows, and to the center of the city on the waterfront, where better-kept and larger Victorian homes housed several government offices, expensive law firms, and the hotel where Arlan had reserved a room. He parked the VW inside the familiar walls of the hotel complex and carried his bag into the lobby of the Fort George Radisson Hotel.

Arlan checked into his room, threw his bag on the bed, and walked to the glass-topped desk in front of the heavily shaded window. He picked up a tourist magazine, the kind of magazine that could be found in any hotel around the world that told tourists where they should go and what they should do. He thumbed through the pictorials and full-page advertisements of the magazine and to the classified section and small advertisements in the back. There it was—*Captain Jay's Dive Shop, Ambergris Cay*. The small ad had a phone number and an address in San Pedro Town.

Chapter 11

El Simpatico entered a sparsely furnished room, tucked into the basement of the twelve-story office building that served as the surveillance center of their Mexico City offices. Joaquin sat in a comfortable chair, watching a flat screen monitor that hung on the wall just above a bank of computers and keyboards. The image on the monitor was as clear as was the audio that accompanied it. El Simpatico took the seat next to Joaquin, who acknowledged his boss with a grunt.

"Look at that fat fuck. He barely fits into the chair," Joacho said. "I hope it falls over."

On the monitor, Alterio's large frame rocked in a stylish black office chair. He swiveled the chair around to the large windows that would have enabled him to see much of the historic part of the city, but it was too dark outside. The monitor showed only his reflection on one side of the oblong conference table. His suitcoat was draped over the back of the chair next to him. His blue and white pinstriped shirt with a solid-white collar looked tight around his neck.

On the other side of the table sat Guillermo, the CEO, and Eduardo, the CFO of El Simpatico's construction company. The third man on their side of the table, Pierre-Pierre, was the person Guillermo had hired to oversee the development of their new island.

"I told you he'd be coming to us, Jefe."

"What have they discussed?" El Simpatico asked Joaquin.

"They're still talking about families and the weather. You haven't missed anything."

"Yes, Joacho, but we almost missed the whole deal."

Joaquin looked at the monitor.

"Are you sure he's going to accept our offer? He won't go back to the Spaniard?"

"Absolutely sure. Spain's economy is in a tailspin. The Spaniard's banks called in his notes. He's going under. He won't be back."

"He should never have been in the picture in the first place, Joacho. Are you sure you can control this deal?"

"Jefe, Alterio is proving to be a little unpredictable. We didn't know he'd made a deal with the Spaniard."

They saw Alterio check his watch and tell the group that he needed to catch the next flight back to Cancun.

"It looks like he wants to wrap this up. Has everything been agreed to, Joacho?"

"Guillermo will finish things up in a few minutes."

"We haven't increased our offer, have we?"

"No. It's still sixty million dollars."

"That's a lot less that the Spaniard offered."

"Yes. The governor's brother told me that Alterio's father-in-law and his attorney are very angry at Alterio for screwing up the deal. Fucking Alterio raised the price hours before they were going to collect ninety million dollars."

"Joacho, if the governor's brother was there, why didn't you know about the offer and the meeting in Spain?"

"Like I said, Alterio is proving to be unpredictable. He invited the governor's brother at the last minute and didn't explain to him why they were flying first class to Madrid."

"You're lucky that Alterio is such a fuck up then, aren't you?" El Simpatico asked Joacho, smiling. "Let's see how this goes."

Both men sat back in their chairs and watched the monitor.

Guillermo, the CEO, said to Alterio, "We see that you have secured the cooperation of the ejido. They have given you control over the privatization?"

El Simpatico knew that he'd chosen well when he tapped Guillermo as the CEO. He had a disarmingly relaxed style that made people across the table comfortable. The sixty-five-year-old former accountant had a round face with soft features—an honest face. But he'd proven years earlier that he was totally corruptible and, so far, trustworthy.

"Yes, and we have contracts recognized by Reforma Agraria and the governor," Alterio answered. "I sent copies to your attorneys last week."

"We know that you and your father-in-law will receive ten kilometers of beachfront and about one thousand hectares of land behind the beach as payment for privatizing the ejido's island."

"Plus two kilometers that we'll use to honor favors we'll need from politicians," Alterio added.

"But you aren't offering any of this land as part of our deal?" asked Guillermo.

"No. Not yet. You can buy into it later, maybe," Alterio said.

Guillermo glanced at the fake smoke alarm on a ceiling panel.

"Okay, Alterio. We'll talk about that later. We understand that each ejiditario will get title to a lot on the beach. And those lots are all the same size?"

"Yes."

"And those lots comprise the fifteen kilometers of beach that we are investing in?"

"Yes. As you've seen in our documents, all one hundred and fifty ejiditarios have placed the lots they'll receive under agrarian law into a trust. Don Francisco and I control the trust. Once the lots are in the trust, we'll buy them from the individual ejiditarios."

"And all of the ejiditarios have agreed to a price for their lots?"

"Yes. I've negotiated with each one. A few, like the colonel, will receive almost one million for his lot. Most will receive two hundred thousand," Alterio said.

"But you just told us that all of the lots are the same size."

"Yes, but some ejiditarios are more valuable to us than others. We will need them to help us purchase the lots near the village and help with the newspapers. They love to write about the poor, down-trodden ejiditarios always being picked on by wealthy Mexicans."

"Yes, down-trodden all right. So down-trodden that they are receiving millions of dollars for land that was recently given to them by the government," Eduardo, the young CFO, said with a laugh.

"The colonel and a few other ejiditarios will help us get permits."

"Let us worry about the permits. That's part of our deal, unfortunately. I, we...," Guillermo said and absentmindedly glanced to the ceiling, "were hoping that we could negotiate the trust."

"I'm sorry. I would like to, but it was Don Francisco and his attorney, Pepe, who insisted that the titles be held by the trust until permits were issued. It's because of your demand to control the project and the permitting process—"

"We're pretty good at getting what we ask for. We have a lot of political contacts here in Mexico City, but—"

Alterio interrupted and said, "But that's why we are only asking for half of the sixty million at the closing and the other half when you get our permits. I look at the permits as a milestone, a hito."

"Okay, Alterio. I think we can get comfortable with the milestone—permits for titles. The titles will be in a trust, which is the closest thing to an escrow here in Mexico. But we're still trying to get comfortable with our investment. We'll be putting in sixty million. But the total amount needed to buy out the ejiditarios is, if what you say is correct, less than forty million."

"Yes, but we have already invested a significant amount of money. We have paid for whatever the ejiditarios needed so that we could stay in good standing and get the contract to privatize the land. We have paid for VCRs, TVs, boats and golf carts, even medical bills and funerals."

"Surely not twenty million dollars worth."

"We have taken all of the risk. We invested long before we knew we would get the contract with the ejido that would enable us to get title to the land. You will be investing in land with clear title," Alterio replied.

"I guess we can agree on that. Risk equals reward. And we should assume that our price for the partnership is still cheap when you compare it with land nearby in Cancun or the Maya Riviera."

"You will make a lot of money from your investment."

Guillermo excused himself and went to the restroom. Alterio checked his phone for messages while Eduardo and Pierre-Pierre made small talk about family and the Mexican soccer team.

When Guillermo returned, Eduardo said, "Okay, we are set with the densities. The governor will approve thirty thousand keys, right?"

Alterio smiled. "We have the governor's approval for twenty-five thousand rooms. We will get more once the governor sees how much money we will spend in his state."

"And the bridge?"

"My family owns the land where a bridge can connect to the mainland. They have agreed to sell it to us," Alterio said.

"And we know the group that builds toll roads around the country," Pierre-Pierre said. "A friend of mine is the president of the company. I know he will jump at the opportunity to build a road from Cancun to Isla X'lak."

Nobody in the room commented.

Pierre-Pierre went on—and on.

Joaquin turned his head from the monitor and said, "What an asshole." He got up to get a cup of coffee from a chrome pitcher that had been placed on a tray on the other side of the small room. El Simpatico watched Alterio check text messages as Pierre-Pierre talked.

Guillermo interrupted Pierre-Pierre and asked if Alterio had any questions.

"Just one thing," Alterio said. "It is very important. When can we close this deal?"

"We have a few more numbers to crunch, and we would like to talk to our lawyers about a couple of things," Guillermo responded.

"Do you think we can close later this month?" asked Alterio.

"If everything is in order we could make that work."

"Good. Thank you," Alterio said with a smile. "Just one more thing."

"Yes?"

"Can we have a closing celebration in Cancun? It is very important that we invite the governor and a couple of ejiditarios from X'lak."

"Of course. We were going to ask for the same thing. We have a few friends we would like to invite, as well."

"Muy bueno. Thank you."

After another ten minutes of niceties and a few logistics details about the closing, Alterio was politely escorted to the door by Guillermo.

"Thank you for coming to meet us here, Alterio. Together, we're going to build the next Cancun," exclaimed Guillermo.

"Yes. And thank you. I will make arrangements in Cancun for the closing and call you with the details in a few days."

Alterio walked out of the offices and into the lobby to take an elevator to the ground floor.

Guillermo walked back into the conference room and dismissed Pierre-Pierre.

Fifteen minutes after Alterio and Pierre-Pierre had left, El Simpatico and Joaquin walked through the glass doors and sat at the conference table.

"Did you hear everything?" Guillermo asked.

"Yes," El Simpatico said, lightly rubbing his chin with his thumb and middle finger of his left hand, his index finger tapping his lips. He asked, not to any of them in particular, "What do you think about Alterio?"

"We've been impressed. He should have gone into politics. He's a natural. And he seems to be corruptible, which is good," Guillermo answered.

"But Alterio's unpredictable... and impulsive," Joaquin said. "Maybe we should bring him in and let him know who's in control."

El Simpatico shook his head. "Joacho, maybe you are the impulsive one. He is as greedy as we are. We all want the same thing. He and his father-in-law have the political juice to get things done without the intimidation factor. We don't want him, or anybody else, to know we are behind this unless it proves absolutely necessary. Besides, we have Pierre-Pierre to control the planning process."

Joaquin rolled his eyes and said, "Pierre-Pierre is as dumb as a shoe."

"That's why he's our project director," Guillermo said.

They all laughed.

"Your project director, Pierre-Pierre, has no idea who I am or that this construction company is a front?" El Simpatico asked Guillermo.

"Not a clue."

"Tell me about him, other than he talks a lot."

"He's naïve. He talks too much to pay attention to what goes on around him. We took your suggestion and found the perfect front man. He is from a wealthy family who made sure he went to the best schools in the US and that he had high-level banking jobs once he graduated from university. His accomplishments at the banks were unremarkable, but he gained a lot of business contacts and can bullshit his way through a meeting. His mother was from a prominent Mexican family, and he's fluent in Spanish and English. He can navigate around both countries well, just as you suggested."

"Is he Mexican?"

"No, Jefe, he's American. But he has FM-2 immigration status. He's almost Mexican," Guillermo said and laughed.

"Have him check out what Alterio has told us about the bridge and the densities. We need both," El Simpatico ordered.

Joaquin cleared his throat and looked at El Simpatico.

"What is it, Joacho? He can't screw that up. It's time to put him to work."

Joaquin snorted and leaned back in his chair, his arms crossed against his chest.

El Simpatico turned to Eduardo and asked, "Tell me again why we don't build an airport."

"We plan a small airport. But a major airlift, the size we will need to move a few million tourists a year, would take up about a thousand hectares, which we can't afford to give up. And there's the noise and we would need customs offices..."

"Okay, okay," El Simpatico said with a wave of his hand. "I've heard all of this before. I don't like it."

"Sorry, Jefe. The island has some limitations."

El Simpatico sighed and said, "That's too bad. Have you finalized the numbers yet? What's our upside?"

Eduardo smiled. He knew the development numbers very well. His family had built hotels and resorts up and down Mexico's Pacific coast.

"Billions," he answered.

"Explain."

Eduardo smiled again and said, "We spent fifty million US dollars on our last resort we built on the Riviera Maya. It was a medium-sized resort."

"But it is so small. It has only seventy rooms. It cost fifty million?" Joaquin asked.

"Yes. It's a five-star boutique hotel and five-star operators expect us, as developers, to spend seven or eight hundred thousand dollars per room. The three-star operators are okay with one hundred to two hundred thousand per room, depending on their brand."

"Do we make money on our resorts?" Joaquin asked.

"Yes. But the operators demand in their contracts that we put profits back into the maintenance and refurbishing of the rooms, which keeps their customers happy. It's typical for the developers who build and own hotels not to make much money until they can sell the entire investment, which doesn't usually happen until the occupancy levels have ramped up to their peaks."

"How long does that take?"

"Three to five years, depending on the strength of the operator and market conditions."

"We're not in this to sell hotels. Remember? We're in it to launder money. And so far, we're behind. We need a larger investment," El Simpatico said.

"We'll do very well with the Isla X'lak investment. Do you know how much of our money we'll be able to launder through our construction company?"

"How much?"

Eduardo's eyes lit up. "Beyond the sixty million we will pay for our partnership share, we'll spend a billion dollars on infrastructure the first two years just to make way for hotel and condo development. Ultimately, we expect two million tourists a year will come to the island. We'll need at least three hundred and fifty kilometers of roads. We'll move over nineteen million tons of sand and dirt and limestone. The potable water demand will be over forty-three million liters per day. We'll need to produce two hundred megawatts of power. The hotels and restaurants will produce over one hundred and fifty tons of trash per day. As you can see, we'll build a lot of infrastructure, over two billion dollars eventually... unless you can get your friend, the president, to get the federal government's tourism arm, FONATUR, to pay for it, like they did when they invented Cancun."

El Simpatico said, "I don't want the government to own anything on the island."

Eduardo said, "Eventually, we'll build over four million square meters of vertical construction. And we'll spend over five billion to do it."

"What's that mean? Vertical construction?" El Simpatico asked.

"We'll build over forty-four million square feet of hotel, condo, villa, office, maintenance, and retail space." Eduardo let that sink in and added, "And that doesn't include the golf courses, marina, and water park. We'll start to see a revenue stream from villa sales and hotel occupancies after year three and start to see return on our investment by year seven—all clean money to do with whatever we wish."

El Simpatico smiled and said, "Let me get this straight. We will launder five to seven billion and have legitimate resort businesses that will give us millions of clean money each year?"

"Si, Jefe. And if we own the ultilities, we will make even more."

"How long will it take to develop the entire destination?"

"It took three decades to build and fill the hotel rooms and villas in Cancun. Because the market already exists we can do it in half the time."

Joaquin leaned forward and said, "I don't like that the titles will remain in the trust until we get permits. That's not right."

"Guillermo tried, Joacho. It doesn't seem that Alterio is calling the shots on that point. His father-in-law is. I can see where he is coming from. After all, we demanded control of the project. It's a small risk to take. We'll get any permits. Our friend, the president, will see to that."

"But should we trust Alterio with the trust?"

"The titles are in Don Francisco's name within the trust. Apparently, even he doesn't trust Alterio. Don Francisco is a well-known businessman who has a reputation throughout Mexico as an honorable man."

"I have no problem with that part of the agreement. What can they do? Try to keep the titles?" El Simpatico looked at Joacho. "Let them. If it goes that far, we'll protect our investment."

Joaquin finally smiled.

"Sign the agreement and set up the closing whenever and wherever Alterio wants it," El Simpatico told Guillermo. He leaned back and looked contemplatively into space. "We need the entire island. Fifteen kilometers of beach is not enough. Fuck the locals. They can move to Punta Eek. Work with Alterio until we get permits. I'll then decide how we will go about taking the rest of the island."

Chapter 12

Arlan took a twenty-minute flight on a local commuter plane from Belize Municipal Airport to Ambergris Cay. The village of San Pedro Town, the only village on the cay, used to be a charming place. He wondered if it still was. As the small plane approached the island, he could see that the little village wasn't so little anymore. As the plane descended, he saw miles of new construction along the beach north of the village. On the leeward side of the island, he saw at least two large excavators dredging mangroves from the shallow bay. He shook his head as the plane bounced on the short runway on the western edge of the village.

Arlan stepped off the plane, adjusted the shoulder strap of his carry-on, and looked at the one-room terminal where he and the other five disembarking passengers were being led. He looked to his right and could see the street sides of several beachfront hotels. He walked the fifty meters to an opening in the short chain link fence on the runway's east side. He stopped and looked around. San Pedro Town used to remind him of an older Cruz Bay on St. John—not physically, but with its immediate sense of place and its personality—slow, funky, friendly, and totally unimportant in the world. He could see now that the *slow* part was long gone.

Arlan dodged a string of golf carts as he crossed a medium-packed sand road that he knew was the main road on the island and walked into the wide-open lobby of one of the scores of hotels lined up south to north along the beach. He passed through the open-air lobby and stepped onto the soft sand on the other side. Waves crashed over the barrier reef less than a kilometer away. He took a deep breath of the fresh Caribbean air and squinted into the sun that was directly above him.

Arlan smiled and took a ball cap from his bag. His vague memory of San Pedro Town suggested that the address of Captain Jay's shop was south, well within walking distance—everything was. He looked down the beach and saw multiple wooden piers that stretched far out into the ocean, dotted with a sea of red and white SCUBA insignias. Most had not been there when he last visited. Some of the insignias were flags flapping on ropes above little wooden buildings that had been built onto many of the piers; some were painted on the sides of the buildings. He walked into the closest dive shop to ask about Jay and was glad to see that a young lady was in charge. When in Captain Jay's territory, it was usually best not to mention his name unless absolutely necessary. Reactions varied.

Arlan stepped to the glass display counter that served as a reception desk and asked about Captain Jay. The young lady looked at Arlan with raised eyebrows and a sly smile and pointed out Jay's shop four piers down the beach.

"He's the best dive master on the island. He's also the busiest."

"Really?" Arlan said. The Captain Jay Arlan remembered may have been the best diver around, but was far too involved with other, more sordid, activities to be the busiest.

"Tell the Captain I said hello," she said as Arlan stepped from the entrance of her shop and onto the beach.

Arlan thanked her and trudged south as best he could through the soft, sugary sand. He smiled and wondered how many young ladies who lived and worked on Ambergris had been caught up by the charms of Captain Jay—probably all of them at one time or another.

He stopped at the beginning of the wooden pier he thought the young lady had pointed to. The metal-roofed shed that had been built to the left side of the pier was about one hundred feet from where Arlan stood, about a third of the way from the end of the pier. Two twenty-foot boats with outboard motors were tied off to the pier near the shed. Arlan recognized the man standing on the pier barking orders to two men in one of the boats, though he'd not seen him in years. He smiled.

"Captain Jay," he said under his breath.

Still chiseled and well over six feet tall, Jay's blond hair was thinner, but his voice, which carried to shore with the stiff Caribbean breeze, was the same—the voice of Elvis.

One of the men in the boat untied it from the cleats, and the other man pushed the throttle forward. The fiberglass boat jumped from the pier and sped away toward the barrier reef. Captain Jay turned to glance at the beach as he walked to the shed. He stopped and stared.

"O'Brien? Is that you?"

Arlan walked down the pier and took his sunglasses off.

"Shit, there goes the neighborhood. I guess I better hide the women... and the children too," Captain Jay said.

"I just came from the Yucatan. I heard you were in the area. I had to see for myself that you're still among the living—and with no bullet holes from the guns of jealous husbands or pissed off girlfriends."

They shook hands. Then Jay gave Arlan a hard bear hug. Arlan thought he felt a rib crack. He stood back and took in a deep breath. Everything seemed to be intact.

"Well, the 'still among the living part is true," Jay said, and lifted his shirt.

Arlan had spent a few years diving and carousing with Jay in the Caribbean. They were roommates for a while. He was not joking about the bullet holes. Jay had several knife and bullet wounds from his rough life as a modern-day pirate. It seemed to Arlan that he'd collected a few more.

Captain Jay was as reckless as he was charming and the most dangerous living man Arlan knew. But he was fun. There was never a boring, or safe, moment when Captain Jay was around.

"You been divin' lately?" he asked.

"I keep up with it."

"Good. We're gonna go to the Blue Hole tomorrow. I'll get my guys to take my payin' guests. You and I are gonna go out together in the other boat. We've gotta lot of catchin' up to do."

Arlan had been to the Blue Hole. For an experienced diver it was not particularly dangerous. But he knew Captain Jay would find a way to make their dive more dangerous than it needed to be. He would find a way to test Arlan. He always did.

"I just got here. I'm not sure I'm ready for the Blue Hole yet."

"So. You ain't gettin' any younger," Jay said, and closed the door to his shop. "Come on, we're gonna get drunk," he said, and walked down the pier toward the beach.

Captain Jay and Arlan toured the island and caught up with their experiences since they last saw each other. Arlan suspected that Jay only told him of the mild events in his life during the past decade. He was sure that there was plenty of blood and guts along the way.

After the short tour, they drank at Jay's favorite bars and Arlan was introduced to several young and not so young ladies who had spent *quality time* with Jay. But their idea of quality probably differed greatly from his. He called them all 'sugar plum' or 'darlin'—standard speech in the Captain Jay charm package. And it always worked. Arlan could never figure out how he got away with it.

Arlan told Jay about Mexico and of Fiona's request for him to help with the development plans for an island controlled by a wealthy family from Madre. Jay told Arlan that he had lived in Madre for a few years and knew the area well. He suggested that, when it was time to return to Madre, Arlan take a shorter route through the center of the peninsula instead of driving the coast to Cancun and then cut across the top. It would save a few hours.

Arlan stayed that night at Captain Jay's place, sleeping on a beat-up cushioned chair in the living room that was infested with something. Maybe fleas, but he couldn't tell. The alcohol deadened the bites.

Too early the next morning and a little hung over, Arlan and Captain Jay left Ambergris Cay and San Pedro Town and motored two hours out to the Blue Hole. The water below the boat was gin-clear. Most of the ride was over deep water and in mild seas.

As they approached the Blue Hole, the dark outline of coral could be seen in ninety feet of water. The water depth lessened as they got closer. In some places the coral was just below the hull. They entered the geological phenomenon from the opening in the reef on the north side. Once through the coral formation, the water turned deep blue. The little boat was swallowed by a perfect circle in the barrier reef that was one thousand feet wide and four hundred feet deep. The aerial photographs of the Blue Hole that were everywhere on the Internet and in every tourist shop in Belize offered a great overview of just how impressive a perfectly round hole in the earth is from a distance, but it is no substitute for being there.

Captain Jay brought them near the rim on the west side. A ledge thirty feet deep allowed them to anchor the boat. Though they had not been diving together in years, their routine was habitual. Jay put the boat in neutral and drifted toward a good anchorage while Arlan prepared to drop the anchor overboard. On Captain Jay's signal, Arlan released the anchor and loosely held the anchor line until it came to a stop. He made one wrap around the bow cleat and held tight while Jay put the boat in reverse, dragging the anchor until the flukes held tight in the sand and broken coral bottom. Captain Jay shut down the engine as Arlan tied off the anchor and returned to the stern to prep his gear.

"What are these things?" Arlan asked, holding up two yellow, hard-plastic boxes. "They look like the battery packs for my Makita drill."

"One is for me. Put the other one in your buoyancy compensator, or BC, pocket."

Arlan took one and inspected it. He turned it over, looking for writing or a label—anything that might identify it. He found nothing.

"It's a battery pack. A shark repellent," Jay said.

"We're diving with shark repellents?"

"You gotta problem with that?"

"Yeah. First, you and I have never had much of a problem just pushing sharks out of the way if they ever got close enough. Second, I've been diving here and have seen plenty of sharks but none were aggressive. Why do we need shark repellents?"

"Do you remember Charlie?"

Arlan nodded, fondly remembering the large, barrel-chested CIA operative who doubled as a dive master on the island where Arlan and Jay had lived.

"Before he died he had asked me to be his partner in his consultin' business. I still work with some of his old clients. We're gonna test these shark repellents for a Defense Department contractor."

Arlan looked at the little box and slid it into his BC vest pocket. "Uh, okay, but we'll be lucky to see a shark that comes within twenty feet. More than likely, we'll have to sneak up on them to get that close."

Jay rolled a fifty-five-gallon plastic barrel from the bow and past Arlan to the stern. Arlan had seen it but didn't ask about it. He assumed it was fuel.

"We're gonna chum 'em in," Jay said. His shoulders heaved up and down with laughter. He pried open the top of the barrel and leaned it out over the water. Weeks-old fish heads and guts, goat parts, and red mush spilled into the sea. The water turned ugly milky red, then green as the smelly mix sank.

Arlan wondered what he had gotten himself into.

"We'll let that settle for a while," Jay said as he checked their gear.

Arlan took the battery pack from his BC and asked, "How do these work?"

"You know how sharks always come around when you have a big wounded fish on the end of your speargun? Right? Well, that's because they're attracted to the low-frequency vibrations emitted by the thrashin' fish. Right?"

Arlan nodded.

"Well, these things put out a high-frequency vibration, which should repel the shark, right?"

"Right."

"See the switch on top? I'll let you know when to turn it on."

"Right." Arlan understood the frequency thing. He also knew that a hundred things could go wrong with this hare-brained idea, but Captain Jay wasn't the kind of guy one argued with. Arlan knew from experience that trying to discuss the scientific theory behind the repellents was useless. Jay couldn't hold an intellectual conversation. His ability to survive was molded by past insular experiences that required a more animalistic approach to life. He never reflected about his past and he never planned very far into the future. Captain Jay was all about the moment.

"What's up, Rookie? You look worried."

Arlan looked at Jay and said, "You haven't called me by that name in years."

"Well, I haven't seen you in years. But just about now you're actin' all scared and stuff."

"Why do you always feel the need to make diving more dangerous than it already is?"

"You got a problem with sharks? I remember when we used to chum 'em in so you could kill one for McQuin's restaurant. What was the name of the chef he had from Trinidad? He marinated the shark meat in milk to take the salty taste out. Remember?"

"I don't see any power heads on your boat to kill sharks with."

"What? You becomin' a pussy in your old age? Just shove 'em out of the way with the spear gun. We've done it a hundred times. That's if we see any sharks at all."

Arlan resigned himself to whatever was going to happen.

Arlan and Jay suited up and prepared to enter the water. Jay's other boat came through the cut on the east side of the coral. The two guys whom Arlan saw Jay give orders to the day before were at the wheel. There were four people sitting behind them, wearing wetsuits.

"What about those guys?"

"They've got my payin' guests aboard. I told them to stay on the other side of the hole today. They won't get in the way. Hey, grab those spear guns in the bow before you put your flippers on. We might as well get dinner while we're here."

Arlan walked to the stern and spotted the two spearguns in the gunwale. They were the mahogany guns made in Australia—his favorite. He pulled them out and returned to the stern.

"Nice guns."

"I thought you might remember 'em. Hand one to me. Ready?"

"No."

Jay smiled, put his mask on, fit the regulator into his mouth, and stepped into the water. Arlan followed. They hadn't bothered with putting air in their BCs so they could stabilize on the surface before descending. When the momentum of their feet-first plunge slowed, they jackknifed underwater and descended head first, swallowing hard every few feet to equalize the pressure in their ears. Jay abruptly stopped, arched his back, bent both knees and, with a long sweeping dolphin kick with both legs, turned his body toward the surface and settled in a vertical position about sixty feet below the boat. Arlan did the same when he was at the same depth. They remained in place by casually moving their flippers up or down or in and out with a simple turn of their ankles, sometimes accompanied with a slight bend of one or both of their knees. Arlan slowly spun around to get his bearings. He couldn't. The water was murky from the blood and mush Jay had dumped overboard earlier. Most of the large chunks had drifted to the bottom. He knew they had entered the water fifty meters from the edge of the hole but, because of the chum, their visibility under the water was less than half that. He couldn't see the wall, only the hazy outline of the boat's hull above.

Old habits kicked in. Arlan placed the butt of the speargun on his stomach, pulled back the three bands of rubber, and locked them in place. He always felt safer with a loaded speargun, if only to use the spear tip to push big things, like sharks, out of the way. He had his back to Jay and saw a flash of a tail in the murky distance. *Probably a kingfish or an amberjack*, he thought.

He heard, and felt, the unmistakable explosive sound of the rubber bands as they released and the tight, bubbly sound of a streaking stainless steel spear through the water. He heard the impact just before he felt the wild thrashing of a speared fish. He turned toward the commotion and saw that Jay had shot a large amberjack. Two others scurried away into the dark blue. They seemed to always swim in groups of three.

Jay let the amberjack thrash. Amberjacks always put up a hell of a fight. Jay hung onto his gun with both hands. The amberjack jerked hard at the end of the taut line and Jay's body jerked with it.

That should attract the teeth.

Arlan scanned the edge of his visibility for sharks. He moved his head from side to side in exaggerated motions, which increased the limited peripheral vision caused by the sides of his mask.

The amberjack tired but still thrashed, but with less determination and strength than before. Jay made no effort to pull the spear in and place the fish in the mesh bag that was tucked under his weight belt. Arlan wasn't sure why they would want to bag it anyway. Amberjacks are notorious carriers of the neurotoxin, ciguatera. He wouldn't eat it.

Arlan noticed the first shark on the periphery. It came and went with a couple of graceful swipes of its tail. It was either a small bull shark or a Caribbean reef shark. It was hard to tell. They looked a lot alike until they reached nine feet or so in length, when bulls grew a lot more girth than their look-alikes. Arlan remained vertical and turned in a slow circle. He spotted three more sharks closer in. They were definitely bulls. He looked up and saw a hammerhead with its wide head moving back and forth near the surface. He saw Jay turning in a slow circle, counting the sharks, poking his forefinger toward each one he could see. Arlan wasn't concerned—yet.

Jay finished counting and looked at Arlan. He smiled behind his mask, gave the universal 'okay' signal with his thumb and index finger, and nodded. Arlan gave Jay the obligatory reply and pointed to the battery pack in his vest. Jay shook his head no.

Within minutes they were surrounded by sharks. Unless some of them happened to have swum through the chum, they had been attracted by the low-frequency thrashing of the fish on the spear. The chum alone would not bring them in, but it would keep them there while they searched for a free meal. A few smaller sharks purposefully bumped into the amberjack, which now hung dead on the spear. One would bite into it and the frenzy would start.

Arlan knew the importance of keeping eye contact with any shark that came close. Sharks were freeloaders. They preferred wounded prey and loved the tactic of blindsiding. Humans are not a normal food source. They're out of their element in water and therefore slow, which causes sharks to hesitate, not sure if something as big and as slow to react as a human is a threat or just stupid prey.

In a few more moments the activity increased. A four-foot shark took a bite of the amberjack and shook it back and forth until half of it was in his mouth. It swam away, leaving bits of fish and more murk. A six-foot, black tip shark grazed the back of Jay's head and knocked his mask off. Jay caught the mask and placed it back on his head. He pushed the top of the mask against his forehead, looked up, and blew hard, forcing the water out. He pulled the strap back over his head and smiled at Arlan. A large bull shark appeared behind Jay but turned back into the distant blue when it saw two large shapes in the water with air bubbles coming from them.

In general, Jay was oblivious to sharks, though he sometimes took offence when they entered his space. Arlan was respectful, but comfortable, around sharks. He'd seen hundreds of them underwater and had spent a few tense moments trying to keep some of them from taking his catch. He knew that sharks rarely attacked humans. They would, however, lose their fear of divers who spearfished in one area for an hour or so and would start to compete with the diver for fish, especially one that had just been speared.

Still vertical in the water, Jay and Arlan instinctively made slow one-hundred-and-eighty-degree turns to see what was going on around them. There were at least eight sharks in their range of visibility. They knew that there would be many more beyond that. Jay smiled around his regulator and motioned to the battery pack. Arlan nodded, knowing that Jay lived for moments like these. They turned on the packs and waited. In seconds, the sharks disappeared as quietly as they had arrived—like ghosts into the murky background. Arlan and Jay looked at each other and shrugged.

Jay pulled the still-dangling spear and what was left of the amberjack up from below. He took the half-eaten fish off the spear and let it spin slowly out of sight toward the bottom. He then stretched the three bands of rubber, one at a time, back to the notch on the topside of the spear-gun in front of the handle and motioned for Arlan to follow. They kicked toward the wall. Arlan checked his air. He had two thousand pounds of air left in the tank—enough to swim to the wall, spear a fish or two for dinner, and get back to the boat. He moved his head in sweeping motions left to right and up and down as he swam to the wall, looking for any sharks that didn't get the message that there were high frequency vibrations in the area. He was surprised that the battery packs worked. Jay led the way. His head was motionless.

They sank to about eighty feet by the time they reached the wall, a vertical plethora of holes and coral heads—perfect habitat for big, delicious fish. Arlan stuck his head in and out of many big coral formations looking for fish—there were a lot of choices. He and Jay were picky about what kind of fish they liked to eat though. Arlan preferred yellowtail snapper, but they wouldn't be hanging out in the coral heads. They would be in the shallow, open water looking for schools of fry. Jay preferred grouper or dog-tooth snapper, both of which would be hiding in the holes.

They had hunted no more than ten minutes when Arlan felt a presence behind him. He looked back and saw several six-to-ten-foot sharks—probably some of their buddies from the chum soup below the boat. Arlan grabbed Jay's fin as he was heading into a large hole. Jay jerked and turned around. His eyes widened.

Arlan checked his battery pack. Jay did the same. There was nothing to check. There was no way to determine if they were working. There was no indicator light that told them if they were operational. Arlan felt a slight intermittent percussion emanating from the vest pocket where the battery pack pushed against his chest. He motioned to Captain Jay and back at himself and pointed to the surface. Jay acknowledged Arlan with a nod and they ascended, keeping the wall at their backs and their masks turning from side to side, tracking any shark that decided to take a run at them. They kept the spearguns straight out in front of them for protection as they rose. When they broke the surface they spit out their regulators, keeping their masks in the water and eyes on the sharks, which swam back and forth along the wall just below them. They lifted their heads out of the water only to speak.

"I think these battery packs are running out of power. The batteries are so low that they're emitting low frequency vibrations. Do you feel it? The sharks think we have wounded fish in our vest pockets—shark treats," Arlan shouted. "We need to turn these things off."

Arlan saw Jay glance at his boat, fifty meters away. They both knew that it was too dangerous to try to swim that distance through the congregation of agitated sharks.

Captain Jay nodded. They switched their battery packs to the off position, put their regulators back into their mouths, and looked below them. The safer place was under water with the sharks—not on the surface where they had limited mobility and the sharks could attack with stealth, which is the way they preferred to attack. Arlan and Jay descended to thirty feet and hung there with their backs to the wall. The sharks swam back and forth in front of them. The aggressive ones swam toward them and, at the last moment, would turn away, drop their pectoral fins, hump their backs, and bolt in a one-hundred-and-eighty-degree turn back toward the two human shapes. Arlan and Jay jabbed them with their spearguns, and the sharks retreated each time. Arlan grabbed his air gauge with his left hand. He had seven hundred pounds of air left. He knew that he breathed a lot lighter than Jay. It was time to do something.

Jay motioned for Arlan to stay. He pointed to himself and then to the surface. Arlan understood. Jay would go to the surface and try to get the attention of his employees on his other boat on the far side of the Blue Hole. A minute later Arlan heard the water-distorted sound of a whistle and shouting from the surface. He kept his speargun out in front to poke at any shark that got too close. Jay rejoined Arlan a few minutes later. They waited, poking at and sometimes hitting the most brazen sharks. Super focused on fending sharks off, Arlan had no idea how long it would take for the other boat to show up, if it showed up. They heard the unmistakable sound of an approaching outboard motor at the same time. Captain Jay looked at Arlan and smiled behind his regulator, as if to say, 'See, I told you so.' Arlan laughed, bubbles escaping from the sides of his regulator.

Arlan had learned years earlier that animals don't like human noises, especially mechanical noises. The approaching outboard motor sent the sharks away into the blue-grey distance.

Arlan and Jay saw the hull close to the wall and swam to the surface. They removed their weight belts and handed them to one of the crew. Arlan stuck his mask back into the water looking for any rogue shark that might take a run at them. He and Jay removed their tanks and waited for the crew to heave them up into the boat. Last were their spearguns. Then they each grabbed the side of the boat and, with strong kicks with their flippers, shot up and over the side and spilled onto the deck.

Jay smiled at Arlan and said, "Just like old times, eh, O'Brien?"

"Right," Arlan replied and looked up at the surprised guests who had backed away to the stern, seemingly not understanding who Arlan and Jay were or why they had just rocketed into the boat. Arlan stood and made his way next to the man at the wheel. The captain's mate handed him a dirty beach towel from below the center console. Arlan used it to dry off everything but his face. He glanced back at the four divers in the stern. They needed an explanation.

Jay came up and said quietly to his helper, "Take us back to our boat." He turned toward the paying customers, put on his big Elvis smile and said, "Excuse us folks, my little brother here..." he pointed at Arlan, "saw a big fish and thought it was a shark. Imagine that. A shark in the Blue Hole. Never seen one here. Hope y'all enjoyed your dive."

Jay turned his back to the guests and stood close to his employee at the wheel. Jay asked what their dive status was before they came to help.

"We'd just put their gear on and were ready to go overboard. They don't know what's going on," he told Jay.

"After you drop us off at our boat, finish your dive." Jay looked into the water and said, "Don't dive here. Go back to the other side of the hole. Offer them a dive tomorrow at half price." Then he added, "Just make sure it's close to the shop."

The captain brought his boat next to the boat Arlan and Jay dove from. The empty chum barrel was at the stern and a few streaks of blood and gore ran down the side that Jay had tipped toward the water. Arlan looked back at the guests. They were wide-eyed and silent. Arlan smiled and jumped into the other boat and Jay followed. They grabbed their gear handed to them over the rails and waved goodbye to the crew and guests as Jay's second boat sped away. The guests never took their eyes off Arlan and Jay.

Arlan pulled up the anchor as Jay pushed the throttle forward. The boat moved out of the Blue Hole and sped back toward Ambergris.

"You know, those repellents suck," Arlan said. "They only worked for a couple of minutes. Your clients need to take that design back to the drawing board or invent better underwater batteries."

"Yep. I'm gonna hang on to them though. I'll put 'em in the shop. Conversation pieces. Hell, maybe I'll let some people I don't like use them. That would be fun to see." Jay laughed. "Ya know, there's only one true shark repellent for people who don't like sharks."

"What's that?" Arlan asked.

"Land."

***

The next day, Captain Jay and Arlan took a morning flight to the Belize City Municipal Airport where Arlan had left Peter's VW. They landed and walked to the parking lot adjacent to the one-room terminal. Arlan opened the door, threw his bag into the back seat, and settled into the driver's seat while Jay closed the door and placed his palms on the roof and leaned down to speak to Arlan.

"I told you that you didn't need to come over here to see me off. You could have stayed on Ambergris," Arlan said through the open window.

"Na. Wouldn't miss it."

"You could at least let me give you a ride someplace."

"I told you on the way over, I got a car I can borrow here at the airport. I supply the security guard with lobster, and he lets me use his car. Besides, there's a pretty local girl who works the counter in there." Jay pointed to the terminal. "And I need to cultivate me a new Belize City girlfriend. The last one found religion and wouldn't screw me anymore unless I went to church with her... and her mother."

"That would be dangerous. Lightning would probably strike the entire congregation just for letting your heathen ass inside."

"Aw, she was gettin' too old for me, anyway. Hell, she just turned twenty-five." Jay laughed and took a step backward. He scanned the VW and said, "O'Brien, this reminds me of when you were the on St. John. You, sittin' in a piece-of-shit car with a shit-eatin' grin."

"I never drove a VW bug."

"No, but you drove pieces of shit."

"We all did—remember? Your Jeep was built of marine plywood and didn't even have a windshield."

"Yeah, I guess you're right. Listen, Rookie, this was a lot of fun. I'll come up and visit you in Madre sometime. My business will start to slow down in May. I can come up durin' the summer for a few days."

"Right," Arlan said.

"You know something, Rookie?"

"What's that?"

"You should write a book about us."

"What...?"

"I've seen your stuff. The stuff you write in your project brochures and shit. It's pretty good."

Arlan laughed and said, "I didn't know you could read."

"Funny, Rookie. Anyway, you should write about us one day... about all the shit we've been through."

"Are you kidding? We'd end up in jail. Well, you would, anyway."

"I've been there. It ain't so bad."

"Right," Arlan said and put the VW in gear.

"Later."

"Later," Arlan said and drove away. He navigated the maze of streets through Belize City and over the open sewage ditches until he crossed over the Belize River and to the road that would take him back to Mexico. He choked back emotion thinking about Captain Jay and how surprised he was that he was still among the living and doing well—as well as could be expected for an aging pirate.

Chapter 13

Fiona and Arlan sat at a table next to the tennis court in the garden of her home in an old neighborhood of Madre. The mid-afternoon heat had chased them off the court and into the shade of one of the many large trees in Fiona's spacious yard. Arlan was surprised by the size of Fiona's estate, tucked away in a non-descript neighborhood near the center of Madre. The white masonry house was not fancy, but it was old. Completely walled in from the city streets, the home and the garden took up an entire city block.

Arlan had called Fiona as he approached the outskirts of Madre. She gave him directions to her home, and he attempted to navigate the narrow city streets. It took forever. Madre was an old city. Arlan had read that it had been continuously inhabited for a couple of thousand years. Before the Spanish Conquistadors arrived, it was a large Mayan city known as T'ho. The story went on to say that the Spanish used the coral and limestone boulders from T'ho and built Madre, while the Mayans retreated to the nearby jungles and small villages. Modern Madre suffered from what most old cities suffer from—haphazard growth with no master plan as to how to get people and vehicles across its sprawl. What confused Arlan the most was that once he found a straight street that seemed to be a major thoroughfare, it changed names with each new neighborhood he drove through. He complained about this as soon as he reached Fiona's home. She met him in the driveway dressed in tennis whites and handed him a racket.

"Can I at least get my tennis shoes from my bag?" Arlan asked as Fiona led him through her house and out to the garden and the court.

Peacocks and chickens and a couple of Jack Russell terriers scampered around the walled-in compound as they walked through the lush gardens surrounding her home. The tennis court was old and the white lines had faded, in some spots blending in with the faded green court. There were no fences; the only ball-stop was the back wall of the compound at the far end of the court.

Arlan removed his flip-flops and put on socks and tennis shoes he took from his bag.

"Sorry, I don't have white shorts. My shirt's beige. Is that okay?"

Fiona laughed and said, "I don't know... it might affect your play."

He grabbed the racket Fiona had given him, picked up one of the six tennis balls in the grass next to the court, and walked to the wall at the far end.

"Let me hit against the wall to get the feel of this racket. Okay?"

"Sure. But don't wear yourself out," Fiona said with a smile.

They talked sparingly while they played. Fiona took tennis seriously. Unfortunately, her skill level was nowhere near Arlan's, but he enjoyed watching her put one hundred percent into every shot and made sure she won a few games. It was her court. Midway through the second set, Arlan feigned fatigue and forfeited the match to Fiona, who he didn't think was overly disappointed. The temperature was over a hundred degrees. They moved to the nearby white, metal table and chairs set up beneath one of the numerous large trees in Fiona's garden. A short, thick-hipped Mayan lady, wearing a utilitarian white dress with floral decorations at the neck and ends of the short sleeves, brought a pitcher of lemonade and glasses before the tennis match started, but most of it had been consumed during the changeovers.

"I'm so happy that you came to visit. How was Belize? What did you do there?"

"I saw an old friend, went diving in the Blue Hole, and saw a lot of out of control development by cowboy developers."

Fiona laughed and asked Arlan if he wanted more lemonade.

"I'd like some of that cold hibiscus tea. What's it called, rosa de Jamaica?"

"Or agua de Jamaica. Either name is correct," Fiona said. She turned and spoke to the young Mayan who had been shagging tennis balls. He scurried away toward the house. The two Jack Russell terriers chased after him. A couple of peacocks near the kitchen entrance scurried away when the boy and the dogs approached.

"That wasn't Spanish."

"He only speaks Mayan. I'm teaching him Spanish."

"But he's Mexican, isn't he?"

"Yes, he's from a village close to here. But about a third of the people from the villages near Madre speak only Mayan."

"And you can speak Mayan?"

"Of course. Now, tell me about Belize and the *cowboy developers*, as you call them."

"Scores of half-built construction sites litter the beach along the road that runs north from San Pedro Town on Ambergris—little condo projects, a few homes, and maybe a twenty-room or so hotel here and there. Just a couple were finished. Most were shut down. Many are just masses of concrete walls haphazardly thrown up with no design in mind."

"It seems to be the same here in Mexico."

"It's forced development. It happens in just about every tourist destination whenever there is a real estate boom. Investors and promoters who have no idea how to develop property clamber to get involved in a hot market before it's too late. The problem is that by the time they hear about it, the opportunities are gone. They just don't know it. Savvy investors and locals have already snapped up the good stuff. All that's left are the dregs. But they invest anyway."

"You'd think they would learn from past mistakes."

"Nobody has ever accused developers of being creative. They're lemmings. They follow each other to the hot location and copy whatever everybody else is doing. Before long there's more of whatever they built than could possibly sell. Those that survive financially come back and do it again on the tail end of the next real estate boom. It's cyclical—and predictable."

Fiona took a drink and shooed away a guinea hen that had strutted under the table looking for scraps. She said, "Why do developers feel the need to build so many of everything. I mean... I guess I can understand the need for housing, but why build so many condos and hotels for tourists in natural areas? They always end up ruining nature."

"Cowboy developers... hell, most investors, for that matter, tend to look at a virgin mountain top or beach and say, 'Wow, this is beautiful. I wonder how many homes I can build there. I could make a lot of money.' They should be saying, 'Wow, this is beautiful. I wonder how I could allow people to enjoy this without destroying it. I could make a lot of money.'"

Fiona took a drink and toweled sweat from her forehead. "What's going to happen to all of those developments on Ambergris? My economist friends tell me that we are entering difficult economic times. Possibly a recession."

"It's a house of cards. When the market slows, which it will, sales will stop. Lawsuits will start. The jungle the cowboys carved their projects from will try to recover."

"But by then it's too late for much of the wildlife."

"This might sound stupid, but sometimes I think that a recession can be a good thing. Like a forest fire—Mother Nature's way of clearing out dead and decaying vegetation. A recession is the business world's way of clearing out dead and decaying real estate projects, especially the poorly planned projects forced onto land where they didn't belong in the first place.

"Development takes a break, and Mother Nature goes to work covering up the mess left in the destructive wake of bad development, bolstering up the defenses of the remaining natural environment, if any, in preparation for the onslaught of the next boom."

"And there's always the next real estate boom."

"It's a see-saw war fought through many battles and usually lost by Mother Nature. But there are a few exceptions," Arlan said. "And there could be more."

"That's pretty optimistic of you, Arlan."

"I was young and optimistic once. Both eyes were wide open then. A few black eyes later, I guess I've lost some hope. But I have my moments."

They laughed and Fiona refreshed their rosa de Jamaicas from a pitcher the Mayan ballboy brought out from the kitchen.

Fiona asked, "How long can you stay? I would like to introduce you to the family that is working with the island ejido to privatize the land. The patriarch is a close friend. His son-in-law is running this for him. I don't know much about him other than he married into the family and has some large retail hardware stores. He may have sold those though. He calls himself a developer. I think he wants to be one. He's very charming, but he doesn't follow through with a lot of what he promises."

Arlan took a long drink and watched the Mayan ballboy try to coax a peacock toward him with a piece of bread. The guinea hen kept interfering. He shooed it away and tried to coax the peacock to him.

"Our organization has some political clout, and we are trying hard to lobby the federal government in Mexico City to declare the island a protected preserve. But that's a long process and it depends on who is president at the time. The current president doesn't sympathize with us. However, his wife supports our efforts. She's a member of our organization. We're working through her to try to get the president to at least meet with us."

"That's good," Arlan said and took another sip. He looked around at the grounds. The peacock strutted onto the tennis court and took a dump near the service line.

"I've asked my friend, his name is Don Francisco, to consider bringing you in as their developer—if you want to."

Arlan glanced at Fiona and then watched the peacock.

"I don't want to see the island developed at all," she said. "But the odds of getting it declared a federal preserve are not good. I would feel better about any development if you were involved."

"I don't know. This ejido thing is a total disaster. Hell, the ejiditarios and the politicians think that the only way to develop land is to squeeze buildings and parking lots on every square meter—just like Cancun."

"Yes, but you'd be working with my friend. He's a prominent Mexican who carries a lot of weight. You could show him a better way to develop the island. He's a very forward thinker. He'll listen to you."

"Who? The son-in-law?"

"No, Don Francisco."

"Is your friend actively involved with this, or is he just backing his son-in-law?"

"Don Francisco is very 'hands-on.' I can't imagine him not staying on top of his investment and controlling his son-in-law every step of the way."

"I'll think about it. But I don't have time to meet with them this trip. I need to get that car back to Playa," Arlan said, pointing toward the driveway on the other side of the house.

Fiona didn't say anything for a while. "You're going to stay here tonight, right? I have a guest room just off the library. It's the largest library of Mayan history in the world. My late husband was much older than I and had spent years collecting books and manuscripts. He was an archeologist and specialized in the Mayan culture."

"I didn't know that."

"Universities often come to use the library."

Arlan hesitated and then said, "Sure, I'd like to stay, if it's no imposition."

Arlan spent the rest of the evening enjoying dinner and wine with Fiona and listening to her describe Isla X'lak and its environmental significance in the world. He had to admit that the island sounded intriguing. Too bad that he had no appetite to work in Mexico again.

It was after midnight when Fiona showed Arlan to the guest room. He was a little disappointed. He thought that he'd seen glimpses of attraction from Fiona during the evening. He didn't push it. He lightly hugged Fiona and kissed her on the cheek before closing the guestroom door, which was an old French door with glass panes that had become translucent with age.

Fifteen minutes later, he pulled back the blanket and sheet on the queen-sized bed in Fiona's guest room. He climbed into the bed and pulled just the sheet up. He turned the bedside lamp off and resigned himself to sleep. The moonlight shone into the library, giving it a hazy aura of importance. A ghostly shadow crossed the library toward the guestroom door. Arlan smiled. He could easily see Fiona's gauze nightgown, and it was—how could he put it—sexy. Arlan found himself getting exited and sat up in the bed. This is what he'd hoped would happen. He just didn't want to push it like he would have twenty years earlier. The divorce, age, and time—all made him more hesitant with relationships, even friendships.

Just before the guest room door, Fiona took a step to her left and took a book from the shelf. She opened it and, evidently satisfied it was the book she wanted, walked back through the dim library and disappeared.

Arlan felt a little stunned and confused. Fiona was coming to the guest room, wasn't she? She had to have known that he could see her, and she didn't seem to be shy about showing off her sexy body. Was she teasing him? Then he smiled at the momentary return of his youthful arrogance. She wasn't coming to sleep with him. He lay back and rested his head on the pillow. Or was she? Maybe she had second thoughts at the last moment. He turned on his side, away from the door and the library, and wondered if he should tell Fiona that he'd seen her. He'd have to figure that out later.

Chapter 14

Alterio left his new partner's office in Mexico City and waited for his flight to Cancun, which was delayed. He used the time to make phone calls, all of which were to people who could unwittingly help him buy time—time he desperately needed. The first was to the governor. He assured him that the money he promised would be delivered within the next thirty days. Then he called Fiona.

"Thank you for taking my call, Fiona. How are you?"

"Very good, Alterio. What can I do for you?"

"I have been thinking about your suggestion for us to bring in your friend from the US as our developer. I've checked out his website and some of the properties he has developed. I agree with you that he would be a good asset for us. Have you talked to him about Isla X'lak?"

"He was here in Madre for the past two days. We spoke about a lot of things, including Isla X'lak. I tried to get him to stay to meet with Don Francisco, but he told me that he didn't have enough time this trip. He drove back to Playa del Carmen this afternoon. But I don't think he is interested in working with ejido land, or in Mexico. I told you that he had a bad experience here a few years ago."

"I am just leaving Mexico City. I was in meetings with our new partners. You would really like them. They have assured me that they are interested in the work your organization is doing, and they want to develop the island in an eco-friendly way."

"I thought you had brought in a Spanish developer as a partner."

"That didn't work out. He wanted to develop the island like Cancun. We had to refuse his offer. Our new partners are bringing in a development director. They seem to understand how environmentally sensitive any development needs to be in X'lak. But I think we need our own developer for our side of the partnership. Somebody with the experience your friend has."

Silence.

"One more thing. Maybe you could call your friend and ask him to stay to meet with me. I am going to be in Cancun tonight and will be there for a couple of days. I could go to Playa to meet with him."

Fiona paused and said, "I'll give you his number. And I truly hope that you can convince him to help you. I think you'll need it. I need to call him first to see if he's interested in meeting you."

"Thank you, Fiona. I will do my best."

***

After leaving Fiona's house earlier in the day, Arlan drove the VW across the Yucatan on the four-lane Autopista. When he was a few kilometers out of Madre, he tried to call Fiona to thank her for a wonderful time. There was no reception, which was fine because he needed both hands on the wheel just to keep the VW on the road, especially when the speeding *doble remoliques* passed him on the left. The blast of wind from tandem trailers made the VW jump a few inches. Arlan watched the trailers wiggle back and forth like giant serpents after they passed. He wondered if the drivers of the trucks that hauled them were in control or if the trailers would gain enough sideways momentum to eventually roll over. He slowed down each time one passed until it was safely ahead of him.

Arlan turned off the Autopista before Cancun and headed toward Playa. He stopped at one of the roadside Pemex stations to get gas. He got out of the car and watched the attendant carefully. The attendant watched Arlan before finally rolling back the pump gauge to zeros, then busied himself by washing the windshield as the gas flowed into the car. Arlan knew what the attendant was planning to do. Many Mexican gas station attendants scam tourists by leaving the liters of gas pumped into the previous vehicle on the gauge, which adds to the amount of gas actually pumped into the tourist's vehicle. The attendants pocket the difference. Astute tourists who catch the scam by calculating that their rental car couldn't even hold the amount of gas purportedly pumped into its tank can do little about it—mostly because of the language barrier. Other times it's because the tourist has a flight to catch and doesn't have time to argue, which is what happened to Arlan on his first trip to Mexico.

Arlan pulled his phone from his bag while the attendant pumped gas. He had two missed calls and a text message. He opened the message. It read: *Hello. My name is Alterio Delgado. I am a good friend of Fiona Anderson. She has told me about you, and I would like to meet with you if you have time. I am in Cancun for several days and can meet you here or in Playa del Carmen. I would like to show you around my country and talk to you about land that my family and I own. We are interested in ecotourism and responsible development. I am sure that you could help us. Please return my call. Thank you. And please excuse my poor English.*

Who the hell is Alterio Delgado? Arlan checked the first missed call and recognized Fiona's number. He called her.

"You made it to Playa okay?" Fiona asked.

"I'm almost there. I've got cell service again and I see that you called."

"Yes. I was going to ask you to meet with my friend's son-in-law, the one I told you about. He called and asked for the meeting. He's in Cancun."

"Is his name Alterio Delgado?"

"Did he call?"

"No. He left a text message. He said he wants to meet to talk about his family's land and responsible development. Is he talking about the island?"

"Yes. And maybe some other family land they own on the mainland. He's very persistent. But I agree with him. You should help with the island. He claims that he has made a deal to form a partnership with a construction company out of Mexico City. That worries me."

"Is he serious about responsible development?"

After a five-second pause, Fiona said, "I don't think he knows what it is. He... we... need your help."

Arlan hadn't even seen the island that was so precious to Fiona. He'd planned to return to the US the next day.

"I'll think about it and will let you and Alterio know."

He drove the rest of the way to Playa not thinking about Alterio or the island. He thought of Fiona. Was there something there, or not? She was so damn... unreadable. But everybody he'd had a relationship with seemed unreadable—the women, anyway. It didn't take much effort to read the guys—they were simpler, and he didn't sleep with them. He wanted to sort this out, and the only way to do that was to stay in Mexico long enough to see Fiona again. He hoped that didn't mean working on a damn project, but looking at it wouldn't hurt.

Thirty minutes later he arrived at Peter's hotel. Peter came out immediately to check to see if his beat-up VW was more beat up.

"I see that you have survived the trip to Belize and back," Peter said. "How did my German car work?"

Arlan smiled and said, "Peter, your German car, the one made in Mexico, operated just fine. But the next time I want a BMW—made in Germany."

"That will cost you," Peter said with a smile. He looked at his watch and added, "It is too late for you to get to Cancun to catch a flight to the US. I suppose you will want a room from me?"

"That would be great, Peter. Can I get the room with the hot tub and ocean view?"

"You are a difficult gringo, my friend. You already know that we have only showers in the rooms and that the only water view you will get is the fish pond in the courtyard."

"But the ocean is fifty meters from here."

"Yes, with a large building in between. You can walk to the beach and look at the ocean every couple of minutes if you need an ocean view. I will even rent you one of my beach chairs so you can stay a while," Peter said with a laugh.

"Okay, I'll take the room. You can keep the beach chair. I'll hang out at a bar on Fifth Avenue. Their chairs are free."

Peter went into his office and came back with a key to a second floor room. Arlan carried his bag up and settled in. He pulled out his computer, got an Internet connection, and checked the weather forecast for the Washington, DC area. More cold and snow—another excuse to stay in Mexico a few days. He grabbed his phone and texted Alterio. He received a message back almost immediately, proposing that they meet in a Playa restaurant the next afternoon. Arlan agreed, hung up, and showered. He went to look for Peter to see if he wanted to join him for a drink. According to the man who sat at Peter's desk, Peter had left for the night. Arlan walked up the street to Fifth Avenue, not giving Alterio another thought.

The next day, Arlan arrived early at the restaurant where Alterio suggested they meet. Just up the block from Peter's hotel, it was a typical Playa restaurant—wide open to the street with tables set up both inside and outside on the edge of the street. It wasn't crowded. Arlan sat at an empty table far from the restaurants entrance and waited for Alterio Delgado. He expected to see a short, stocky Mayan with a starched white shirt and dress pants walk in and introduce himself. He looked around. Every man near the restaurant, except the tourists, fit that description.

A large, barrel-chested man with a friendly face and Spanish features walked into the restaurant and said something to the maître d' who pointed to Arlan. Arlan watched the man approach. He wore a starched white shirt and dress pants.

"Hello. Please excuse my poor English. My name is Alterio Delgado. Welcome to the Yucatan. I would like to talk to you about some land my family and I own. But first, I must show you a proper Yucatecan handshake," he said through a smile. He held out his hand. Arlan did the same. They shook. Alterio smothered Arlan with his corpulent body and then stood back and held his hand out a second time.

His English was perfect.

Chapter 15

For such a large and out-of-shape man, Alterio had boundless energy. And he used much of it to show Arlan everything there was to see on the peninsula—especially anything that had to do with the Mayan and the more recent colonial cultures of the Yucatan.

"I am very happy that you agreed to allow me to show you the Yucatan Peninsula. It is very important that you understand our culture and history," Alterio told Arlan the first day of their three-day excursion.

"Forget Chichen Itza or Tulum. Too touristy," Alterio told Arlan. He took him to places with names like Labna, Ek' Balam, Izamal, Dos Ojos, and a dozen colonial haciendas with no names.

"Just one more thing that you need to see," Alterio said each time he wanted to show Arlan another ruin or cenote, the Mexican term for *sinkhole*. "It's just thirty minutes from here," he would add before they bounced down bumpy roads for three or four hours.

This day was no different.

They had lunched at a village restaurant that had been built into the side of a large cenote. While they ate, they watched cliff divers perform forward two-and-a-half somersaults in the tuck position, back one-and-a-half somersaults in the pike position, and multiple other dives from a limestone ledge twenty meters above the water. When they finished eating, Alterio announced that there was 'just one more place you need to see.' Another dilapidated hacienda—the fourth of the day.

He continued giving Arlan lessons in Yucatecan architecture and history. A few times Alterio made references to the development of Isla X'lak but didn't push it too hard. Manipulation was an art form to Alterio. *He should have gone into politics*, Arlan thought. He didn't understand why it was so important to Alterio that he help plan the development of an island. Alterio could get a dozen different developers to help him. He shrugged it off and decided that he'd enjoy the adventure while it lasted. Knowing that he'd either be back in the cold US or visiting Fiona in a few days, he sat back in his seat and watched the jungle go by.

The flat topography throughout the area was difficult for Arlan to get used to. He could see for miles across the flat cornfields of the Midwest, where he grew up. On the volcanic mountains of the Caribbean, where Arlan had spent many years, every turn in a road opened up to a photogenic vista of beaches and the sea and islands in the distance. The interior of the Yucatan Peninsula was different. Low-canopied jungle enveloped the roads on either side. There was an occasional opening in the jungle where the locals had planted mangos or bananas or corn, but there were no hills or overpasses to see out over the top of the thick vegetation.

When Alterio finally did call a halt at one of the'touristy' ruins, and while he and Flaco sat on a bench and smoked cigarettes, Arlan climbed the pyramid with the most steps, according to Alterio. One hundred and twenty uneven steps later Arlan reached the top. He took a deep breath. He could see forever. There were no buildings or clearings to view—just the bright-green top of the jungle canopy in the midday sun. But it was refreshing. Alterio had told Arlan that the Mayans built pyramids to be closer to the gods. Arlan was convinced that they were built so that the Mayans could climb above the claustrophobic jungle to be closer to sanity.

Arlan climbed back down the pyramid. A rope had been tied from the top of the steps to the bottom, and most people used it to help them get back to the bottom. Originally built by the Mayans from unequal-sized limestone, the steps had been plastered so that the risers and treads were consistent sizes. Over time, though, the plaster had worn away, and what remained were steps that varied from four to nine inches high, with some treads wide enough for only the ball of the foot. What was a fairly easy ascent became a very difficult descent. What the Mexican government never advertised was how many serious injuries and deaths resulted from tourists who had fallen on the way down.

Arlan reached the bottom where Alterio and Flaco still sat on the bench smoking cigarettes. They all walked back out to the parking lot, where Juan waited with the SUV.

"Arlan, I have one more thing to show you. Have you been on the Mayan canals south of Tulum?"

Arlan smiled and said, "That's what brought me here. I never got to see them though. The guy who was going to show me had some last minute business issues and had to cancel."

"I have a boat and a captain from Punta Eek waiting for us at a small ruin south of Tulum. We can drift down the canals to his village."

"How long will this take?" Arlan asked, and sneaked a look at his wrist watch.

"Just a couple of hours. No more."

Arlan sighed. He knew that was bullshit. He wouldn't see Playa until the next day.

On the one-hour drive to Tulum, Alterio asked, "Arlan, how did you become a developer?"

Jesus, where did that come from?

Arlan had to think about how to answer. Maybe it was time to throw some manipulation back at Alterio, who looked at him expectantly.

"That's a good question," Arlan replied, laughing. "I guess I stumbled into it, like every other developer. It took me several projects before I considered myself a *developer*. At first, I thought I was a builder—until I realized that I was creating projects from scratch and doing everything from analyzing the land, designing the project, building the project, selling the product, and managing the property once it was built."

"I know some developers from Madre. I don't think they do all of that."

"The word 'developer' is used pretty loosely. I mean, a lot of people who buy and sell land call themselves developers. But, really, what do they do? They don't develop anything. They don't build anything. They produce nothing to be proud of."

Arlan saw a sheepish smile from Alterio before he turned to look at a passing sign. He mumbled something to Juan. Juan acknowledged whatever Alterio said and continued down the road.

"But how did you learn to be a developer?" Alterio asked.

Arlan thought for a moment. *What is he after?*

"Developers don't go to college to study *development.* That degree doesn't exist. They have no pedigree. They are mutts. There is no licensing, no tests, and they have no, or should have no, specialized expertise. But the good ones have a unique talent."

"But one thing," interrupted Alterio. "I have a cousin who graduated from Tulane, and he develops time-shares in Cancun. He makes a lot of money."

"What was his degree in?"

"I don't know. I think archeology."

Arlan thought about time shares and how ridiculous they were for the consumer. Marketing companies who work on behalf of timeshare developers frequently use cheap gimmicks to goad unsuspecting tourists into an emotional and regrettable purchase of a hotel room for one week a year in paradise. The marketing companies clean up financially. The developers sometimes make money but more often get stuck with a lot of unsold inventory after the marketers sell the best units during the most popular times of the year and then leave. The buyers never, ever, see a return on their purchase.

"Development is all about being profitable, no?"

"It's about a lot of things, profitability being one of them. But so is doing what's right for the community, offering quality projects for your employees, and building a business philosophy that they take pride in. It's about maintaining architectural integrity and creating sustainable projects that respect the intrinsic environment and local cultures. It's about projects that live well into the future and leave a positive legacy."

"Excuse me, Arlan. Just one minute, please." Alterio turned to Juan and said, "Necesito comida y una cerveza. Deja alli en la tienda."

Juan braked hard and pulled the SUV up to a small roadside store.

"Arlan, are you hungry or thirsty."

"Sure. I'll have a beer."

Flaco got out of the SUV and walked around to the front passenger window. Alterio handed Flaco a wad of pesos.

"Me trae dos cervezas y un taco. Rapido!"

Flaco walked through the open front of the store and disappeared into the poorly lit interior. Arlan saw no door and wondered how the store was ever locked up. Alterio pulled his cell phone from his pants pocket and looked at the screen. He started to thumb a message and said to Arlan, "I'm sorry. Could you please continue? You were explaining about development."

"Are you really interested in this?"

"Yes. Very much. I told you that my family has a lot of land. But we are not developers. I would like to know how it is done. I have asked many other developers, but they just shrug and tell me to buy and sell land."

Arlan went on to explain about the legal, financial, and planning parts of development and explained about due dillegence and project financial models, called *pro formas* and how timing and luck were as big a part of successful development as location.

"But I can go to college to learn how to become a developer, no?"

"No, Alterio. There are no *development* degrees offered in college. Being a developer is less about a specialized education and more about being a quick study and having a flexible mindset. Sprinkle in enough experience to fend off the bullshit and you might have a start."

They rode down the road in silence for a while. Alterio checked his phone for messages and gave Juan a couple of instructions that were muffled by the wind coming in the open windows.

Alterio put his phone in his lap and said, "My family and I have a lot of land. And we have very good political contacts. I've been trying to decide if I should become a developer or go into politics."

"Maybe in Mexico they're the same thing," Arlan said before he realized he might have insulted Alterio.

Alterio laughed and said, "I have just one more question. Why do you choose to work with eco-tourism development?"

"I don't call it eco-tourism development. I would rather call it low-impact development or nature-based development. Buzz words like green and eco become overused and meaningless as soon as they hit the mainstream. They become worthless promotional words used by people and corporations who don't understand or abide by them but think that they create a softer, friendlier identity for themselves or their product."

Alterio laughed and told Arlan about a movie theater in Mexico City that is named Eco Theater. It was deemed *eco* because it recycled plastic bottles.

"I started as a builder in the Caribbean. I was fresh out of college and far too young and inexperienced to realize that I could trust my instincts. I found myself building projects that were conventional—ideas and designs handed to me by architects and partners. I was just a cog in the wheel of a copycat business. After a couple of projects, I realized an important thing—I wasn't building places that I would live in. They were wrong for the island... just as a project that catered to an island lifestyle would have been wrong for New York City. I set out to correct that."

Alterio looked at his phone again and again mumbled something to Juan. He turned his head as far as he could to the back and asked, "So what did you do?"

"I began to develop projects that maintained a sense of place—projects that blended in."

After a long pause, Alterio asked, "Can you develop an entire island as a low-impact destination?"

Either Alterio was a quick study, or he was blowing smoke up Arlan's ass.

"That's a good question. I've done it many times with small-to-medium-sized projects within a destination. But I have never seen this type of nature-based, low-impact development implemented for an entire tourist destination. *That* would be a great project that would require a lot of vision."

"But we have a vision plan for Isla X'lak. Last year we hired one of the world's largest land planners to help us understand what we could do with X'lak. They came to the island for ten days and came up with the vision plan."

"That's a little different, Alterio. But I'd like to see it someday."

Arlan looked out the window at the endless vegetation. He liked Alterio. He had a great intellectual curiosity and an even better sense of humor. And he was comfortable traveling the back roads.

Chapter 16

The SUV pulled off the paved road and into a bumpy gravel parking lot. It came to a stop next to a small ruin, about the size of a two-car garage, only taller. Arlan could see a small wooden dock in a lagoon beyond the mangroves on the edge of the parking lot. A long, single-hull, fiberglass boat pulled up. The captain stood at the stern holding a three-foot piece of plastic that had been placed over the outboard motor's throttle. A helper had jumped to the dock and tied off the boat. The boat had no top. Arlan was glad he had brought plenty of sunscreen.

Alterio, who had climbed back into the SUV while Arlan and Flaco climbed the ruin, climbed back out of the SUV in shorts and sandals, which looked out of place on him. Alterio told Juan to carry a cooler from the SUV to the boat and then instructed him to drive the SUV and their bags to Punta Eek overland, which would take several hours. He motioned for Arlan and Flaco to follow him to the boat, where he introduced the captain to Arlan. There was no need to introduce Flaco—the captain seemed to be an old friend. After they were all situated, the captain's mate untied them from the dock, and the captain slowly motored through the shallow water of the lagoon.

They reached the ancient limestone canals an hour later and spent the day drifting, motoring, and swimming with the gentle current of the gin-clear water several kilometers to the south. In a few places along the way, the canals gave way to wide lagoons. Wildlife was everywhere—in the water beneath them as they swam, in the thick jungle that enveloped them on both sides, and in the sky, where hundreds of species of birds flew overhead. They even had a close encounter with a crocodile. Flaco claimed he was a crocodile expert and tried to tickle the underbelly of the nine-foot beast. In one violent motion, the crocodile turned with a wide-open mouth, hissed loudly, snapped its jaws shut, and stormed away, its explosive bite missing Flaco's arms by inches and Arlan's head by a foot, close enough for Arlan to feel and smell its foul breath.

Late in the day, the lancha left the canal system and motored through a wide bay. Arlan could see the flat terrain of the mainland on his right. On the left was a strip of land that he knew was the tip of a long peninsula. Within minutes the lancha rounded the tip, and Arlan could see the open ocean. The captain hugged the shore until they came to a small village. He beached the bow of the lancha, and Arlan jumped over the side and into the gin-clear shallow surf. Alterio exited the lancha with a lot less gracefulness. Flaco helped the captain carry a cooler up the gentle slope of the beach and to a sandy road that appeared to split the narrow strip of land down the middle—the beach on one side and mangroves and the bay on the other. A sprinkling of small palapa shacks populated both sides of the road. Juan had already arrived with their bags and had parked the SUV under a group of palm trees just off the beach in the center of the small village.

Arlan walked through the soft sand and between two beach palapas. They and a couple more on either side were identical—small, one-room wooden shacks with thatched roofs. Each had an inviting seaside porch and hammocks.

"Those hammocks look pretty good about now," Arlan shouted back to Alterio, who trudged up the beach twenty meters behind Arlan. "Are these rental rooms?"

"Yes. A friend of mine owns them. I thought that we could spend the night here. The road to Playa is bad. It will take hours to get there."

Arlan continued to walk toward Juan and the SUV and the setting sun. He caught a whiff of his shirt, pungent with tropical sweat, and knew that he needed a shower. He was fine with staying.

"Fine, Alterio. Can we rent one of these places?"

Alterio rented two of the four beachfront palapas—one for Arlan and one for Flaco and himself. Juan stayed with a cousin. That night they sat around a plastic table in plastic chairs and enjoyed a late fish dinner in the open roadside restaurant of the funky hotel. The restaurant had no walls. It had no floor—just sand. The conversation was sparse. Everybody was beat.

After dinner, Arlan walked across the sandy road to his beachfront palapa and rolled into a hammock slung between two posts that held up the porch roof. The stiff breeze from the ocean kept the mosquitoes away and caused the hammock to sway gently. He was happy to be back in the Caribbean, if only for another night or two, and had liked the excursion with Alterio. He fell asleep with a smile.

The next morning, Alterio and Arlan sat at the same table they had eaten dinner at the night before and ate scrambled eggs with tortillas. Arlan struggled to keep his plate from blowing off the table. The breeze was stronger than it had been all week. The napkins had blown away as soon as the waiter put them on the table, only to be stranded by the wind against a nearby black mangrove. Nobody moved to pick them out of the mangrove branches and throw them into the trash. There were no trash containers. But there was a lot of trash on the ground and in the mangroves, something he hadn't noticed the night before.

The natural beauty of the village was scarred with unnatural trash haphazardly thrown everywhere, the lighter trash having blown into the mangroves, the lagoon, and a dilapidated burgundy and lime-green concrete structure on the beach a few dozen meters from where they sat. It was the all too familiar sight of the third world crapping in its own nest—the ubiquitous, squat concrete building looking absolutely out of place in the middle of a rustic fishing village. Unfortunately, Arlan had first-hand knowledge that crapping in one's nest is not reserved for third worlds. The developed world has plenty to go around: concrete strip malls that have replaced once marvelous historic architecture; Wal-Mart Super Stores built on the outskirts of many small towns in the US that suck the life out of historic downtown areas; and rambling aluminum sided residential communities that pop up just outside towns and cities, taking away forest or farmland and destroying any character and warmth that might have exisisted before they were built.

Ugliness—designed by idiots and paid for by fools, Arlan thought and shook his head.

After Alterio had sated his appetite, he announced, "I would like to show you some property near here. I think it would be a very good hotel site."

"Alterio, I appreciate your hospitality. I've had fun and have learned a lot from you about your country, but I think I need to get back to the US. I've neglected things there for longer than I should have."

"But you still need to see Isla X'lak. After we see my land near here, I plan to take you to the island. Have you ever been swimming with whale sharks?"

That piqued Arlan's interest. He'd heard about these behemoths, the largest fish in the world, but had never seen one. He and Captain Jay stumbled onto the rotting corpse of a basking shark on Tortola's north shore once. But the largest fish he ever swam with was a thirteen-foot tiger shark. He knew that the much more harmless whale sharks could reach more than forty feet. He also knew that Alterio wasn't going to make it easy to turn him down.

Flaco and Juan walked up to the table with a short, stocky local man. He looked a lot like Juan and was angry. Alterio made no effort to shake the man's hand or acknowledge him. Flaco leaned into Alterio, motioned to the man, and told Alterio, "El primo de Juan quiere hablar con usted." It was Juan's cousin.

Juan stood a couple of steps from the table.

"Eres un ladron. Robo mi tierra!" Juan's cousin said to Alterio in a loud voice. His face was red. His eyes darted back and forth from Alterio to Juan to Arlan. A few nearby villagers noticed the confrontation and stopped what they were doing to watch.

Arlan decided that this conversation was about to get ugly and was none of his business. During breakfast he'd noticed a house that was being built, Yucatecan style, a few meters away on the beach side of the road. This would be a good time to take a closer look. He stood and walked away from the table. Behind him he heard shouts. Juan's cousin called Alterio a thief. Flaco told the man to lower his voice, and Juan told his cousin to treat Alterio with respect.

Arlan put the argument out of his mind and focused on something less stressful. The house under construction was about thirty feet long and fifteen feet wide. Alterio had told him during their travels that all homes and haciendas in the Yucatan Peninsula were designed with the omnipresent hammock in mind. Rooms tended to be fifteen feet wide at some point. Hooks or stubby wooden notched pegs were built into the walls at about head height to hold the ends of the hammocks.

Arlan stood on the side of the road and watched the men work. The house had been framed from large branches and logs cut from the nearby jungle. There was no milling or sanding. The wood went into the structure as is—bark, bugs, and all. Arlan didn't see a tape measure. A small man eyeballed a log and cut it with a chain saw. It was then hoisted into place on the roof by two other men and tied down with small flexible vines, also taken from the jungle. Another man layered dried palm fronds as roofing and tied them in place with even smaller vines. Arlan smiled.

The construction method was primitive, but appropriate. Architects often use ego instead of logic and make the mistake of bringing first-world designs, which need first-world construction methods, to a third-world labor force. This always produces poorly built and quick to deteriorate buildings that look out of place before they were even finished.

"You knew I owed back property taxes," Arlan heard Juan's cousin shout from the restaurant.

Arlan tried not to listen, but it couldn't be helped. Even the construction workers stopped their work and watched the activity across the street.

"You had your notario make up a false title that put the ownership into Juan's name. The public registry accepted the new title because you provided the receipt from the municipio that showed that you paid the taxes," the man shouted.

Alterio denied the accusations. Flaco tried to calm the man down. Juan fended off his cousin's wife, who had arrived and was equally pissed. Arlan walked farther down the beach and out of earshot. He looked out into the turquoise water of the Caribbean. He'd spent thousands of hours under its waters. Its lure was magical. The promise to swim with the whale sharks near Isla X'lak later that day was too good to pass up. He had no idea when he might be back in the area. He guessed that the price was visiting Alterio's *hotel* site—and delaying his trip back home. A small price to pay for the opportunity to get in the water with big fish.

***

"This is not a hotel site," Arlan told Alterio after walking as much of the land as he could and reviewing the plat of the property Alterio had given him.

"But we have offers from a couple of Spanish developers who want to build an all-inclusive hotel here."

"Are you kidding? An all-inclusive? Here?"

"These are big developers," Alterio said.

"Big developers who haven't put much thought into this land, or its location."

"But they have other hotels in the Maya Riviera."

"Look, Alterio, this is a good piece of property. Great beach, a protected bay in the back. But it has a lot of mangroves, which means only about a quarter of the land is buildable. It is better suited for a few beachfront palapas."

"But we can clear the mangroves. I see developers do that all of the time in the Maya Riviera."

"That's too bad."

Alterio looked confused.

"Listen, even if you did scrape the land clean, there's no way an all-inclusive or any other type of hotel will work here."

"But they work in Cancun and on the Maya Riviera, no?"

"Who says they work?"

"But, they must work. Look how many have been built," Alterio said and took his cell phone out of his pocket. There was obviously no signal. He continued to hold it in his hand.

Arlan despised all-inclusive hotels. Maybe it would sound too much like a lecture if he told Alterio that the all-inclusive model was started by the Spanish developers. They built scores of them. The Spanish developers are notorious for stripping a property of all of its natural habitat and paving it over with concrete. Arlan called it *scrape and rape*. All the developers needed to do was to pay off a local politician for permits to build in a mangrove forest, build a four-hundred-room hotel, bring in managers from Europe, hire a few locals to make the beds and cut the grass, bring Spanish and other European tourists over on discount airlines from Europe, collect the tourist's money in Spain, and make the hotel an all-inclusive experience so the kitchen can cook up large vats of high-carb food that can be used and re-used in all kinds of cheap food recipes throughout the week, effectively ensuring that the tourists don't leave the hotel to infiltrate the local economy. The Spanish hotel owners want all of their guest's money, preferably with none of the euro dollars ever seeing Mexico. And Arlan had seen on this trip that the four-hundred-room model was slowly growing into eight-hundred-room models, and more, as the airline industry added more and more flights to Cancun from many cities around the world, especially the US and Europe.

No, that would be too much for his new ambitious friend to take. He seemed to think his land would be the home of an all-inclusive, as ridiculous as it was. Arlan decided to change the subject and said, "Alterio, do we still have time to swim with the whale sharks today?"

"Yes, we will have plenty of time. But one more thing. Please explain why this land cannot be developed. It is very important."

"Alterio, I didn't say that it couldn't be developed. I said it's not a hotel site."

"But..." Alterio started to ask a question and looked at his phone again.

"I don't think the reception is going to improve anytime soon," Arlan told Alterio with a smile. "Okay, Alterio, listen. First, all-inclusive hotels and all of the hotels in Cancun or on the Riviera Maya rely on easy tourist access to fill their rooms. It is critical that they be located within an hour or so from a major airport. And there needs to be a lot of things to do—tourist things, like shopping centers, water parks, golf courses, bars, restaurants, and more bars."

Alterio nodded.

"How far are we by car from the Cancun Airport? My guess is that we are several hours away."

"About four hours. Longer in the wet season."

"The only type of hotel that would consider this location would be a boutique hotel, one that specializes in nature-based activities—fly fishing, birding, kayaking, diving—"

"I really like the Four Seasons. Have you ever been to Bora Bora or Bali? I would think that they would be interested in this land, no?"

"No. Even if you could interest a major boutique operator in this location, you would have a number of problems. One would be employees. Boutique hotels are all about service. In Mexico they would expect to be able to afford about three employees per room. Most boutiques are between one hundred and eighty to two hundred and twenty rooms. Even if you only had half that, ninety rooms, that's two hundred and seventy employees. Where would they come from? Punta Eek? There aren't that many adults in the village. The next closest village is how far away?"

"About three hours by car," Alterio said. "But we could move employees here, no?"

"And where would they live? There is no room in the village. You would need to build housing and services for the employees and their families. There is nothing here."

Alterio stammered and looked at his phone.

"You have less than ten hectares. That's less than twenty-five acres. Even a small boutique hotel needs at least twice that to fit the rooms, lobby, and the back of house operations."

"What is this *back of house*?" asked Alterio.

"That's the operations part of the hotel—trash, maintenance, laundry, storage, management housing, and so on."

"Okay. But just one more thing..."

They spent another hour on the land and returned to Eek. Alterio told Arlan he had some business to attend to and left with Juan driving the SUV. When the sun began to set with no sign of Alterio, Arlan figured he'd be spending another night in the hammock on the porch of the beachfront palapa. It could be worse. He walked across the street to the restaurant and ordered ceviche and a beer.

***

Alterio sat in the mayor's very small house at the south edge of Punta Eek. The mayor's wife was busy in the kitchen with a servant. She had promised Alterio a meal of baked fish with an appetizer of brazo de reina. The mayor and Juan sat at the table with Alterio.

"What did the developer say about the hotel property?" the mayor asked Alterio.

"He said it was a great location and that it is worth a lot of money."

The mayor looked at Juan and smiled.

"Juan's cousin is very angry that you stole his land. He may cause trouble."

"I didn't steal it. The land is in Juan's name."

"Yes," the mayor said, "but now that we know it's worth a lot of money, he will come after it."

"He'll never know it's value. That's why you're involved. You will keep him happy and continue to entertain the potential buyers I send to you."

"But Alterio, I need money to entertain your buyers. You insist that I take them fishing and cook meals for them. It is expensive."

"But you'll be paid well when the land sells. Don't worry."

The mayor smiled.

Alterio looked at his cell phone. Still no service. He looked at the phone on the wall in the kitchen.

"May I use your phone? I need to make an important call."

"Si."

He called Jose Manuel, his notario. Jose was the best investment Alterio had ever made. Alterio was glad he'd convinced his father-in-law to back the new governor's election campaign. In turn, Alterio asked that the governor appoint his friend, Jose, as notario. The state had a federally mandated quota for the number of notarios allowed to practice. The quota was based on population. But who really knew the population of the state of Quintana Roo? The governor made it up. As a new notario, Jose spent his days producing titles to land. He would then provide the necessary notario stamp and record them in the public registry. It was a lucrative business, and Jose had become wealthy, almost exclusively from the deals that Alterio brought to him. Consequently, Jose gave Alterio anything he requested. Scruples and ethics were of no concern.

"Did you get the gringo to agree to work with you on Isla X'lak?" Jose asked.

"Not yet. But I will. Once I get him to the island he'll be hooked—just like everybody else."

"You've not taken him yet?"

"No. He had booked a flight back to the US tomorrow. I delayed the island trip so he'd miss the flight. Maybe he won't be able to get another flight for a few days. More time I'll have to convince him."

Jose asked, "Why not hire another developer? Better yet, why hire any developer? Your new partners are developers."

"They're builders. They've never had to plan a resort destination. But that is good. It will slow them down. Plus, they've hired an idiot as the project director. I think he is a banker. All he does is talk and doesn't seem to know anything about development. That's also good for us. But we need to ensure that the planning goes slowly, Jose... unless you've heard from Alejandro that he is ready."

Alterio had literally bumped into his old friend, Alejandro, at the Mexico City Airport while returning to Madre from his first meeting with Guillermo and Eduardo. Alterio and Alejandro had grown up together in Madre but hadn't seen each other for years. They both had a few hours to kill before their flights and spent the time in an airport restaurant. Alterio learned that Alejandro had been working for the Mexican consulate in China for over a decade, where he had developed friendships with many wealthy Chinese politicians. Alejandro instantly became Alterio's best friend and, by the time their conversation was over, they had hatched their plan.

Jose said, "He's working on it. He thinks he's found the right group. But it will take more time."

"Push him, Jose. You know that once our partners get permits, the titles will be released from the trust and transferred from Don Francisco's name and into the partnership."

"How does Fiona's gringo friend help us buy time?"

"Arlan O'Brien is perfect for us. He's into low-impact eco projects. And he's not shy. My partners want another Cancun. The gringo will fight it and he makes good points. Equally important is that Fiona and her environmentalists won't fight us as long as he's involved."

"Why would that matter?" Jose asked.

"Jose, Isla X'lak is well known. It's in the newspapers all of the time. Alejandro would hear about the controversial project that threatens the environment and hesitate to bring his group to Mexico. The Chinese don't want to get involved with controversial investments, particularly when they are just breaking into a new market."

"I don't understand."

"We need to appear to work with my new partners. But we need to slow them down. They cannot get permits until we're ready. And we need to keep things calm—no controversy. Entiendes?"

After a long pause Jose said, "Claro. But we need some immediate cash. What did the gringo say about our hotel land near Eek?"

"He's not convinced that it's a good site. But he's wrong. The Spaniards will buy up everything up and down this coast. And they'll pay millions."

"What about Juan's cousin, the man we took the land from?"

"Juan and the mayor can handle him. I have promised the mayor part of the profit from the sale. The title is secured in Juan's name, no?"

"Si."

"And you can receive the money from a sale without sharing any of it with the mayor, no?"

"I can make the deal so complicated that he would never be able to find out how much was paid for the land. You can tell him anything you want."

"Okay. Very good. We'll start to promote the land through brokers in Cancun. It will sell. I want you to raise the price to three million dollars US."

"No hay problema."

Chapter 17

Arlan looked at the snorkels, masks, and flippers in a dark blue mesh bag on the floor in front of the center console of the lancha. Then he looked around at everybody's feet—Mexican feet. He looked down at his big feet and hoped he could find a pair of flippers that fit.

The lancha beat into a slightly choppy sea. Arlan, Alterio, and Flaco sat on hard seats that had been molded into the body of the lancha along either side of its interior. They all leaned forward with their palms pushing against the edge of the seat so that they could adjust their bodies to absorb the rhythmic blows of fiberglass against water. The captain and his first mate stood at the center console and bent their knees each time the bow hit a wave. The combination of the wind rushing by and the loud outboard motor made it impossible to talk without shouting. Arlan turned his head and watched Punta Eek fade away. They were heading into the open sea to swim with the sharks.

Alterio pointed out Isla X'lak as they motored past the island. He told Arlan that they would be dropped off on Isla X'lak after they swam with the whale sharks. The island was flat and unremarkable from the sea. Arlan had seen the island on maps and knew that it was shaped like a fat snake with a slight bend toward the open sea. The closest end was probably a kilometer from the mainland. The village was located on the bay side in the middle of the island and was ten kilometers from the mainland. Arlan saw nothing but mangroves on either side of the village on the bay side of the island. Once they were past X'lak and well into the open sea, he looked back and saw nothing but beach and jungle on the ocean side of X'lak.

The whale sharks fed on plankton that arrived with an up-welling from the continental shelf to the shallow waters of the Gulf. Fiona had told Arlan that there were about one thousand individual whale sharks that visited the waters off X'lak each year and stayed for about five months. They usually swam in pods of up to twenty or more but sometimes solo.

Everybody in the boat seemed to be on high alert. The captain used his hand-held radio to talk to captains of other boats in the area who were also carrying passengers and searching for the whale sharks, *tiburon ballenas*, as the captain referred to them. His first mate and Alterio searched the horizon in all directions.

Flaco flashed a knowing smile and told Arlan to watch for an-imals. Arlan shrugged and thought that Flaco's request was strange. Of course, they were looking for animals—whale sharks. But he quickly learned that they had entered an area filled with all kinds of sea life. They began to see breaching manta rays that could easily grow a wing-span of more than twenty feet. They had the ability to propel their entire body out of the water, expose their snow-white underside, perform a half-twist, expose their black topside, and flop back onto the surface with a large splash. In just a few minutes they spotted eight breaching mantas and an occasional massive black shape of a manta swimming alongside or below the lancha.

Arlan started rifling through the mesh bag to find gear that would fit him and a mask that might not leak. He heard shouts from the captain, followed by Flaco and a more excited Alterio. Arlan dropped the bag and looked over the bow. A school of small golden rays, none more than two feet across parted as the captain slowed the lancha so that it is just stayed up on plane. There were hundreds of them on all sides of the lancha. It was an unbelievable sight. The sea resembled a large, flat lawn in New England in the fall, blanketed with golden-brown leaves.

Within minutes, Flaco pointed out several large shapes about a hundred meters in the distance. They were dorsal fins—the largest Arlan had ever seen. The captain motored into the center of a pod of about twenty whale sharks from fifteen to well over forty feet long.

Arlan had heard the term *domino* associated with these large animals. He saw why. Golf-ball-sized white dots spotted their black sides and broad snouts.

They didn't school, not in the way people think when they see schools of small fish swimming in the same direction. This was more unorganized. They stayed relatively close to one another but swam in different directions and collected plankton in their large open mouths. They seemed to be barely movingIt couldn't be very difficult to swim with them.

Arlan put on a pair of flippers that were a size too small, but they were the largest in the bag. He grabbed a mask and pushed it against his face without pulling the strap onto the back of his head. He breathed in hard to check to see if it would leak. A little air sneaked in. He tried a few other masks. They all leaked, but not enough to cause a problem.

Flaco and Alterio waited their turn to enter the water. They let Arlan go first. The captain said that there was a trick to getting in the water with the whale sharks. It was to figure out which way the shark was swimming and then maneuver the boat so that the swimmer could be dropped directly in its path—and its gaping mouth. This didn't sound right to Arlan, but he shrugged. It wasn't like these things had teeth.

The captain gently maneuvered the boat into the path of a large shark. "Vamos! Rapido!" were the last words Arlan heard before he dropped over the edge of the lancha and into the water. It was cold and murky. The thick plankton limited his visibility. Underwater, through the mask, he could see nothing. He raised his head out of the water and saw a huge dorsal fin, at least three feet tall, fifteen meters away and moving directly at him. The top of the shark's mouth rose and left a small wake as it was pushed through the water by the bulky mass behind it. Arlan placed his mask back into the water and breathed through the snorkel. He still saw nothing. He raised his head again. The shark's dorsal fin and mouth were closer. Arlan put his mask in the water and back-pedalled a few feet. He heard the motor and muffled voices from above and turned his head to look for the hull of the boat. He heard the loud click of the propeller pushed into gear, and the voices faded. His head still under water, he turned back toward the direction of the whale shark.

About five meters from him a large open mouth appeared from the murk. It was on a collision course with Arlan, who was wondering what it would feel like to be swallowed whole. There was no panic or suddenness in the shark's movement as it gracefully slipped below and then past Arlan. Arlan turned to swim with it. The shark wasn't slow. That was an illusion. The shark moved deceptively fast. Though an excellent swimmer, Arlan couldn't catch it. He saw its slowly swishing gigantic tail, and then it disappeared in the plankton-rich murk.

Arlan eventually managed to catch up to several large whale sharks that afternoon. As one glided by, he kicked with all his strength but could stay even with it for only a few seconds. He reached out and grabbed its dorsal fin and was surprised that it didn't seem to mind the passenger. Maybe it was so large it couldn't feel him. The shark took him far beyond the boat and started to dive deeper, where the deepest water was no more than forty feet. He wasn't worried about depth—he was worried about the cold. As the shark took him deeper, the water was noticeably colder—much colder. It was Atlantic upwelling water. Arlan wore no wetsuit and almost let go but held on as the shark started to surface. As they neared the surface, and nearly out of breath, he let go of the dorsal but grabbed the shark's tail as it sped by. Again, the shark didn't seem to mind, and Arlan rode the gently swishing tail until his lungs were ready to burst.

Besides the whale sharks, the breaching manta rays, and the schooling golden rays that he'd already seen, green turtles and dolphins swam in and around the pod later in the afternoon. They were a lot easier to see from the lancha than through a mask in the murky water. Arlan was pretty sure he had seen the long caudal tail of a passing thresher shark on one of his swims. He had spent thousands of hours diving and snorkeling in the Caribbean, but he'd never seen this much large sea life gathered in one place. When he climbed back into the lancha for the last time, he felt as though he had just left a giant underwater party for all nearby creatures.

Alterio, with Flaco's help, swam with the whale sharks for twenty minutes. Afterward, the captain steered the lancha toward Isla X'lak. The ride was considerably smoother going with the sea, which had calmed into long swells that lazily rolled the bow of the lancha up and down as they made their way to the distant shoreline. The first mate chopped onions and tomatoes on a cutting board he'd placed on top of a cooler in the stern. He put the pieces into a Tupperware bowl that he moved out of the way so he could open the lid of the cooler and pull out two fifteen-inch fish they had caught on trolling lines while on their way out to swim with the whale sharks. He held one of the copper-bronze fish up for Arlan to see. It resembled a small sea bass. The mate smiled broadly and shouted, "Corvina." Arlan was familiar with the name, which included a variety of salt-water fish species that tasted great in ceviche, which was what the mate was preparing. After cleaning and chopping the fish into small chunks, he mixed them into the onions and tomatoes. He added a little vegetable oil from an old Mazola bottle that looked as though it had been under the center console for years. He threw in chopped cilantro and then cut a dozen limes on the cutting board and squeezed the juice into the bowl. When all of the ingredients were swimming in citric acid, he placed a lid on the bowl and put it into the cooler.

Twenty minutes later they anchored near the beach that Alterio said he and his partners owned. The captain unfurled a canvas roof tarp on an aluminum frame that had been attached to the center console top and tied it down at the bow cleat. Flaco handed Arlan a paper cup full of ceviche and a bottle of Sol. He brought the same to Alterio and grabbed a cup full of ceviche and a beer for himself. He placed a bowl full of tostados next to them on the fiberglass seat. For the next thirty minutes, they sat in the shade of the tarp, drank cold beer, and used tostados to scoop ceviche from their paper cups. The lancha swayed up and down in the gentle surf. The beach stretched for miles on either side of the lancha, with no sign of habitation. *It couldn't get any better,* Arlan thought, and took another cup of ceviche from the cooler.

After they had eaten, Alterio insisted that they swim to the beach so Arlan would see what the land was like on this side of Isla X'lak. The water was shallow and much clearer than the plankton soup the whale sharks swam in a few kilometers offshore. It was laced with beautiful turquoise, blue, and green striations. The captain protested, but Alterio jumped over the side anyway and half swam, half walked toward the beach. Flaco followed Alterio and was halfway to the beach when Arlan figured that he should join them. It was a short swim of fifteen or twenty meters, mostly in water shallow enough to wade through. They walked out of the water and onto a hard-packed beach. It was wide, at least twenty-five meters to the first dune.

"Everything you can see," Alterio pointed up and down the beach, "is ours."

"How much land do you have?"

"There are twenty-five kilometers of beach and about five thousand hectares of land behind the beach."

Over fifteen miles of beach and over twelve thousand acres of jungle behind the beach Arlan thought. That's a lot of land... undeveloped land, so close to a major tourist destination and airlift. Unheard of in a world in love with developing beaches.

"Does that include the village on the other side of the island?" Arlan asked.

"No. The ejiditarios own their homes and the land around the village."

Arlan walked up the dune to get a better look at the vegetation. The dune was covered with bitter panicum, cord grass, bluestem, sea grapes, and other common vegetation that was critical for the dune's protection, which, in turn, was critical for the protection of the island during tropical storms.

The jungle was impenetrable, but it *had* been impacted. Alterio told Arlan that, years earlier, the coast of the island was a coconut plantation and there was a road behind the dune. The lethal yellow disease had wiped the coconut palm out several decades earlier. Only a few hardy survivors remained, and they were easy to spot. Their tall, skinny trunks supported clusters of palm fronds and coconuts and towered over the rest of the jungle. There was no longer any evidence of a road or buildings. Once abandoned, the jungle had swallowed them up.

Arlan marveled at Mother Nature's healing abilities. Left alone, even after heavy impact, some places, given enough time, will recover. Most times, though, the recovered landscape is a far different place than what it once was, forever changed by invasive species introduced earlier.

Arlan looked around. This was the prize. Fiona and her group wanted to preserve it. Alterio and countless others wanted to profit from it.

There were three ways this island could evolve. The first possibility was that the island would be left alone to continue to evolve as a thriving marine and terrestrial ecosystem, which is what it had been doing for decades. The second possibility, and one that he'd seen a lot on the Yucatan Peninsula since the privatization of ejido land, was that the locals would clear mangroves and other island vegetation over the next decade or so and sell land. The result would be gradual, haphazard development—an abandoned project here, a finished project there, a few local shacks in between, insufficient infrastructure, and trash everywhere. It would be environmental chaos. The third possibility would be full-scale development and total environmental alteration. This threat was very real. The island was too beautiful, too close to Cancun, and surrounded by an abundance of investors, land owners, and developers who operated through greed and arrogance. Arlan gazed into the jungle. His mind could easily conjure up future high-rise hotels, four-lane boulevards, golf courses, and hundreds of people on the beach.

Arlan heard the distant sound of an aircraft. He looked up but didn't see anything. But the sound grew louder.

"Do you have title from the ejido?" Arlan asked Alterio.

"Yes, but it's complicated. My father-in-law and I privatized the land and received some of the beach from the ejido in return for our work. We are bringing in a partner from Mexico City to help us buy the rest of the beach from the ejido. We are signing a contract with our new partners in a couple of weeks. I would like it very much if you could come to the closing."

Alterio and Flaco looked up and squinted.

"You can meet my partners and the project director... and the governor will be there."

Flaco pointed to a black speck coming out of the east. It had the unmistakable half whining and half chopping sound of a fast-moving, jet-engine helicopter. The sleek, black machine passed over them in a loud blur and continued down the beach at a low altitude, its nose tipped slightly forward. It disappeared as quickly as it had approached—the sound going with it.

Arlan couldn't give a rat's ass to have a chance to meet the governor, or the president, or any other politician stupid enough and corrupt enough to allow a place like this to be destroyed. He looked toward the disappearing black speck. "That must be an expensive tour."

Alterio looked to the horizon where the helicopter had been and started to say something but was distracted by a large fly that buzzed his head. A second fly buzzed Arlan and landed in his hair. He had left his hat on the lancha.

"Ouch!" Flaco shouted and swatted the air.

The fly that landed in Arlan's hair bit him.

"Ow! Shit. That really hurt." He tried to smash it with an open hand and ended up slapping his head instead. The fly escaped and continued to buzz around him. "This damn thing won't go away."

Alterio fought his own battle and swatted flies with both arms flailing.

"Tabanos!" The captain shouted from the lancha and laughed. "Te lo dije."

Alterio and Flaco ran toward the water. Arlan saw at least ten flies buzzing around their heads as they ran down the slope of the dune. The flies must have called in reinforcements. Arlan was bitten again. He ran. He passed Alterio and dove into the water. Flaco was already there. The captain continued to laugh from the lancha and pulled up the anchor. Arlan had to duck his head under the water to keep the flies from biting. He heard Alterio's body splash into the sea next to him.

"What are these... flies on steroids? They look like deer flies, but their bite is like a blow from a hammer."

"Tabanos," Alterio answered and ducked his head under the gentle surf. He brought his head up after a moment, his mop of dark hair flattened by the warm salt water that ran down his face. "They come out this time of the year for a few weeks. I forgot."

The three of them duck-walked in three feet of water back to the lancha, which the captain had brought in closer to the beach. They climbed into the lancha, and the captain made a quick escape. The tabanos didn't follow.

Alterio told the captain to take them to the village but to take them to the lagoon that separated the island from the mainland first. He continued to look up in the sky.

As they paralleled the beach, Alterio pointed out what he thought was his land and where he thought the joint venture land with his new partners started. It was hard to tell. The beach and vegetation behind it was the same. The scale of this land was overwhelming. Arlan had not seen this much undisturbed beach anywhere near the Caribbean for decades. The only place that came close was the north shore and National Park of St. John. But even it had been blighted with new mansions built on the mountains above the park by the multi-millionaires who had recently discovered the island and seemed to need to impress each other and the world with the sizes of their homes.

They rounded the outer end of X'lak and motored into the shallow lagoon. The captain took his time and drove the lancha close to the island's shore and then several kilometers to the shore near the mainland before returning across the bay to the island. Dolphins raced the lancha as it crossed the bay to the mainland where they went in and out of estuaries and a short way into the mouth of a canal. Flaco pointed out two small crocodiles on the shore near the bank of the canal.

Arlan was astounded. The shorelines of the island and the mainland were teaming with wildlife. The small bays on the island were full of pink flamingos. Fiona had told him that the area hosted well over four hundred and fifty different types of birds.

The lagoon was a large outdoor aquarium with no walls, marred only by the occasional net strung out into the water by local fishermen. He would ask about this destructively indiscriminant practice later, when they were out of earshot of the captain. Arlan could only guess how many juvenile turtles, manatee, dolphins, and other sea life died in these nets and how long it would be before nets like these would obliterate any hope of a sustainable fishing future for the children of the locals who set them.

Alterio shouted, "Vamonos. Al Isla X'lak." The captain turned the lancha toward the village.

Chapter 18

Arlan was wrong about the village having only mangrove on either side. As they approached in the lancha, he could see a fairly large beach to the right of the village. Several fishing boats, lanchas just like the one they rode in, had been pulled up onto the sand. Others were anchored stern to shore in the bay a few meters off the beach.

The captain landed at a concrete pier and everybody disembarked. Alterio handed the captain a wad of pesos and told him that Flaco would let him know when they would need him to take them back. Alterio then turned and barked orders at two men who sat in the drivers' seats of dirty, beige, gas-powered golf carts. One of the men was handed their bags from the lancha by the captain. He put them in his cart and then drove away, presumably to a house or hotel where Alterio had arranged for them to stay. He guessed that the other cart was for them.

A few locals approached Alterio and Flaco with smiles and questions. Arlan didn't stick around in the midday sun to listen to conversations he didn't care about. He drifted over to the beach and some commotion near the shore.

Several fishermen stood around a lancha on the edge of the beach jabbering and laughing. Arlan approached and peered over the heads of two of the short men. He noticed a couple of tourists on the other side of the lancha doing the same. Their eyes were wide, and they shared a frightful glance at each other. Dead sharks were stacked in the hull of the lancha. A glassy-eyed hammerhead lay on top of the heap with five or six bull sharks beneath it. All

of the sharks were between eight and ten feet long. The blood that
spilled from their mouths indicated that they had been caught on
long lines that had probably been baited the night before. The tourists on the other side of the lancha had come to Isla X'lak to swim
with the whale sharks. After seeing a boatload of real sharks, with
real teeth, he wondered if they would get in the water. He walked
back to where Alterio held court near the golf cart.

"Vamos," shouted Alterio.

Arlan was given the front passenger seat. Alterio drove and
Flaco sat in the rear seat, facing backward. They drove away from
the pier and toward the center of the village on a potholed, hard-
packed road. The land on either side of the road, and as far as Arlan
could see, was the same grade as the road. There were no ditches.
Arlan couldn't imagine how rainwater would ever drain off the
road. It would have to percolate through it, which would take time.
One of the first buildings they passed, no more than fifty meters
from the pier, was an ugly brown and white concrete building that
housed the island's generator, which was running with a lot less
noise than Arlan expected. From then on, either side of the road was
sprinkled with palapa-roofed and some corrugated, metal-roofed
shacks.

They bounced through several potholes and passed the man
who had driven the cart to the pier. Flaco said something to the man,
and the man laughed but continued walking.

"I will show you around the village and then we'll get something to eat, if that's okay," Alterio said, turning to the right off the
main sand road and onto a narrower sand road with more potholes.

"Fine with me. I'm just along for the ride."

The place was a mess. On the right side of the road were mangroves, and on the left were small homes. Most of the homes were occupied but unfinished, with trash and construction materials strewn
around. Seemingly functional golf carts were parked on the sides of
the road, while broken down golf carts sat in the sandy yards. Laundry hung from clothes lines attached from the homes to half-dead
palm trees in the yards. The homes were wide open, and hammocks
could be seen hanging on the dimly lit interior walls. Some were occupied with sleeping bodies that wore white tank tops and had large

bellies. Occasionally, children could be seen chasing dogs and cats through the houses and into the yards.

Alterio drove the golf cart as far as he could before he had to turn to the left. Again, mangroves were on the right, and homes and an occasional small store were on the left. They were circumnavigating the village, though neither Alterio nor Flaco had any time to tell him this. They were busy talking to locals along the way. Flaco made jokes and asked about family. Alterio answered questions about money: 'When will we get more money?' 'My boat needs a new motor. Can you pay for it soon?' Each time Alterio smiled and promised that they would receive money very soon.

Alterio pulled the cart in front of a small store and sent Flaco inside for some beer. Arlan peered into its open front. It was a small space with shelves packed with all sorts of randomly stacked food and sundries, typical of many island provision stores that Arlan had seen in other places around the world. Arlan saw Flaco take several cans of cold beer from a cooler on the floor next to the cashier and put them in a plastic bag, the whole time carrying on conversations with a few of the local residents in the store. While they waited, several locals walked by the cart and acknowledged Alterio with a smile and a few pleasant words, then asked about money. Alterio was very popular.

The village was home to about two thousand people. It didn't take much time to see it all.

It was all the same: sand roads, golf carts, scooters, and the ubiquitous yellow-orange bicycles with large wooden carts on the front that carried goods and passengers. Small houses throughout the village were built directly on the sandy ground, and all doors, if there were doors, were wide open. The locals had perpetual smiles. A few tourists with backpacks strolled through the village.

Alterio drove Arlan to areas outside the village. There were only three roads, all littered with trash. One road led to the beach on the other side of the island, and two others led to either tip of the island. Close to the village on all three roads, Arlan saw locals cutting and burning mangroves and driving posts into the ground around the clearings. The posts were painted red with a hand-drawn name of the ejiditario owner nailed to one of them.

"Are they going to be building something out here?" Arlan asked.

"No. They recently received titles to the land from the government. They're clearing it."

Arlan looked at the cleared land. Nothing was left standing. "Why?" he asked.

"Locals commonly clear their land as soon as they receive titles. It's done throughout the peninsula. It's their way of delineating what is theirs."

"Why don't they build a fence, or simply place metal pipes or concrete markers at the corners of their land?"

Alterio shrugged and asked Flaco if he had remembered to tell the mayor they were coming.

They bounced back toward the village on a road that had rippled sand running across it. The condition was commonly called *washboarding* and was caused by the separation of small and large sand particles on the roads surface. It was jarring—and slow.

They passed a road that led inland and was littered with black plastic bags of trash. Some of them were broken open and being fed upon by birds and a couple of dogs. A hand-painted wooden sign on a post had the word *basura* on it.

"The dump is right here?" Arlan asked.

"No. It's down that road about one hundred meters. I guess some people don't want to go that far," Alterio said with a smile.

"Is it a landfill?"

"No, it's just a place where everybody throws their trash. Sometimes it's hauled away to the mainland."

Arlan wondered how much trash floated into the ocean during a tropical storm, when much of the low island must be inundated.

"I call those dumpster dogs," Arlan said, pointing to three similar-looking dogs lying on the side of the road. They raised their heads to watch the golf cart go by, but apparently it was too hot for them to try for handouts.

"Those things?" Alterio asked. "My grandmother used to poison them at our beach house north of Madre. They're all over the place."

Arlan winced and said, "I read an article once about a multi-year experiment that showed that, after several generations, all pedigree of dogs—poodles, beagles, German shepherds—left to fend for themselves in urban or rural environments, tend to evolve ancestral features that the article claimed were more natural for survival—medium weight and wiry, short to medium brown or tan hair, an up-turned tail, and large, pointed ears—similar to dogs depicted in ancient Egyptian hieroglyphs... just like those dogs," Arlan said and pointed his thumb in the direction of the dogs they had just passed.

"They're big rats," Alterio said and almost hit another dog that ran in front of the cart. He didn't aim for it, but he didn't slow or try to avoid it either.

Arlan tended to judge the health of a third-world village by its dumpster dogs. If they were fat and happy, so was the village. Around the world that was rare. The dogs here, though, were healthy. He watched the locals take time to greet the dogs with a pat on their heads or a shred of whatever food they might be carrying.

That night Arlan and Alterio stayed in a house on the beach just outside the center of the village. Flaco stayed with friends but came to the house in the morning with a cooler full of cash. Arlan tried to ignore them as they divvied out the day's allocation. This was a pattern Arlan would get used to over the next few days.

Arlan was invited to the ejido office to meet the president, the colonel, a small man with beady eyes and a thick mustache. He wore a white sailor's outfit and couldn't have been more deferential to Alterio. After a brief discussion, Alterio handed him a thick roll of pesos.

A lot of time was spent in the restaurants around the plaza in the center of the village. They must have had the same interior decorator. All were appointed with plastic tables and chairs, checkered plastic table cloths, and neon-colored, fuzzy portraits from the seventies on the walls. But all of them served great ceviche. Alterio held court in these places—sometimes lunch and dinner in one long sitting. He insisted that Arlan sit with him. Men and women who were introduced to Arlan as ejiditarios came to speak with Alterio. Arlan heard the phrase *Seremos la proxima Cancun* several times from many of ejiditarios. Alterio sometimes handed out pesos. Sometimes he promised pesos. The colonel, always dressed in a white sailor's outfit, spent a lot of time sitting with Alterio. They spoke in hushed tones, and Alterio handed him money each time he left the table.

The time in the restaurants bored Arlan. When he could get away from Alterio, he walked through the village and observed the locals' activities.

Isla X'lak was a very friendly and safe place. Many times Arlan saw small children laughing and running a block or two ahead of their parents on their way through the village. Ten year olds and younger often drove golf carts by themselves. He never heard an argument or saw a fight. At the same time, it was a quirky place with some strange traditions. The village had a feel that was not quite Mexican. It felt partially Caribbean. Some of the homes were typically Mexican thatch-roofed palapas. Others were painted in bright colors and had metal-hipped roofs. Arlan learned that the island had been settled by pirates in the nineteenth century and had been isolated from the rest of the Yucatan Peninsula culturally and politically for decades. Perhaps that's where the quirkiness came from. Or maybe it came from the days and weeks these fishermen and their ancestors spent together in small fishing boats many kilometers from civilization—and women.

On one of his strolls through the village he ran into Flaco, who had just come out of the house where he stayed.

"You look lost."

"Hard to get lost on an island. I'm just enjoying the sights."

Flaco looked at his watch and said, "Let's go visit the cantinas. They just opened."

"What's a cantina? Isn't it just a bar?" Arlan asked and looked down at his own watch. It was two in the afternoon.

"No. No. There are a lot of things about Mexico that you need to learn," Flaco said and pushed Arlan along the road.

They walked a few blocks from the central plaza and into the residential part of the village. Two large wooden shutters had been pushed back against the concrete exterior walls on either side of the two streets that bordered the cantina and exposed a brightly lit, one-room interior full of plastic tables and chairs. Flaco led Arlan in and introduced him to the owner, the colonel's brother. He was handed a bottle of Sol and led to a plastic table. A plate of salt and a small bowl of lime slices were placed on the table. Flaco joined Arlan and the cantina filled rapidly with fishermen.

Arlan leaned toward Flaco and said, "There are no women in here."

"They are not allowed. That's why it's a cantina, not a bar."

Several fishermen came by the table and were introduced to Arlan. All were friendly, and drunk. The empty beer bottles began to pile up on the tables.

"Does the owner not have enough help?" Arlan asked.

Flaco looked confused.

"These tables, they're full of empty beer bottles. Doesn't anybody come to take them away?"

Still confused, Flaco said, "No," and turned to talk to a man that Arlan had met the day before at his tortilleria, which was a small open room with a conveyor belt that moved tortillas into an oven. On the other side, his wife and daughter picked up a few dozen tortillas and wrapped them in brown paper. Villagers lined up outside the window to buy the daily staple, so important in Mexico's diet that the prices are government controlled. Alterio bought a package and offered Arlan a freshly baked tortilla. It had a warm, plain taste. It needed something in it.

"What's that fat lady doing here? I thought women weren't allowed," Arlan asked Flaco.

Flaco laughed and introduced Arlan to a man named Loco. Loco had short, curly, grey hair and wore a lot of gold jewelry.

When asked if he was a fisherman he answered that he rarely fished. He told Arlan that he recruited the whores for the cantinas and pointed to the fat lady who led a much smaller fisherman through a back door. They returned fifteen minutes later. Just a little surprised, Arlan asked where he recruited them. "Desde los barrios pobres de Cancun," Loco answered.

The afternoon passed, and more empty beer bottles crowded the tops of the tables. Some had fallen onto the floor. Arlan saw a few men stagger out into the street and to their homes—or another cantina. The fat lady made it to their table where Arlan got his first close look. *She* was a *he*. Flaco told Arlan that this was not unusual and then jokingly accused Loco of being a mariposa and that he was the cause of the other fishermen becoming gay as well. Loco protested, saying that they were the pitchers, not the catchers—therefore, not gay.

At six thirty in the evening the colonel's brother started to count empty beer bottles at each table and on the floor around the tables. He then told the men at that table how much they owed for the beer. At seven he kicked everybody out and closed the doors.

The next day, Alterio announced that it was time to head back to the mainland—but not before lunch. Arlan and Alterio sat at an outdoor table in Alterio's favorite restaurant on the plaza. Flaco had gone to arrange for a lancha.

They had just quietly finished a beer, the first of the day. Alterio didn't have much to say, which was a first also. They sat with their chairs close together on one side of a plastic table. The large Coca-Cola umbrella that was propped up on a pole that rested in the hole in the center of the table gave them welcomed shade—as long as they both stayed on one side.

"Who is that guy?" Arlan asked Alterio.

"Uh, who?" Alterio answered and looked around.

"That guy. The one standing next to your golf cart talking to the colonel. He looks mad, and he's shaking his finger at you, or me. I don't know him. It must be you he's pissed off at."

"That's my cousin," Alterio answered, "I'm surprised to see him on Isla X'lak."

"You have a lot of cousins."

The cousin came to the table and sat down. Alterio made the introduction.

"This is my friend, Arlan," Alterio told his cousin.

"Arlan, this is my cousin. We call him El Tenador. He is a chef. His real name is Fernando."

Arlan nodded. Fernando gave Arlan a brief smile and turned to Alterio.

"Why do you think my land is yours?" Fernando asked Alterio.

"It was our grandfather's land and..."

"And he gave it to my father, who gave it to me and my sister. It is not your land," Fernando said. "Now I learn that you are promising to build a bridge on my land. A bridge to this island. Are you crazy?"

"But we tried to make a deal with you and your sister."

"You had your notario contact us. He's as crooked as you. Ladrones, both of you."

"But we can buy the land from you. Or we could be partners."

El Tenador glared at Alterio.

"Neither my sister nor I would be partners with you. Not in a million years. You still owe us for our land that you stole in Madre. We have taken precautions with this land. We have placed heavy restrictions on it. It will never be sold to you or to anybody. Our children will be the only ones who will ever get that land. And it will never be used as a place to build a bridge. Are you on drugs or something?"

Fernando stormed away from the table. Alterio smiled. Arlan was embarrassed by the confrontation.

"Not that it's my business. You're going to build a bridge?"

"I had to promise my new partners a bridge. They wouldn't invest otherwise."

"Do you know how preposterous that is?"

"I have gone over it with some engineers. It can be done."

Arlan sighed and leaned back in the plastic chair. He said, "We can go to the moon too. That doesn't mean we should put a McDonald's on it."

After a long pause Alterio said, "You could help me with this. I know we shouldn't have a bridge. I need some time to show them how the island could be developed without the bridge."

"It doesn't seem that you have the land to build a bridge anyway. It's your cousin's land, and he's not selling. Didn't you hear him?"

Alterio paused and looked around to see if anybody else had heard the conversation.

Arlan put the bottle of beer to his lips. It felt light—and warm. He pulled the bottle from his mouth and pointed it toward the man behind the bar. "Una mas."

***

Arlan sat alone in the bow of the lancha that sped them back to the Punta Eek. Dolphins raced the lancha, bobbing in and out of the water just ahead of the bow. Arlan needed to digest all that he'd seen and heard in the past few days. He realized how precious and how fragile the island was. It was not a tourist destination—not yet. But the tourists were coming. And they would come for all of the right reasons—fly fishing, swimming with whale sharks, birding, befriending locals, and visiting regional ruins and cenotes—all nature-based activities that would promote sustainable growth. The island desperately needed a thoughtful development plan and some infrastructure improvements to help satisfy the experiential traveler demand.

Alterio and his partners were going to develop the island, and Arlan didn't believe for a second that Alterio wanted a sustainable destination. He was sure that Alterio didn't understand the term or how it could be applied to the island. The type of development Alterio had promised his partners would require an airport or a bridge to bring the number of tourists required to make it economically viable. But anything close to the densities on Cancun or the Maya Riviera would destroy X'lak. The charm and character of the remote island would disappear, suffocated by the heavy footprint of mass tourism and its accompanying infrastructure. And one more of the world's premier ecosystems would be gone.

It wasn't hard to figure out that Alterio needed help—lots of help, and Arlan figured that Alterio could use his help to fend off development opposition from Fiona and her organization. He also knew that he could use that plan to argue against turning the island into another Cancun, if he could prove that his plan could be profitable. He didn't think he could trust Alterio, but he couldn't figure out why he would need to. Money controlled decisions, and Alterio would rely on his father-in-law and his new partners for money. Arlan assumed they were successful businessmen and would make logical decisions based on profitability. But he'd seen egos and convention ruin projects many times before.

Arlan watched more dolphins race the bow of the boat. He sensed an opportunity. X'lak could become the perfect destination—a global showcase of a low-density development that teaches sustainability and respect for the natural environment and local cultures. If successful, the model would be copied in other parts of the world, saving thousands, maybe millions, of acres of habitat while allowing travelers a high-quality experience with Mother Nature.

He didn't know if he could wrestle control of the planning process, but he might be able to put his stamp on it.

The island was poised to be exploited. It was in the shadow of Cancun, but maybe just far enough out of its reach to maintain its peaceful tranquility. A big enough push though, like the promise of wealth, cloaked in short-lived promises made by short-sighted promoters, could push Isla X'lak over the edge and on its way to oblivion. Alterio was just the person to give it that push.

Arlan looked back at Alterio, who stood next to the captain and was in an animated conversation. Alterio was an entertaining pirate, similar to Captain Jay, but in a different way—less physically intimidating, more intellectually challenging.

Arlan knew at that moment that he'd been sucked in.

The next Cancun.

Right.

Chapter 19

Juan drove the SUV past a green sign with white lettering that read,"Balam, Pop. 10,000." He continued through the narrow roads of the village, bouncing over speed bumps, or topes, as they are called in Mexico, and dodging dogs and children until he reached the central plaza. Alterio looked at the three dilapidated buildings on the west side of the plaza and saw the mayor's brand new, black Volkswagen Jetta parked in front of the middle building. She wanted a red car, but Alterio's father-in-law's Volkswagen dealership had only black models on the lot. Alterio told Juan to park next to it. He pulled a plat map from the rear seat and studied it.

"Are you sure this is the most recent parcel map of the ejido land near the coast?" Alterio asked Juan.

"Si. Jose got it from the Reforma Agraria office in Chetumal two days ago."

"Bueno," Alterio said, with his head hunkered close to the map on his lap. He studied it for a few more minutes, then rolled it up and tossed it in the rear seat. He exited the SUV and looked around. A group of men sat at a rickety table in the dirt and played cards under the largest of three trees that helped to shade most of the small, grassless plaza. A couple of short-haired brown dogs with weary eyes came over to the SUV and wagged their tails. Alterio stomped his foot and yelled, "Vamos!" They scampered back into the plaza. He looked beneath one of the other large sapodilla trees in the plaza and saw the overturned rusted pot that he'd heard was used more than a century ago to make chicle, the precursor to modern-day chewing gum. The round pot was at least two meters in diameter and a meter tall. Alterio first spotted it a year earlier and thought that it would make a great conversation piece if placed in the foyer of the home he hoped to build once he made his money from the island. During his last visit to Balam, he'd asked the same group of men who were playing cards to try to lift it. They couldn't move it even a millimeter. He realized then that he would need a front-end loader or a backhoe and a large truck to move it. And he would need to build the foyer around it. The problem was that he didn't know where he would be building his house.

The men playing cards noticed him and waved. He waved back and walked up a flight of unfinished concrete stairs of the building in the center. Unannounced, he opened a door that led into the anteroom of the mayor's office. The mayor's assistant rose from her desk and greeted Alterio.

Alterio looked toward the open passageway that led to the mayor's office and loudly asked, "Is the mayor in?"

"Si, she is in," the assistant said. Within seconds, the mayor appeared in the passageway.

"It's very nice to see you again, Alterio. I didn't know you were coming, but, as you know, you are welcome anytime," she said.

"Thank you. And thank you for meeting with me with no appointment, but I have had a busy schedule and didn't know exactly when I would be in Balam," Alterio said and greeted her with a hug.

"Please come in and sit," the mayor said and nodded toward the opening to her office.

Alterio sat on an old, worn sofa that had been pushed up against a sliding glass door that led to a concrete balcony. Alterio peeked through the slightly-parted, heavy, purple drapes that had been haphazardly hung above the door to keep the bright sun out and saw that the balcony had no railing. The mayor's assistant joined them and sat in a metal folding chair in the corner opposite Alterio.

"I understand that you are signing your deal with your new partner from Mexico City this week," the mayor said.

"Yes. It is very important. The governor will be there, and I have asked the colonel to come." He saw a sideways glance from the mayor's assistant. "I'm sorry that no more guests could be invited. But I'll bring my new partners to meet with you very soon."

"Good. You know that we will support your project in any way we can," the mayor said.

Alterio thought about the new Jetta and hoped he could make good on the other promises he'd made to the mayor, at least until he didn't need her anymore.

The mayor continued, "I saw the e-mail you sent earlier in the week. What is this about a support town?"

"Yes. That is why I wanted to meet with you. We will need a place for the employees to live who will work at the resorts on Isla X'lak. There could be several thousand by the time the development is finished. They will have families. I have suggested to my partners that we build a support town on the mainland across from Isla X'lak."

The mayor smiled and waited for more.

"Services for the new town will be needed—stores and schools and medical services. The people who provide the services for the new town will also have families. We might need to build a town that could accommodate one hundred thousand people."

"I never thought about that," the mayor said. "I can see now why you would look for an area on the mainland instead of Isla X'lak to build a support town."

"I was wondering if there was land near the coast that we could buy for a future support town."

"Of course, Alterio. But you already know that most of the land near the coast is Balam ejido land."

"Yes, of course. But you and your husband are ejiditarios, no?"

"Yes, my husband is the president of the ejido."

The mayor smiled and told her assistant to get the plat map.

"Your ejido has already privatized this land?" Alterio asked.

"No, not yet. But we've gone through the process of subdividing it amongst ourselves. The next step, the legal work needed to obtain titles from Reforma Agraria, is very expensive, as you know," the mayor said.

"Yes, but we could help with that," Alterio said.

The mayor smiled again and asked, "How much land do you need for a support town?"

The mayor's assistant returned with a large map of the municipio. She placed it on the mayor's desk. The three of them huddled around the map.

"It will need to be very large. What about that parcel?" Alterio asked, pointing to a large parcel just off the road to Punta Eek. "How large is that?"

"It's five kilometers by five kilometers."

"Twenty-five kilometers squared. That's perfect."

"Do you know the ejiditario who this lot had been assigned to?" asked Alterio.

"Si. It is my husband."

"Muy bueno. I'm sure you can convince him to sell it to us, no?"

"I'm sure we can work something out."

Alterio said, "I will come back with our planners to meet with you after the closing. They will need to design the town. It will take time, you understand."

"I understand. But you will buy the land first, right?" She paused and added, "I mean once we have titles."

"Yes, we can do that. Just one more thing."

"Yes?"

"Don Francisco's attorney was here this week."

The mayor glanced at her assistant.

"I know because my driver and his driver are brothers. I was just wondering what he wanted."

"He came to negotiate the land values on the island for property tax valuation. He wants me to keep them at the same value that is on the purchase contracts."

Alterio wasn't surprised. Most of the money on any land contract in Mexico was paid in cash to avoid taxes. The purchase prices for the land on Isla X'lak, according to the contracts, were low. She wouldn't know how much was actually paid and would find it difficult to increase property taxes without re-assessing the land at a higher value.

"But, as mayor of the municipio, it is up to you to assess the land and place a value on it for tax purposes, no?"

"That's correct," the mayor answered. "But your father-in-law's offer is too low. You and your partners will be building a new Cancun. We have been researching land values in Cancun and they are much higher than his offer. We are a poor municipio, and you and your father-in-law are very wealthy. I assume your new partners are wealthy, as well."

"Do you know how much value you'll place on the land?"

"We're still reviewing it, Alterio. We'll get this year's tax bill out soon."

"You know that we're still negotiating with some of the ejiditar-ios and have not purchased their land yet."

"We can only tax non-ejido land. Your land."

"I understand that. But can you please talk to me before you send our partnership the property tax bill? As your friend, I want you to know that I will see that it is paid."

The mayor and her assistant looked at each other. "Thank you, Alterio. And thank you for coming to meet with us. Please let me know when you will be visiting again."

Alterio walked down the stairs and got into the SUV. He was happy. As the Americans say, he just killed two birds with one stone.

He told Juan to take him to Cancun. Things were moving along smoothly. He called Jose, his notario.

"How did your meeting with the mayor go?" Jose asked.

"It was too easy. She has no idea how to negotiate."

"But that is good, no?"

"Si. We'll get to look at the property tax bill first. And I think I can get her to charge us for the land we haven't bought yet. She knows that it's inevitable that we will."

"But we can negotiate the price, right?"

Alterio laughed and said, "Since the property tax revenue from the municipios mostly goes into the mayor's pockets, that won't be a problem."

"And the land for the support town?" Jose asked with a laugh.

"She bought into it, just as everybody else has."

"That's good, because we have promised a lot of land on the is-land in return for favors. We're running out of land," Jose said.

"Don't worry, Jose. Once the word is out that we need a support town, the speculators will be begging us to buy into it."

"But one thing, Alterio. How are you going to pay for the land for the support town?"

"My new partners will pay for it."

"But, Alterio, maybe you're losing sight of the big picture. Why do we want to screw around with a support town?"

"Jose, you don't understand. We don't know how long it will take for Alejandro to find the right group of investors. We need money now. We can get control of the land for the support town quickly."

"But it doesn't have title yet."

"So? The people we owe land to for favors won't know. They won't take the time to check titles. Even if they do, we will tell them that we are working closely with the mayor, and the titles will be ready in a month or two. They'll accept the land and go about their business."

Jose didn't respond.

"And the land we haven't promised already we can sell to the speculators."

"Muy bueno, Alterio. I understand."

Chapter 20

El Simpatico, Joaquin, and Guillermo sat in a private lounge area in one of Cancun's most luxurious hotels. The top two floors of the hotel were reserved as club rooms and had their own elevator access, private lounge, brunch areas, and special room service, which included a concierge on both floors. El Simpatico's group had taken every room on the top floor for themselves and their security. It had been designed so that all of the rooms were on the periphery of a large, open area filled with palms and other tropical plants that grew out of the garden in the center of the floor below.

"What's with that totem pole?" Joaquin asked and pointed to a colorful pole that was the centerpiece of the garden. It rose from the floor below and stretched thirty feet to a stained-glass dome that was the garden's ceiling. "It's ugly. I get all of the Mayan symbols stacked on top of each other, but that head on the top? It's modern and wearing glasses. It looks like the head of an accountant. What the fuck is with that?"

El Simpatico said, "That's the owner of the hotel, or was anyway. You remember him, Joacho. He *was* an accountant. He represented a large US subsidiary in Mexico. He set up false documents and eventually stole the company. He sold it for a small fortune and used a lot of the money to build this hotel."

"I remember. He didn't pay off the right people. We were supposed to whack him."

"*You* were supposed to 'whack' him, Joacho."

"Well, I couldn't. He got out of the country before we could get to him. Who owns the hotel now?"

"We do."

"Oh."

Eduardo walked up to the group and greeted them. "Good to see you, Jefe. How was your trip?"

El Simpatico made no effort to be nice. He said, "Joacho and I arrived a couple weeks ago. We flew over the island on the way. It is quite large. I saw no noticeable infrastructure—just a very small village. Have you and your engineers worked out all of the development logistics?"

"Not yet. It is a large project. It will take some time to plan all of it and produce detailed plans for permits. We're going to be building an entire destination, another Cancun, from scratch."

"Don't worry about permits," El Simpatico said. "Are we set for the closing today?"

"As much as we can be," Guillermo answered. "Eduardo and I will attend as the owners of our construction company. Pierre-Pierre will be introduced as our project director and will give the presentation. Alterio, his father-in-law, and a couple of their attorneys will be there. Alterio has also given us the names of the ejido president and another island resident he has asked to attend. The governor and his entourage will be there. We call his entourage the *Men in Black*."

"The what?"

"You'll see why. We've learned from Alterio that he is bringing his own development director. But he has assured us that Pierre-Pierre will remain the overall project director."

"Who is this new man?" Joaquin asked.

"His name is Arlan O'Brien. A gringo. We've checked him out. He specializes in low-density resort developments. Alterio calls it ecotourism."

"Well, we can't have that bullshit on our island," Joaquin blurted out. "That means a few campgrounds and some trails and shit. Who wants that? And how does that help us launder our money? A campground would only cost us a few hundred pesos."

"Joacho. You are so impatient. Let our partners and their new developer argue whatever type of development they want. We control the planning through Pierre-Pierre and—"

"But—"

"Stop. We'll get whatever we want. This man is no threat. Alterio wants the same thing we want. Who cares why he brought in this man, O'Brien. Maybe Alterio is a closet gay. Maybe he and the gringo are lovers. Who gives a shit?"

El Simpatico looked thoughtfully toward the garden and said, "Do you know that the name, O'Brien, has strong ties to Mexico? It's Irish. We had a president once whose name was Obregon. The name is derived from the Irish name, O'Brien. There used to be a city in Sonora called O'Brien City. It's now called Ciudad Obregon."

"Well, this man is close to Fiona Anderson," Guillermo told them.

"That bitch? The turtle lady? She and her group are a pain in the ass. She's trying to get our island declared a federal preserve. We should bury her in one of her turtle nests."

"Joacho, you are lucky that I am around to control your anger. Fiona is a prominent lady who is liked and respected by a lot of politicians and wealthy Mexicans. We don't need to bring her and her work to the forefront by killing her and making headlines. She and her environmental group represent no threat to us. We've even contributed to her group through one of our fronts. She'll never get Isla X'lak turned into a preserve."

Guillermo continued, "You and Joaquin can monitor whatever is said in the meeting and the lunch afterward. We have bugged the private dining room and placed a couple of cameras in the ceiling vents... unless you want Joaquin to sit in. He can be introduced as an advisor."

"No. Alterio has seen him with me at the ex-president's beach palapa south of here. It would needlessly alarm him."

"But Jefe, we should bring him in. He's a pendejo. He won't care if his new partner is El Simpatico. If he does, we will threaten to kill him," Joaquin said, and saw the glare from his boss. "Or maybe break a finger or two... or, better yet, the sharks will like his fat ass, Jefe," Joaquin said.

Before the meeting broke up, El Simpatico said, "The president called me this week and wants us to hire the son of one of his advisors."

"To do what, Jefe? Is he a killer?" Joaquin asked and smiled.

El Simpatico stood to leave and said, "He recently graduated from university with a degree in some kind of environmental bullshit. Pierre-Pierre can hire him as an assistant. It will be just one more favor the president will owe me." He then walked out of the lounge, down the hall, and to his room.

Chapter 21

A pretty receptionist with perfect English handed Arlan an envelope with two room card keys and two similar cards that allowed him the use of beach towels at the pool and nodded to a bellman who stood near the front desk. Arlan sighed, shouldered his only bag, and walked to the private elevator that she said would take him to the eighth floor, one of two floors reserved as *club* floors. The bellman tagged along with begging eyes and his hand out as if to take his bag. Arlan gave him ten pesos at the elevator and told him to go away. *God, Mexico seemed to be built on tips, propinas.* Every restroom he entered, every gas station, every gym—even the people who bagged groceries, somebody waited at the door with a wanting smile and a hand out. What *was* cute and maybe even gratifying at first had become annoying.

The elevator had four buttons—Lobby, 8, 9, and STOP. Arlan pushed 8. The fast-moving elevator stopped, and the doors quietly slid open. Arlan exited and looked around. The design was typical. Rooms were built around a large center courtyard garden. Trees from the garden grew up to the next floor. A pole with Mayan shapes stacked on top of each other had been erected in the center of the garden. It was about eighteen inches square and stood thirty or more feet tall, tall enough to expand through the open area in the floor above. Arlan craned his neck to see where it ended. It seemed to stretch beyond the ninth floor and to a stained glass dome. The shape on top of the pole was a human head, with modern glasses and a pompadour hair style. Arlan didn't think it was Mayan.

He walked along the hall to the other side of the garden and his room. Once inside he tossed his bag on the bed next to large bath towels that had been folded into the shapes of swans, or ducks. He couldn't tell.

He turned off the AC, pulled back the blinds that had been closed to keep the sun out of the room, and opened the window that looked out at the ocean. He sat on a cushioned chair and called Fiona.

"I'm so happy that you're going to help Don Francisco. Will you be coming to visit?"

"More than that... I'm moving to Madre. Alterio insists on it. But we need to talk."

"You're moving to Madre? I hope Alterio offered you a good deal."

"He did, but he made a big deal about the contract being guaranteed by his father-in-law. I'll get a house, a car, consulting fees, and expenses. I think that's a good offer. But I really don't know. I've never been a consultant. I've always been the owner and developer."

"Alterio always uses his father-in-law's money and integrity to get what he wants. We need to find you a nice house. There are plenty around. I'll show you around and introduce you to some of my friends. We'll be able to play tennis." She paused and then said, "When you tire of my tennis, I will introduce you to a friend who owns a club. He played professionally for a while."

"We'll see. But listen..."

"My sister will be sad to see you leave the flounder."

"I know. I talked to her already and told her it might happen. But I need to ask you a couple of things. I'm in Cancun. Alterio and his partners are going to finalize their partnership tomorrow. It's a big deal. But you know that everything with Alterio is a big deal."

"That's true. Will Don Francisco be there?"

"According to Alterio, everybody will be there—the new partners, some big shot Reforma Agraria people, the colonel... and the governor's coming. Maybe even Santa Claus and the Easter Bunny," Arlan said and laughed. "Alterio seems to be all about image. From what I've seen, it's a Mexican thing."

"Yes, image is important here."

Arlan laughed and said, "I hope they don't mind my khaki pants and jungle shoes."

"Arlan, you need to dress better than that," Fiona said.

"I travel light. I don't have anything else. I didn't think I'd need to make a fashion statement."

"You'll make a statement all right," Fiona laughed. "What about the new partners? What are their plans?"

"I don't know. I suspect they'll want another Cancun. Doesn't everybody?"

"Not everybody, Arlan. That's why you're there—I hope."

"Well, let's see what I can do. This is a big group with a lot of money. But tell me, how are you doing with your efforts to get X'lak turned into a preserve?"

"We're picking up support. But it'll be difficult. We're pressuring the president. But we may have to wait until the next election. Why do you ask?"

"I have an idea about the development of the island."

"Can you tell me about it?"

"I'm still trying to figure out how it will work on such a big scale. I need to know more, especially about Alterio's intentions. Plus, if you get the island declared a federal preserve my idea won't work. I'll be out of a job." Arlan laughed.

"I'm sure you'll be fine. Like I said, I doubt that we'll succeed. It's too political. And we don't have the funds to pay the politicians."

"If there were restrictions in place for the island that couldn't be changed by payoffs, I'd have an easier time making my case for a different type of development."

"Well, we are pushing a mangrove law at the federal level. The way it's proposed, it will restrict the cutting and removing of any mangrove. It's been around for a few years and hasn't gone anywhere."

"Half of the island is mangrove. A law like that would play hell with plans to turn it into another Cancun. But you'd better get that law passed pretty fast. There may not be any mangrove left to protect. The locals have already cut much of it."

"Yes, unfortunately. What about Alterio? You can't find out what his intentions are?"

"He's evasive as hell. He seems to be in love with the planning process. He doesn't know a thing about development. He seems to only focus on securing a partnership. I'd like to know more about what his father-in-law thinks. I hope he doesn't want another Cancun."

"I suspect he's following Alterio's lead. But I've known him to be smart and pragmatic. He'll do what's logical, not necessarily what his son-in-law wants. But with all of the other people that you just mentioned involved, you'll have your hands full."

"I know. I'll meet them tomorrow and let you know what I find out. I don't think it'll be much. I expect a dog and pony show with a lot of toasts and handshakes."

"Good luck."

"Gracias. And please keep me informed about the proposed mangrove protection law."

Chapter 22

Arlan and Alterio met at the hotel restaurant, which served a breakfast buffet. They were both dressed casually. Arlan was not a breakfast eater. He preferred a good workout. He knew that Alterio was not much of a breakfast eater either—not because he didn't like food; he was pretty certain that Alterio spent half his life in restaurants, but rather because Alterio was rarely up early enough for breakfast. Arlan looked at his watch. He had plenty of time to get a workout. The partnership closing celebration wasn't starting until two in the afternoon.

After the waiter took their room numbers, they walked to the buffet. Arlan returned to their table with toast and juice. Alterio arrived several minutes later with two plates of food. The restaurant's walls were glass, which gave every seat a panoramic view of the pool on the right and the sea straight ahead. Arlan saw Alterio staring to the far left of the view where a sleek, black helicopter sat on a grassy area beyond the tennis courts. Arlan had already spotted it.

"That looks like the helicopter that flew over us on Isla X'lak," Arlan commented.

Alterio smiled and took a bite of omelet. "This is really good huevos motuleños. You should try it. It's a special dish from the Yucatan."

Arlan finished his juice and toast. Alterio had gone back for thirds.

"After breakfast we should go to our rooms and change into our suits. I want to introduce you to Don Francisco and our attorney before we meet our partners."

"Suits?"

"You have a suit, no?"

"Alterio, I haven't worn a suit in—forever."

"Here in Mexico it is very important to dress impressively. You don't have a suit?"

All on the front end, Arlan thought as he remembered the common West Indian term.

"Yeah, and a tie that hasn't been tied for years. I just slip it over my head when I need to wear it. They're at my house in the US."

"We have to get you a suit."

Alterio motioned for Juan, who appeared out of nowhere, gave him a credit card, and told him to take Arlan to a clothing shop in Cancun Centro. A few instructions from Alterio later, and Juan said that he knew where the shop was located. As Arlan walked away from the table, he heard Alterio on his cell phone pleading with the haberdasher to drop everything and fit his friend with a suit *mas pronto*. Three hours later, Arlan, dressed in his new suit, met Don Francisco and his attorney in a lounge area just outside the private room that had been set up for the presentation and lunch. They talked for an hour. Arlan liked them both immediately. Alterio's father-in-law was engaging with a good sense of humor, and his attorney was similar but a little more subdued.

Just before two o'clock, they were escorted into the dining room by a hotel employee dressed in a tuxedo. The negotiations between the partners had been completed earlier in the day, and the attorneys for both sides had approved the final documents, which were spread out along with vases of flowers and a multitude of shiny, gold ink pens, on a long table that had been set up in the back of the room for the official signing.

Nobody had taken a seat. The governor hadn't arrived yet. Alterio introduced Arlan to the two new partners. He had then introduced Arlan to a tall, baby-faced man with two first names. The names escaped Arlan, but the man's appetite for talking didn't. He talked and talked—mostly about himself. He looked as though he could have been an athlete as a young man, and his muscle had turned to flab that was not well hidden under his tight dress shirt and slacks.

The governor entered the room surrounded by three men wearing black clothing. Not suits. One was dressed like a cat burglar without the cap—the other two like cowboys. The governor walked comfortably through the room and greeted everybody with a handshake and a smile. He was treated like a rock star. In return, he was as magnanimous as politicians are, especially when they know that the men they were there to meet represented a lot of money, some of which would find its way into their pockets. The men in black remained stoic and unfriendly. They didn't navigate the room or mingle with anybody but themselves. They kept an eye on everybody.

The colonel arrived in his sailor's suit, late and drunk. He carried a bottle of rum. It was almost empty. A man built like a fire hydrant, whom Arlan had seen on Isla X'lak, followed the colonel into the room. He carried a half-empty bottle of orange juice and some plastic cups and was dressed as though he was going to work in an auto repair shop. If this embarrassed anybody in the room they didn't let on. Everybody except the men in black smiled politely at the duo as they sat down at the table with the legal documents. The fire hydrant used his forearm to shove the closest stack of documents out of the way and set his juice bottle and plastic cups on the table. Alterio said something to the man dressed in a tuxedo. He approached the colonel and his friend and escorted them to the dining table.

Everybody kissed the governor's ass before he was led to his seat in the middle of the table. People still standing scrambled to a seat. The presentation started. The baby-faced man with two first names, whom Arlan now remembered as Pierre-Pierre, stood and talked... and talked. He praised the governor, the partners, and Alterio for making it all possible. He even managed to praise himself. He then presented the vision plan that Alterio had told Arlan about.

It was a hand-sketched depiction of a large marina near the center of the island, several golf courses, a shopping center and sports arena at the north end of the island, several hotels and residential projects scattered around the marina and golf course, and a bridge to the mainland. The plan had been masterfully created. The use of green colors and the depiction of trees and shrubs throughout the plan presented the viewer with an optical illusion. A high density design for the island was deceptively made to look like medium, almost low density. It took a trained eye to recognize it. Arlan suspected Alterio saw it, but he beamed as Pierre-Pierre told the crowd that this was an *ecological* development and that they had hired the *best-in-class* planners and engineers and economists to help bring the vision to fruition.

We're a dog show, thought Arlan.

While Alterio listened, he ate candy from one of the bowls placed in the middle of the table.

Pierre-Pierre went on to talk about the prominent Mexicans who had invested in the project... how committed they were to the island's environment, and how this project would economically empower the local people.

After an hour, even the governor seemed tired. Throughout the presentation, Arlan saw him try to discreetly send text messages or e-mails from the smart phone he held in his lap. Mercifully, Alterio interrupted Pierre-Pierre and suggested that lunch be served. There was an audible collective sigh that led to happy chatter around the table. Pierre-Pierre stood with a dejected smile. Lunch was served.

After everybody had eaten and the plates were removed, the partners were asked to sign the documents. A big deal was made of it, and everybody in the room received a shiny, gold ink pen. Afterward, people milled around the governor, who was the center of attention. The new partners talked and politely joked with Don Francisco, who seemed to enjoy himself. The men in black stood in one corner and scowled. Alterio continued to munch on candy. Arlan fended off questions from Pierre-Pierre who didn't seem to understand why Alterio had invited him or what his participation in the project would be. It was obvious that the new project director was in way over his head.

***

The party broke up and people bid adios to each other. Arlan returned to his room and realized he'd left his new gold ink pen back in the dining room.

El Simpatico sat in a comfortable chair in his hotel suite. Smiling at Joaquin, he closed his laptop and pulled out the cables that connected his screen to the cameras and microphones that had been placed in the room where the closing had taken place.

"That went well," said El Simpatico.

"Except that idiot Pierre-Pierre. He talks too much. And what's with those three men in black?"

"Don't worry about him, Joacho. Don't know what is up with the men in black—other than they look silly. This was an important milestone. Since nine-eleven it has become increasingly difficult to find ways to launder money. Cash is virtually useless. This is the perfect vehicle and a way to become respected more than feared."

"I like fear," Joaquin said.

"Our cartel will become Mexico's most successful developer, and nobody will know it." Fernando called his pilot and told him to have the helicopter ready to go in an hour. Then he called the captain of his yacht and told him to be prepared to leave for a long weekend. "Now that this is done, we have different business to attend to, Joacho. A competitor is trying to move into our territory. It's time for you to earn your money. I've heard of a seven-meter tiger shark down at the Banco Chinchorro reef. We will grab this hijo de puta, take him to the reef, and chum up the tiger. Whatever part the shark doesn't eat we'll put it in our trophy room."

Chapter 23

Arlan sat on the front edge of a large sofa across from two empty matching chairs. There were three other identical furniture arrangements in the carpeted lobby of the Miami hotel—the same tropical-colored upholstery and the same squat, glass-topped coffee tables between the fluffy furniture. A bronze-colored metal vase with tall, freshly cut flowers sat on the floor beside a large coffee table. Arlan needed to make space for the vision plan he had unrolled before Alterio stepped away to talk on his cell phone.

Alterio had brought the plan to the lobby because he wanted to look at it again with Arlan.

It was the same tired, one-page vision plan that had been presented at the partnership closing and that Alterio had shown to countless people, from the governor, to the ejiditarios on X'lak, to his gardeners and drivers—anybody he thought would be impressed.

The plan had been drawn a year and a half earlier by a world-renowned land planning firm, and Arlan was in Miami to finally meet them—along with a plethora of other professionals ... *the team,* as Alterio referred to them. They had gathered at the planner's offices in Miami at the request of the new partnership to begin the process of turning Isla X'lak into the next Cancun—all except Arlan. He was there to prevent it. But that was a secret—for now. Arlan missed the first two meetings with the development team because, just after the partnership celebration, he'd returned to the US to prepare for a long-term commitment to Alterio and Isla X'lak.

Alterio remained standing, talking on his phone. Arlan looked down at the vision plan. If used properly, a realistic vision plan could be a powerful tool that could attract investor interest and add credibility to the project. What was rolled out on the coffee table in front of him was a very high quality vision plan—but totally unrealistic for Isla X'lak. It was a graphic rendering of the property from a birds-eye view that depicted an idea, a vision of what might be developed sometime in the future, based on an owner's or planner's want, with no concern for environmental, logistical, legal, financial, or market feasibility issues. Unfortunately, Alterio treated this flawed version as a master plan, ready for the bulldozers. It was his badge—his ticket to credibility as a developer.

Arlan shook his head. He had a lot of work to do.

Alterio finished his phone call with only a little bit of shouting and returned and sat in a chair across from Arlan.

"What time is the meeting?" Arlan asked.

"In thirty minutes at the planner's offices. It's just a few blocks from here. We have plenty of time."

"Tell me again, Alterio. Who will be at the meeting?"

Alterio took another minute to thumb another text.

"The development team," Alterio said, without taking his eyes from his phone.

"Who is on the team, again?" Arlan asked.

Alterio looked at Arlan and said, "Besides us, I asked the planners to put together their own team. They invited a marine engineering firm and a design team from one of the top golfers. I forget which one, Norman or Nicklaus, maybe both. I met most of them when we were working on the vision plan."

Alterio read the screen of his phone and busied his thumbs again. "And Pierre-Pierre has invited a team of economists and marketing people."

"You're kidding, right?"

Alterio looked at Arlan with his head cocked.

"Alterio, this is all backward. This, or whatever it is, that you have brought together is a waste of time. These people may be the best in the world at what they do, but we need to understand what we can do with the island before we call in these types of experts."

"What do you mean? Isn't this what developers do?"

"We'll utilize all of the consultants sometime during the proj-ect, but not all at once—and certainly not yet." Arlan swept his hand toward the plan on the coffee table. "I mean, look at this vision plan. It's garbage."

"You don't like the plan?"

"It looks great, but it's a pipe dream. We don't know yet if it's even feasible to build all of this."

"We can build anything we want to build," Alterio told Arlan. "It's our island."

Arlan looked down at the plan and then back to Alterio. "We have far too much to learn about the island before we can come up with a workable plan. We don't know what can be permitted. We don't know enough about the kind of structures the soils will take. We don't know enough about the island's flora and fauna or the to-pography. We don't know how we're going to get heavy materials across that shallow bay," Arlan said and pointed to the plan. "We can't just stamp a bunch of hotels and roads arbitrarily on a map and then expect to build them there."

Alterio tilted his head and said, "But that's why we're here. The planners have been working beyond the vision plan and have come up with a preliminary development plan."

"Based on what? What studies have been done? I'm not aware of any."

"What studies do we need?"

"Alterio, it's irresponsible to plan this project without under-standing the island's physical and environmental constraints—other than the obvious."

Alterio answered another text, or pretended to.

"Alterio, isn't that why you invited me to work with you on this project—because I don't use cookie cutter plans? Because I work with the land, not against it?"

Alterio didn't respond.

"Alterio, I dropped everything I was doing in the US and moved to Mexico to help plan and develop an island. This is my first meeting with the development team. You told me that you don't want anoth-er Cancun. But you don't speak out against this," Arlan said, pointing to the plan again. "We have a lot of work to do to get everybody on the same page."

Alterio busied himself with his phone.

"Alterio, this is pissing me off. You're not paying attention. I can't work in the dark. I need some answers."

Alterio put his phone down but continued to look at the screen. "What do you need to know, Arlan?"

"Okay. A bridge? Why do you continue to promise them a bridge?"

Alterio looked up from his phone and said, "I've already told you. I had to promise they could build a bridge or they wouldn't have invested. But you already know that I'm not in favor of a bridge."

"Not in favor? You can't build one anyway. Have you told them why?"

Alterio looked at his phone again.

"What else did you promise them?"

"Just a few more things. It was the only way to get their money. Now I have to figure out when to tell them the truth. They still owe us a few more million dollars, which they'll pay when I meet certain milestones."

"What milestones?"

"One is that I get a letter from the governor that approves the bridge."

"Even if you had the land to build a bridge, can the governor alone approve it? Wouldn't the federal government have something to say?"

Alterio smiled and picked up his phone. He walked toward the entrance with the phone next to his ear and his right hand cupped over his mouth as he talked. Arlan had no idea if anybody was on the other end of the phone call.

Alterio returned a few minutes later.

"Alterio, your partners are developers. I assume they've checked all of these things out."

"No, they're builders. You pointed out the difference to me the first time we met. I don't think they understand much about island development."

This was crazy. But Arlan knew that the new partners were equally at fault. They should have done a better job of due diligence and not simply taken Alterio at his word. The complexities of buying ejido land, even recently privatized, are immense. Add the difficulty of island logistics and severe environmental restrictions, and one could easily surmise that this was not a game for amateurs—or first-time developers.

"What else did you promise?"

"I told them that we could build twenty-five thousand."

"That's a lot of hotel rooms. How did you come up with that number?"

"That's a deal I made with the governor," Alterio said.

Arlan shook his head and said, "If seventy-five percent of the rooms are occupied, that's over thirty-seven thousand guests. Add to that the employees and service people needed to keep the resorts operating, and add the number of employees at the shops and restaurants, and the number of people on the island will easily multiply by ten. With those kinds of numbers, you will need a bridge or an airport that can handle commercial airlines."

Arlan could visualize the four-lane boulevards, high-rise hotels, shopping centers, and services needed to meet the demands of a destination that size.

"I know that it is a problem. But I had to promise these things so they would invest. What would you have told them?"

"How about telling the truth?"

"But Arlan, this is Mexico. The truth doesn't always work."

"I'm starting to figure that out. But, Alterio, you know there is going to be no bridge. Why would you even want one?"

Alterio busied himself with his cell phone again.

"And a couple of other things. I've seen you pay cash out to a lot of people. I assume that they are bribes. I don't understand bribing dynamics. I know it's part of your business culture, but I don't do it. Never will. I don't come from a business culture that depends on corruption to work."

Just when Arlan was sure he wasn't paying any attention, Alterio looked up from his phone and smiled.

"Well, not at any level I'm familiar with," Arlan added.

"Your corporations don't send lobbyists to pay politicians for favors?" Alterio asked.

"Corporations pay for influence all of the time. But they hide it in the form of campaign contributions."

"And that's not corrupt?"

"What's that got to do with this?"

"It's no different in Mexico," Alterio answered. "If we don't pay the politicians, we don't get what we want."

"Maybe, but I have seen you pay people who aren't politicians."

"I pay who I need to pay, Arlan. It's how I get things done."

"I'm simply telling you that you invited me to the party to help you plan and develop an island. I'm not going to participate in bribes. But, in order to do my work and not run around in circles, I need to know what promises you've made and who you've made them to. And if I find that you're lying to me, I'm gone."

"You don't trust me, Arlan?"

"Does it matter?" Arlan answered.

Alterio's phone rang. He answered it.

When Alterio was finished with his call, Arlan asked, "What about your project director, Pierre-Pierre, the guy with two first names? He doesn't know a two-by-four from a broomstick. He talks all of the time and says nothing. Why is he involved with this project?"

Alterio smiled and looked toward the entrance, at nothing in particular.

"You know I'm going to fight his bullshit, right? Are you going to support me when I do?"

"When the time is right, yes, I'll support you. But I can't fight with my partners yet. They owe us too much money."

"I'm still fighting it, Alterio. This plan will be a disaster, not only environmentally, but financially. You'll never get enough people to the island to support this much infrastructure."

"I want you to fight it. Pierre-Pierre doesn't like you. I think he's intimidated. But let him think what he wants about the project and about you. It's my partner's responsibility to obtain permits for the project. They could be controversial—"

"I can guarantee there will be controversy with anything that has to do with developing that island. And it won't come just from Mexico."

"But don't you see, Arlan? We'll eventually get what we want."

"And what is that?"

Alterio didn't answer. Instead, he said, "He only has a two-year contract with our partnership as the project director."

"He can do a lot of damage in two years. He could cost you the project. I can't understand why you or your father-in-law would agree to have a person who is way under qualified to be you project director."

"But you are our development director."

"Titles. Big deal. They're meaningless."

Alterio's phone rang again, and he walked toward the hotel entrance with the phone next to his ear. Arlan rolled up the plan and placed the flowers back on the table. He stuffed the plan under his arm and heaved the strap of his computer bag onto his shoulder.

Arlan walked out of the hotel entrance and expected to find Alterio outside waiting to walk with him to the planner's office. Alterio had opened the rear door of a taxi and climbed in. He looked back to Arlan, nodded his head to the other side of the rear seat, smiled, and shouted, "Vamonos."

Chapter 24

A couple of minutes after they left the hotel, the taxi turned into a driveway in a residential neighborhood that led to a compound of several two-story contemporary buildings, all attached with glass breezeways and surrounded by lush gardens. It looked to Arlan as though it had been built in the fifties and was probably a school at one time. Now it housed the offices of thelargest planning firm in the world.

Alterio and Arlan exited the taxi and entered a reception area. The receptionist immediately smiled at Alterio, stood, and said, "Please follow me, Mr. Delgado."

They were led from a reception area, through a short breezeway, and to the glass doors of a conference room. Arlan could hear laughs and multiple conversations from the room when Alterio opened the door to enter.

A bald man in his early seventies at the far end of the large, rectangular table smiled, looked at his watch, and asked Alterio, "Did your car break down?"

Arlan glanced at Alterio, who apologized as though he really meant it and walked toward the bald man and Pierre-Pierre, who sat next to him.

After Pierre-Pierre and the bald man, who Arlan was to learn was the lead planner, finished listening to Alterio's apologies, everybody took a seat. Pierre-Pierre introduced everybody who had been waiting at the table and told what their respective consulting specialties were. Alterio introduced Arlan.

The planners, who hosted the meeting, were represented by one of the firm's principals and a junior staffer. Others present included a marine engineering firm—*one of the largest in the world*, according to Pierre-Pierre, a major hospitality accounting firm, a branding company—*the largest in the US*, and a marketing company that specialized in branded residential floor designs—something Arlan had heard about but had never used. Two competing golf course designers represented two famous golfers, a consultant represented the environmental certification of golf courses—*if that is possible*, thought Arlan—and there was an anthropologist from Madre who specialized in all things Mayan, invited by Alterio to teach all of the other consultants why any name associated with the project had to have the word 'Maya' in it.

The last person introduced was a young man with a handsome face and infectious smile. He didn't have a title and seemed to defer to Pierre-Pierre. His name was Hilario.

Most of the people around the table represented firms that had been involved with thousands of resorts around the world. The firms were well known and respected by lenders and investors. Place their names as participants on a project brochure for a new development and an audience with any large investment banking company is a given.

It was an impressive gathering of talent, and Arlan started to question if he was up to the task of being the development director for one of the two partners of this project.

After several minutes of pleasantries, Pierre-Pierre started. "We represent two of the most important businesses in Mexico. We have assembled the best consultants to plan and permit the project—the best in class. We have a very environmentally friendly project. We will be economically empowering the poorest county in the state. We have to be given permits... and we know the president."

This sounded familiar.

Pierre-Pierre had an assistant project manager who put an image of the island on an overhead screen that was attached to the wall next to the entrance doors. As he talked, the assistant scrolled through another few slides. The third image was that of an organizational structure for the partnership. It listed the names of the planners and engineers and other consultants who would work on the project. It was meant to impress, not inform. At the top of the page, Pierre-Pierre was listed as the *Master Developer*, a term Arlan had never heard. Arlan glanced at Alterio. They both smiled.

Another fifteen minutes of pep talk and Pierre-Pierre finally let the planners present their new plan. Using the same overhead projector and accompanying plans that had been spread out on the conference table, they presented a glorified version of the vision plan. There were also enlargements of different parts of the plan with more detail added.

Arlan listened to the presentation, which was as he expected—well rehearsed and very professionally presented. The new drawings were equally impressive and used the same designer's trick that had been displayed on the vision plan. The golf courses and the marina were colored in with green vegetation and blue water and showed large yachts in slips or entering and exiting the marina. Trees were drawn around the buildings that obstructed the full impact of their footprints on the land. Small portions of the roofs of the homes and hotels peeked through the multi-shaded green canopy. The plan was designed to appear to be 'green.' In reality, if the observer thought about what it took to create the roads, the golf courses, the hotels, the marina, and shopping areas, they could then visualize what the island would look like during construction. From overhead, the island would look like the site of a nuclear explosion. The surface of the entire island would have been scraped away, ready to be shaped and molded into a new mass tourism resort.

"This looks great," Pierre-Pierre beamed.

Everybody smiled and offered glowing comments about the plan.

"It is unique. It's very eco-friendly," Pierre-Pierre said and looked directly at Arlan.

Arlan was a bit off-balance. Many of the experts in the room certainly had to know that this plan had no sustainable qualities whatsoever and was far from *eco-friendly*. Didn't they? How could they not see the obvious flaws in the plan? Should he bring them up or be quiet? Arlan looked at Alterio for some direction. Alterio glanced at Arlan and turned to talk to the head planner. Arlan was on his own.

Fuck it, he thought. I'll either be booted or I'll make them think.

"What is with this road system running down the middle of the island?" Arlan asked and pointed to the six-lane highway system that cut the island in half length-wise.

"That's the *spine*. It's a continuation of the bridge and will carry all of the cars from Cancun. The island's infrastructure will be built alongside—power, water, and sewer."

"Oh."

After a brief discussion about the spine, Arlan pointed to the large marina basin depicted in the center of the island and asked, "Why is that labeled 'Mega Yachts'?"

One of the marine engineers talked about the demand for marinas south of the US into the Caribbean and South America where the mega yacht owners wanted to travel.

"Interesting."

"Why did you decide on a bridge?" Arlan asked.

"It's the only way to get the densities we need," answered one of the accountants.

"But there is no road from the airport to where you show the bridge connecting to the mainland," Arlan replied.

"We have contacts in the construction company who built and own the Autopista. They will build the road for us," Pierre-Pierre said.

"Who owns the land that this road and bridge will be built on?" Arlan asked.

"Alterio's family owns it," replied Pierre-Pierre with a broad gotcha smile.

"Oh," Arlan said and looked at Alterio.

There was more chatter around the table. Arlan asked, "Why three golf courses?"

The lead planner nodded to one of the golf course designers. "We are only showing three. But we are studying the market. We might eventually need five," he said.

Pierre-Pierre pointed out the hundreds of homes and condos depicted around two of the golf courses and said, "We need the golf courses to help sell real estate. They're called *residential* courses."

"Why does the other golf course—"

"The third golf course is a *core* course. It takes up less area because there are no homes on the fairways," Pierre-Pierre interrupted and smiled at one of the golf course designers. "Do you see the hotel next to it? The hotel will be a five-star boutique hotel, and we will build villas for them to sell branded residential units."

Arlan wondered if Pierre-Pierre had just recently heard those terms from the planners.

He asked about the shopping center and sports arena and was told that 'we are a mixed-use development' and 'they are required.'

"Who requires them?" Arlan asked.

Pierre-Pierre stared at Arlan. The lead planner looked at the accountants. One of them said, "That's the way it's done. We have to have shopping and amenities in resort areas." He looked toward the lead planner and then to Pierre-Pierre.

Arlan looked at Alterio and then at the people around the table and asked, "Why would you even want a bridge?"

Pierre-Pierre glared. The lead planner looked sternly at Arlan.

"We've talked to many of the operators. They want a bridge," an accountant answered.

"Of course some would *want* a bridge. But they don't *need* a bridge. You promised them a bridge and they grasped at it."

Pierre-Pierre looked as though he wanted to charge at Arlan.

Arlan said, "A bridge completely changes the personality of the island and will cause irreversible changes, not good ones. Most important, the island will lose its exclusivity."

Pierre-Pierre stammered, and Arlan assumed that he was trying to add something thoughtful, which he knew wasn't possible.

"It's a matter of filling the hotel rooms," one of the accountants said. "Bodies have to be brought to the island in mass. The trip from the closest major airlift, in this case Cancun Airport, has to be no more than forty-five minutes."

"But you show an airport on the plan," Arlan pointed out.

"It's just for small commuter planes from Cancun," one of the accountants said.

The lead planner said, "We have to rely on the Cancun Airport and a bridge. It would be impossible to fit an international airport on the island and still have enough room for the development."

Arlan stopped asking questions. The accountants then threw out acronyms that measured a hotel's performance like Rev Par and ADR. They talked of absorption rates and compared the island to five-star resorts in Mexico, Costa Rica, and the Dominican Republic.

Arlan couldn't blame the consultants for not seeing the obvious. Their jobs were to plan, not to be the developer and take all of the risks. It was really Alterio's and the project director's responsibility to insist that a plan be feasible. And they weren't doing their jobs—Pierre-Pierre because he had no idea how, Alterio... who really knew?

The bridge was steering the planning process, and Arlan knew that it would steer it into the abyss.

He brought it up once more.

Pierre-Pierre looked at Arlan and said, "You are just an ecologist overreacting to a bridge. We must have a bridge or the hotel operators won't come. You heard the consultants. We need the bridge."

Arlan looked around the room and said, "That's bullshit. Half the people in this room have worked on boutique hotel projects located in remote places. Have you been to the Caribbean? Hawaii? The Greek islands? Ever seen a bridge there? The operators will come to X'lak. Most will come because they'll figure out that they'll make more money without a bridge. There just won't be as many hotels as you've planned for."

Pierre-Pierre said, "You don't know what you're talking about. I'll take the advice of the people in this room who have decades of experience over your advice any day. You're crazy if you think there will be no bridge."

Right.

Arlan shut up.

The meeting ended with another *best in class* speech from Pierre-Pierre. Everybody complimented each other on the outstanding work they were doing, everybody except Arlan, and they adjourned with a promise to meet in one month to further the planning of Isla X'lak.

After the meeting, as everybody walked into the parking lot, Hilario approached Arlan and formally introduced himself. He told Arlan that he had recently graduated from a university in the US with a degree in environmental sciences and really appreciated his questions. Arlan thanked him, and after a few niceties they parted and told each other they looked forward to the next meeting.

Arlan wondered why Hilario was at the meeting. Nice guy, but he seemed out of place—just a little more than himself. He shrugged and thought that Hilario was probably related to one of the partners from Mexico City. But maybe he had found an ally.

*****

Arlan and Alterio met later in the hotel lobby to discuss how each thought the meeting went.

"Alterio, why don't you straighten these guys out on the bridge? There'll never be a bridge. Not only that, a bridge will bring exactly the kind of tourist Isla X'lak doesn't need. It's not the right market."

Alterio smiled and busied himself with his cell phone.

"And a mega yacht? That's absurd. I thought these people were *best in class* planners? Where's their homework?"

Alterio looked up from his phone and said, "Do you think a marina is a bad idea, Arlan?"

"No. A properly located marina that can accommodate boats appropriate for the island is needed. But a marina basin that takes up one quarter of the island? For mega yachts? Come on. It's not even possible."

"Why is it not possible? There are marinas all over the world that are larger than the one proposed on the plan," Alterio said.

Arlan leaned forward in his seat and said, "Most mega yachts have a draft of over twenty feet. I assume this marina was proposed to be at least that deep. The water around Isla X'lak is nowhere near that deep. It's twelve feet deep, max, for at least a kilometer out. The depth then gradually increases to between twenty and forty feet all the way to the continental shelf. On the lagoon side, the depth is six feet, in some places less. So, what's the plan? To dredge the entire ocean?"

Alterio smiled and said, "I didn't know that." He looked up from his phone and said, "That's why I asked you to come onto the team. You know about these things. But you came on a little strong today. I think some of the consultants are upset."

"They should be."

"But you can slow down a little. There will be plenty of time for you to present your ideas."

Arlan sat back in his chair.

"Why do you think PP called me an ecologist?" Arlan asked Alterio.

"Who's PP?"

"Pierre-Pierre, the man with two first names."

Alterio laughed and said, "He was very concerned after he met you at the closing. I think he feels threatened."

"What did you tell him about me and my involvement with the project?"

"I told him that you were an environmental expert and that you are close to Fiona and other NGOs, which would help with permits."

"You didn't tell him that I'm a developer?"

"He knows that you are our development director. But I didn't give him much more than that. I didn't want him or my new partners to feel as though we are trying to take over the project. I need for them to feel good about their investment and to know that we are working together as a team."

"And what does PP contribute to the team?"

"He's the *Master Developer*," Alterio said with a laugh and answered another text.

Arlan laughed too.

Chapter 25

Arlan stepped between the two-foot-thick concrete columns that supported a Moorish-style portico on the backside of the hacienda and onto an expansive lawn. Americans would call it a back yard. To Mexicans, it was a garden. It was as large as a third of a football field, surrounded by an eight-foot-tall limestone and coral wall. Pink and red and white bougainvilleas covered much of the wall. Large trees, many as old as the one-hundred-fifty-year-old hacienda, shaded most of the lawn. The only sunny area was the hacienda's original cistern on the far west side of the garden that had been converted into a pool. Enrique, the gardener, was cautiously skimming leaves from the pool's surface, careful not to get too close to the edge. Like many Mayans from small villages in the Yucatan, he couldn't swim.

Arlan watched a three-foot iguana do a few push-ups and scamper up a tree that was covered with vines that had leaves so large they looked prehistoric.

Arlan was to travel to Miami the next day to meet with the development team, which he had affectionately named *the Train*. He needed someone to stay in the hacienda while he was gone.

"Puedes quedarte en la hacienda hasta mi regreso?" he asked Enrique.

"Si. No hay problema."

The hacienda had fifteen architecturally magnificent rooms. They all had their original tiled floors, large wooden shutters on the windows, thick wooden doors, walls painted with lime-mixed paint to give them a warm patina, and ceilings sixteen to twenty feet high. Throughout the hacienda were heavily weathered wooden pegs built into the walls at eye level to hang hammocks. Living there was like camping in a museum. Arlan had time to buy furniture for just three of the rooms. Its size and lack of furniture couldn't diminish the overall historic warmth it exuded though. And it was incredibly wide open to the elements and impossible to close up, just the way Arlan liked it. It reminded him of the Caribbean home he used to live in.

But openness came with problems, depending on one's tolerance of wild animals.

In the Caribbean, Arlan would sometimes return to his home to find an iguana or two making themselves comfortable in his living room. Once a wayward goat decided to make himself at home in the kitchen. But the Yucatan had a lot more bio-diversity than an island in the Caribbean. Besides iguanas, which weren't as colorful as they were in the Caribbean, there were bats, birds, opossum, coati, feral cats, squirrels, scorpions, tarantulas, and snakes. The hacienda had been there so long that the animals' ease at making themselves at home in it was probably instinctual, handed down generation after generation. Every time Arlan left the hacienda for more than a few days he would return to a zoo.

As Arlan walked back to the hacienda to prepare for his trip to the US, his phone chirped.

"O'Brien. I heard you moved into the neighborhood."

"Captain Jay?"

"You betcha."

"News travels fast. Belize is a little far to be considered the same neighborhood, isn't it?"

"Nah, it's just up the road. I told you that I lived in Madre for a while. I even have a little boy there someplace."

"Is there any country where you haven't sired a child?"

"Only the countries I haven't been to. So, where you livin'?"

"In a hacienda. It even has a chapel. It's on the north side of the city and is called Hacienda Murcielago. It's the only word in the Spanish language that uses all five vowels. That's what I hear, anyway."

"It means *bat*. I know where it is. It's one of the only haciendas in the city. It's a big yellow thing next to the periferico."

"That's the place."

"I need to come up there and visit my son. I haven't seen him in a year. My wife will kick me out after a day or two, so now I've got a place to stay when she does."

"You have a wife?"

"Too many," Captain Jay said.

Maybe he's not kidding, Arlan thought.

"You know you're welcome to stay here. When are you coming?"

"Summer's comin' up. Business'll slow down. I'll come then."

"I'm usually pretty busy. You'll need to give me some notice."

"Aw, fuck it, Rookie. I got plenty to do in Madre while you're *busy*. I'll surprise you."

Arlan knew that was too true.

***

Three hours later, Fiona and Arlan sat at a concrete coffee table in the portico of the hacienda. The sun had set but it wasn't quite dark yet. It was the mosquito hour. They weren't bad, but Arlan turned on the low-hanging ceiling fans to help keep them away. Bats flickered by near the high ceiling to grab any mosquitoes that buzzed above the fan blades. A half empty bottle of Amarone sat on the coffee table. Another one waited in the kitchen.

"This is my favorite red wine," Fiona said.

"Mine too. But it's pretty strong."

"Have you been to Italy to see how this wine is made?"

"I guess I'm more of a third-world traveler."

"You've been other places. We've talked about them."

"Well, I've never been to Italy," Arlan said and emptied the bottle into their glasses.

"Thank you," Fiona said, and toasted Arlan. "This wine is made from dried grapes. That's why it's so strong."

"Is that also why it's so expensive?"

"Probably. Where did you get it? I've never seen it here in Madre."

"I picked up a couple of bottles the last time I was in Florida, when I was playing big shot developer and hanging out with the *best of class* consultants. Maybe that's why I felt I could afford Amarone."

Fiona laughed and said, "Besides being responsible for great wine showing up in the Yucatan, is anything else productive coming out of your meetings?"

"Not much. It's all show biz and all wrong. We'll start another round of meetings tomorrow in Miami. All of the sexy development disciplines will be there."

"Development is sexy?" Fiona asked.

Arlan smiled and said, "Everything is, once you understand the nuances." He took a drink and continued. "High-paid consultants who specialize in all sorts of development disciplines will be there— planners, accountants, marine engineers, marketing specialists, hotel operators, golf course designers... At this stage in the planning process it's ridiculous to have all of those types of consultants on board."

A small thud came from the fan above them.

"Did you hear that?" Arlan asked Fiona.

"Did a bat just get hit by a fan blade?"

"I think so," Arlan answered. "Don't they have echolocation?"

Arlan looked around on the floor for a dead bat but didn't see any. He'd find it in the morning. It wouldn't have been the first time he'd found bat carcasses on the portico floor.

"Why are the partners wasting their time and money?"

"Damned if I know. Alterio is in no hurry. The project director is, but he has no clue how to proceed."

"But you do. Won't they listen to you?"

"No. I'm poison in that room. I'm an *ecologist*, the worst thing imaginable in a room full of consultants who make their money cramming two-dimensional drawings of resorts on three-dimensional beaches and jungles. The only reason I'm there is because Alterio insists on it. The project director would have me thrown out in a minute if he could."

"How can they continue to plan a project that may not be able to be built?"

"Fiona, these guys think they can do anything. They have unlimited funds and are like kids in a candy shop. For the most part, the consultants are nice guys... smart guys. But the arrogance in the room during the meetings is astounding. They think the island is simply a playground for whatever development whim is currently popular or purportedly profitable. It's like a child's board game. The real players in the game—the island's inhabitants, the flora and fauna, and the island's future—are expendable... or interchangeable."

"Well, some people say that they have a presentation of the project and that it's environmentally friendly."

"It's not. Nowhere close. My guess is that Alterio has been showing off some of the presentation info at dinner parties."

"Do the materials he shows off state that the project is a green project?"

"Most of the presentation garbage does, yeah. It's a smoke screen. The consultants and Pierre-Pierre hide behind buzz-words like *green* or *eco*, or *environmentally sound*, or *sustainability*.The plan is a wolf in sheep's clothing Cancun in disguise."

"It's that bad?"

"Yeah. But the strange thing is that these guys are oblivious to it. They all think that they are doing what's right. Miami Beach and Cancun are the templates for everything they design. And they think that as long as the new place has a different name, it's unique."

"Sounds like you're frustrated."

"You know, this is my first venture into the big leagues. I've been a fairly small, hands-on developer. These guys are very good at what they do. But they each specialize in specific parts of the planning of a development. When their part is done they move on to another project. None of them see the big picture. So, yeah, it's really frustrating."

Fiona asked, "Alterio doesn't support your position?"

"Who knows what he supports. He plays both sides, and when things get dicey, he gets on his phone or announces that he needs to meet somebody somewhere."

"It sounds like he's using you."

"I think he uses everybody. But at least I have my foot in the door. And I've brought in some help... Mauricio Sanchez," Arlan said. "You must know him."

"Mauricio?" Fiona asked, her face flushed.

"Yes."

"I know him well. How did you get him to help you?"

"I convinced him that we can change the direction of the planning. With Don Francisco's blessing, I've started to work out a different plan for the island and plan to bring Mauricio in on it as soon as I can get him acquainted with the consultants. Nobody but Mauricio and Don Francisco will know of my plan. When the time is right, I'll present it. The toughest part will be to prove that it can be profitable. That's the only way they'll accept it, and they'd be right."

Arlan was a little surprised at Fiona's reaction that he had enlisted Mauricio to help with Isla X'lak. It could have meant a lot of things, but he assumed that the two had crossed paths frequently while fighting the good fight against mangrove clearing and over-development of Mexico's coastlines. He hoped that she didn't have anything against him.

Fiona fidgeted with her watch and took a sip of wine. She finally asked, "Arlan, do you think, even with Mauricio's help, you'll be able to get them to understand the island and your sustainable approach to development?"

"I don't know. I don't know if they can make a clean break from convention. First, I've got to prove that their way won't work on Isla X'lak." Arlan paused and said, "The partners need to build what will work on the island or pack up their consultants and go home. Financially, they're heavily committed. They're in quicksand up to their noses. They can't simply stop and sell out at this point—they're still working on securing some of the titles, and they need to secure permits. No investor will be interested in purchasing the land until the partners have both of those things in place. It's too risky. The partners have to move forward or they'll lose a lot of money. It's my plan or PP's plan. It'll be a battle."

Arlan paused and took a sip of wine. He then said, "I suspect that I'll be visiting Miami a lot in the foreseeable future."

"Good," Fiona said, and raised her glass. "We'll be having more Amarone in the future." Arlan had already blown any possibility of asking Fiona to stay the night by telling her that he needed to get up early to travel. Maybe she had opened the door for something down the road.

Chapter 26

A Toyota Landcruiser drove up to the entrance of Hacienda Murcielago. Arlan grabbed his carry-on and computer bags and walked down the steps as Mauricio pushed open the passenger side door. Enrique raked leaves near the entrance of the hacienda. Arlan thanked him once again for agreeing to stay in the hacienda and handed him five hundred pesos before stepping up into the Toyota.

On the driver's side sat Mauricio Sanchez, a tall, handsome man, who reminded Arlan of a famous Hollywood movie star from the fifties. He couldn't remember the star's name. Arlan had met Mauricio the first time he came to Mexico a few years earlier when he found out the land his friend purchased from an ejido was taken back and sold to another developer. Mauricio worked for the law firm who represented his friend. He was polite and professional and the only Mexican he felt he could trust at the time. Mauricio told Arlan that he specialized in environmental law, but that he understood ejido law well. He took the time to explain to Arlan the complexities of buying ejido land and was truly sorry that his law firm could do very little about the land scam, which seemed to be a common occurrence. Arlan told himself that if he ever did anything in Mexico again he would contact Mauricio.

By chance, Arlan ran into Mauricio at a local engineer's office a couple of months earlier, soon after he moved to Madre. Alterio owed the engineer money and asked Arlan to look at the work he produced to see if it was worth the invoiced amount. Mauricio was in the reception area when Arlan entered. They spent quite a while catching up. They had known since they first met that they shared a love for the sea, though Arlan's was beneath it and Mauricio's was on the surface. Anything on top of the sea that required a board was his passion.

Mauricio told Arlan that he had recently quit his job representing three of the major environmental groups. He was worried about his health. He had successfully stopped several major hotel proposals that would have wiped out vast areas of mangrove forests, and the developers and land-owners weren't happy.

"Why don't you come and work with me on Isla X'lak?" Arlan had asked Mauricio. "I need to understand everything there is to know about environmental laws and permitting in Mexico."

"I've seen the vision plan... that's what Alterio called it anyway. I don't like it."

"Give me a month. I'll show you how we can change it."

After a long discussion, Mauricio agreed to work with Arlan. Arlan convinced Alterio to bring Mauricio onto the development team by telling him that Mauricio's presence would cause even more NGOs to hesitate before voicing opposition to a project on Isla X'lak. Mauricio was now on his way to be introduced to the Train.

"Hey, Mauricio. Como estas?"

"Bien. Y tu?"

Arlan made himself comfortable for the three-hour drive to Cancun.

"The hacienda looks great, Arlan. I wish Alterio would rent one for me." Mauricio laughed.

"Yeah, it's a great place. I haven't had a lot of time to enjoy it though. It seems that I'm always in Miami for meetings with the Train."

"What's the Train?"

"It's what I call the development team. You'll see." Arlan looked at his watch. "This is a long drive just to fly an hour to Miami. Too bad flights out of Madre are so damn limited. You'd think we live in a third world."

"Arlan, look around. We do."

Mauricio drove toward the periferico. He looked over at Arlan and said, "You are very polite to your gardener."

"I hope so. I see the way Alterio and some of his family treat the help. It kind of embarrasses me."

"Don't worry about it, Arlan. It's typical in the Yucatan for wealthy employers to treat their domestic employees with indifference. The employees don't mind. They seem to expect it. The higher paid domestic helpers have their own employees that *they* treat indifferently in *their* houses. And those employees have employees."

"Are you kidding? They must not be paid much."

"No. It goes on down to the next rung on the employee ladder until it reaches the bottom. You'd think the lowest rung employee would have ill-feelings toward the people on the rungs above them. They don't. They try to raise their status so they too can have their own employees to kick around."

"You're not comfortable with it?"

"No. I don't have any employees."

They rode in silence for a while.

"What about Alterio? Is he coming?"

"He's in Cancun already. He'll meet us at the airport. He left a couple of days ago. He told me that he needed to meet with the head of the municipio. Something about a support town on the mainland for the employees of the hotels and resorts to be built on Isla X'lak."

"Is he working to privatize the ejido in Balam?"

"I don't know. But the whole thing makes no sense. I mean, it's irresponsible for a developer not to address the needs of the resort employees. But this is different. First, if we get our way there will be no need for a support town. We'll have a fraction of the number of hotels and businesses that Alterio and the Train plan. About one tenth or less of the employees. We'll be able to hire people from the village and Eek and Balam. Second, gringos who visit a destination frequently, which is the market we would target, like to meet and befriend locals. It gives them a feeling of belonging and keeps them coming back. Alterio and his partners don't want any employees living on the island. That's arrogant. They want the island to be their own Mexican gated community."

"Have you seen how the local employees in Cancun or Playa live?"

"Yeah, they live in barrios. The developers and the government that created the destination should have provided for the growth of the employee population. Tourists may not admit it, but I'll bet they feel a little strange when they drive through squalor on their way to their five-star hotel and the beach."

Once they were on the Autopista Arlan opened his laptop. He wanted to show Mauricio as much of any up-dated plans as he could before they arrived in Miami to meet the Train.

The sun was bright, and Arlan couldn't find a good position for the screen of his laptop. He moved it up and down to try to eliminate the glare.

"Does the group we're meeting with know I'm coming?" Mauricio asked.

"I cleared it with Alterio. Evidently, he had a hard time convincing the project director to bring anybody else to the meetings. It's a big group. Most of the people in it aren't needed, especially the project director, as far as I'm concerned. PP, that's what I call him."

"PP?"

"Short for Pierre-Pierre."

Mauricio frowned.

"You'll see why when you meet him. Anyway, he's already weary of Alterio's choices of team members. He despises my presence. I think it's because he knows that I'm a real developer and can see through his bullshit. It could be, though, that he doesn't like that I'm trying to shrink the project into something about one-tenth of what they are proposing. Alterio brought a friend to the first meeting and introduced him as part of the team."

"A friend?"

"Yeah. He painted houses for a living."

"That sounds like something Alterio would do. Maybe he liked the houses he painted."

"Close. He liked his choice of books."

"Is he still part of the team?" Mauricio asked.

"No. I couldn't use him and PP wouldn't pay him, so Alterio told him to go back to painting houses, I guess."

Arlan pulled up the vision plan on his laptop. He had a lot to go over with Mauricio, especially explaining the bridge fiasco.

"Did I tell you about the first time I saw Alterio's plan?" Mauricio asked Arlan.

"No."

"It was very funny. It was on Isla X'lak about a year and a half ago. Mexico had declared a National Ecology Day, and the president came to give a speech. A tent had been set up on the beach just in front of a home rented by Alterio that he used as an office for his early work privatizing the ejido."

"That little beach by the pier?"

"Yes. I was invited into the house before the speech and saw these really large plans, like three meters long, set up in the house."

"Alterio wanted the president to come to the house for a presentation?"

"I think Alterio wanted to be seen as somebody close to the president by the ejiditarios who were going to decide if he would get the contract to privatize the island. Or maybe he had the contract and just wanted to impress the locals.

"Three huge, white helicopters landed on the beach," Mauricio said and laughed. "They kicked up a lot of sand. A thousand people who traveled to the island to hear the president speak were ducking and wiping sand from their hair and eyes. One of the white helicopters stayed in the air and constantly circled the island."

"Must have been the gunship."

"When the president finished, he was escorted by security through the tent and back to the three waiting helicopters. He had a lot of people with him—his wife and a bunch of advisors. Alterio approached the president, and it looked like he begged him to walk over to his office. I couldn't hear everything that was being said, but I could tell the president didn't want to go with Alterio. His advisors were pointing to the helicopters and to their watches. Alterio was relentless."

"Sounds familiar."

"I guess a compromise was made. Alterio started barking orders to all of his employees who were there with him. They ran to the office, about fifty meters away. The president and his entourage waited just inside the shade of the large tent shaking hands and making small talk to some of the people in the crowd."

"The crowd stayed?"

"Yes. We didn't know what was going on. Most people figured that this was part of the presentation, I guess. Some drunks staggered back to the village for beer. Alterio and his employees came out of the house carrying boxes and easels and rolled up maps. They placed small maps with cardboard backing on the easels. The large three-meter map was strung between two tent posts and attached with tape. Alterio was really animated when he explained the plan to the president. The security detail looked nervous. One of the entourage whispered into the president's ear, and most of them walked to the helicopters and climbed in. The president and a few others stayed to listen to Alterio."

Mauricio let out a snort and laughed.

"The fourth helicopter, the circling gun ship, moved close to the three parked helicopters, probably to escort them away from the island."

"I'm sure this was pre-planned down to the second. Security must have been going nuts," Arlan said.

"The gunship hovered just behind the presidential helicopter, the closest to the tent. I guess because the gunship pilot was nervous or maybe because he was trying to see what the holdup was, he maneuvered his helicopter alongside and a little higher than the presidential helicopter." Mauricio laughed again. "The blade wash was too much for the big map taped to the tent posts, and it flew into the crowd. It barely missed the president and wrapped itself around several people near him. The cardboard-backed maps on the easels flew like square Frisbees in all different directions. Some flew into the tent. The rest flew down the beach or into the water. The boxes tipped over, and hundreds of papers flew down the beach. Sand hit everybody."

Arlan's eyes watered with laughter.

"The gunship pilot must have seen what had happened and backed out farther over the water, but it was too late. The president's security team rushed him to his helicopter. Alterio followed as close as he could and he was still talking. I couldn't hear him, but I saw his lips moving and his arms flapping. The security guys pushed Alterio back and the president's helicopter flew away."

"That is a funny story... and typical of Alterio."

For the next hour they reviewed the plan. Arlan mostly talked about its ramifications for the island. They had traveled for two hours and were in the middle of the Yucatan Peninsula, surrounded mostly by jungle with a few small villages sprinkled here and there. Arlan was the first to mention the wall of smoke several kilometers ahead of them.

"Looks like a roadblock. Maybe there's an accident."

"No. See the bomberos? It's a fire. The ejiditarios are burning the jungle."

Two police cars were parked on the side of the Autopista. Their blue lights flashed. Policemen stood outside of the cars and one waved for Mauricio to stop. Arlan could see firemen milling around near the two fire trucks a few meters beyond. The smoke was thick in front of them. Through it, Arlan saw flames jump across the highway. Mauricio and the policeman had a brief conversation that Arlan didn't follow. Mauricio rolled up his window and looked at Arlan.

"It's voluntary. We can go through it or turn back."

"It's a long way back, and we have a flight to catch," Arlan said, staring ahead at the smoke. "It's a straight road. Just keep the wheel pointed ahead—and floor it."

They both laughed as Mauricio plowed through the smoke.

It was dicey. Smoke filled their view. Twice, flames jumped across the highway and hit the Toyota.

"It's getting hot in here. I hope it didn't blister your paint," Arlan said.

Mauricio kept the Toyota straight and didn't let up on the gas. They could see nothing. The smoke was too heavy. "What if there is a car ahead of us?" he asked.

"We're screwed."

In a couple of minutes, they cleared the fire and smoke and broke into the bright morning sun on the other side. Arlan looked across the burned out median to the other side of the highway. He saw a fire truck and two police cars. A line of cars heading in the opposite direction formed to the east. With a three-point turn, the second car in line broke formation and bolted through the smoke and toward Madre.

"Was that a forest fire or are ejiditarios burning their land?" Arlan asked Mauricio.

"Both," Mauricio said. "This land is being privatized very quickly, mostly by one of Alterio's main competitors. The ejiditarios clear the land as soon as they get titles—rainy season or dry season. It's dry season now and their fires are out of control."

"Is that allowed?"

"No. They just do it. Nobody does anything about it."

"Why doesn't the government stop it?"

"The locals are treated with, what is the English term? *Kid gloves.* They are poor farmers and fishermen. Everybody feels sorry for them. They are left alone to do what they want."

"Even if they are poor, that's no excuse. And if they're getting free land they're not poor anymore, at least on Isla X'lak they're not. The ejiditarios have sold a lot of the island for a fortune, yet every time I'm on the island I see mangroves being cleared."

Mauricio looked at Arlan and smiled. "It's Mexico."

"Maybe privatization is good. It seems to make some people rich. But wow, it's pretty bad for the environment. I guess it should have been easy to predict that privatizing beachfront land would bring the bulldozers in to build resorts, but I don't think anybody is prepared for the scale of slashing and burning of inland property by the locals."

Mauricio said, "Most people don't even know that they are doing it. They think that these fires are natural."

Arlan looked at the scorched landscape and said, "A few dozen machetes in the hands of experts, and the locals seem to be machete wielding experts, can do just as much damage as one bulldozer—just a little slower. Cleared habitat is cleared habitat no matter how it gets there."

Chapter 27

Arlan and Mauricio sat together at the planner's conference table. Alterio sat next to PP. The rest of the Train sat where they had set up their laptops. A set of plans lay in front of them. Mauricio had been introduced, and everybody was enjoying casual conversations amongst themselves while the overhead projector was being set up.

"So, why do you call them the Train, Arlan?" Mauricio whispered to Arlan.

"All of these world-renowned, high-powered consultants gather in this room every month, like clockwork. Every meeting is the same. They toot their horns and start the meeting, barreling down the same track with no deviation. Nothing in their way is safe—not the law, not the environment, not the people. Collectively, they're a powerful locomotive that knows one thing—how to chug along the same beaten path, its destination a foregone conclusion. There's really no reason to meet. You'll see."

PP stood and started the meeting. "We are the best in class. We represent two of the most prominent businesses in Mexico. We have an environmentally sound plan, and we will economically empower the poorest county in the state. We know the president..."

Mauricio leaned toward Arlan and whispered, "Jesus, does this guy ever shut up?"

"When he runs out of breath and sucks in air you can interrupt, if you have something to say. But he doesn't normally say anything that elicits a response."

PP continued. He finally let the planners give their dog and pony show, mostly for Mauricio's benefit, since he was the newcomer. Arlan was sure that the Train expected little from Mauricio. But Arlan knew that Mauricio was his new best weapon. Convincing the Train that the plan needed a one-hundred-and-eighty-degree turn was going to take time. The moat of arrogance that surrounded the group was hard to penetrate. Mauricio understood how the federal authorities worked and he understood Mexican law. Most importantly, he knew how it might be applied by the authorities with respect to Isla X'lak. He would simply explain the way things were in a calm, non-combative fashion. He wouldn't be considered a firebrand, as Arlan was.

Before the meeting, Arlan had warned Mauricio not to address the bridge or any of the other more ridiculous aspects of the drawings. "Just let them ride for now. But be careful. Take a position against anything and you'll be labeled an ecologist, a fate worse than death in this room. You're here to address much bigger issues than their imaginary bridge."

As usual, the planners put on a great show. Arlan was as impressed as anybody in the room. They spared nothing when presenting the latest version of the same plan, with minor changes here and there. The graphics were unbelievably good. As usual, there were stacks of drawings on a large side table, from which any page could be brought onto the main table and reviewed and marked up as desired by whomever held the markup pen. The result was always illegible until the person who made the notes tried to explain their meaning, none of which mattered today. The planning process was about to be stood on its head.

When the initial presentation was almost finished, there was a knock on the conference room door. Caterers came in carrying two flat boxes and plastic bags. They were escorted into a kitchen area adjacent to the conference room. The junior planner said, "So that we can keep working we've had a caterer bring food. It's ready anytime you're hungry." He pointed to the kitchen.

People got up in twos and threes and brought food and soft drinks or water back to the table. While they ate there were few pertinent conversations. It was good not to let the meeting venue change because of food. Maybe something would get done today. Arlan never could understand business lunches. Food ruined meetings and meetings ruined food. He preferred to meet until the work was done, then eat, or not.

PP came over and sat next to Mauricio and Arlan with a plate full of food. He opened up the conversation in Spanish. Mauricio listened patiently.

"Your Spanish is really good," Mauricio told PP, chewing on a bite of tuna sandwich.

"My mother is from Mexico," PP answered through his own bite of some kind of sandwich. "I'm half Mexican."

"And half idiot,"Arlan said under his breath.

"We're thinking about taking a tour of the east coast of the US to visit resort destinations that rely on bridges. You should come with us," PP told Mauricio.

Mauricio looked at Arlan and smiled. He busied himself with another bite of tuna sandwich. Arlan got up to find Alterio. He found him smoking a cigarette in the courtyard adjacent to the conference room. Alterio usually ate large quantities of food when nervous. He smoked when he was really nervous.

"Alterio, PP is planning an east coast trip so that we can be convinced that we need a bridge. This is out of control. Have you received the rest of the money from your partners? You need to stop this bridge bullshit."

"No. But I can see that I need to tell them. I am kind of nervous. I don't know how to do it. This is the tough part."

Yeah, it's much easier to lie.

For the next few hours the train discussed densities and total impact. Mauricio was invaluable for this part of the discussion. Arlan told the Train that the ultimate permit, the Manifesto de Impacto Ambiental, the MIA, issued by the federal government, trumped all state and local permits and was the key to the project. The rest of the group, especially PP, not believing him, put up a mild argument and promised to look into this. Without Mauricio's confirmation, the group would have simply dismissed it. There would be no discussion. Mauricio added that an MIA approval might require very low densities and a total impact of less than ten percent of the land.

This didn't sit well with the Train. The implications were obvious, but no one was willing to accept them. The arguments started.

"What's the definition of low-density? We're already low-density."

"Look at the plan. There is hardly any impact. It's mostly green," PP said.

"Low-density to the federal environmental authorities has always meant one or two keys per hectare. And they usually have frowned on any development impact beyond ten percent of the surface of the island," Mauricio said and shrunk back into his chair to avoid the storm of questions and outbursts from the consultants.

"Units or keys?" Mark, the assistant planner, asked.

"Keys," Mauricio said, and added, "In Mexico, one hotel room is one key. One villa equals two and a half keys."

"So, it's the same as most other places," Mark said, clarifying the math for everybody in the room, whom he'd worked with before.

Arlan had some one-on-one time with Mark after their last meeting and was impressed that he seemed to understand the need for a more sustainable plan. But he'd admitted that he was just an assistant planner and couldn't force the idea onto the group, or his boss. At least he was an ally.

"That's ridiculous," interrupted PP. "We have the best in class designing this project. We will be hiring local people from the poorest county in the state."

The discussion became heated, mostly with the consultants arguing with each other about what their definitions of low-density were and what meant. "Look at the plan," PP said. "The golf courses are green. There is no impact there."

"Uh," Arlan grunted, "in order to build the golf courses you need to first destroy the existing vegetation. That is an impact."

PP interjected, "But that is crazy. Golf courses are beautiful. We need them to attract boutique hotel operators and to sell homes."

"Tell that to the plants and animals you will destroy in order to build them. I am not convinced that golf courses make sense for Isla X'lak. We won't attract golfers. They'll stay on the Rivera Maya, where there are lots of golf courses."

"But we will attract them," one of the accounts said. "There are already three golf courses near Cancun with several more being planned. With the bridge, the guests staying in the hotels on Cancun and in the Maya Riviera can easily get to our courses."

Arlan glared at Alterio.

Alterio hesitated, and then said, "Just one thing. It is very important."

As usual, this silenced the group.

"Um, the... the land where the bridge connects to the mainland is not owned by my family."

More silence, and a few nervous glances.

One of the engineering consultants broke the silence by saying, "Well, that's a game changer," which drew a few nervous laughs.

"What are you saying, Alterio?" demanded PP.

"I was meaning to tell you. My family's land stops on that north-south line that separates the two municipalities," Alterio said, as he stood up and ran his finger along the county lines on a map on the conference room wall.

"This piece of land that juts out into the lagoon where you propose to place the bridge is my cousin's land," Alterio said.

"We'll buy it," PP said.

Alterio answered, "We can try, but he won't sell. He told me that he has it locked up legally so that only his children will get the land."

"But that's the only place the bridge can go. We've studied the rest of the shoreline and lagoon basin, and this is it. This is the place," the engineer stated.

"What's that land next to it? It looks like it would work," the head planner said.

"That's federal land," Mauricio said.

"Then we will get a lease from the federal government," answered PP. "We know the president."

Mauricio looked at Arlan. Arlan nodded.

"It's a federally protected wildlife preserve. No bridge or road will be allowed on it," Mauricio said.

The Train broke into chaos. Everybody was out of their seats pointing to whatever map they were closest to trying to figure out a magical solution to this new problem. The problem was far from new. It was just new tothemMauricio leaned into Arlan and said, "Wait until I tell them about the mangrove protection law that is being talked about in Mexico City."

"Is it going to happen?"

"It has a good chance of becoming law very soon."

"How restrictive will it be?"

"As it reads now, all four mangroves will be protected. No cutting, not even a branch. And no mitigation."

"All four? Red, white, and black are all I've seen in the Yucatan."

"And botoncillo."

"Buttonwood? That's an upland plant. They're all over the place."

Mauricio shrugged. "It's Mexico."

"That could really help us. I think you'd better hold off though. Let them digest the bridge issue for a while. Throw another fly in the ointment and PP will implode."

The planning session lost all momentum after Alterio's revelation, and everybody left to lick their wounds, but not before they got to listen to the fact that they were still *best in class,* Arlan thought. The jury was probably out on Mauricio. He was too new to the group. Alterio was, for now, definitely out of the dog show.

That evening, at the hotel the Train used when in Miami, Arlan sat in the lobby waiting for Mauricio to come down from his room. They planned to dine at a restaurant a few blocks from the hotel. PP and the accountants nursed drinks at the lobby bar a few paces away. Hilario came into the lobby and spotted Arlan. He invited himself to sit across from Arlan on a sofa and said that he appreciated Arlan's passion for sustainable development. Arlan thanked him, and they briefly discussed some of the logistical and environmental problems of the proposed project. Hilario told Arlan that he would like to work on the type of plan that Arlan had suggested in the meeting. Arlan invited Hilario to join him and Mauricio for dinner, but Hilario politely declined, indicating he was going to visit an old friend but would be happy to join them for a nighcap later. They shook hands and Hilario walked away. Arlan looked over to the bar. PP glared at him and then watched Hilario walk out of the lobby.

Chapter 28

El Simpatico sat in the chair behind Guillermo's desk in their Mexico City offices. Guillermo and Joaquin sat across from him with a medium-sized cooler at his feet. They waited for Eduardo, the CFO, who told them that he would be on a conference call with Don Francisco's attorneys for the first part of their meeting.

El Simpatico looked at his watch and said, "Let's get started."

"Our project director came to Mexico City yesterday, directly from his planning meeting in Miami." Guillermo hesitated and said, "We may have a problem."

He told them about the land where the bridge was to be built.

"I thought he was to check this shit out," Joaquin said.

"Pierre-Pierre said that Alterio showed him title to the land. It was in his father's name."

"Did the idiot check the public registry to see if the title was real?" Joaquin asked. "What the fuck is due diligence for, anyway?"

"So his cousin owns it. No problem. Make him an offer he cannot refuse," El Simpatico said.

"Alterio claims the land is legally locked up. It can't be sold."

"Check that out. And check out the federal land next to it. Maybe I can get ownership to it from my friend."

"A federal wildlife preserve?" Joaquin asked.

El Simpatico glared at him.

Guillermo said, "We'll check it out immediately. But that's not the only problem. This man, the gringo, Arlan O'Brien, has brought in an environmental attorney... a Mexican. We have run up against him before with one of our all-inclusive hotels we tried to build south of Cancun. He represented an environmental group that didn't want the mangroves cleared. He won."

"So?" Joaquin said.

"He's pretty influential and—"

"We should whack him. The gringo too. I could send Raton and Nacho. They need something to do."

"It seems that your friend's son, Hilario, supports him, as well," Guillermo added, looking directly at El Simpatico.

"What the fuck," Joaquin said and looked at his boss.

Guillermo continued. "According to Pierre-Pierre, the attorney supports O'Brien's low-density sentiments for the island. He claims that the MIA, the environmental authorization from the federal government, will require low densities and minimal impact, which might eliminate the golf courses."

"Bullshit," Joaquin said.

"Joacho, settle down. Don't worry about permits. We knew that MIA authorization would be required. We knew that we would need to submit plans and apply the normal way. It's part of our low profile. We can't be seen as forcing permits through. That would be a boon for the newspapers. I'll take care of the MIA. The bridge worries me. Guillermo, tell your project director to work with the planners to see if this thing can work without a bridge."

"Pierre-Pierre? That pendejo. Let me hurt him too."

"Joacho. You are impatient. We need Pierre-Pierre and his contacts in the financial world when we take our development company public."

"Public?" Joaquin asked.

"Yes. I have worked it out with our accountants. We'll not only launder several billion of our money through development costs, but once we are up and running, even with just a few hotels, we can raise hundreds of millions of clean money through a public offering."

"A public offering of what?" Joaquin asked.

"Of a development company that we'll spin off from our construction company. We'll own the majority and have management control."

"There are people who specialize in that sort of thing, no? Why do we need him?"

"Joacho, we need a man who can navigate easily between the US and Mexico... a man in the industry with contacts... and a man we don't need to worry about trusting because he is far too inept to be calculating. A man we control."

Eduardo entered the office and sat in the only empty chair. El Simpatico looked at him and raised an eyebrow.

"I just got off the phone with our partner's attorney. He received this year's property tax bill for our land on Isla X'lak. It is very high. It's more than twenty million pesos."

"Pay it," Joaquin said.

El Simpatico turned to Eduardo and asked, "What do you think?"

"It's excessive, but we are in this to spend money. Our partners don't want to pay it. They want to argue the high land evaluation. They have a point. If we cave in, the municipio will forever have their hands out for more and more money."

El Simpatico thought for a moment and said, "These are our partners. Fifty percent partners, for now. We need to let them think that they have equal say. Let them fight the tax bill. But don't let them take too much time." He paused and said, "Guillermo, I want you to call a board of directors' meeting. Make sure it's in Madre. And I want a plan ready to submit for MIA authorization. You and Eduardo will attend, along with Pierre-Pierre, who will make the presentation. Joacho, I want you to keep an eye on our friend, Alterio... and send your goons to rough up Hilario. Let him know that he works for Pierre-Pierre, not the gringo."

El Simaptico let that settle in and then said, "Before we go... Joacho, show our friends my newest trophy."

Joaquin placed the cooler on the table. Eduardo and Guillermo exchanged glances. Joaquin smiled, pulled out a human head by its hair, and held it out for the others to see.

"Look," he said with a grin. "His eyes and mouth are fixed in a permanent scream. But he looks tired. You would think he was screaming for a day."

"He screamed a long time, Joacho," El Simpatico said and admired the head of his most recent competitor.

"Even the sharks wouldn't eat the stupid pendejo's head. They probably thought if they ate his brains they would get stupid too," Joaquin said and laughed.

El Simpatico watched as Guillermo and Eduardo let out nervous smiles and glanced at each other. He smiled and said to Joaquin, "Joacho, take the head to the freezer in the trophy room."

Chapter 29

Arlan and Fiona sat across from each other at a table in the atrium section of a popular Madre restaurant. The restaurant, and the three others owned by a successful American, included his name in the restaurant moniker. This one was frequented often by the who's who of the city, especially for lunch. It also served some of the best food in town.

"I was so happy that you told us about the turtle migration," Fiona told Arlan.

"It was really unbelievable, Fiona. I've never seen anything like it. I don't know if too many people have."

"They might have been Ridley turtles. They're known to mass like that. But there aren't many left. Edmundo thinks they were green turtles. We have heard about this phenomenon from local fishermen, but we've never been able to document it. You were very lucky to have seen it."

"That's what it was? A migration?"

"That's what Edmundo thinks. They come together from the Gulf and the Atlantic to mate. It's too bad you couldn't get close-up photos."

"That would have been impossible. We were in the small helicopter, heading to X'lak from Cancun. It was just Alterio, me, and the pilot. We weren't more than a couple of kilometers from Isla X'lak when we started to see groups of a dozen or so sea turtles swimming on the surface. Within a minute we started to see groups of fifty or more. That's when Alterio got excited and ordered the pilot to get closer to the water and fly this way and that way. The pilot wasn't going to argue—Alterio pays him well. I was dizzy. It didn't matter where the pilot flew. There were turtles as far as we could see in all directions. Even if I had a professional camera with a zoom lens I think the photos would have been blurry."

"We would have loved to see documentation of this. It would be one more piece of ammunition to help preserve the island."

"As we flew away from the turtles, I told Alterio I was going to ask you about them. He wanted me to keep it a secret." Arlan laughed.

"That sounds like Alterio. He's always manipulating something for the development of the island. I think he tries too hard to impress his father-in-law."

"I'm not sure that's what it is. It's something else that I can't pinpoint."

"Money," Fiona said. "Isn't that why he wants to develop the island?"

"If he wants to develop the island, he should be more focused on the planning process, which he isn't. It's almost as if he doesn't care."

"One of our supporters sent a copy of the development plan to our office. It's not as bad as I thought it would be."

"That was probably the old vision plan. Alterio passed copies of that plan to everybody."

"Is there a new plan?"

Arlan thought for a moment and laughed. He said, "Yeah, but the new plan is the same—just a lot more detail."

"Well, it looks nice."

"Of course it does. You know, Fiona, and I mean this with no disrespect, but environmental groups and academics should try to understand drawings and the development process better. Just because an architect or a planner has a degree and can draw pretty pictures, it doesn't mean that they know what they're doing."

"So the plan I saw is bad?"

"It's a great drawing. But it hides the truth."

Fiona sighed and sank a little in her chair.

"What's hidden on the plan I saw?"

"Not exactly hidden... they're disguised with trees and green and blue charcoal."

"So, what did I miss?"

"Multiple golf courses and as many hotel rooms as Cancun. The plan also includes a sports arena. But the best thing is the deep water port for mega yachts."

"Mega yachts? How are they going to get there? Isn't the water too shallow?"

"Yep."

"How could they not know that?"

"Because they don't care. They're not developers... they're planners. They don't have to build what they design. They'll be done with their work long before construction begins."

"Does Alterio support this plan?"

"He's like a kid in a toy store. He seems to be having a great time—traveling, eating in fancy restaurants, living large. He loves being called a developer. Who knows what he supports. He doesn't fight for or against anything on the plan."

"What about Don Francisco? Does he support it?"

"I'll be meeting with him before I head to Miami tomorrow. So far, he's not very happy with what I have told him about it. He thinks that it is not unique and doesn't represent the island."

Fiona took a drink from the glass of water, which had condensation running onto the white table cloth even though the restaurant was air conditioned.

"What's happening in Mexico City? Will there be a mangrove law?" Arlan asked.

"We're working on it. The legislation has been around for a while. It needs a push from the president to pass. He's popular, and politicians who are on the fence would follow his lead if he chose to support the bill. I've told you that the president's wife is our friend. She's made a pretty strong case for us. But he has close advisors who are totally against any environmental legislation. They claim that it will hurt tourism. We'll see who wins the battle. The president adores his wife."

"Mauricio is pretty sure that it will pass."

Fiona smiled and took another drink of water.

"Does that mean that you have a chance to get Isla X'lak to be declared a protected preserve too?"

"I wouldn't go that far."

"If you do, I'm out of a job."

"You'll find another one," Fiona said.

Arlan took a drink of water and said, "I think you'll like the plan Mauricio and I are coming up with. With it, the island may not need protected status."

"We'll see, Arlan. I truly hope you can come up with a good plan and that it's adopted by the partners. But I have my doubts that even your plan, as good as it may be, can control the future of the island. There's too much money to be made by the land speculators and developers. They'll figure out a way to change whatever you do and build their high-rise condos eventually."

Arlan looked down at the table. He didn't want Fiona to see his disappointment.

Fiona and Arlan finished lunch, making small talk about her horses and his lack of time on the tennis court lately. When they finished lunch, they stood and walked through the restaurant toward the rear exit and the parking lot. Arlan paused to let Fiona step in front of him and said, "Speaking of the devil." He nodded to a small alcove on one side of the restaurant. Alterio sat with another man at a semi-private table separated from the rest of the restaurant by a couple of columns, which Arlan thought strange. Alterio always held court front and center in this restaurant.

Arlan and Alterio made eye contact. Alterio quickly looked away. Whatever he was trying to avoid, if anything, backfired when Fiona stepped up to Alterio's table. Alterio looked surprised and stood. His companion looked up from a menu and stood.

Alterio gave Fiona a hug. He then gave Arlan a Yucatecan handshake.

"Have you eaten?" Alterio asked.

"We've just finished," Fiona said.

"Very good." Alterio stood back and gestured toward the man with him. "Permitame presentarle mi amigo, Alejandro. El no hable Inglese."

Alejandro held out his hand. Fiona and Arlan each shook it in turn.

"Mucho gusto," they each said.

Alejandro was as large and barrel-chested as Alterio. They could have been brothers.

"Si, yo solo hablo espanol," Alejandro said. He then added, with a laugh, "Y chino."

Alejandro pulled out two business cards from his sport coat pocket and handed them to Arlan and Fiona. Each politely thanked him. Alterio gave his friend a disapproving look. Arlan did as he always did when handed a business card—shoved it into his pocket without looking at it. Fiona held onto the card she had been handed.

"Alejandro and I have known each other for years. He's from Madre but hasn't lived here for twenty years," Alterio said.

Arlan and Fiona smiled at Alejandro. He nodded back.

"How was your lunch?" Alterio asked.

"It was very good. Try the tuna tartare."

"I will. Thank you. Are you going to Miami tomorrow?" he asked Arlan.

"Yes. You're coming?"

"No, I have business here. You and Mauricio are on your own. Don't be too hard on PP."

Fiona tilted her head questioningly.

Arlan looked at her. "I'll explain later. We should get going."

"It was good to see you both. Arlan, please call me when you return."

They all said polite goodbyes.

Arlan and Fiona walked to the parking lot behind the restaurant. Arlan held the passenger door for Fiona and went around the car to the driver's seat. He backed from the parking space. Fiona opened her purse and started to put Alejandro's card in it.

She paused and said, "This is Chinese." She turned the card over. "This side is in Spanish."

"What does he do?"

"It says that he is a Mexican consulate officer to China."

"Do you think Alterio is doing something in China?" Fiona asked. "He's always seemed to me to be a man constantly looking for a business venture."

"He hasn't mentioned anything to me about China. But I doubt that he and his friend were meeting for old time's sake. That's not anything Alterio would do."

Arlan pulled the car out of the parking lot and onto a crowded Madre street. He looked in his mirror at the angry driver he pulled in front of and said, "With Alterio, who knows?"

Chapter 30

Joaquin and El Simpatico were seated behind heavily tinted windows of a black Suburban as it sped down Circuito Interior toward the Mexico City Airport. Five minutes later Joaquin pulled the big SUV into the parking lot of a modern warehouse on the north side of the airport and parked near a small entrance door. They got out. Joaquin looked around and pulled his jacket collar up around his ears to keep out the cold breeze.

"What time will the truck be here, Joacho?" El Simpatico asked.

Joaquin looked at his watch and said, "Within an hour, depending on traffic."

El Simpatico grunted and walked through the unmarked entrance door and into the warehouse. There were no stacks of crates or boxes against the walls and the concrete floor was clean enough to provide a shadowy glare from the dim overhead lights. The warehouse wasn't for storage. It was for transferring cargo—drugs and human. It was large enough for two semi-tractor trailers to drive into one of the large doors on one side of the warehouse, park unseen from the outside for as long as necessary, and drive out again through the large doors on the far side. One semi was already parked in the warehouse. It was empty and its driver nowhere to be seen.

Today they were moving Central American emigrants through Mexico to the US and were expecting a semi-tractor trailer truckload of smelly, frightened Salvadorans, who had been crammed into the trailer for three days. When the truck arrived at the warehouse, the Salvadorans would be transferred to the empty trailer and hustled up to the border and to several drop off points where coyotes who worked for El Simpatico waited to offload the cargo and escort them across the river and into five smaller trucks on the US side of the border. The trip would take two more days. There would be no light in the trailer. No air. No bathroom facilities other than buckets stacked up in one corner of the trailer. There was little water and less food.

El Simpatico followed Joaquin up a steel stairway to the mezzanine level of the warehouse where they kept a large office, which was often used as an interrogation room. He wasn't happy. He was expecting a truckload of Asians, mostly Chinese, who had paid twenty-five thousand dollars apiece to be smuggled into the US. Salvadorans paid less than ten thousand each. Besides the fee for each body, El Simpatico took a reasonable commission from the sale of the drugs strapped to the bodies of many of the emigrants. The drugs weren't his. El Simpatico saw the drugs as a loss leader—they allowed small-time dealers to pay the fee for the emigrants and recoup their money on the other side of the border.

With one hundred and fifty bodies being moved it was a profitable venture for El Simpatico. The more profitable Asian transfer had been delayed for a month, and that's why El Simpatico was in a foul mood.

Joaquin opened the door to the office and stepped back to let his boss go in first. The interior was brightly lit and smelled of sweat and blood and urine. The truck driver stood with his back against a wall. He laughed as Nacho and Raton took turns beating Hilario, the son of a prominent politician and newest member of PP's development team.

El Simpatico stopped just inside the door and said, "Jesus, Joacho. I told you to have your goons rough him up. Look at him. He's practically dead. And why the fuck are they here? They should have done this somewhere else—not in our warehouse. What a fuckup."

"Sorry, jefe," Joaquin said.

The driver saw El Simpatico first. He straightened up and shuffled to the door under the menacing gaze of Joaquin. Raton and Nacho turned and saw Joaquin and El Simpatico. They stood back and smiled, admiring their handywork. Joaquin sneered at them.

They backed away, afraid.

Joaquin said, "What the fuck are you two idiots doing?"

The two thugs were speechless.

El Simpatico thought for a moment, walked to a nearby sofa and sat. "It's too late," he said with a smile and his head slightly cocked, looking at Hilario.

Hilario had been tied to a chair, his hands and feet duct-taped. A ball of cloth had been stuffed into his mouth. His eyes were swollen shut and fresh blood ran down his face over dried blood that likely was the result of a beating before Hilario was dragged to the warehouse.

Nacho and Raton glanced at each other, not sure if they should run or say something. Nacho looked to Joaquin, searching for an answer. Joaquin shrugged.

"Continue," El Simpatico said. "And make it fun to watch."

Nacho smiled, stepped forward, and grabbed a finger on Hilario's left hand. He pulled it back until it snapped. Hilario screamed through the gag. El Simpatico noticed that all of the fingers on Hilario's right hand had already been broken.

"Take the gag out," El Simpatico ordered. "Nobody can hear him."

Raton leaned forward and removed the bloody gag while Nacho snapped the next finger.

"Hey. Wait until my hand is out of the way," Raton shouted and jerked his hand away.

El Simpatico smiled.

Joaquin stood near the door, looked at his watch and said, "Jefe, we need to get this done. The truck might get here early."

El Simpatico looked over at Joaquin and said, "Relax, Joacho. You look nervous."

"But, jefe, do you remember who his father is?"

"It doesn't matter anymore. Those two goons shouldn't have brought him here," El Simpatico said with a nod toward Nacho and Raton. "He's seen too much. If we had more time we'd take him out on my boat and let my pretty sharks finish him off."

Hilario screamed again and El Simpatico looked back to the chair and the blood and piss and sweat that pooled below it.

"Joacho's right. Finish him off," El Simpatico ordered.

Raton stepped in and pummeled Hilario's face with a pair of brass knuckles he'd pulled from his pocket. Hilario groaned. More blood ran to the floor, now mixed with broken teeth. Raton continued to beat Hilario until he tired. Nacho took over and threw heavy body punches into Hilario. El Simpatico could hear bones break. Hilario remained conscious.

El Simpatico yawned. He stood and walked to Joaquin as Nacho continued to throw punches and Hilario continued to groan.

"Give me your weapon."

"But jefe..."

"Now."

Joaquin reached under his shirt and pulled out his nine millimeter Glockmeister handgun and handed it to El Simpatico, who calmly walked over to the chair and shot Hilario in the groin. More blood spilled onto the floor as Hilario squirmed and screamed.

"How can this pendejo still be alive?" El Simpatico asked with a smile.

El Simpatico leaned into Hilario, who was delirious, and said, "You little asshole. You work for me. But you weren't smart enough to know what that means—were you?"

Hilario groaned and whispered a barely understandable, "But I don't understand..."

El Simpatico took aim and shot his left ear off. The noise was enough to break Hilario's eardrum. What little blood was left in his body leaked down onto his neck and shoulder.

El Simpatico leaned into Hilario's right ear and shouted, "I don't give a damn who your father is. He'll never know that it was me who killed you."

Hilario moaned. El Simpatico shot Hilario's left knee, which caused Hilario to jump against his restraints.

El Simpatico waited a couple of minutes and said, "Jesus. This pendejo should be dead by now. The shock alone should have him comatose." He looked at his watch and said to Hilario, "You didn't follow orders when you were healthy and don't follow orders now, either. You won't die properly."

El Simpatico placed the barrel of the Glock on Hilario's forehead and pulled the trigger. The back of Hilario's head exploded.

"Get this little prick out of here before the truck comes," he said to Joaquin and handed the handgun back to Joaquin as he walked toward the door.

"Jefe, what do you want us to do with the body?" Joaquin asked.

He turned back to Joaquin and said, "Steal a car from our competitor here in Mexico City. Put the body in the trunk and call in an anonymous tip to the authorities. Tell them where they can find it."

Nacho and Raton busied themselves cleaning up the mess. Joaquin supervised. El Simpatico walked out the door and back down to the lower level of the warehouse.

Chapter 31

Arlan pushed the intercom button outside Don Francisco's office and, after announcing his name, was buzzed in. He walked up a stone path with tall plants on either side and to the door of the hacienda that led to a small foyer and a receptionist. He let himself in. The receptionist smiled at Arlan and told him that Don Francisco and Pepe were expecting him. He opened the heavy wooden door behind her desk and entered. Don Francisco and Pepe were huddled in two large chairs behind Don Francisco's desk. Both smiled and welcomed Arlan. Arlan unrolled the new development plan for Isla X'lak, the Train's plan, and placed it on the round, glass-topped table opposite the desk. Don Francisco and Pepe rose from their chairs and stood on either side of Arlan.

Arlan looked around and said, "I have a question."

"Si?" Pepe and Don Francisco said simultaneously.

"I come here all of the time and never see bodyguards."

Don Francisco laughed and said, "There are a couple on call here at the hacienda, but I only use a driver when I'm in Madre. When I travel to Cancun I take two guards and my driver. But when I travel to Mexico City I take all six."

"That many?"

Don Francisco laughed again and said, "Yes, and my oldest son gets two bodyguards. My youngest son gets one. My daughter, Alterio's wife, gets none."

Arlan cocked his head.

"Kidnapping," Don Francisco said.

"What?"

"In Mexico, kidnappers will go after the oldest son first. There's more money in it. They never take a daughter."

"Oh," Arlan said and focused on the drawings.

"Your partners want to present this plan at the board of directors' meeting in a couple of weeks."

"You've told me about it. Please show us the details," Don Francisco said.

Arlan spent ten minutes going over the plan. Don Francisco and Pepe let him speak uninterrupted.

"I agree with you, Arlan. When Alterio brought me into this project, I thought we were going to create something unique. I had hoped that we could keep some of the island's character. This looks like all of the rest of the resorts I've visited all over the world. I don't want to be responsible for ruining Isla X'lak."

Pepe's cell phone beeped, and he stepped away from the table and spoke into the phone with his hand cupped around his mouth.

Arlan looked at Don Francisco and asked, "Do you want me to put a stop to this plan?"

"We know you have been giving Pierre-Pierre some difficulty. And it seems that he deserves it. But we want you to go a little easy for now."

"I thought you just said you don't like this plan."

Pepe finished his call and said, "We don't. But we have a problem with Alterio that could turn into a liability for Don Francisco."

Arlan had wondered why Alterio wasn't there.

Pepe continued, "We're not sure yet, but we think that he has taken money from the trust that we set up to buy the ejido land on the island."

"How much?" Arlan asked.

"Five million."

"Pesos?"

"Dollars."

That surprised him. How could he get his hands on that much money?

Pepe said, "Our partners don't know about it. They know that the negotiations with the individual ejiditarios have slowed. We haven't been able to pay the last dozen or so ejiditarios the price that was negotiated. Some of the ejiditarios we have paid have spent the money and are looking for more from us. We should have expected this."

"Expected what? Alterio taking money? Or some of the ejiditarios demanding more money?"

Don Francisco laughed and said, "Both."

Pepe said, "At this point, we can't afford to get into a legal battle with our partners. If they knew that Alterio stole from the trust they would sue us and probably win. There might even be criminal charges."

"What does Alterio say about it?"

"He denies everything. You know him," Don Francisco said. "It was either he or I who took the money. We are the only people with access. And I am the one who put money into this deal. I'm not going to steal from myself."

Arlan thought about Alterio and what he might do with five million dollars. He would spend some on himself. Some he would use for bribes. The way he burned through money it wouldn't last long. The sloppy bookkeeping he had seen so far from Alterio's accountant would make deniability easy.

Arlan said, "If Alterio did steal the money, he's not taking it and running, not with a mere five million. Alterio has to have another motive."

Don Francisco said, "While checking into this, we found some problems with the documentation that Alterio and his attorney produced for the privatization. He might be working with the ejido—the bad ones anyway. We don't know for sure, but we think they are trying to re-claim ownership of the land we received."

"Why would Alterio work with the ejiditarios who want their land back?"

"We don't know."

"But it was my understanding that all of the titles were in your name, not Alterio's name."

"They are. But we need to be careful. Any document in Mexico is legal if it is signed and recorded by a notario, and a lot of them are unscrupulous and will sign and record anything—for a large fee. We found out last week that Alterio has been working with an attorney who is a notario in the municipio that controls Isla X'lak. We have heard rumors that he is crooked."

"There's only one notario in Balam? That's Alterio's attorney? I thought he was the attorney for the ejido?"

"He is."

"Isn't that a conflict of interest?"

"Yes. And your point is?" Pepe said.

Right. This is Mexico.

Arlan sat back in his chair. He knew it would be fruitless to confront Alterio about the money. He would deny that any money was missing from the trust.

Don Francisco said, "The legal part of this project has become very complicated. Just keep up with your work. Try to change that plan without making too much trouble, and we'll try to find out about the titles and the money."

"You want me to fight this plan without really fighting?"

Don Francisco answered, "As you know, Alterio made representations to our partners. Pepe found out about them at the closing in Cancun. We could have stopped the closing, but at the time we didn't think it would be a problem."

"You're talking about the bridge?"

"And the densities," Pepe said.

Arlan thought for a moment, pointed to the plan, and said, "I can't help much with my hands tied behind my back. PP means to force this plan down our throats."

"Can't you delay it for a while without causing too much trouble?" Pepe asked.

"PP and the consultants are digging a deeper hole with this plan." Arlan looked at Don Francisco and said, "It's your money they're wasting. You'll go broke letting PP continue with this nonsense."

"I don't think so," Pepe said. "There is only a little over a year left on the project director's contract. How much damage can he do?"

"He's already done a lot of damage." Arlan thought about Alterio and the money he had purportedly taken. "But he's not the only one we need to be worried about."

Chapter 32

Arlan walked into the planner's conference room and sat next to Mauricio, who had arrived in Miami on an earlier flight. This particular planning session was important for two reasons. First, the planners were going to present an alternative to the bridge, though its possibility was still being kicked around, especially by PP. Second, this would be the plan presented to the partners at the upcoming board of directors' meeting, the first presentation to the partnership since the Train started working together.

Arlan smiled at Mauricio and opened his laptop. He had decided as soon as he left Don Francisco's office that he wasn't going to take it easy on PP or anybody else who insisted on a development plan that would ruin Isla X'lak. He wasn't sure what a lawsuit with the partners would cost Don Francisco, if it ever went to litigation, but he *was* sure how much Don Francisco would spend on planning and consulting fees for a project that would never be approved or built. The way Alterio, PP, and the Train were burning through money, he should welcome a lawsuit, if only to stop the financial bleeding.

PP stood and, with a somber voice, announced that Hilario was killed the previous week in Mexico City. He made a brief speech about Hilario's attributes and how important he was to his father, a key advisor to the president, and that the president would attend the funeral. He offered no details as to how Hilario had met his death other than the police suspect a botched kidnapping. Arlan looked around the room and saw that the news gave everybody a jolt. None knew Hilario well, but he had made a positive impression on everybody with his gregariousness and intellectual curiosity. Arlan felt sad not only for Hilario, who reminded Arlan of a younger version of himself, but that the small opening on the other side of the partnership that might allow more sustainable development discussion had just closed.

PP paused for an appropriate time and, with a smile, started the meeting. "We are best of class. We are an environmentally sound project and we know the president. We're going to economically empower the poorest county in the state."

Arlan's eyes weren't the only ones that rolled.

Eventually, PP pointed to the small, wiry man who sat next to him and said, "I have asked Ricardo to join us today. He is an economist and works with the largest construction management company in Mexico, which is owned by our partners in Mexico City. He has come up with some preliminary costs and general numbers for the project." PP stared at Arlan and added, "He also came up with the number of boat trips per day in order to build and operate with no bridge."

Ricardo opened his computer and connected it to the overhead projector. He started his presentation with a statement that, without a bridge, the boat traffic in the lagoon would be substantial, maybe impossible. He described the huge quantities of construction materials and equipment that would be required to build out all of the infrastructure, hotels, and villas and the number of corresponding boat trips. He eventually told the group that thirty-two trips a day would be needed to bring people and materials back and forth from the mainland.

Arlan and the planners laughed.

"That's all?" Mark asked.

PP and Ricardo looked at each other. Ricardo went on to talk in great detail about the planned luxury fishing camp on an isolated part of the island. Not only were his projected costs for the thirty huts ridiculous at thirty-five million dollars, he projected that the paved parking lot would cost three million.

Mark and Arlan looked at each other. One of the engineers let out a small laugh.

Arlan asked, "How do cars get to the fish camp? It's only accessible by boat or helicopter."

PP and his construction manager had obviously forgotten that there was no longer a bridge planned that would have allowed cars and vans to drive from Cancun directly to a fish camp on the island, trampling everything on their way.

The lead planner stood and switched the overhead screen to the island and a new canal planned next to the spine that ran through the center of the island. The canal would allow a water experience from the mainland directly to the guests' hotels. Ricardo took over and talked in detail about the length of the canal and that it would be built of concrete with overpasses to allow traffic.

Arlan couldn't believe his ears and eyes. He asked, "You want to build a fifteen-kilometer-long canal out of concrete? First, if you really think you need a canal, let the mangroves secure it on the sides. They'll do a better job and provide terrestrial and marine habitat. Second, how long will it take a guest to travel fifteen kilometers at five or eight kilometers per hour?"

Most people in the room understood immediately. PP didn't.

Arlan looked at PP and said, "Your accountants have been fighting for no more than a forty-five-minute ride from the airlift to a hotel. Now, in addition to having to drive from the airlift to Punta Eek, they have to endure a two-hour boat ride." Arlan smiled and said, "I'm all for it, but I don't think you have thought this out very well. It pretty much flies in the face of your mass tourism model. Further, the disembarkation port that you show on the mainland is on Alterio's cousin's land. Haven't we been over that?"

After a long pause and huddled conversations, Ricardo stood to continue his presentation. The discussion moved to boats and dredging needs in the shallow bay. Mauricio suggested that dredging may not be legally possible because of the Isla X'lak's status as a protected area.

"What's a natural protected area?" Mark asked.

Mauricio answered, "It's land or water with special environmental status. In some cases it can be developed, with limitations, but permits are more heavily scrutinized."

"What kind of limitations?" asked the head planner.

"They vary. There are not specific laws. There are subjective decisions at the federal level to help protect the environment. It depends a lot on the plan."

"Is there anything else we should know about?" Mark asked Mauricio, after giving PP a look of annoyance.

"You should keep tabs on the proposed mangrove protection law that is being discussed in Mexico City."

"What mangrove law?" Mark asked, and looked at the head planner, who shrugged his shoulders.

"It won't pass," PP said.

"I'm not so sure," Mauricio said. "The president may push it through."

"If it does pass, we'll get permits to cut a few mangroves. It's for the greater good. We know the president."

"It's a very restrictive law."

"Then we need to get this plan permitted before it passes," PP said.

"That will be difficult. Environmental authorization, the MIA, requires a lot of very specific detail. It's time consuming. Every square meter of the island that will be impacted by future construction must have flora and fauna studies. Biologists are required to sector the areas and physically count and measure each tree. All animals must be catalogued..."

One of the engineers pointed to the plan on the table and said, "That would take forever. The entire island is impacted by this plan."

Arlan laughed and said, "And we don't have any idea where or what to build in the second or third phases of the project... unless one of you has a crystal ball and can tell us what the market will demand ten or twenty years from now."

"Phase two, three? What are you talking about?" PP asked.

"You don't think you can possibly build and have the market absorb everything proposed on this plan all at once?"

Ricardo interrupted and said, "It will be more cost-effective to build the entire spine and all of the infrastructure up front."

"Are you serious? Only governments can afford to do that."

"Or drug cartels," one of the engineers said, which solicited laughs from around the room.

Arlan said, "The cost would be in the billions. Further, we don't have a clue what villa buyers or hotel guests will want in the future. Why would you devastate the island with highways and canals and buildings that may never be used?"

Everybody was quiet. Even PP said nothing.

Arlan then asked, "How much money, other people's money, are you willing to put into expensive infrastructure that might sit for decades before being needed? By which time it could be out-dated or dilapidated. Where is the financial return on that?"

PP spoke up, "But we are best of class. We represent two of the most prominent businesses in Mexico. We are going to economically empower the poorest county in the state—"

Arlan interrupted and said, "We need to think about a different plan... a plan that doesn't rely on millions of tourists. We'll never get that many tourists to Isla X'lak. Why try?"

PP said, "But we need the densities."

"Use your head. You're not going to get them."

"Alterio promised us permits for twenty-five thousand hotel rooms. It's in our contract."

"So you simply crammed all of the rooms that Alterio promised into this plan without first doing you homework." Arlan shook his head and added, "Alterio promised a bridge too."

The accountants fidgeted.

"But..." PP stammered.

Arlan said, "When the federal government shrinks your densities, you can always show the president your contract with Alterio. That'll fix it."

Ricardo had been busy with his computer. He half raised his hand and without looking up from his computer, blurted, "Using three different formulas, based on what you just said, I calculate that this project will reach full absorption in one hundred years."

"Where'd that come from?" one of the engineers asked with a laugh. "Haven't we decided there would be no bridge?"

"What's that mean—full absorption?" Mark asked.

"If there is no bridge, it will take one hundred years to sell all of the proposed number of villas, condos, and lots on this plan, given the absorption rates quoted by the accountants."

Arlan laughed and said to PP, "I wouldn't show up at the board meeting with those numbers."

"But we know the president and are representing two of the most prominent families in Mexico. We are economically empowering the poorest county in the state. This is an environmentally sound project—"

Arlan interrupted PP and said, "There's a logical solution. You all are designing X'lak for a mass tourism market. Permitting issues, logistics, and the environmental challenges point to a different type of project—a low-impact model... one based on nature, not golf courses and shopping centers."

"That's impossible. You won't make money," one of the accountants said. "You've got to have golf courses to attract the boutique operators."

"Why?" Arlan asked

PP said, "Golf courses aren't an impact. They're beautiful and very environmentally friendly."

"Voodoo ecology," Arlan said.

"What?"

"Scrape the jungle away and bring it back to life with different vegetation."

"What?"

"Never mind."

The accountant commented, "The hotel operators want the view corridors. That's why they want golf courses."

"Are you kidding?" Arlan said. "The jungle canopy is so low on X'lak that a second story room will have views to the ocean or the bay. All of the buildings should be raised a meter or two above the ground, anyway."

"Why?"

"To get up in the breezes and away from the mosquitoes."

"What mosquitoes?"

"Jesus. You guys need to visit the island." Arlan looked at the lead accountant and said, "I know it takes at least twenty thousand rounds of golf for a normal course, one in the US, to break even."

The accountant sighed and said, "This golf course will lose money. We know that."

"How much money do you expect the golf course to lose?"

"We had estimated one million dollars lost per year."

"And that is for the first golf course. You're planning two more," Arlan added.

PP said, "We've already signed a contract for the first golf course design. We signed the contract with Norman."

"What? That contract hasn't been vetted by our attorneys. Mauricio and I have warned youthat the chances of getting a golf course permitted on X'lak would be slim," Arlan said, and looked around the room. He focused on PP and asked, "Does Don Francisco know about this?"

"The partners called him about it this morning."

Arlan laughed and said, "You just bought an imaginary golf course—to be managed by Harvey the Rabbit, I guess." He added nothing during the rest of the meeting.

Later, as Arlan and Mauricio walked out of the meeting Arlan said, "The all important board of directors' meeting is a couple of weeks away and theTrain has painted itself into a corner."

"It seems that way, Arlan."

"PP and the consultants have a square peg to place into a round hole and are hell-bound to force it in."

Mauricio smiled and said, "The upcoming meeting might be fun."

"Yeah, worth the price of admission just to watch PP hang himself. Let's go get a beer."

Chapter 33

Arlan parked his black VW sedan on the third floor of the hotel's four-story parking garage. When he had first moved to Mexico, and before he moved into the hacienda, this hotel was his home. It was the largest hotel in Madre and one of only two in the city that catered to business travel. The other was on the same block across the street.

Arlan exited the VW and walked toward the elevator. He carried the jacket Alterio bought for him at the partnership closing in Cancun over his shoulder. He was glad he hadn't worn a tie. It was ten in the morning, and beads of sweat already ran down his forehead. He raised his right arm and saw that moisture had started to form on his shirt under his arms. The elevator offered no relief. He rode it alone down to the lobby, which was crowded but, thankfully, air conditioned.

Arlan walked toward the stairs that would take him to a mezzanine that housed the business center and conference rooms. He slipped his jacket on along the way. Just before he reached the stairs he heard, "Arlan, where is your Guayabera?"

Arlan stopped and turned to see Alterio walking toward him wearing dark dress pants and a white Guayabera shirt.

"Didn't you get my message?" Alterio asked.

"What message?"

"You were supposed to wear a Guayabera to the board of directors' meeting today."

"I thought I was supposed to impress people with my suit."

"That's in Cancun or Mexico City. In the Yucatan we wear Guayaberas."

"Oh."

"There is a clothing store here in the lobby. They sell Guay-aberas."

They walked a few meters down a short hall just off the lob-by to a small, glass fronted and brightly lit clothing store. All of the clothing in the shop was made locally. And it was all linen. Arlan found the rack of embroidered shirts and pulled out a blue, short-sleeve Guayabera to try on.

"No, no. It must be white and long-sleeved," Alterio said and took a shirt from another rack.

Arlan didn't bother with the dressing room. He took off his jacket and dress shirt and put on the white Guayabera. He thought the embroidery would be scratchy. It wasn't. He stepped up to a full-length mirror. *Perfect,* he thought. He turned to Alterio and said, "It looks as though we're going to a Cuban wedding."

Alterio paid for the shirt. Arlan placed his coat and dress shirt into a bag, and they walked up the stairs to the mezzanine.

Alterio huffed up the last step and said, "I want everybody on our side of the partnership dressed in Guayaberas. We'll look like a strong team."

They walked down the hall a short distance, turned the corner, and stepped into a large conference room. It seemed that Alterio had invited everybody. The Train was there. The accountants and Ricar-do the economist were in the room, huddled together with PP. The planners had set up large hardboard maps and drawings on easels around the room. The partners Arlan had met at the closing sat at the far side of the long conference table. Don Francisco, his attorney, and Mauricio, all wearing white Guayaberas, were talking to the partners. The colonel, the mayor of Balam, and her husband stood in one corner of the room eating pastries that had been set out on silver platters. The mayor wore a colorful dress. Her husband wore a white Guayabera. The colonel wore his white sailor suit.

"I thought this was a board of directors' meeting," Arlan said to Alterio.

"We're going to have a presentation first. Afterward, we will have a private meeting with just the partners, the attorneys, you, and Pierre-Pierre."

Alterio mingled. Arlan walked over to talk to Mark from the planners' offices.

"You guys going to a wedding?" he asked.

"Funny. This is Alterio's way of having his team from Madre look menacing. Are you menaced yet?"

PP told the crowd that the presentation was to start and everybody should sit. Alterio had all the Guayaberas sit on one side of the table. They looked like a group of parochial school students. The Train took the other side. Guillermo and his CFO sat near the head of the table, next to Don Francisco and Pepe. There were a few empty chairs on both sides of the long table with bowls of candy placed at three- or four-foot intervals. Alterio sat next to Arlan and un-wrapped a piece of candy. The mood in the room was festive, but Arlan wondered how long that would last.

PP stood at the far end of the table and pointed to a projector screen. On it was the name of the partnership, PMS, and a Mayan symbol that Arlan assumed was supposed to be a logo. Under it were the names of the partners and the businesses they represented and PP as the *Master Developer*.

PP started talking. "We have assembled the best in class to come up with this model. We represent two of the most prominent businesses in Mexico. We have put together an environmentally sound project that will economically empower the poorest county in the state."

Arlan looked at Mark and smiled. He turned to see Mauricio doing the same. PP's presentation droned on. He finally asked the head planner to present the master plan. He and Mark stood, walked to the far end of the table, and placed the hardboard plan and easel in front of the projector screen. It was the same plan Arlan and Mauricio argued against at the last planning session. Faint traces of an erased bridge remained visible. The disembarkation port on Alterio's cousin's land was still there. The fifteen-mile canal was still there. There were two noticeable changes. First, the word *mega* had been removed from the yacht basin, and the center part of the plan had been outlined in red. Below the outline was "Phase 1." It seemed to be an arbitrary outline with no logic as to why it was to be the first part of the island to be developed.

The planners' presentation was representative to their pay-scale. It was good. During their presentation, Alterio had moved to a seat on the other side of the table. Arlan saw him put his hand into the closest candy bowl and pull out a piece of candy. He looked into the bowl next to him where Alterio had been sitting. There was no candy, just wrappers.

When the planners finished, PP invited the accountants to talk. One of the accountants stood up and went through hotel densities and occupancies and golf course gobbledygook. Other than PP, nobody seemed too interested. PP then asked Ricardo to make a presentation. Arlan leaned forward, thinking there was no way he'd present his absorption numbers to this group.

Ricardo stood and said, "I will be presenting the economic efficiency of the project over time using data collected from several business schools and real estate research companies." His presentation sounded like an economics lecture. He continued, "This graph shows the overall absorption rate for the entire destination given that there is no bridge. Therefore, sales over time adjusted over the past forty years using empirical data gathered and researched by various real estate economists in the US, Europe, and..."

Arlan looked around the table. Only the accountants were still paying attention to Ricardo. The room filled with hushed conversations and laughs.

"So it is therefore an accurate analysis to assume that the time needed for total absorption of the project will be one hundred years. And..."

Arlan looked toward the end of the table where the partners and Don Francisco sat.

"What did he just say?" he heard one of the partners ask, not loudly and to no one specifically.

The commotion at the partner's end of the table increased. Guillermo and Eduardo huddled. Arlan couldn't hear their whispered conversation. Don Francisco said something to Pepe, who got out of his chair and approached Arlan. He leaned down and whispered, "What does absorption rate mean?"

Ricardo continued, using another complicated graphic. One of the accountants argued Ricardo's interpretation of the graph and how it applied to Isla X'lak. Nobody could follow their argument. The presentation disintegrated into multiple conversations. Mark asked Mauricio for his opinion of the pending mangrove law and how it could affect the project. Mauricio described the law as it had been proposed and the other conversations around the table started to quiet down. Within a few minutes everybody in the room was listening to Mauricio.

"The law will be very strict," Mauricio explained. "Half of the island is mangrove. The project you propose will need to be changed."

"If passed, will the law be enforced?" Pepe asked.

"Isla X'lak is already under a microscope. It gets a lot of attention because of the whale sharks and the chit palm."

"The what?" PP asked.

"Thrinax radiata," Mauricio answered. "It used to be everywhere on the peninsula and was used for decades for palapa roofs. Now it only grows on Isla X'lak."

"But we can use locals to cut out the mangroves. They cut mangrove all of the time. We can hire them to cut a few here and a few there. Nobody will know," PP said. "It's for the greater good."

Arlan looked around the room. Most nodded their heads. He stood and walked to the far end of the table and pointed to the master plan on the easel. He said, "All of these hotels here, and the marina, and all of the spine... and everything you have drawn as back of house operations are presently mangrove forests. You'll need bulldozers to take them out. It'll be a major operation. You'll hide it from no one."

"You're just a tree hugger," PP said.

"Yes, I am. And I'm a developer. But the poor mangroves, they have such a bad reputation."

"That's because they're in our way."

"Do you have any idea what the mangroves do? If our grandparents and uncles and aunts had sent us post cards from Florida with mangroves on them instead of palm trees, we would like them better. They are a far more valuable species. They're the reason the island has uneroded beaches. They're the reason there is a healthy reef. They're the reason we have clear water for the tourists to swim in. Without mangroves you wouldn't have any sport fishing in the area—there wouldn't be any fish!"

One of the engineers evidently agreed and explained the scientific merits and structural qualities of mangroves.

"So do you think we will need to save all of the mangroves?" Mark asked Mauricio. "Can't we cut through some of it?"

"If the law passes, we will not be able to touch any of it."

"We need to look at alternatives, guys," Arlan pressed.

"But won't that alter densities?" PP asked.

"Yes," Mauricio answered.

"But we're the best in class. We represent two of the most prominent businesses in Mexico. We will economically empower the poorest county."

Guillermo suggested they break for lunch and come back for the formal board meeting. The consultants were told they might be needed later in the day and should stick around. If not, they would be welcome at a dinner that had been arranged for the group in a private dining room later that night.

***

Don Francisco was the first to speak when the partners reconvened without the Train and the other people not directly associated with the partnership.

"Even if the mangrove law doesn't pass, this project is too big. It's not right for the island."

Arlan saw PP's mouth open, but nothing came out. PP wasn't the verbal bully he normally was when in the presence of his bosses.

Guillermo said, "But we've heard what the accountants say. We need the proposed densities to be profitable."

Don Francisco said, "Maybe Arlan is right." He looked at Arlan and asked, "What alternative project do you have in mind?"

"I haven't thought out all of the details. I would need some time, but I could redesign the plan so that it could work without touching mangroves and still be profitable."

"But it would be a much smaller project," PP said.

"Yes, and a lot less cost. But it will be a plan that would fit the island better and have a better chance of approval from the federal government."

"How could that be?"

"Because we have a unique island and an opportunity to capitalize on its exclusivity. Hotel rooms, villas, lots... will command premium prices and attract travelers who want to experience the island as it is. They want authenticity. I could point out several examples."

"How long would you need to come up with a new plan?" Don Francisco asked.

"A month."

"But the mangrove law could pass by then," PP said.

"It won't matter. Like I said, my plan won't touch the mangrove."

"I'm against it," Guillermo said. "We need the densities in order to make money."

"Let's let Arlan and Mauricio come up with a new plan and a financial model. We can decide then if it makes more sense," Don Francisco said.

Guillermo and Eduardo exchanged concerned looks but remained cordial during the rest of the discussion. Don Francisco and Pepe politely argued the merits of the plan Arlan described in very general terms. PP, Eduardo, and Guillermo just as politely argued for the Train's plan.

Pepe said, "But neither plan has been vetted financially. The financial model for both will need to be validated by one of the large hospitality accounting firms."

Don Francisco added, "Then we'll compare the plans and their ability to make money after Arlan completes his work." He looked at Alterio and asked, "Is that all right with you?"

"Si, Tio," Alterio said, staring at the floor.

Arlan smiled. There it was—an impasse... and a big one. What really confused Arlan was why Guillermo and Eduardo couldn't understand that an alternative plan would be needed. Even taking the mangrove law out of the equation, the Train's current plan wouldn't work. There was going to be no bridge, and there was no way to build a major airlift on the island. They were not going to get masses of tourists to Isla X'lak. They had designed far more hotel rooms than could possibly ever be filled and far more villas than could ever be sold.

With nothing resolved, the partners politely agreed to stop the meeting, but only after Pepe brought up the recent property tax bill.

"We need to pay it," Guillermo said.

Pepe replied, "No. We know the mayor. She is trying to get rich. We need to set a precedent and negotiate a lesser amount. If we don't, we will be stuck with high taxes every year."

"What are the risks of not paying it?" Eduardo asked.

"None. Mexican law doesn't allow foreclosure for unpaid taxes. We let them build up for a year or two, until the mayor gets desperate for money and agrees to less. She'll take it."

"Okay," Guillermo said. "Let's enjoy the dinner tonight and discuss what we have learned today. I think we should have a partnership meeting very soon so we can keep the planning process moving forward. Is that all right with everyone?"

The partners agreed and stood to leave.

"Just one more thing," Alterio said, and looked directly at Guillermo. "Do you have a black jet-engine helicopter? I saw one at the airport when I arrived last night. I think I have seen it before."

Guillermo glanced at Eduardo. He turned to Alterio and, with a laugh, said, "I wish. That would be a nice way to travel. Maybe we can make enough from this project to both have helicopters."

Chapter 34

El Simpatico sat on a sofa in his three-room suite in the hotel across the street from the hotel where the board of directors' meeting took place and where most of the Train and other consultants had checked in. He had stayed at both hotels in the past and had no preference for one over the other, but he wanted to stay clear of the board meeting.

Joaquin and Guillermo were led into the room by a large security guard. They sat in the chairs opposite El Simpatico. Listening devices and a hidden camera had been placed across the street in the room where the board meeting had taken place, but the reception was poor. El Simpatico wanted an immediate report from his second in command and CEO of his construction company.

Guillermo told El Simpatico what had been said during the presentation and afterward in the formal board meeting.

"Did you know Pierre-Pierre was going to ask Ricardo to make a presentation?" El Simpatico asked Guillermo.

"Ricardo works for our construction management company. He and I reviewed his analysis, but he had not told me that he had been asked to present it by our director."

"That fucking Pierre-Pierre. He's an idiot," Joaquin said. "One hundred years. That scared the hell out of our partner and his attorney. We need that bridge."

"You've checked on Alterio's cousin's land?"

"It's as Alterio said. His cousin has placed restrictions on the land. We can't buy it. Even if his cousin met a premature death, the restrictions would survive."

"Why don't we just kidnap him? Force him to change the restrictions while he's still alive. Or maybe we take his wife and keep her until he gives us what we want," Joaquin said.

Guillermo said, "The cousin has set up a trust to own the land. Any change would take the signatures of all of the trustees."

"So?" Joaquin said with a smile. "We can get ahold of all of them and make them change their minds."

"Joacho, a lot of people know of the development plans for the island. Alterio has made sure of that. Even a rumor that a cartel forced the sale of land that enabled a bridge to be built would kill our chances for a success."

Guillermo said, "But we need to do something... and we need our plan to be permitted before restriction on mangrove clearing becomes law."

"We'll get what we need. But we have to move fast. This gringo, O'Brien, and his attorney friend, Mauricio, are a problem?"

"Don Francisco has asked them to come up with an alternative plan—no bridge and no mangrove clearing. Densities would be reduced dramatically. Our ability to launder several billion dollars would disappear. We would be lucky to spend more than a half a billion—total."

"Did you argue against an alternative plan?"

"Not hard. I didn't want to create ill feelings with Don Francisco. No sense getting into a fight with our partners at this point. I assumed that you would solve the problem."

"That was the wise thing to do. What did Alterio think of an alternative plan?"

"He didn't say much during the presentation or the meeting afterward," Guillermo said.

"It looked like the fat ass just sat and ate candy," Joaquin added. "We need to get control of this project. Our project director can't control anything. I feel like slapping him around a little, the pendejo."

Guillermo added, "By the way, Alterio asked if I owned a black helicopter."

El Simpatico leaned back on the sofa and looked at the closed window drapes. He rubbed his chin, leaned forward, and asked, "How much time until your dinner tonight?"

Guillermo looked at his watch and said, "Four hours."

"Bring Alterio to me."

Joaquin's eyes widened. "Are you sure, Jefe?"

"Yes."

"It's about time," Joaquin said and smiled. He looked over at Guillermo. "I think you should be the one to invite him here. I'll wait in the lobby." Joaquin smiled at El Simpatico and added, "Just to make sure he gets up here safely."

***

Alterio sat alone in his room assessing the meeting. The presentation and board meeting had gone as he'd expected. The master plan was flawed, but he didn't care. He didn't like that his father-in-law had asked Arlan to come up with an alternative plan. He welcomed the additional time it would take, but he didn't want opposing plans floating around. He wasn't sure what to do about it yet. He would sleep on it. He closed the blinds and lay down fully clothed on top of the king-sized bedspread. The phone in his room rang.

It was Guillermo.

"I'm very sorry to bother you, Alterio. But there is somebody I would like for you to meet before our dinner tonight."

"Is it important? I'm tired."

"It is very important, Alterio. The man I want you to meet is a major investor in our construction company."

Alterio agreed to talk to the investor, and within a few minutes met Guillermo in the lobby.

"Thank you for agreeing to meet on such a short notice," Guillermo said. "Do you mind walking to the hotel across the street?"

Alterio looked across the street and smiled. "There is a very good bakery on the first floor of that hotel. They make good pastries."

They left one hotel for the other. Guillermo went into the lobby first. They were met by a short, wiry man with reptilian eyes and a large man who wore a suit and a sneer. Alterio looked closely at the smaller man. Guillermo didn't introduce either of them. Alterio glanced at the short-wiry man. .

They all got into an elevator. A tourist tried to squeeze into the elevator as the doors closed, but the large man pushed him back into the lobby. Guillermo pressed the button to the tenth floor, and Alterio knew they were going to a luxury suite.

The doors opened and another large man stood outside the elevator.

"Levante sus brazos, por favor," he told Alterio.

Alterio looked at Guillermo and then to the other two men in the elevator. They nodded. He raised his arms and the man patted Alterio's large frame through his Guayabera and pants.

"Bueno," the man said to the shorter man, who sneered at Alterio. His eyes blinked—slowly.

Alterio remembered, and his eyes widened.

Joaquin smiled.

Alterio was led into the suite at the end of the hall. A tall, well-dressed man with a shock of white hair rose from the sofa and walked to Alterio, holding out his hand. Alterio hesitated. It took all of the self control he could muster to keep fear from creeping onto his facial expression. With a weak smile, Alterio shook hands. He didn't offer a hug, nor did El Simpatico.

"Hello again, Alterio. Please come and sit with me," El Simpatico said and led Alterio to the sofa.

Guillermo and Joaquin each sat in opposing chairs. The large man with the sneer stood by the door.

"You do remember me, no?"

"Yes."

"And do you remember Joacho?"

Alterio looked in Joaquin's direction and nodded. He didn't make eye contact.

"Our mutual friend told us about the possibilities of ejido land privatization a few years ago. Of course, land is not my normal business. I have other, how should I say it, different business ventures. But, based on what our friend told us, I calculated that if the right piece of property became available I could do very well in the land development business. So, I put things into motion and waited for the right opportunity. And, thanks to you, it has presented itself."

Alterio thought back to his meeting with Mexico's ex-president.

"You see, my young friend, we are partners."

El Simpatico ran his fingers through his hair.

Alterio watched with fascination. *How did this happen?* he asked himself.

El Simpatico said, "I am proud of my white hair. It reminds me how long I have survived in a very dangerous business. I attribute my survival to good business instincts. I choose my partners well... and I prefer a non-violent route to riches whenever possible."

Alterio heard a snort from Joaquin and saw El Simpatico give his lieutenant an almost imperceptible glare.

"Please bring us something to drink," El Simpatico said to the man at the door. "Would red wine be okay?" he asked Alterio.

"That would be fine... thank you."

"I trust that you will not tell your father-in-law or consultants about me. As far as they are concerned, Guillermo and Eduardo are your partners. And it must remain that way. Do you understand this, Alterio?"

Alterio hesitated before answering. This was a new wrinkle in his plan, but he was sure he could deal with it. He would need to be more cautious though.

Joaquin stared at Alterio, as if daring him to say *no*.

"Yes." Alterio answered.

"Good."

Two glasses of red wine were placed on the coffee table in front of El Simpatico and Alterio. Guillermo and Joaquin were each handed a glass.

"Salud!" El Simpatico said. They all raised their glasses and took a drink.

"Now, let's talk about our partnership," El Simpatico said and set his glass back on the table. "It seems that we have a few problems with the planning of our island. We need your help... and I am confident you will cooperate."

Joaquin cleared his throat and shifted in his chair.

El Simpatico said, "First, I need for you to control your gringo friend. We need *our* plan to be submitted for approval. No changes. We need the densities *we* have proposed and that *you* promised. We also need the plan to be submitted and approved before a new mangrove law can be implemented by the government. Understood?"

"Yes. I agree. But approvals take time. There is no guarantee we can get the current plan, or any plan, approved before the mangrove law takes effect, whenever that might be," Alterio said.

"Let me take care of the approvals. You just get your people under control. We don't have time to waste on alternative plans. We don't want an alternative plan. If you can't get your development director under control, I will let Joaquin talk to him."

Alterio looked over at Joaquin. He saw a real smile and thought that if he waited long enough he would see Joaquin drool at the possibility of hurting somebody.

"We also need that bridge. We understand that the land needed for it on the mainland belongs to your cousin and that he has placed restrictions on it."

"Yes."

"Can you convince your cousin to sell or lease his land to us? I understand that it is controlled by a trust. This is something you should understand well, my friend. Do you know all of the trustees your cousin has appointed?"

Alterio thought for a moment. They could kill his cousin, but that wouldn't get them the land. They could threaten to kill the trustees, but his wife's father owned one of the largest newspapers in the area and constantly reported on cartel doings, which is why he traveled with six bodyguards. El Simpatico must know these things. He needed Alterio. Need equals leverage and leverage buys time.

"My cousin and I are close. Our grandfather used to own the land. It ended up belonging to my cousin after a dispute between our fathers. I can get him to cooperate," Alterio lied. "It might take time, though, as well."

"I only care that it is in our control by the time we are ready to build," El Simpatico said.

"I'm sure that I can get his cooperation," Alterio said and smiled.

"I hope so. I would hate to have a more serious discussion with him. I will not see you at dinner tonight. I will not see you much at all in the future. Joaquin will be my contact with you. I know you won't disappoint us."

"Just one more thing," Alterio said.

"Yes?"

"My cousin's land will be very expensive. And we might need to pay some of the trustees for their cooperation."

El Simpatico dismissed Alterio's statement with a wave of his hand and said, "Whatever it takes. Go through Guillermo."

Alterio smiled and said, "Just one *more* thing."

El Simpatico leaned forward. "Yes?"

"Why do you want to be partners in a real estate deal? Especially if you have... different business interests?"

"Let's just say that I want to expand into the finance business. Our partnership will need a lot of money to build a destination that rivals Cancun."

With that, El Simpatico declared the meeting over and had Alterio delivered back to the lobby.

Alterio crossed the street to his hotel without pastries from his favorite bakery and walked through the lobby and into the bar. He needed some time to compose himself and ordered a scotch with crushed ice and club soda. Three drinks and twenty minutes later, he used the phone in the lobby to call the mayor's room.

"Hola, Alterio. And thank you for inviting us to the presentation today and dinner tonight. Your partners seem to be very nice men."

Alterio shook his head at the irony of what she had just said. He asked, "Can we meet tomorrow in Balam? It is very important. It's about the property taxes."

"Yes, of course, Alterio. I'll be back in my office by early afternoon tomorrow. Is that all right?"

"Yes, but one more thing. The partnership has agreed to pay the taxes and I will be there with the funds tomorrow. Can you have all of the necessary paperwork ready?"

"Well, certainly, Alterio. This is very good news. When I asked Pepe about the tax bill yesterday, he told me that we would need to negotiate."

"The partners gave me permission to pay the taxes. And, because I'm paying them so quickly, I would like to pay a little less. But we can talk about that tomorrow."

"Yes. That sounds fine. Thank you, Alterio."

Alterio hung up and called Jose.

"Jose, can you get any more money from the trust?"

"No, Alterio. Five million was all I dared take. The accountants think that the money is going to pay more ejiditarios. There aren't that many left to buy out. Any more money and they would be suspicious."

"Claro. I will try to get the mayor to accept two million. But we will need to move our plans up. I just found out who my partner is."

"It's the construction company. We have known that. What's the problem?"

Alterio told him about his meeting in the hotel across the street.

"El Simpatico! No. We need to leave the city. We need to leave the country."

"We will be fine. We just need to move faster."

"Are you crazy? We need to get out of this deal. You know how this man deals with people who cross him, even those who don't. They are fed to the sharks. And I've heard that he keeps heads of his enemies in a big walk-in freezer."

"That is a rumor, Jose. You don't know that for sure."

"I've heard it from multiple sources. And that hitman who accompanies him everywhere... Joacho... he's a sick man."

Alterio wasn't listening to Jose. He was thinking. With less conviction than he had at the the beginning of his conversation with his notario he said, "I... we can handle this. Call Alejandro and tell him to hurry things up."

"I don't know. I think..." Jose started to say, but Alterio had disconnected the call before he could finish.

Chapter 35

Arlan and Mauricio huddled in Mauricio's office. They had spent the past six hours pouring over Arlan's multiple development scenarios for Isla X'lak and their legal implications under Mexican law. They had been doing this every day except Sundays since the board of directors' meeting two weeks earlier. Sundays were reserved for Mauricio to spend time with his daughter and his wind-surfing and kite-surfing hobbies.

"Permits are usually bought in Mexico. But Isla X'lak is under a microscope, and permits for the Train's plan will be difficult. To purchase them will require political contacts at a very high level. It will be expensive, even for Alterio and his family."

"Can't we get permits based on the project's merits?" Arlan asked.

"Everything here is political. The only reason people go into politics here is to make money. Merit doesn't count."

"That's unfortunate."

"It's Mexico," Mauricio said with a shrug.

Arlan sat back in the black office chair that rocked and swiveled but was a clear step or two below the quality of the chairs he and Mauricio sat in when in meetings with the Train. They were sequestered in Mauricio's small office in a four-story office building in an old neighborhood on the north side of Madre, working on Arlan's development plan.

Arlan knew that he could turn Isla X'lak into a sustainable destination. All of the natural ingredients were there. And protecting those ingredients would make it profitable. His previous development experiences and island life were cumulative stepping stones that groomed him to be in a perfect position to attempt to design a sustainable resort destination on a large scale.

It always irked Arlan that resort developers tended to suffer the same lack of understanding of the natural environments they impact and the lack of imagination to come up with a plan that allows humans and nature to inhabit the same space, opting instead to stack condos and hotel rooms along thin stretches of beach, isolating guests from intrinsic natural features and local culture.

For there to be any understanding or respect by the masses of natural environments, people and nature must co-mingle in ways that allow nature and the local culture to be the focal point of guest experiences. Nature shouldn't be a zoo exhibit viewed from behind protected glass and fences. It needs to be personally experienced. One must touch it, feel it, and smell it in order to appreciate it or to miss it when it's gone, or understand the things that threaten it.

Arlan and Mauricio had established a productive working method whereby Arlan proposed hypothetical development scenarios and Mauricio used his legal and political expertise to punch holes in them. Through this process, they had come up with a realistic development model for the island—one that had a good chance of getting permitted, according to Mauricio.

Once Arlan and Mauricio were happy that they had a feasible development plan, Arlan drew it up and added pretty green trees, just like the Train did. The difference, though, was that Arlan's green represented existing vegetation—not the scrape and rape alternative. Over ninety percent of the island under his plan would remain in its natural state—forever.

Arlan knew that all the planning in the world meant nothing unless the plan could be validated, and the ultimate validation would be market acceptance and copycat imitations in other parts of the world. For that to happen, the project had to be built. First, though, he needed to present a plan that would be approved not just by Don Francisco, but by Alterio and the partners from Mexico City.

***

Mauricio and Arlan drove together to Don Francisco's office. On the way, Arlan's phone rang.

"Hey, O'Brien, you there?"

"Captain Jay. Listen, I can't talk long. I've got a meeting in a few minutes."

"No problem. I just wanted to tell you that I'm comin' up to visit next week. You gonna be around?"

"Hell, I don't know. Probably. What day?"

"Late in the week. I'll call you when I get there."

"Fine. But what day? I don't know..."

Jay had hung up.

Mauricio looked at Arlan and said, "Problem?"

"No. Yes... it's a good friend. He's coming to visit."

"That doesn't sound like a problem," Mauricio said.

Arlan drove a block and said, "You don't know my friend."

***

Arlan and Mauricio were led into the conference room with a large overhead projector and comfortable seating that had been arranged in a circle near the room's periphery. Arlan had convinced Don Francisco and Pepe to allow Fiona and another influential NGO head to attend the presentation. Pepe balked at the idea, saying that the plans for the island were none of their business. But Mauricio pointed out that all of the major environmental organizations in Mexico would receive copies of their plans as soon as they requested federal permits and that the heads of the NGOs carried a lot of political clout. Most NGOs and environmental groups would dismiss any development plan for Isla X'lak without reviewing it. Fiona could cause the other NGOs to take notice if she liked the plan.

While Don Francisco, Pepe, Fiona, Mauricio, and Jorge, the head of the second largest NGO in Mexico, socialized, Arlan rolled out a twelve-foot-long plan and opened the digital version on his computer. Alterio was late.

When everybody was seated, Arlan stood at a small podium in the center of the room and started his presentation.

"Please allow me to give you some background information as to why we think the concept of a sustainable tourism destination is feasible for the island of Isla X'lak. Last year there were approximately one billion tourists in the world. It is estimated by the World Tourism Organization that this number will reach one point six billion by 2020. The vast majority of this is mass tourism that can be broken down into business and leisure travel. You all know the difference. I don't need to expound on it. We are only interested in leisure travel. The experiences one finds in mass tourism markets—theme parks, casinos, beaches—are considered to be flat experiences. That's because there are thousands of these types of experiences world-wide that are easily accessible, and they tend not to exceed the five-per-cent-per-year growth, which is the normal rate of annual tourism growth for the entire industry. However, there is a market segment in leisure tourism that has been labeled *experiential travel,* which exceeds this growth rate. Experiential travel has been categorized into a lot of different types, but the most popular are nature-based and cultural-based travel—exactly what is found on X'lak and in many other places close by on the Yucatan Peninsula. This market has been growing world-wide at a rate of twenty percent per year for over a decade and a half. It's a small segment, but its depth is still being analyzed. The experiential tourist will travel farther and spend more money to get to places where outstanding natural environments and cultures still exist. Many feel they need to visit these places before they disappear."

Alterio walked into the conference room and apologized for being late. He sat in an empty seat near a large bowl of candy. He pulled out three pieces and popped them into his mouth.

Arlan continued, "When I first got involved with this project I had to ask three questions. First, why develop Isla X'lak at all? Second, why is our plan the best plan for the island? The third question, and most difficult, is how do we keep the next generation of developers from destroying the island through over-development?"

Arlan answered each question in detail and went on to discuss the merits of the proposal. He described how ninety percent of the island will be placed in permanent preservation to be co-managed by the developer and Fiona's NGO. The cost of preservation would be paid for by a two percent surcharge tacked onto every sale, resale, and room rental.

The island will see just a ten percent development impact. Everything designed and built, including infrastructure and roads, will comply with leading edge construction and operating methods that protect the island's environment. Hotel and tour operators will have specification manuals that will require them to learn how to operate their hotels with environmental efficiency and teach their guests how to respect nature and the local culture.

"What does ten percent impact mean? Is a golf course an impact?" the ever skeptical Pepe asked.

"Impact is any disturbance to existing habitat or vegetation."

"What about the pending mangrove law? How will it affect this plan?"

"As you can see, the mangrove law doesn't come into play with this plan. We're not going to touch any under any circumstance—ever. Using only ten percent of the land, we can easily work around them."

Arlan pointed to the site plan on the overhead screen and decribed how the island might eventually have three or four small villages near the beach, but that all structures will have a one-hundred-and-twenty-meter setback from the water.

"That's unheard of," Fiona remarked.

"That's how we protect the beach and the dunes. Believe me, guests won't complain once they walk up and down the beach and feel like they're lost on a desert island. With no structure more than two stories tall, they'll never see them from the beach.

"We'll ask that your group help us design raised walkways to get people from the villages to the beach so they don't trample the dunes."

Arlan switched the screen to a closeup on a village and told the group that the only transportation allowed will be bicycles and golf carts. Service roads behind the village will be built for construction and supply vehicles, and those will be limited in size.

"And what will be in the village for tourists to do?" Alterio asked.

"The village core will be the focal point, the gathering place for guests. We plan to have a few small shops and restaurants, a lecture hall, and interpretive centers. We'll invite biologists, anthropologists, and other professions to work and speak on the island. Many travelers will want to come to learn and maybe participate in their work. During the day, they'll be at the beach or on excursions—hiking, birding, fly-fishing, kayaking, touring Mayan ruins and colonial haciendas on the mainland, swimming with whale sharks, or discovering new cenotes. Or they could drive a golf cart to the old village and hang out with locals. There are a hundred wonderful things to do within an hour or two of Isla X'lak. At night they'll have the village core to enjoy food and drinks and music.

"One of our biggest challenges is to ensure the village doesn't come off too slick—Disneyesque. Villages with character build up over time, sometimes hundreds of years. We'll hire different architects and mix up materials and designs. If we have a few blemishes, we'll keep them."

Arlan switched the screen back to the plan of the island.

Alterio asked, "What if your plan doesn't work? Isn't that a big risk to take."

"Less risk than the Train's plan. They want to build out the entire island. That, Alterio, is risky. We'll start with a baby step—the first village, and only a portion of it. If our plan doesn't attract the market we think it will we'll stop, having only impacted a small footprint.

"I see no golf courses," Don Francisco said.

"There aren't any. We won't attract golfers. Why try? That's not the market we want anyway."

Jorge said, "I see large lots on the plan near the village periphery. They are labeled *Preservtion Lots*. What is a preservation lot?"

"Once our message, our identity, is out there, we'll attract buyers and investors who want to leave a legacy. I call it baby boomer guilt. There are thousands of very wealthy baby boomers. They'll always visit the Cancuns and Hilton Heads of the world, but when given an opportunity to buy into a preservation development model, they'll do it. It gives them bragging rights. 'I'm helping to save an important island from over-development' is what they'll tell their friends. We have set aside large lots, one or two hectares, on which we will allow a single small palapa to be built. We'll choose where it can be built based on vegetation, wildlife, and hydrology studies. The remainder of the lot goes into preservation. They'll own it, but they can't do anything with it—other than enjoy Mother Nature."

Jorge then asked, "Are you going to rely on solar power?"

"No. Collecting energy has become easy. Storing it when you're off grid, as we are, is a nightmare. Battery technology is antiquated. When a guest, who pays eight hundred dollars a night, demands AC, you'd better provide it—consistently. Unfortunately, diesel generators are the only resourse for us at this scale. We'll experiment and allow others to use our project as a guinea pig if that will help us eventually provide all of our power needs through renewable resources."

Arlan concluded his presentation a few minutes later. Don Francisco talked quietly with Pepe. Fiona and Jorge listened to Mauricio talk about environmental authorization from the federal government. Arlan soaked it all up.

Don Francisco said, "I like this plan. I would like for you to get one of the major hospitality accounting firms to vet your model, both from a design-and-use perspective and financially—especially financially. If it proves profitable, it will be easier to sell this concept to our partners."

Alterio stood and said, "Thank you Arlan and Mauricio for the presentation. You have done a great job showing us how we can better develop the island. If you will excuse me, I have to meet with somebody. It is very important. Just one more thing. Will you be presenting this plan to our partners?"

"That's up to you and Don Francisco."

"I'll call Guillermo when we are finished here and set up a meeting," Don Francisco said. "I think it is better coming from me rather than you, Alterio."

"Very good," Alterio said and shook everybody's hand before he left.

The meeting went on for another thirty minutes, mostly centered around Fiona and Jorge and their work on the island.

***

Alterio stood behind the desk in his study and placed documents into plastic boxes. He thought about how he would handle his next move. He couldn't delay anymore. Arlan and Mauricio's plan was far too logical to try to convince his father-in-law to not support it. His phone rang. It was Joaquin.

"I received a call from Guillermo a few minutes ago. He was contacted by your father-in-law today. It seems that he has been presented with a new development plan from the gringo and his attorney, and he likes it enough to have asked that our plan be put on hold."

"Yes. I was there. It was an impressive presentation."

"You need to tell me about it."

Alterio did. When he finished the basic details, Joaquin let out an audible sigh.

"It seems that you are not in control of your developer. I will take this news to my boss—your partner." He hung up.

Alterio assumed that things could get ugly for Arlan and Mauricio. Maybe even Fiona. But none of that was his concern. They had served their purpose. Alterio picked up his cell phone and called Jose.

Chapter 36

After Arlan and Mauricio's presentation, Fiona asked Arlan to come with her to Isla X'lak to swim with whale sharks. He didn't need an explanation, but Fiona gave him one anyway. Some wealthy birders from the US were visiting the Yucatan, and Fiona had convinced them to take a couple of days to see the whale sharks. She told Arlan that she felt obligated to visit with them because they were financial supporters of her environmental organization and concerned about the habitat destruction of the northern Yucatan, which was the seasonal home to a couple of hundred species of migrating birds.

They arrived on Isla X'lak the next afternoon and walked through the bustling village. They had time to sightsee. They would swim with the whale sharks the following morning.

"This place is changing. There's construction everywhere," Fiona said.

"Yeah, but take a close look. These are ejiditarios spending the money they have received from Don Francisco and his partners. They're putting additions on their homes and building apartments in their back yards," Arlan said and jumped with Fiona to the side of the sand road as a golf cart sped by.

"What was that?" Fiona asked.

"A golf cart on steroids. That thing is as fast as a car."

"One thing I meant to ask you about during your presentation was what happens to this village once you have put another village full of resorts on the other side of the island?"

"We need to protect its cultural heritage and help rebuild their school, which was destroyed a few hurricanes ago, and improve roads, which are nothing but ditches every time it rains, and improve solid waste removal. The landfill here is a joke. Have you ever seen it?"

"Unfortunately."

"We have a responsibility to help this village and its residents—if they want it. But look around. It's astounding what damage a boat-load of money given to a poor fishing village can do. What looks like progress is the slow destruction of the island's social fabric. This used to be the friendliest place I'd ever seen. On the surface it still is. But there's trouble here in paradise."

"What do you mean?"

"About two-thirds of the ejiditarios have sold their land on the other side of the island to Alterio. Some are still waiting to be paid. Most of those who sold made a lot of money. I'm talking millions. Remember, this wasn't even their land. It was communal land that the government gave to them. So it's not like they had mortgages or notes on the land that needed to be paid off. And they had a special agreement with the government. They were able to keep all of the money—tax free. None of the money from the sales went to help the island or its people who happened not to be ejiditarios, which is most of them. The ejiditarios bought newer and faster golf carts, new boats, homes in Madre or Cancun, and built additions to their island homes. I heard that one them bought a Porsche. It can't be driven on these sandy roads. It's stored and rotting away in a dilapidated garage in Punta Eek."

"I can see evidence of that," Fiona said and skittered out of the way of a large three-wheeled motorcycle.

"Some who have pissed through the money banded together through an attorney friendly to one of Alterio's competitors and are suing Alterio and his partners for more money. They are convinced that they should get their land back and sell it again—without returning the money they received from Don Francisco. The attorney is using the newspapers to portray the partners as wealthy men who want to destroy the island and saying that their clients want to protect the island from environmental devastation."

"I've seen those stories. They seem convincing."

"Yeah. They are the same ejiditarios who, at this very moment, are slashing and burning mangroves around the village to make way for little lots to sell to tourists." A small scooter drove by them with a teenage girl driving, a toddler nestled between her legs, and a young boy sitting on the flat wire back of the scooter where books or groceries would have normally ridden. They giggled and laughed at villagers as they passed. "Nobody here wants to save the island from development. They all want the same thing—money, and lots of it. The whole ejido system and its privatization is flawed and corrupted beyond belief. These people are lottery winners. Do you know the history of lottery winners? Far too unsophisticated with finances to understand how to manage windfall profits, they go broke."

"But there are only one hundred and fifty or so ejiditarios," Fiona said.

"And they've taken all of the money. Flaco has told me that the younger generation is angry at their mothers and fathers who are the ejiditarios. They have sold their heritage. They'll see nothing from the windfall profits—no land, no money, and no infrastructure improvements."

"That's where the anger comes from that you talk about?"

"Some of it. But there'd plenty to go around. The ejiditarios who didn't sell are angry at those who did, or want to. I mean, this is brother against brother and sons against father shit. The ejiditarios who are suing the partnership for more money are against everybody—even each other. The entire population seems to be living up to its cutthroat pirate ancestry. It's all about money. They all want what Alterio has promised—a new Cancun."

They walked together through the village and stopped for ceviche and broiled fish at one of the funky restaurants on the plaza. Afterward, they walked across the plaza to their hotel to meet with Fiona's birder friends and eventually get some rest for an early morning swim with the whale sharks. Arlan hadn't asked about the room arrangements on the way in. Fiona had simply told him that she had booked some rooms at a popular small hotel on the plaza. It was late when they finished their last bottle of wine with Fiona's friends, who walked up the wooden stairway to their rooms in the same sixteen-room hotel. Fiona led Arlan to the room she had booked on the ground floor.

"Do I have a room?" Arlan asked.

"No. You can stay with me. I have two twin beds in the room."

"Oh. Okay," Arlan said, and they spent the night in separate beds.

***

The next morning Flaco showed up with Loco and his lancha. They loaded up their gear and headed out into the open sea. It was the same routine they had done many times.

An hour later Arlan said to Flaco, "We're pretty far out."

"Loco told me the whale sharks have been migrating closer to Cancun this year."

"Does he know why?"

"He and some of the other fishermen think that the food they eat is moving. A group of scientists was here last year and hired Loco to take them out to where the whale sharks feed. They came back to follow up on the study last month and said that, in addition to the plankton, the whale sharks might be feeding on eggs from fish that spawn offshore."

"What kind of fish?"

"We don't know. It's not one we fish for."

"All the more reason to learn more about these animals before we screw up their habitat."

Loco shouted and pointed to a group of boats a couple of kilometers ahead. They approached and saw at least thirty people in the water swimming around one small, twenty-foot whale shark.

"I thought only two swimmers were allowed in the water at one time," Fiona said.

"These captains are all from Cancun," Loco told them.

"We've worked with the captains on Isla X'lak for years, training them how to swim with the whale sharks responsibly. These captains aren't respecting the animals," Fiona said.

Arlan watched the people in the water laugh and grab at the shark as it lumbered through the water gulping down millions of miniscule plankton. They might as well have been on a Disney ride. It was a disturbing sight. Arlan glanced at Flaco and motioned that they should leave. There was no way he was going in the water to further molest this poor shark. He was sure everybody in the boat felt the same. Loco turned east to look for more, hopefully larger, sharks.

Arlan sat next to Fiona and said, "I don't understand why that whale shark was putting up with the abuse. It could have easily swum away. It was as though it was chosen by the entire X'lak whale shark pod to be the sacrificial lamb for the day. The pod said to the whale shark, 'You go out and get molested by these stupid tourists today, and the rest of us will be left to eat in peace. Tomorrow it will be somebody else's turn.'"

Fiona laughed. It was a sad laugh.

They found a group of five much larger whale sharks within twenty minutes and spent time swimming with the gentle giants. Arlan noticed the captain of a passing boat grab his radio microphone. Within minutes the six boats full of tourists who were molesting the lone whale shark had all converged on their location. A minute later more than twenty people were in the water.

It was disappointing. They left the area and motored toward Isla X'lak. Loco trolled for and caught a few fish and prepared ceviche. He anchored off the beach now owned by Alterio and his partners. The ceviche was delicious. Afterward, they motored back to the village and Arlan used the white noise of the fast-moving lancha moving into the wind to think about what they had just seen.

Suppose he was successful in creating a true sustainable destination, one steeped in nature and culture, that attracted the experiential traveler who comes to the destination to enjoy and respect the things the destination has to offer. Suppose it becomes popular, written up in travel magazines, and talked about on travel shows and word of mouth conversations around the world. More people arrive, people with no understanding of the place beyond the truncated version they heard in a thirty second sound bite on CNN or a Sunday Travel Section article that promotes *the next new safe adventure*. Swimming with the whale sharks offers just that. The masses will come and the destination could easily spin out of control and turn Disneyesque.

How can the destination be protected from being loved to death? How is it prevented from evolving too quickly and to its demise? Is it education? Education takes time. It took the US a generation to learn to stop throwing trash out of their cars and onto the country's roadways. Is the answer to limit the number of tourists who can visit the destination? Most resort destinations are an assembly of privately owned land with many owners with different interests. There would never be a consensus to limit tourism. Government-owned land controlled through agencies such as the US National Park Service can limit tourism numbers, as they do in many places. But they don't need to answer to market demands or make profits. One-owner destinations can limit the numbers of tourist visits if they want to also limit their revenue stream. But how many one-owner destinations exist? Very few. Isla X'lak is one of them. Maybe it has a chance. It would take tremendous vision and conviction on the part of all of the Island's stakeholders to maintain a sustainable destination. Was that possible? He didn't discuss it with Fiona. He knew how she would answer.

Chapter 37

El Simpatico sat in a private corner of the VIP lounge area at the Mexico City Airport and listened to Joaquin's report about his phone conversation with Alterio. His helicopter pilot stood nearby and waited for instructions. Raton and Nacho sat on a nearby sofa, within earshot.

"According to Alterio, the gringo's presentation went well. Even Alterio thinks his alternative plan might work... that it would be profitable."

"That's not the point, is it Joacho? How many keys does he propose?"

"A little over three thousand. Maybe my math is rusty but that's twenty-two thousand less than our plan. The cost of his plan would be a fraction of ours."

"That's a big problem," El Simpatico said. "We don't have time for this nonsense. What's Alterio think? Don't tell me he's supporting the gringo's plan."

"Who knows what he thinks? Who cares? The gringo has hired one of the big accounting firms to critique his new plan. Don Francisco wants the plan presented to our group after that's done. And that turtle-loving bitch wants them to make a presentation to her environmental group, including the president's wife."

"Tell Guillermo to get Pierre-Pierre to finish up *our* master plan."

"Claro. Did you talk to your friend?" Joaquin asked.

"That's why we need to move fast. His wife and some key senators are pushing him—hard. He can't hold off much longer. The damn law's going to pass. It's a matter of when. He told me that he'll use his advisors to push our permits through quickly. Once permitted, we're grandfathered. We need our plans finished and the permits formally applied for as soon as possible."

"What about the gringo?"

El Simpatico sighed and thought about his new favorite tiger shark at Banco Chinchorro. But that didn't seem to be an option. He said, "Get rid of him. And his attorney friend too."

"It's about time," Joaquin said and winked at Raton and Nacho.

"Leave Fiona alone. She's no threat."

"I don't know."

"I said no, Joacho. Make this look like an accident. Have Alterio somehow get them in the same car. You know what to do. This cannot come back to us."

***

Alterio was on the phone with Joaquin for the second time in as many days. This time Joaquim had called with instructions. Alterio hung up and thought about the ramifications of the instructions. He felt an unusual sense of guilt. It didn't last long. He shrugged and called Alejandro.

"How was the flight from China?" Alterio asked.

"Long. My clients finally gave in. They've agreed to the price."

"Very good. I've been waiting for this news. Now we can move forward."

"They'll be coming to Mexico as soon as you're ready. But they are still uncomfortable with some of the things you have presented."

"What things?"

"The permits and the densities. Most important, though, seems to be the bridge."

"I've told you before that these things are not a problem. The governor has promised me the densities and permits. You can meet with him when you come to Cancun. You can have your clients talk to him by phone. They have an attorney in Mexico City, no?"

"Si. He is a friend of mine."

"Make sure he is on the phone call with the governor. You have given him the documents from Jose, no?"

"They have all of the legal papers and seem to be satisfied."

"Bueno."

After a long pause, Jose asked, "And the bridge?"

"My family owns the land. They are eager to make money from the sale."

"Claro. I'll be in Mexico City for a few days and will talk to my client's attorney. When should I return with my clients?"

"Two weeks. No more... and one more thing."

"Yes, Alterio?"

"We'll meet your clients in Belize, not in Mexico."

Chapter 38

Alterio sat at a table in the atrium section of his favorite Madre restaurant with Arlan and Mauricio. He'd asked them there to discuss a major boutique hotel's interest in Isla X'lak.

"They like your plan, what I was able to explain to them anyway. One of their top executives is on his way from Miami to Brazil. I have convinced him to stop in Cancun for a day. I'm supposed to meet him tonight. The helicopter will take us to X'lak tomorrow morning at eight."

"That's pretty short notice, Alterio," Arlan said.

"We would need to leave tonight and spend the night in Cancun," Mauricio said. "I have a meeting later today here in Madre that I need to attend."

Alterio's phone rang. It was Joaquin. Alterio pulled the phone close to his ear with his right hand and cupped his hand over his mouth with his left.

"Did you make up a story?"

"Yes."

"Did they buy it?"

"Yes."

"Good. Excuse yourself and go to the restroom. There will be a large man wearing a yellow Polo shirt near the door to the men's room. Introduce yourself to him. Make sure he sees you return to your table and sit down. He needs to recognize Arlan and Mauricio. Do they each have a car at the restaurant?"

"I think so."

"Find out who'll be driving and what time they will leave for Cancun."

Joaquin hung up.

"No problem, Don Francisco," Alterio said loudly into his phone and smiled at Arlan.

Alterio looked at Arlan and Mauricio and said, "That was Don Francisco. I told him about the hotel's interest in our project. He's eager to sign them up. It's one of his favorite boutique chains." He excused himself and walked toward the men's room outside of the restaurant seating area. He introduced himself to the man with the yellow shirt and walked back to the table and sat.

"I think it's better to stay at a hotel in Cancun rather than getting up at four in the morning," Mauricio said.

"That would be good," Alterio said. "We can have breakfast and talk about your plan before we fly. We'll need to take the big helicopter. It's difficult to talk in it. The headphones never work well." He looked at the restaurant entrance and saw the man with the yellow shirt enter and look around. He glanced at their table but didn't make eye contact with Alterio.

"I'll drive," Mauricio said to Arlan. "Your little car is too uncomfortable. I'll pick you up at eight this evening."

They finished lunch, and Alterio told them that he would see them for breakfast the next morning in Cancun. He waited outside near the restaurant entrance for Juan to pick him up and take him to his house. He called Joaquin. "They're leaving at eight tonight. Mauricio is driving."

"Good. That'll put them near the rest stop around ten." He hung up.

As Juan brought the SUV up to the entrance, Alterio saw the man with the yellow shirt in the passenger seat of a black sedan in the parking lot of the restaurant. He heard the man's cell phone ring and saw him place it next to his ear. Alterio was close enough to hear the man say into the phone, "Si, the taller one. The Mexican. I'll see what car he drives and we'll wait for him on the Autopista at the oasis. Claro." Alterio guessed that Arlan and Mauricio represented a threat to El Simpatico's plans. He wasn't sure what would happen to them. He didn't care.

***

Arlan drove back to his hacienda to pack for a day or two in Cancun. His phone rang.

"O'Brien!"

"Captain Jay. What trouble are you in today?"

"None yet. But we're gonna change that."

"We are?"

"You betcha. I'm in Madre."

Arlan had forgotten all about Captain Jay's scheduled visit.

"I told you that I had a kid here. I was visitin' him—until my ex-wife booted my ass out. So now I'm gonna come and see you. It'll be a short visit though. I need to get back to Belize tomorrow."

"Well, you can stay here but I'm leaving for Cancun tonight." Arlan thought for a moment and asked, "Did you drive up?"

"Yeah. It's a shitty drive too."

"Hey, if you could give me a ride to Punta Eek tomorrow morning, I'll stick around for the night. But we'd need to leave pretty early."

"Fuckin'-a, tweety," Captain Jay responded. "I'm there."

Arlan smiled. He never understood what any of that meant.

"You remember where I told you I lived?"

"Yeah, I know where it is. I'll be there in a little while."

Arlan hung up and called Mauricio. "You're going to have to drive yourself to Cancun. An old friend of mine is in town. He'll give me a ride to Punta Eek tomorrow morning. I'll ferry over to X'lak and meet you and the helicopter there."

"Alterio won't like it."

"Let him wait for once. You can handle the breakfast discussion."

Mauricio laughed and said, "Okay. See you tomorrow."

***

The drive on the Autopista from Madre to Cancun was as straight-forward and as boring as they get. Mauricio had done it hundreds of times. There were two exits between the two cities—one at Chichen Itza and the other a rest stop, an oasis, at about the halfway point in the center median. The oasis consisted of a gas station and a strip of eight ugly, concrete one-room restaurants open to both sides of the Autopista. East-bound customers exited the highway, diagonally parked, and entered the restaurants through the south openings, west-bound customers through the north. All of the restaurants served the same greasy tacos, panuchos, and tamales. Some served tortas, the closet thing in Mexico to an American sandwich. Mauricio and Arlan laughed every time they stopped at how similar the restaurants were. 'I think the same family runs all of these food shops,' Arlan had once commented. 'Everything is exactly the same in every store.'

Mauricio stopped at the oasis and bought a taco and a bottle of water and continued to Cancun. It was dark. There was little traffic, which was normal. The toll road cost as much from Madre to Cancun as locals made in a day.

A man in one of two black sedans that had been parked in the lot of the oasis watched Mauricio pull away from the food shop and make a phone call.

"The Toyota just left."

"Is the truck ready?"

"Si."

"Ok. You and Raton know what to do. Call me when it's finished," Joaquin said and hung up.

***

An hour later Joaquin sat in his car shouting through his cell phone at Raton. "What do you mean there was only one man in the car? You pendejo! El Simpatico told me that you could be trusted to take care of this problem. You went back to check it, right?"

"Si, Mr. Joaquin."

"Puta! Explain to me what happened."

Nacho said, "The Toyota left the oasis and got back on the Autopista. Raton and I had him trapped. Our cars were side by side in front of him. He couldn't pass us. We took up both lanes. The truck was behind the Toyota—just as planned. We slowed down to let our truck catch up. The Toyota stayed in the right lane. The truck driver moved beside him in the left lane and steered into the Toyota. It ran off the road and hit a big kapok tree. It burst into flames, but the collision alone would have killed him. Saved me a bullet."

"Are you sure there wasn't another person? Maybe the passenger was thrown from the Toyota."

"Absolutely sure, boss. We checked all around the crash site."

Joaquin paused and said, "How could you not tell that there was only one person in the Toyota when you were on the road?"

"It was dark. The windows were tinted."

"Where are you now?" Joaquin asked.

"We are back in Madre, waiting for instructions."

Joaquin hung up and called Alterio. "Where's the gringo? He was supposed to be with the attorney."

"I told them to be in Cancun. Mauricio said he would pick him up at eight. Maybe he decided to drive tomorrow. I don't know."

"Where does the gringo live?"

Alterio told him. Joaquin hung up and called El Simpatico.

"Do I have to do this myself, Joacho? Send Raton and Nacho. Have them kill him there and take his body to the jungle and let it rot. Nobody will miss the gringo." El Simpatico paused for a moment and thought about his sharks, but he knew it would take too much time.

"Something else, Jefe?"

"No." El Simpatico hung up.

Chapter 39

About the same time Mauricio had left Madre for Cancun, Captain Jay showed up at Arlan's hacienda in a beat-up truck with Belize license plates. He wore his trademark flip-flops, shorts, Polo shirt, and sunglasses. Other than a Speedo that he wore when diving, Arlan had never seen Captain Jay wear anything else. They shared a couple of beers and went out to a bar a short distance from the hacienda—walking distance, or staggering distance as it turned out. They sat at a plastic table in the funky neighborhood bar and ordered Sol con limon. Captain Jay was himself—funny, loud, and going out of his way to charm every female within striking distance, regardless of age, size, or disposition. Fortunately, he didn't hit on anybody's wife—at least not while their husbands were present, or none that their husbands cared about. There were no fights. Arlan spent the time updating Captain Jay on Isla X'lak and Alterio.

"Your friend, Alterio, sounds like a complete asshole."

"Na. He's ambitious and manipulative. I don't trust him, but he's harmless. It's because of him that I have an opportunity to develop a great project."

"So? He's an asshole. Watch your back."

They staggered back to the hacienda around midnight. Arlan showed Jay one of the guest rooms just off the large open portico. It was the only guest room with a bed in it. He walked through the portico and the two-story library and into the master bedroom, which was four times larger than his entire flounder back in Virginia. He fell onto his bed for a couple of hours sleep.

Arlan woke up to a loud thud—a thud that resonated through the hacienda's concrete structure. He sat up. It was still dark but the sky was brightening. He heard a couple of grunts and slaps and then a gurgle. He half ran, half walked through his bedroom and library and into the portico.

"What the...?"

Captain Jay was squared off with a man holding a knife. Another man was lying awkwardly near the steps to the lawn. His body was draped over the side of the old concrete cattle trough that served as a fish pond. His head was face down in the water. Even in the dim light Arlan saw that the water was red with blood. There was a handgun lying on the step next to the body.

Arlan shifted his eyes back to Captain Jay and the man with the knife. Captain Jay, much larger and more powerful than the man with the knife, was crouched in a defensive position between the dead man and the man with the knife, whose back was against the portico wall. He took three quick swings at Jay with the knife. Jay jumped back with each one, but it looked as though the third caught him on the left side of his torso. Arlan shouted and went for the handgun near the dead man, keeping his eyes on the fight. The man slashing at Jay glanced at Arlan, and that was all the opening Jay needed. He attacked and shoved the man hard into the concrete wall of the portico and pounced on him. Arlan grabbed the handgun and looked for an angle to fire from without hitting Jay, which was impossible at the moment. Jay was all over the man. He had grabbed the wrist that held the knife and jerked it behind the man's back, which forced the man's body around, his face hitting the wall hard. Jay grabbed the knife with his right hand and stuck it into the man's neck. The man slouched to the floor with the knife still in his neck. Blood pooled immediately around his head.

Arlan couldn't believe what he was looking at. He and Jay had gone through a lot when they lived together in the Caribbean. Arlan had been shot at and threatened with knives. Death was not normal, but it happened. It was one thing to come across a fatal accident or drowned bodies in the ocean or maybe a bloody knife fight, but when confronted with two fresh bodies in your home, floating in their own blood, your mind tends to go to a surreal, far away place—

as if you are witnessing the bloody scene through a filter. Arlan was sure that his mindset would be far more focused on reality if he'd been the one doing the killing.

Captain Jay was out of breath. He was bent over with his hands on his knees. He smiled at Arlan and said, "These stupid fucks were tryin' to kill me. Imagine that O'Brien."

"Well, I guess you showed them."

"Who the fuck are they?" Jay asked. "Friends of yours?"

Arlan looked at the man with the knife sticking into his neck and said, "I don't think so." He shook his head and asked, "What the hell happened?"

"I heard footsteps. Got up and saw them sneakin' around. That shithead," he pointed to the bloody fish pond, "was carryin' a gun. I came out onto the porch to see what they were doin'. When they saw me they attacked. I gave the shithead with the knife a kick in the gut and fell back against the wall. I went after the gun, got that asshole's arm behind him, and rammed him head first into that column." Captain Jay looked at the dead man's head bobbing lightly in the water. He smiled and said, "Guess it was a bit too hard for him."

"The bastard with the knife knew how to use it. The fucker cut me."

"Yeah, I saw. How bad is it?"

Captain Jay pulled his shirt up and pointed to a long but not too deep cut on his ribs. "Can you believe it O'Brien? He cut me. Pissed me off."

With his shirt still lifted, Arlan saw the familiar scars from long ago knife and gun fights next to the cut. This one wasn't deep. It probably wouldn't even leave much of a scar. He looked at one dead man and then the other. *These guys messed with the wrong man.*

"You don't know these guys?" Arlan asked.

"Nope."

"Who'd you piss off on this trip?"

"Only my wife. She knows some bad asses around Madre, but she wouldn't do this. I still send her money now and then. I made a few enemies when I lived here. But none knew I would be here. Maybe they're after you."

"Me? I'm just a developer. What threat am I to anybody?"

They stood with their hands on their hips, Jay breathing normally again. "Maybe it was a robbery," Arlan said.

"Then why not wait until you were gone durin' the day?" Jay glanced around the portico and said, "Doesn't look like you can lock the place up."

Arlan stopped asking questions. He couldn't figure it out. "Maybe it's as Mauricio says... it's Mexico. What do we do now?"

"I ain't hangin' around Mexico to see. We're not reportin' this, either. You and I are gringos. No matter what it looks like, we'd be the ones goin' to prison. Help me put them in my truck. I know of a cenote a couple of hours south of here. I'll dump them there. But I'm gonna continue the back way to Belize. I'm not comin' back here for a while. You'll have to find another ride to Punta Eek."

Arlan hesitated. Captain Jay was right. He didn't see any other choice.

Arlan helped Jay wrap the bodies in the two bedspreads. They loaded them one at a time into the back of Jay's truck, and they used logs and branches left in a pile by the gardener to cover up the bedspreads.

Jay put his hand on Arlan's shoulder and said, "You look scared. Don't worry about it, O'Brien, or should I call you rookie again. There are assholes all over the world. They deserved it." He looked into the bed of the truck, saw the bedspreads and logs, and laughed. "You're just lucky I was here to save your ass—again."

Jay got into his truck and closed the door. He started to drive away. Through his open window he shouted, "Just like old times, eh, O'Brien?" Then he was gone.

Arlan stood and watched the taillights disappear. *Not really,* he thought.

But he knew he was very lucky that Captain Jay chose that day to visit—and that the bad guys chose the wrong day. He wondered if he'd ever find out who they were or why they'd chosen his house to rob.

***

A few hours later, Arlan tried to call Mauricio and got no answer. The same with Alterio. He wasn't going to Cancun or the island after what had happened. He needed some time to sort out his mind. It wasn't every day that two thugs were killed in your house. And it wasn't as though he could ask about them or tell anybody.

He was spraying down his portico and replacing the water in the fish-pond when he got a call from Pepe.

"Mauricio was found dead in his Toyota late last night on the Autopista. It seemed that he ran off the road and hit a tree. The Toyota caught fire and burned. Mauricio didn't have a chance."

Arlan couldn't believe it. Two seconds ago he was worried about the bloody mess on his portico and if Jay got the bodies to the cenote, or if he got caught with them, all of which was stressful enough. But this? This was beyond his comprehension.

"Are you still there?" Arlan could hear Pepe's voice in the phone that was in his hand and held near his thigh.

Arlan raised the phone to his mouth and said, "Okay. Thanks for calling, Pepe. I need to get back to you a little later. I need to absorb this news a little."

"I understand, Arlan. This is hard for all of us. Call anytime you want."

The news hit Arlan hard. He finished his tasks with his mind a million miles away. He forgot all about Captain Jay and the two dead thugs and went about grieving for his closest friend in Mexico.

***

El Simpatico sat across from Joaquin and waited for an answer. They were in a luxury hotel suite in Mexico City.

Joaquin punched his phone to off and said, "It's been two days and I haven't heard from Raton or Nacho. Neither one is answering their phones. The gringo could still be alive."

"We would have to assume so if your men haven't reported in." El Simpatico paused and said, "Is the gringo that good? Or is he lucky? Raton and Nacho are natural killers."

"Maybe the gringo had help," Joaquin said.

"His help must have been very good."

"Maybe Alterio told him they were coming and he is hiding."

"No way. He knows who he's dealing with. He values money and his life. He's not loyal to friends. He has no friends. Find your two stooges. If the gringo is still alive, tell them to find him and follow him—for now. If you can't find Raton and Nacho, you go to Madre and tell me about the gringo. We need to sort this out."

El Simpatico stood and walked to the window. "What have you heard from Guillermo?"

"Nothing much. He told me that Don Francisco's attorney called and wanted to know if we paid the property taxes."

"What's that about?"

"I guess he went to Balam to negotiate the tax bill with the mayor and she told him that it had been paid."

"That makes no sense. Somebody is mistaken. Check it out and get back to me. What is the status of our plan?"

"Guillermo is going to Miami to meet with the planners and Pierre-Pierre in two weeks. The attorney's funeral is this week."

El Simpatico looked to the ceiling and exhaled. "Just see that the damn plan gets finished— *our* plan, Joacho."

Chapter 40

After Mauricio's funeral, Arlan traveled to Mexico City. The hospitality accounting firm he contracted to appraise the island and review his financial model for the project had some preliminary numbers and was ready to meet. He needed solid information and informed opinions that either supported his plan or didn't.

The firm had a strong international presence and a large database from which to work. What they didn't have on file they could get with a phone call. They were accustomed to analyzing single resorts or hotels, but to analyze an entire destination of resorts was a different matter. New destinations didn't pop up in the world very often. They normally grew into a destination after decades of tourism growth. Their task was a difficult one, and they had suggested that Arlan stay in Mexico City at least two nights. They would need an entire day to present their work.

Arlan met with three of the top accountants of the firm in the conference room of their downtown offices. They started with a discussion of the low-density, exclusivity model that Arlan had proposed, and though uncomfortable not maximizing densities, as they would recommend in any resort destination, they generally agreed with the model, given the special status of the island under Mexican law.

"But why not develop the entire beach?" they kept asking. "And why do you propose to set the buildings back so far from the sea?"

"Turtle nesting, beach dunes, and indigenous flora that no longer exist in other places throughout the region, a strong sense of privacy, and the island's uniqueness need to be protected in order to keep the destination authentic. That's what will attract our market—a market that couldn't give a damn about Cancun, or any place similar."

They continued their discussion and talked about background data, product mix, and costs. The discussion came back to the beaches.

"It doesn't make sense to us," one accountant said. "Beaches are the most valuable places in resort locations to build hotels or villas."

Another accountant added, "We would have to lower the value of the beachfront where there's no development."

"Have you ever been to St. John in the Virgin Islands?" Arlan asked them.

Everybody nodded. Two had been and the other was familiar with it.

"It's about the same size as Isla X'lak. It's mountainous, whereas X'lak is flat, but there are a lot of similarities. The Rockefellers bought most of the island in the fifties and donated the land to the Department of Interior. Two-thirds of the island became a national park, protecting most of the island's beaches from any type of development."

"That's where Caneel Bay Resort is, right?"

"Yes. And you should look at that reasort as a model beachfront hotel—no golf, no marina, historic ruins renovated or used as focal points, lots of open space, and very popular.

"I lived on the island and developed properties there for fifteen years. My development costs were forty to fifty percent higher than the neighboring islands of St. Thomas or Puerto Rico. That was because of the logistics of moving materials and labor to St. John from the larger islands, similar to what would be needed on Isla X'lak.

"But my sales prices and average daily rates for hotel rooms were one hundred to two hundred percent higher than on any of the neighboring islands. Do you know why?"

The accountants shrugged.

"It wasn't because of the beaches. The other islands had beaches just as beautiful as those on St. John. The difference was that our beaches were empty. Every buyer I sold anything to on St. John and every tourist who rented my rooms had one common strong reason to seek out St. John and continue to come back. The beaches were protected by the federal government from any development—forever. There were very few beachfront homes on the island. They don't have to be beachfront to be valuable. They simply need permanent access to protected beaches."

After another hour of discussion, they took a break. Arlan used the time to catch up on e-mails. The accountants huddled in an outer office. Two hours later the discussion resumed in the conference room.

"We have reviewed all of the numbers you sent and, of course, your plan for the island," the financial expert said. "And we all agree that the development approach that you propose is the best way to go. And we agree substantially with your financial forecasts."

"It's really the only way you can take the project," the head accountant said.

"I have a group of planners and economists in Miami who wouldn't agree with you," Arlan said. "They're trying to plan another Cancun."

"I can't imagine who would have that kind of money. Only governments can afford to sit on those kinds of start-up costs."

"Or drug cartels, as one of our team members remarked recently," Arlan said with a smile. This elicited shallow laughs. The joke fell flat. Arlan realized that this was Mexico, and these men knew not to take any discussion about cartel dealings lightly. All walls could have ears, and anybody, no matter how well you thought you knew them, could be involved with or threatened by a cartel.

"We have worked up a preliminary report for you. You can take it with you and review it. We'll go over it with you when you're ready."

Arlan was handed a thick report. The word *preliminary* took up most of the cover page. He thumbed through it. There was far too much detail to go over in one sitting. He placed it on the table and was handed another report. It had three pages.

"You also asked us for an appraisal of the island... one as is, which is simply the land with nothing on it, and another built-out version that assumes that the island is fully developed. For our purposes, we address the built-out of the first phase only."

"That's fine," Arlan said as he looked at the appraisal.

After a cursory look, he said, "I can't disagree with your *as is* appraisal, but the value you place on the *built-out* version seems very low."

"There's a lot of beachfront that is not being developed with your plan. We can't place the same value on it that we place on developed beachfront."

"But the undeveloped beach makes everything else more valuable," Arlan said.

"But that's not conventional thinking."

"Exactly."

"How can we justify that?"

"You didn't listen to what I told you about St. John and the national park influence on values," Arlan said.

"We talked about it. It helps increase the value somewhat."

Arlan was quiet for a few moments. How could he get these guys to understand exclusivity?

The accountants seemed to be waiting for Arlan to respond.

Arlan slapped his hand on the table and said, "What's Central Park worth?"

The accountants looked at each other.

Arlan continued, "It's open space... mostly usable open space. It can't be developed. It's a park, the most famous park in the world—an oasis in a desert of concrete. If it didn't exist what would the values of all of the real estate around the park be? Even if you could develop the park into additional condos and hotels and apartments, the value of the additional real estate wouldn't come close to the value of all of the buildings and real estate on the park and within a couple of blocks of the park. It's the open space that gives the surrounding real estate its high values."

The accountants looked at each other and said nothing.

"Do you propose that the island of Isla X'lak is worth more if we line up structures, like a ribbon, from one end of the beach to the other, impacting every linear foot of beach? Where, then, is our Central Park?"

The accountants asked for the rest of the day to discuss the appraisal and possibly adjust some numbers. Arlan returned late in the afternoon to review the new report. The accountants sat in the conference room with sheepish smiles. Arlan opened it to the first page—the summary. He smiled. The value of the island developed as a low-density, sustainable destination far exceeded that of a high-density mass tourism destination. Not only could the mass tourism model not be developed logistically and legally, lot and villa sales and hotel room rates couldn't come close to prices of the model based on exclusivity. Validation—finally... at least on paper.

Now it was time to prove it. He had to build the destination.

***

Arlan returned to Madre and visited Fiona, whom he hadn't seen since Mauricio's funeral. It was late afternoon. They stood a short distance across the net from each other on her tennis court and casually hit tennis balls back and forth. Arlan called it a short game. It was usually for warm-ups. The object was to hit as many soft slices back and forth as possible, keeping the ball within the service court area. Neither felt up for a competitive match, and lethargy dominated even this little exercise. Both had been hit hard by Mauricio's death and they had yet to discuss it. After twenty minutes of heat and silence, they retired to a nearby table and a pitcher of lemonade a kitchen servant had brought when she'd seen that they had finished hitting. Arlan lightened the mood by focusing the conversation on the island and telling Fiona of his trip to Mexico City and his meetings with the accountants.

Fiona filled their glasses with lemonade and said, "Congratulations, Arlan. It looks as though the partners will have to listen to you now."

"I don't know. Don Francisco seems to care enough about it that he's asked me to find money for the development. He still has to sell the idea to his Mexico City partners."

"Don Francisco can't raise the money?"

"No. We've gone beyond his ability to raise money. He can find a few million here and there, but we'll need a couple of hundred million dollars for his half of the development costs. I'm working with a banker who lives in Houston. He's Mexican and knows Don Francisco. He thinks we can find money in China. We plan to travel there to make presentations next month."

A peacock strutted by and onto the tennis court.

"What are the chances of the partners in Mexico City accepting your plan?"

"They should embace it. It makes sense for the island and is a lot less expensive to develop. I can't imagine why they would choose the more costly route." Arlan paused and took a long drink of lemonade. "You know, Alterio may be the key, and I still don't know what he wants. I can't even find him."

They heard what sounded like a loud "help" from the garden around the side of Fiona's house—then another.

Arlan stood to run toward the sound and asked, "What the hell? Is somebody in trouble?"

Fiona laughed, spitting lemonade around the sides of the glass she'd started to drink from. Arlan saw why a moment later. The peacock that had screamed strutted around the corner of the house in full bloom and made its way to the tennis court, where the less colorful female waited.

"That's what peacocks sound like when they're interested in sex."

"Jesus, it sounded like someone in distress. I hope I don't sound like that," Arlan said and sat down.

Fiona wiped her mouth with a cloth napkin and said, "I haven't seen Alterio lately, either."

"He missed the funeral, which I thought was strange. I hear he's been traveling. He's probably looking for money."

They sat in silence for a moment and watched the peacock courtship taking place where they had just been playing tennis.

"Of course, if you're going to get the island declared a wildlife preserve, I shouldn't waste any time or money traveling to China," Arlan said, fishing for information about her efforts.

"Do I pick up a little sarcasm, Arlan?"

"It's just..." Arlan looked down and tried to collect his thoughts. "It's just that I'm so close to being able to develop a sustainable tourism destination—one that will raise the bar around the world with respect to environmental protection and education. One that will be financially successful and copied by other developers."

"I'm very proud that you were able to come up with a plan for the island that will protect it. But you know that I don't trust its future. We've discussed that aspect. This is Mexico, after all."

"But, Fiona, putting a project together on paper doesn't prove anything. I need to build it."

"I hope you get the chance. But my priority is to see the island a federally protected preserve. You know that, Arlan."

"I'm serious, Fiona. If you're close to getting the island declared a preserve, then I should cancel my trip and start looking for a new job."

Fiona took a drink. She set her glass on the table, smiled, and said, "I think you better keep your plans. We're going to get the mangrove law passed but maybe not much more. It's difficult. But we're still trying. We have a few more rabbits up our sleeves." She stood and said, "I need to take a shower. Are you going back to the hacienda?"

Arlan hesitated and asked, "Is your guest room available?"

Fiona sat back down and took a drink. She chewed on one of the few small chunks of ice that had been floating in the lemonade and kept her gaze on the pitcher. When the ice was gone she bit her lip.

"I saw you," Arlan said.

Fiona looked up, cocked her head, and raised her eyebrows.

"The last time I stayed. I saw you come toward the guest room and turn around and leave."

"Oh. I was just looking for a book," Fiona said, and offered a tight smile.

They sat in silence for a few minutes and watched the peacocks continue their mating ritual.

"That's not true," Fiona said, staring down at her glass.

Arlan waited.

"I coming to your room, but..."

"Why did you change your mind?"

Fiona took another drink and watched the peacocks scurry away when one of her Jack Russell dogs chased an iguana up a tree on the other side of the court.

Fiona looked back to Arlan and said, "I need to tell you something."

Arlan waited.

"I feel just horrible about Mauricio's death."

"We all do, Fiona."

Fiona sat up and crossed her arms on the wet table. "Wait. Let me finish. I didn't come into your room that night because of Mauricio."

"What?"

"Well... That night I did get cold feet. I didn't trust my feelings toward you. I haven't since we met. But every time since the night in the library that we've been together I've shied away because of Mauricio."

"What?" Arlan knew this meant that they had, or were having, an affair. He hoped there was another explanation, but his gut told him to expect the worst.

"It's not what you think. I met Mauricio years ago when he was just out of law school and working with an NGO that I work with occasionally."

Fiona took another drink. She put her glass on the table and stared at it. She looked up and said, "My husband had been dead a couple of years by then. I think I was over my grief, and Mauricio had something that was special. You recognized it too. You two had become close friends in a very short time. Anyway, I was lonely, and Mauricio and... we had an affair."

Arlan sat back, as far back as he could in the upright metal chair. He didn't expect that. After a moment he smiled.

Fiona's face reddened. "You're laughing."

"No. I'm smiling."

"This is funny?"

"No. But I'll bet you thought that I would be angry."

"Well?"

"No. Not at all. I think you two would have been a perfect fit. I can see why it happened."

"Except for the age difference. My God, Arlan, this is Mexico. More than that, this is Madre—a city of almost a million people with the small town gossip like a town of two hundred. Mauricio was ten years my junior. Had the affair been found out, he would have been laughed out of town—a young lawyer from a prominent family hooked up with older gringa, head of a national NGO."

"What about reputation?"

"I'm gringa. We don't have to live with the same social formalities expected from the Mexicans, especially the Yucatecans."

"What? Are you kidding? Most of the prominent men in Madre have mistresses. Hell, there are scores of those funny hotels around the beltway that cater to afternoon trysts. They drive in through a gate, talk into an intercom to order a room for an hour or two, a carport door automatically opens next to the room, they drive into the carport, and the door closes. When they're finished, a buzzer to the front desk brings a servant who places a bill on a lazy susan on the wall of the hotel room. The man, or woman, rotates the lazy Susan, pays the bill, and they leave, never having seen, or been seen by, another human."

Fiona looked shocked. "Arlan, you sound like an expert on these hotels."

Alan smiled and said, "No. I'm not. But a friend of mine is." Arlan thought back to Captain Jay's description of them. "I've wanted to check them out..."

Fiona looked even more dismayed.

"No, no. Not like that. I meant..." Arlan stammered. His joke had backfired. He said, "I mean... what a real estate play."

It was Fiona's turn to smile. "Can you be serious for a moment longer, Arlan?"

"I'm sorry," Arlan said, relieved that he'd made a fast recovery. Then he said, "I just don't get the double standard in this culture."

"It's not just culture. But your story about the hotels makes my point—affairs are not flaunted here, and there's big trouble if they are."

"So what does this have to do with Mauricio?" Arlan asked.

"You two were close and, my God, you worked together so well and were doing so well with the plans for Isla X'lak. I was afraid that if we were together it would come out eventually that Mauricio and I had an affair. I was afraid that it might damage your relationship with either me or Mauricio, or both."

"Was this an ongoing affair?" Arlan asked.

"No. It was short and happened years ago, before Mauricio was married and had a daughter. But we've worked together on many projects since. He's always been a gentleman and never brought it up. He was friendly, but professional. It just made me so happy to see the way you two worked together," she repeated and looked down into her lap.

"Fiona, you're just a few years older than I am. But that attitude is old-fashioned. Give me some credit. We've all had relationships or marriages in the past. Big deal. This is *now* and Mauricio is dead." Arlan hated to be so blunt, but something told him that Fiona needed to hear it.

They watched the male peacock strut back onto the tennis court with a weary eye, watching for the dog that had disappeared around the side of the house. It kept strutting until it reached the other side of the court, where it fed on insects at the base of a large bearded ficus tree and its multiple aerial roots.

The female peacock returned, and the two birds continued their mating dance. The cock turned his back to the hen and ruffled his tail feathers. The hen responded by not running away, and the cock fanned and vibrated his blue and yellow plumage. The hen strutted back and forth a few feet from the cock. The female paused and moved closer.

Fiona broke the silence and said, "I just needed to get that off my chest. Nobody else has ever known about it." Fiona rose from the table and said, "The guest room is not available."

Arlan, dejected, said, "Oh."

Fiona came around to where Arlan sat. She bent down and kissed him. She straightened back up and said, "My room is available though." She smiled and walked toward the house.

Arlan called after her, "Aren't you afraid of your reputation?"

Fiona turned and said, "Hell no. You're gringo. I think most people we know have been expecting this for a while."

"Damn," Arlan grunted and walked toward the house.

***

The next morning Joaquin called El Simpatico.

"Jefe, Raton and Nacho have disappeared. I am in Madre, outside the gringo's place. It's a big hacienda. I have been coming by off and on for the past two days. There is no activity here except a gardener, who told me that he had seen the gringo come in briefly yesterday with a travel bag and then leave. I came back last night, but the gringo did not return. He must have spent the night some other place."

"So, he is not dead, Joacho? Do you think he took out Raton and Nacho?"

"I am not sure."

"Drive to Cancun. We will meet on my yacht tonight and make a plan to deal with this mess."

Chapter 41

Alterio and Jose sat at a table in a far corner of the Cancun Airport VIP lounge. Alterio hadn't been back to Madre since Mauricio was killed. He felt just a little remorse. Not enough to lose sleep. He wondered how the hell Arlan had escaped Joaquin and his killers. It didn't matter. He doubted he would ever see him again. And it would be a while before he would return to Madre.

"These are all of the tax receipts from the mayor?"

"They are all in front of you. All in your name," said Jose. "Are you sure you want it that way?"

"For this deal I do."

"Claro. I see you got her to take a little less than two million. But how did you get her to let you pay taxes for the lots still in the trust?"

"She figured we were eventually going to buy them. I told her it would save time, and I let her raise the tax amount a little. She needed the money to buy a house in Madre. I'm glad we squeezed more money from the trust though."

"Me too. Taxes for those lots just cost you another five hundred thousand. But with them, you have the whole island—everything outside the village anyway." Jose pointed to the documents on the table and said, "I created titles for the additional lots."

"Are they real?"

"They have my stamp on them. That is all you need."

Alterio smiled.

"They will hold up until somebody checks the public registry." Jose then said, "You will need to sell the land quickly."

Alterio signed a document in front of him and put it on the stack next to him on his right.

"That's the last one. Are you taking these to the public registry this afternoon?"

"Yes. They're closed for lunch until four thirty." Jose looked at his watch and added, "They're open until seven thirty. I'll stamp them and get them all registered today." He placed the stack of documents in his briefcase.

Alterio said, "I'm leaving for Belize in an hour. I will meet with Alejandro and his clients tomorrow."

Jose pulled a file from his briefcase and handed it to Alterio. He said, "You have an unrestricted offshore account at Bank Caribelize. It's set up and ready to go. I placed the money that didn't go to pay real estate taxes in the account."

"Claro. One thing, how long do you need to make up more original titles to bring to Belize?"

"I'll need two days... I assume that you will need some time to negotiate."

"I won't need any time. The price is set—four hundred million dollars." Alterio leaned forward and placed his right elbow on the table. He put the back of his index finger against his lips and stared out onto the deck.

"You just thought of something else?" Jose asked.

"Maybe... but I'll tell you later."

Jose fidgeted.

"What is it, Jose?"

"What about your family, Alterio?"

"I have arranged for that. My wife may not want to join me after this is done, but I will have my children join me in Belize next week. They will be escorted across the border by a friend who works for immigration in Chetumal."

"Okay. I'll see you in Belize the day after tomorrow. The Fort George Hotel, no?"

"Si."

***

Alterio sat alone in the second row of the turboprop plane owned by a Belizean airline. The new flight from Cancun to Belize City made traveling back and forth a lot easier. He didn't like the road from Cancun to Belize any more than anybody else. The road was bad, the drivers were bad, and there were too many military checkpoints.

The plane landed at Belize International Airport, and Alterio grabbed his bag from the overhead compartment. He traveled light, expecting he would only be in Belize for three or four days. Then he planned to go to Europe, where he would buy any clothes he needed. He took a cab to the Fort George Hotel and gorged himself with an early dinner.

The next day, after a late, room-serviced breakfast, Alterio left his room and walked down an exterior hallway to a flight of stairs that led to a side entrance of the lobby. He was one hour late for his meeting with Alejandro and his Chinese clients. The lobby was crowded, which didn't bother Alterio. He wasn't worried about privacy, not here anyway. The room was filled with people making all kinds of deals—some legal, some illegal. Some of the people in the room would get rich. Most just talked about getting rich. Alterio was there to get rich. He was there to finally hit a financial home run—one he'd been planning since he and Alejandro hatched the plan several months earlier.

Alterio spotted Alejandro sitting on a large, cushioned sofa looking nervously around the room. Two Chinese businessmen sat in cushioned chairs across from him. To Alterio, they could have been twins, right down to their polo shirts, khaki shorts, and loafers. They both had sweat rolling down their chubby faces.

Alterio walked up to the group and apologized for being late. Alejandro stood to make the introductions. As far as Alterio could tell, only one of the Chinese men spoke Spanish, and not well. After a few pleasantries, they sat down. Alterio switched to English, which both seemed to understand. Alejandro's English was bad though. The language problem complicated the discussion.

"Alejandro has explained to me that you represent one of the largest construction companies in the world."

"Twenty largest," the man on the left said.

"He also said that you are interested in setting up business in Mexico to bid on large infrastructure projects sponsored by the government."

"Yes. We in Africa and Central America now. But we have hard time getting into Mexico."

"Buying Isla X'lak makes a lot of sense then. You could use the Isla X'lak project and our contacts as stepping stones for bigger projects."

Alterio translated the discussion for Alejandro in Spanish.

Alejandro nodded his head and smiled. Alterio translated what he had said. He turned his attention to the Chinese and said, "Alejandro told me that resort and tourism development is not your company's main focus, but that you have built a few hotels and casinos in Macau."

"Yes."

"Perfect. But you know you will not be able to build casinos on the island."

"That fine. We see your plan and it small for us, only twenty-five thousand keys, but we think it large enough to move our top management people to Mexico. Then you and Alejandro will help us get government projects," one of the Chinese said.

He smiled at Alejandro. Alejandro smiled back.

This was news to Alterio but a good negotiation strategy on Alejandro's part. If he were to stay in Mexico, he and Alejandro could make a fair amount of money introducing the Chinese to their political contacts. But Alterio wasn't staying in Mexico.

"Why we no close the deal in Mexico?" the man on the left asked Alterio.

"Taxes. You understand, no?" Alterio said with a smile.

They both laughed. Alterio told Alejandro what he had said in Spanish. Alejandro shook his head and offered a nervous laugh.

The men smiled and started conversation with Alejandro in Mandarin.

"Alterio, se preocupan por los permisos y el puenta," Alejandro said to Alterio.

Alterio looked at the men and said, "There is no problem. Alejandro and his attorney in Mexico City explained that to you and your attorney. No?" Alterio paused. "You have seen the letter from the governor that approves the project, no?"

"But we not know if you have permits."

"You will get permits. The governor's letter guarantees it. But you must design your project first. Permits are issued only to the owners of the land. They are not transferable. It would do no good for us to get permits and then sell the land to you."

"But we could buy your corporation that owns property," one of the Chinese men said.

These men are smart, Alterio thought. He said, "I own the land. It is not owned by a corporation or a partnership."

The two Chinese men looked concerned. One asked Alejandro a question in Mandarin. Alterio interrupted and explained to Alejandro in Spanish what he'd just told the Chinese. He didn't give Alejandro a chance to respond to him or the Chinese.

Alterio turned to the Chinese and said, "The attorney in Mexico City explained all of this, no? We have been working toward the development of the island for a long time—until you came along and decided to buy it. We have a development plan that we were going to submit for permits, but it might be different than what you want to develop. I will see that you get copies of everything."

Alterio translated for Alejandro, who nodded his head in agreement. The men talked in Mandarin for a while. Alterio saw smiles and assumed that they were comfortable with his explanation. They asked about the bridge.

"The bridge will be permitted by the governor, and the land where it will be placed is owned by my family. You have been given all of the documentation. My attorney will be here tomorrow with titles and a letter from the governor that approves the bridge."

They talked more between themselves. One of the Chinese men pulled out his cell phone and made a call. He looked at Alterio and said, "We have money ready to be wired as soon as we close deal."

Alterio smiled and looked around the room. He wasn't sure how to tell them what he was about to say. He hadn't told Alejandro yet. It was better to make this kind of change at the eleventh hour. *It was simple psychology*, Alterio thought. Once the purchase was envisioned in their heads it was hard to take a one-hundred-and-eighty-degree turn and back out. Besides, five hundred million was a better number—it was a round number.

"Just one more thing," Alterio said. He paused and said, "The price is five hundred million dollars."

He watched the Chinese men talk rapidly to each other in Mandarin and then to Alejandro. Alejandro tried to calm them down. He looked at Alterio. "Como? No era el acuerdo."

"Lo cambie."

"Mierda."

Alterio listened to the argument. He understood none of it. He didn't care. He had just made another one hundred million dollars.

***

Jose arrived in Belize the next day and called Alterio from the airport.

"I have everything we need. All of the land is registered. I talked to our new banker here in Belize and told him to expect a large amount of money to come in from China in the next day or two."

"Very good. Did you tell the banker how much money to expect?"

"Four hundred million."

"Call him back and tell him five hundred million. Then fly to Ambergris and meet me at Ramon's Village Hotel. There has been a delay. We are going to go diving."

"But, Alterio..."

Alterio had hung up.

Alterio had flown to Ambergris Cay soon after he'd given the Chinese the news of the price increase. Before he left, Alterio had met with Alejandro. Alejandro would babysit the Chinese for as long as it took for them come around. Alterio told him not to worry. They would pay the five hundred million. He told him that the Chinese stood to make that back times ten if they got the government contracts they coveted.

Alterio had been to Ambergris many times. He liked Belize and thought it might be a good place to live and invest. He had checked into Ramon's late in the afternoon and was led to a room on the beach. He kicked back on the bed for a late siesta and started to leaf through the promotional brochures in his room. There were a lot of advertisements for dive operations and much written about the Blue

Hole. He'd never been there but always wanted to. He called the front desk and asked for the manager.

"Captain Jay. That's who you want. He's the best," the manager told Alterio.

Alterio decided to forego the siesta. He put on his shorts and sandals and walked fifty meters down the beach to a pier where the manager said Captain Jay's Dive Shop was located.

Alterio stepped up onto the wooden pier, kicked the sand from his sandals and walked to the dive shop, which had been built a few meters out onto the pier's left side. Two dive boats tied along the pier across from it were riding gentle waves that continuously stressed and then relaxed the bow and stern lines. Each had dive tanks resting in wooden saddles that had been attached to the gunwales.

"Can I help you?" a voice shouted from inside the shop. The door was open, and Alterio stepped through it and into the small, crowded shop. The unpainted interior walls were adorned with scuba gear and underwater photos. Swimsuits and T-shirts hung from clothing racks in the center of the shop. Various flip flops and dive footwear were on display on shelves on one side of the shop. A tall, blond man stood behind a glass counter counting money from a shoebox that seemed to serve as a cash register.

"You lookin' for somethin' particular?" the blond man asked.

"Hi. My name is Alterio Delgado, and I understand that you are the best diver in Belize. I would like to go diving."

The blond man looked for a moment at Alterio, as if he was trying to remember where he'd seen him before. "Alterio Delgado. You Mexican?"

"Yes, I am from Madre, in the Yucatan. Have you been there?"

"No, other than trips for provisions across the border in Chetumal, I've never been to Mexico." He looked outside at the setting sun and said, "It's a little late for divin'."

"No, I mean tomorrow. I am here in Belize to close on a real estate deal, but the negotiations have been delayed for a day or two. I thought that I would finally take time to see the Blue Hole."

"Well, , you're in luck. I have a dive to the Blue Hole planned for tomorrow morning."

"Very good. My attorney will be coming in tonight. He would like to come along. Do you have room for both of us?"

The blond man opened a notebook lying on the glass case top.

"I know this is late notice. Price is not an issue," Alterio said.

"Sounds like you're makin' a killin' from your real estate deal. Are you sellin' land in Belize?"

"No. I am selling land on Isla X'lak. That is an island near Cancun. I am selling almost the entire island."

"Wow. It must be worth a fortune. Who has that much money to buy an island?" the blond man asked with a smile.

Alterio smiled and said, "The Chinese. They'll buy anything."

"Good for you. How did you get ahold of so much land, anyway?"

Alterio smiled again and said, "It is a long story, but I can tell you that my attorney and I made some savvy deals to get control of the land."

"Wow," the blond man said and finished counting the money from the shoebox. He shoved the cash into a pocket in his shorts and looked up at Alterio. "What are you gonna do with all of the money you're makin'?"

"I have thought for a long time about investing in Belize. It is close to Mexico and far easier than Mexico to get clear titles to land."

"Well, you should stand in line. There are a lot of investors comin' into Belize these days."

"Really? Maybe you can introduce me to somebody who can show me some properties for sale. I would be interested in hotels."

The blond man smiled and held out his hand. Alterio shook it. "My name is Captain Jay. I need to know the name of your attorney so I can put it into my schedule," Captain Jay said and pointed to the notebook.

"Yes, very good. His name is Jose Manuel."

Captain Jay wrote the name in the notebook and said, "Okay. You're both set for tomorrow. Seven in the mornin'."

"Just one thing, captain. How much does the dive cost?"

"Don't worry. You can afford it. We'll do two tanks. It's a long way to go for a one-tank dive. I'll make you a special deal."

"Very good. Thank you," Alterio said and started to leave. He turned to the captain and said, "Just one more thing... is a dive business lucrative?"

"You betcha. In a lot more ways than just makin' money."

"Very good," Alterio said and walked out of the shop, having not understood the captain's answer.

Chapter 42

Arlan sat at the table in the portico of his hacienda with his laptop open. He was making plans to travel to Miami to meet with the Train and then to the US and possibly China to find funding for Don Francisco. He pondered something Fiona had told him on the phone a couple of hours earlier. She was in Mexico City lobbying for Isla X'lak and was heading into a meeting with the president's wife. Don Francisco's attorney, Pepe, called, interrupting his thoughts. He told Arlan that they needed to talk—immediately.

Arlan drove to Don Francisco's office and was led into his private conference room.

Pepe and Don Francisco were seated at the small round table with documents spread out in front of them. Don Francisco didn't wait for Arlan to sit. He said, "Alterio has taken our land."

"What land?"

"All of it. All of the land from the trust and our partnership."

Arlan plopped down into the chair next to him.

"How did he do that?"

"We should have seen it coming," Pepe said. "He paid the property taxes last week. We thought our partners paid them. They didn't."

"How does that give him the land?" Then Arlan remembered the argument he overheard in the village of Punta Eek when he first met Alterio.

Pepe continued, "All you need in Mexico is a crooked notario and a lot of balls, and you can steal any land you want. Having a receipt that shows you paid the property tax along with the fake title convinces the people at the public registry that you own the land. They don't question it. Alterio and his notario, Jose, are pros at this sort of thing. In this case, though, they bolstered their claim with an expired power of attorney that Don Francisco gave Alterio years ago. Jose changed the dates, notarized it, and Alterio used it."

"But you brought in partners. They must have required that the titles be put into the partnership name, right?"

"Those were not the terms of our partnership agreement."

"There were contingencies?" Arlan asked.

"The titles to the land on Isla X'lak were to remain in Don Francisco's name until permits for the project were awarded by the federal government. They would then be transferred into the partnership. We insisted on that when they demanded that they be in charge of the permitting process and brought in Pierre-Pierre as the overall director."

"Alterio had alluded to something like that when I questioned him about the partnership. But I never knew the details."

"If we had received permits and the titles to the land put into the partnership, Alterio couldn't have used the doctored power of attorney."

Arlan slumped in his chair.

Don Francisco said, "We didn't know. You were right to fight the project our partners wanted."

"Do your partners know about this?" Arlan asked.

"We called Guillermo this morning as soon as we found out."

"What are you going to do?"

"Find Alterio. Have you heard from him?"

"Not for a while."

***

Arlan left Don Francisco's office. He wondered what shit storm would come from Alterio's latest escapade. He would need to cancel his plans to go to China. Hell, he thought, he'd need to cancel his plans for everything in Mexico.

Arlan's phone rang as he pulled up to the hacienda. He answered it.

"O'Brien. You still among the livin'?"

"Thanks to you I am, for now. Jesus, captain, you won't believe what has happened." Arlan figured that keeping things to himself applied only to those involved with the project. He told Captain Jay about Mauricio's death, Alterio, and the land.

"Your friend, Mauricio, died the same night we were attacked?"

"Yeah. I never thought about it that way. A coincidence."

"Right. You're still a rookie, O'Brien. What are you doin' to find the asshole who stole all of the land?"

"I'm doing nothing. I suspect that Don Francisco and his partners are looking everywhere."

"Well, you're one lucky rookie. I'm callin' you because I wanted to tell you that your buddy, Alterio, and a friend of his, named Jose, have just signed up for a dive trip to the Blue Hole. He's a big barrel-chested guy. A real talker. Real polite and shit, right?"

"Sounds like him."

"I know it's him. How many Alterio Delgados are there in the world? I just wanted to make sure. He sat in my office and gave me a boatload of information."

"What kind of information?"

"Let's just say that you need to watch your ass, O'Brien. I think he's got help. And I think those guys at your hacienda were part of it."

"Bullshit. Alterio's not violent."

"Jesus, Rookie."

"What are you going to do?"

"You just watch your ass. I'll take care of this."

Arlan paused and thought about this. He was pretty sure it was bullshit.

"You need to call the police," Arlan said.

"You kiddin', O'Brien? What the fuck are the police gonna do? You think they give a shit? This is Belize."

Arlan figured he could call Don Francisco and Pepe, but what could they do? They had no political clout in Belize, and Jay was right—a land theft in Mexico wouldn't upset the Belizean authorities. He absent-mindedly said, "Maybe he'll be eaten by a shark."

"Maybe," Captain Jay said and hung up.

A moment later Arlan thought, *Shit, I need to call him back to tell him that I was just kidding.*

Fiona called.

"You'll never believe it," she said.

"The mangrove law passed."

"That's right. But there's more."

"More?"

"I just left the president's wife. Arlan, I'm so excited. It will be announced tomorrow or the next day. The island will become a federally protected preserve."

Arlan's shoulders slumped. He held the phone away from his ear. That one sentence made him realize how deeply competitive, and selfish, he'd been with respect to Isla X'lak. The ejiditarios, Alterio, the partners in Mexico City, and countless consultants had been fighting for the island to become the next Cancun. Arlan had been fighting to showcase an internationally recognized sustainable tourism destination. Fiona had been fighting for simple preservation—and had just won the war.

Arlan raised the phone to his ear and said, "That's great, Fiona. I am very happy for you."

"Just be happy for the island," she said. "I'll see you tomorrow."

Arlan hung up and thought of the ramifications. They were endless.

Arlan tried to call Captain Jay but there was no answer. He tried again the next morning and still couldn't reach him.

Chapter 43

Alterio and Jose left the hotel dining room where they had just finished breakfast and walked to the beach toward the pier that housed Captain Jay's Dive Shop. Both wore baseball caps, white tennis shoes, and shorts they had purchased at the hotel's tennis shop the night before. Their T-shirts were too small for their large frames and their white legs looked as though they had never seen the sun.

As they struggled through the sand, Jose belched and said, "There's only one boat tied to the pier. Maybe they left without us. We should go back to our rooms."

"Jose, we have a day or two to kill. Then we'll be wealthy. What else is there to do here? I thought you liked to dive." Alterio wiped the sweat from his forehead with the back of his forearm.

"I enjoy shallow water close to shore. This Blue Hole thing scares me."

"Plenty of people dive in the Blue Hole. It's safe. Stop worrying. What could go wrong?"

They continued to trudge through the sand toward the dive shop, stepping over anchor lines tied to palm trees on the beach and the sterns of a couple of dive boats bouncing in the surf just offshore. The boats were held fast by bow lines anchored farther out in the sea. Each time the boats rose with a wave, the line tied to the palm went taught and rose a foot above the sand. Alterio timed his step and just barely made it over the line before it tightened. Jose's back foot got caught by the line, and he stutter-stepped forward with his front foot. But it wasn't enough and he fell onto the sand. He got up, looked around, and brushed sand from his knees and palms. Alterio laughed at his notario's clumsiness but didn't say anything.

"Are you sure my briefcase is all right in the room? Maybe I should go back and see if the hotel has a safe," Jose said and used his shoulder to wipe sweat from his brow. "All of the paperwork is in it."

"It's safer under the mattress. Besides, the titles for the Chinese still need your signature and stamp to be legal. And my titles are copies of the originals in the public registry, no?"

"But, Alterio, the bed looks funny with such a large lump under the mattress. Maybe I should stay with the briefcase."

"Don't worry, Jose. The maids won't take a briefcase full of papers, and nobody from Mexico knows we're here, except Alejandro. And he won't tell anybody. He'll make a lot of money when we close the deal."

They were almost to the pier when Alterio saw the tall blond man he had booked the dive with. He came out of the dive shack built into one side of the pier and dropped two large blue mesh bags into a center-consoled dive boat tied alongside the pier opposite the shop. Alterio pointed and said, "I think that's the owner of the dive shop. See? They haven't left yet. Come on."

The captain watched them approach as the two Mexicans stepped up onto the wooden pier. Jose caught his new shoes on the edge of the pier and stumbled forward, regaining his balance before he fell. Alterio saw the captain rest his hands on his hips and shake his head.

"Hello, captain, do you remember me from yesterday?" Alterio shouted.

Alterio and Jose stopped in front of the captain. Jose peered down into the boat.

"I remember. You're late."

"I'm very sorry. I had an emergency," Alterio lied. "This is my friend, Jose."

Jose held out his hand. Captain Jay ignored it and walked over to his shop to close the door.

"Are we still going to the Blue Hole to dive?"

"Did you bring any gear?"

Alterio shrugged and said, "We don't have any gear. I'm very sorry." Alterio looked into the boat. "What kind of gear do we need?"

"Most people who come to Belize to dive have their own masks and flippers. Some have their own regulators. The captain pointed to the mesh bags and dive tanks stored on the boat and said, "No problem. I have all of the equipment y'all gonna need."

"Yes, that's fine. But one thing..." Alterio pulled his cell phone from his pocket and asked, "Will we have phone reception?"

"No. We'll lose service a few minutes after we leave the dock."

"How long will two tanks take? I need to be able to call somebody by tonight."

"That's not a problem. I can have y'all back by five, maybe six in the afternoon."

Captain Jay walked across the twelve-foot-wide pier to the dive shop and closed the door. He looked at Alterio and Jose and asked, "Ya'll ready?"

Without waiting for an answer, he stepped next to the boat and jumped down onto the deck. The boat rocked when he landed. Alterio followed and the boat rocked hard toward the pier. He fell back and was caught by Captain Jay before falling in the space between the boat and the pier.

"Thank you, captain. I almost fell."

"That wouldn't be good. We wouldn't want you to get hurt, would we?"

Captain Jay looked up at Jose and asked him to sit on the pier and slide into the boat. Once aboard he told them to make themselves comfortable.

"Are there other divers coming?" Alterio asked.

"No. A young couple on their honeymoon had signed up, but I guess they're still gettin' to know each other." The captain laughed. "They canceled."

"Very good. And one more thing, do we stop for lunch someplace?"

"I've got lunch and drinks in the cooler."

The captain started the engine and untied the boat from the metal cleats on the pier. He pushed off, stepped back to the center console, and pushed the throttle to forward. The boat was up on plane in ten seconds, a little longer than usual.

Jose sat in the back on a cushion he placed on the hard plastic seat. Alterio sat across from him. The wind rushed passed their heads, making a normal conversation difficult.

Alterio leaned close to Jose and said, "Why are you sulking, Jose? We're going on a great dive."

"I don't like long boat rides. And I don't like diving in deep water."

"Relax. I'll be with you and our captain seems competent. He is the best in Belize."

The boat beat into three-foot waves. Alterio stood and wobbled toward the center console. He reached out to an aluminum rail that ran down the side of the console and grabbed it before he fell.

"Captain, thank you for taking us out. I'm sorry that we were late."

"No problem," the captain said and stared ahead at the sea. "You and your friend better hold on. We're headin' into some open ocean for a while. We'll hit a few large waves before we reach the hole."

"Will there be calm water where we are going to dive?"

"Smooth as a baby's butt."

"Good. Jose sometimes gets seasick."

"Just tell him to stick his head over the side." Captain Jay adjusted the trim on the motor to compensate for the heavier surf. With one hand on the wheel and one on the trim button, he looked behind the boat at the wake. He turned to Alterio and asked, "Are you both certified?"

"I am. A friend of mine owns a dive business south of Cancun. He gave me a certification card."

Captain Jay nodded and said, "How 'bout your friend? Can he dive?"

"He doesn't like it as much as I do. But he has been diving with me before."

Captain Jay put both hands on the wheel. He looked straight ahead and said, "That'll do."

They rode in silence for a while, something Alterio was never comfortable with.

"Captain, what is in that plastic barrel on the bow?"

"Fuel."

"Oh, okay," Alterio said. He looked beyond the bow to a large wave cresting just ahead of them and bent his knees to take the blow. He asked, "Will we need it?"

Captain Jay smiled. "It's for emergencies."

After ten minutes of bouncing into the seas Alterio asked, "Captain, can I ask you a question?"

"Fire away, it's your nickel."

"You gring... Americans... have many strange expressions of speech," Alterio said with a laugh. He braced himself for another large wave. The boat shook when it hit the valley of the wave. He looked back at Jose, who'd just turned back from the side of the boat. His face was white and vomit dribbled from his chin.

Captain Jay drove the boat into another large wave. Alterio looked to his right and saw what seemed like calmer water. He pointed south and asked, "Isn't the water calmer over there?"

Captain Jay glanced in the direction Alterio pointed and said, "Too many coral heads close to the surface. Can't take the boat over there."

Captain Jay turned to look straight ahead, but Alterio was sure he saw the captain smile.

They bounced in silence for the next twenty minutes. Alterio staggered back to sit with Jose. An hour later the captain let up on the throttle, and the boat came down from its plane to a much slower speed. Alterio could see coral just under the surface on all sides. Some of the stag horn coral breached the surface between the shallow wave crests. They motored over the coral for a few minutes until it abruptly disappeared, and they were in deep blue water.

Captain Jay drove the boat a couple of hundred meters and shut off the engine. They drifted slowly to the west.

"Okay, caballeros, here we are—the Blue Hole."

"Do you speak Spanish, captain?"

"I know a few words."

"Have you been to Mexico?"

"Only across the border to Chetumal. I shop there for provisions sometimes. It's a pain in the ass to get in and out of the two countries though. Maybe I should drive up there sometime. I'd like to see Cancun. And I keep hearin' about an island near Cancun where the whale sharks congregate. They say you can swim with them."

Alterio looked around. There was no land. No boats. Just the calm Caribbean Sea protected by the barrier reef.

The captain continued, "You know, we have whale sharks here late in the winter. They come to mate, I think. I've looked for them underwater near Glidden Cay, but I've never seen them. I think I'll go to Mexico, to the island near Cancun to swim with them. What's that island called? Isla Ex lax? Something like that."

Alterio looked around and said, "I don't see any other boats."

"This time of the year y'all may not see another boat out here for days."

Alterio looked down into the water. "This is really blue. How deep is it here?"

"Four hundred feet," the captain answered and walked to the bow to grab the mesh bags.

Alterio looked back at Jose. He didn't look happy. Alterio walked to where he sat. Jose looked up, his face still white.

Jose leaned toward Alterio and said, "The captain doesn't seem very friendly."

"He's just gringo."

Captain Jay brought the bags to the stern and tossed them in front of the Mexicans.

"Find some gear that fits. I'll get the tanks to the stern. I'll drop the dive tray, and once you've found gear that fits I'm gonna want y'all to sit down with your backs to me with y'all's legs in the water. I'll put your tanks on you. All y'all will need to do is buckle them up and slide into the water. Got it?"

Alterio and Jose took their snorkel gear to the tray and sat on its edge. They donned the flippers they had each chosen and placed the masks over their heads. The masks already had snorkels attached to the head straps.

"Excuse me, captain. What will we see in four hundred feet of water?"

"Y'all are likely to see all kinds of sea life if you stay in one place long enough. But we're driftin' toward the eastern edge of the hole. By the time I put y'all in the water y'all will be close to the wall. There's a lot more small fish in the holes in the wall."

"Just one more thing. I don't see any dive equipment for you. Aren't you diving with us?"

"Nah. Y'all are certified. The water's too deep to anchor. I'll stay with the boat and follow your bubbles. When y'all get down to five hundred pounds of air, come up. I'll get y'all back in the boat, and we'll prep for the next dive."

"But, one more thing. How deep should we dive?"

"Stay around sixty or seventy feet. There'll be plenty to see."

The captain placed the tanks and buoyancy compensators on the Mexican's shoulders and reached around to fasten them in place with the Velcro straps and plastic buckles.

"Let out some slack in your straps," he told them both.

Alterio's Velcro belt barely closed around his stomach.

The captain handed each of them one of the small yellow boxes Alterio had seen him put on the boat earlier.

"What are these?" Alterio asked.

"They're shark repellents. They're the newest thing. They emit high frequency vibrations which repel any shark that comes too close."

Jose had already put his mask over his face. It had fogged up, but Alterio saw his eyes widen at the mention of sharks.

The captain opened a pocket on their vests and told them to put the boxes inside.

"Are there sharks down there?" Jose asked.

"Y'all are likely to see one or two. But they won't bother you. They never do in the hole. But since I'm not gettin' in the water, I want y'all to feel comfortable. So, if you swim with these y'all don't need to be worried about sharks. But y'all should wanna see one or two anyway. It always makes the dive more excitin'."

"Okay. Thank you. I had a friend once, a gringo like you... Sorry, I didn't mean to call you a gringo," Alterio said.

"I *am* a gringo. I've been called a lot worse."

"My other friend was a diver and spear fisherman. He had told me about sharks being attracted to speared fish because of the low frequency vibrations they give out when thrashing around on the end of the spear."

"He was right."

"Do we turn the repellent on now or only if we see a shark?"

"Go ahead and turn them on now. There's a switch on the top. Ya see it? Here, I'll turn them on for you," Captain Jay said and reached into each vest pocket and flipped the shark repellent switches.

"Now, y'all see that button on your buoyancy compensator?"

They each looked around and were slow to find the buttons. Captain Jay leaned over and pressed the button on Alterio's vest first. The button opened a valve and air was forced into the vest from the tank. He did the same for Jose.

"Now, when y'all get in the water make sure your masks don't leak and that y'all's regulators work. Then hold this hose up." He placed the hose that had been attached to the vest with Velcro so it wouldn't flop around in the water into each of their hands. "When you press this button on the end, the little bit of air I put into y'all's vest will escape, and y'all are gonna sink. Got that?"

The two divers slid off the dive platform and clumsily bounced around on the surface for a minute. Alterio hadn't been diving for a while and kicked his flippers back and forth like mad to try to stabilize his body and the heavy tank on his back. The captain shouted and gave them an okay signal by making a circle with his thumb and index finger. Alterio returned the signal and lifted the hose on his BC and pressed the button. He looked over and saw that Jose had done the same and also had the sense to clear the fog from his mask with sea water. His face showed pure fear. They sank into the blue as the air was released. Both of them kicked wildly on the way down as they tried to get comfortable with the tanks and the buoyancy compensators. Instead of a controlled, feet-first descent, they slowly rolled and somersaulted their way down.

After clearing the pressure in his ears for the fifth time, Alterio felt as though he was in better control of his descent. He reached for the hose on the left side of his BC, the one he knew had a depth gauge and showed how much air the tanks had in them. He couldn't find it. He reached over his left shoulder, found the base of the hose, and was able to slide his hand down its length and to the gauges on the end. Sixty feet. Just under three thousand pounds of air.

Jose was in free fall and floated just past Alterio. Alterio reached out, grabbed his BC, and pulled him up. Jose had a little blood swishing around the bottom of his mask. He hadn't cleared the pressure in his ears properly on the way down, and the lining of some blood vessels in his nose burst. He didn't seem to know it, and Alterio wasn't going to communicate it to him.

They stabilized at seventy feet. Alterio looked around. He saw nothing but blue. There was no wall and he wasn't sure which way to swim to find it. He thought about going back up when he glimpsed a shadow on the far reaches of his visibility. It had a large tail. It swished twice and was gone. He turned a slow circle and saw a trio of large fish swim by. Maybe they wouldn't need to find the wall to see fish.

Alterio had just relaxed enough to enjoy the dive when he saw another dark shadow come out of the blue. This was definitely a shark. Jose hadn't seen it yet. Alterio watched as it swam within thirty feet of them. It turned, giving Alterio its full measure, then disappeared like a ghost in the same direction it had come from. He was glad the captain had given them shark repellents.

Alterio was happy to stay below the boat and not swim blindly to find the wall. Just as the captain had said, he saw several large fish swim in and out of the limits of their underwater visibility. Even Jose seemed to relax. Alterio saw him smile at a small school of curious fish as they swam by.

A couple of minutes later, chunks of something from above floated past them on their way to the bottom. Each one left a trail of milky green goop in the water as it sank. Most of it was unrecognizable, but Alterio was sure that he had seen fish heads and what looked like animal hooves in the mix. Within minutes, the water around them was a cloudy, milky green, diminishing the visibility. Alterio felt for the shark repellent in his vest. It was pulsating, something it hadn't come when he had turned it on.

Alterio had no idea what was going on, but he was pretty sure that it was time to get out of the water. He looked over at Jose to get his attention. A four-foot-long shark came out of the murk and hit Jose in the back of his head, knocking his mask off. Jose panicked and started to thrash toward the surface. Alterio followed him up.

The water was cloudier the closer they got to the surface. Alterio felt something large bump against him. He turned to see a large shark a few feet from him. It slowly swam away.

Alterio heard a bubbly scream. It was Jose. A six-or-seven-foot shark had his left calf in his jaws and was shaking it violently, the whole time pulling Jose into deeper water. Alterio felt real fear. He needed to get back to the boat.

He kicked as hard as he could and clawed at the water with his hands. Bubbles from his regulator rose to the surface faster than he swam. He had to get out of the water and into the boat. He was going to be rich. He felt another bump and kicked out as hard as he could. He made contact with something. He looked down through the bubbles and the murk and saw that it was Jose. Blood still spewed from his leg. He had to get away from Jose. He was bleeding and attracting the sharks. Alterio kicked out at Jose again. He looked up. Just a few more feet and he'd be on the surface, and the captain would save him. He looked back down. Jose had disappeared. He saw a couple of large, thrashing tails in the murk beneath him where Jose had been.

Alterio broke the surface and turned in all directions to look for the boat. He didn't see it. He turned a circle and frantically looked for a boat, any boat, or land, anything that would get him out of the water and to safety. All he saw was the plastic fuel barrel bobbing up and down with the light surf. Its lid was off, and it listed at such a steep angle that, with each bob, seawater gushed in and came back out red. Alterio reached out for it, but it filled with seawater and sank just below the surface. Behind where the plastic barrel had been, in the distance, he saw their boat. It was speeding out of the entrance to the Blue Hole. The captain had left them.

My money. I have to get out of this water.

Alterio felt a bump from below. He put his mask back into the water. A large shark with light, almost invisible, wide stripes on its side brushed him and swam a few feet in the opposite direction. It slowed and seemed to have dropped its pectoral fins and simultaneously humped its back. It turned toward Alterio and charged him with lightning speed. Its jaws grabbed onto Alterio's upper right thigh. Alterio felt no sharp pain, just unbearable pressure on his thigh and hip. The shark shook Alterio's body like a rag doll as it swam downward. Another shark had bitten the top of the regulator next to the back of Alterio's neck. It hung on and shook for a few seconds before it released what was obviously not food. Bubbles of compressed air blasted from the broken hose. Alterio felt another shark clamp onto his left forearm and shake hard, back and forth, as it tried to separate his arm from his body.

But I'm going to be wealthy. I can't die here.

Alterio's world went black before the frenzy reached eighty feet.

Chapter 44

El Simpatico walked with Joaquin to his helicopter. He was seeth-
ing, not so much at losing sixty or seventy million dollars, but at
losing it to that pendejo, Alterio. And the way he lost it. He was
out-maneuvered.

"You find that bastard. Bring his head to me. I want his balls
stuffed in his mouth."

"What about the gringo and the turtle lady?" Joaquin asked.

"You'll get nothing from them. Leave them alone. I'm going
to meet with my friend, the president, and his two advisors who
are on our payroll. I would like to find out what happened to their
cojones. They lost them somewhere. They'll pay. I think we'll drop
a few dead bodies at the border and tell the US where to find them.
That'll keep the president and his advisors busy. And we'll keep
doing it until they find us another opportunity."

***

Arlan met with Don Francisco and Pepe, and they told him that the
partnership with the Mexico City group had been dissolved. Once
it was established that Alterio had stolen their land, the government made a deal with both partners. They offered them, in lieu of
cash compensation for their land on Isla X'lak becoming a federal
preserve, a tax credit that could be carried forward anytime over
the next ten years. The tax credit amount was equal to their total
investment—what they could prove. Arlan knew that extortion
money and bribes wouldn't be disclosed or credited.

"What about the locals?" Arlan asked Don Francisco.

"The ejiditarios are angry at the government for turning their island into a preserve. You know those guys. They were trying to get the land back from us so they could sell it again and again. It seems that they can't do that now."

"What about Alterio?"

"We don't know. Rumors are that Alterio and Jose have disappeared to Cuba."

"With what money? Do you think he was able to sell the land he stole before it was declared a federally protected preserve?"

"Nobody has come forward to make a claim, not that it would do them any good. But he stole titles to ejido land near the village too. Who knows how much the land is worth. Maybe a couple of million dollars."

"That wouldn't last him very long."

"No, it wouldn't. We've also heard that he and his notario stole land near Punta Eek by paying unpaid taxes and falsifying titles. We think they sold it to a Spanish group for three million dollars."

"That still wouldn't be enough for *Alterio* to disappear."

Arlan wondered if Alterio had made it to Cuba, or if Captain Jay might have taken Alterio for the swim of his life. He was pretty sure it was the latter. Captain Jay squashed anything he considered a problem, whether a person or a mosquito, with equal lack of compunction. Arlan wasn't about to share any of his thoughts with Don Francisco, or anybody else—ever.

***

Arlan and Fiona met in Punta Eek. They hadn't seen each other for months. After a warm hug they stepped onto the ferry to Isla X'lak. Thirty minutes later, they checked into a hotel on the plaza in the center of the village. After a lobster pizza dinner they shared a bottle of wine in the hotel lobby.

Fiona asked, "How is the flounder?"

"It's good. Just like I remember. I'm glad that you and your sister allowed me to use it again."

"I was sorry to see that you gave up the hacienda."

"I didn't need it anymore. I was spending most of my time at your place."

"Well, then I was sorry to see you leave Mexico."

"I'm back."

"Temporarily," Fiona said.

"The project is kaput. I need to find something new," Arlan said. He didn't mention Captain Jay's warning and that he'd grown tired of looking over his shoulder for threats that would be hard to recognize and harder to do anything about. It was Mexico.

They sat for a while, sipping their wine. Fiona asked, "What are you going to do now?"

"I'm not sure. I might write a book."

"Really? You should write about this island and your experience here."

"I don't think so. It's too fresh. You know... the *tragedy plus time* thing."

"It would be a good story," Fiona said.

"Yeah, it would. But I'm thinking of a different story." Arlan took a sip of wine and asked, "Have you ever been to Belize?"

Fiona cocked her head.

"There is somebody there I would like you to meet. He's quite a character and has saved my butt more than once."

***

Early the next morning, Flaco and Loco brought Loco's lancha to the ferry dock where Fiona and Arlan waited with mesh bags that contained snorkeling gear, towels, and sunscreen. A cooler full of drinks and ingredients for ceviche was on the boat. After a round of hugs and handshakes, Loco motored the boat around the island and into the open sea.

On the way out, Flaco approached Arlan and said, "Loco's father is ejiditario. He wants to know why you and Fiona fought so hard to turn their land into a wildlife preserve."

Arlan looked at Flaco and then to Fiona. Flaco didn't have his facts quite straight, but he deserved an answer, if there was an answer.

Flaco said, "He wants to know why they can't profit from their land the same way other ejiditarios have. Why can't they sell their land?"

"Flaco, most of the ejiditarios on Isla X'lak sold the land they were given by the government. They made a lot of money from Alterio and his partners."

"But Loco's father was one of the ejiditarios who didn't sell to Alterio."

"Flaco, the land is gone."

"But they are entitled to their land. It is their heritage."

"Their heritage? It wasn't their land in the first place. They didn't buy it. Their fathers didn't own it and pass it down to them."

"But their fathers *did* own the land."

"No. Nobody owned the land. It was communal land *for the people*. But a few villagers were lucky enough to have been named ejiditario when that crap was invented by the government in the nineteen-thirties. And they passed their made-up ejiditario status down to the next generation, and the next. And when the government allowed the land to be privatized, the ejiditarios were given titles to the land and could do with the land whatever they wished. It was a gift. They won the lottery."

Arlan took a drink of water from the bottle he was holding and looked at Fiona, hoping that she would smile or say something that would ease his building anger. Mauricio was dead, and the social fabric of the village on Isla X'lak was in tatters—those who sold out against those who didn't. Other villagers were pointing fingers, blaming anybody they could find for losing their ability to cash in on the next Cancun.

Arlan said, "And what did they do with the millions of dollars they received from Alterio and his partners? I don't see any improvement to the island. All I see are the ejiditarios with flat-screen TVs on the walls of their palapas, bigger golf carts, and new boats. Oh, and a Porsche rotting away in a shed in Punta Eek." Arlan paused again and asked, "How many ejiditarios are on the island? One hundred and fifty? And how many people live on the island? Two thousand? What did the people get when the money rolled in? Nothing."

"But Loco and his father want to know why they aren't allowed to make money by developing their land into a resort like Cancun."

"They already made money. They sold the land that was gifted to them by the government." Arlan paused and said, "They'll still be able to fish and offer whale shark tours. Tourists will still come to the village."

"But that is a small business. It doesn't help Loco or his father put food on the table. Most of the ejiditarios got just a small amount of money for the land. It is gone. They cannot build large hotels. They see their cousins in Playa del Carmen or Isla Mujeres and wonder why they cannot be as wealthy."

"It's all about the money, isn't it, Flaco?"

"They need to survive. There are not enough jobs to go around. Their children will move to Cancun or Madre to find work."

"Then they shouldn't have sold out to Alterio. There were other options."

"But he promised..."

"What he and everybody else promised wasn't sustainable. Maybe if the ejido had insisted on the protection of the environment things would have been different. Fishing, swimming with whale sharks, the beaches, the turtles—all the things people come to see now could have been developed on a larger, controllable scale on the other side of the island. Loco and his children, and their children, and all the people of the village could have opened small businesses that catered to the tourists who would have come to fish or swim with the sharks or simply hang out in the village. It wouldn't make the ejiditarios short-term millionaires, but it would provide lucrative and productive work and a stable economy for the island for decades to come. And the village and its culture would be preserved. That's *sustainable*." Arlan placed his hand on Flacco's shoulder and said, "They got greedy, Flaco."

"But they were promised... now it is a wildlife preserve. It cannot be sold."

"You mean, it cannot be sold again," Fiona said.

"Fiona's right," Arlan told Flaco.

Fiona said, "I think that many people, including the president, were tired of the circus that surrounded the island. The vultures gathered as soon as they sniffed out the rumor that Isla X'lak would become the next big tourist attraction. None saw Loco or the village or the flora and fauna. They saw only dollar signs. Arlan's plan was a good one, and it might have worked if he had the control and cooperation he would have needed from the locals and the government. As Arlan often says, greed, arrogance, and stupidity are powerful contributing factors that destroy too many places just like Isla X'lak. The risks of those factors becoming the dominant force that would control the future of the island were too great. Many of us felt that something needed to be done, including several influential people close to the president."

Arlan said, "The ejido sold out to developers who wanted to build a new Cancun. If left unchecked, the island would have been over-developed, and the turtles and the whale sharks would be gone. All that would be left would be the beach—and that, too, would disappear as soon as developers started to replace the protective dunes with their hotels. And there might eventually be a bridge to the island. A lot of people would have been made rich, but none of them would be islanders. The islanders would have been displaced and forced to move to Punta Eek or farther away."

The conversation drifted and then petered out completely when they realized that there were no easy answers. The mood brightened, though, when they spotted a pod of fifteen sharks. They swam, unmolested by other boats, in the same area for almost three hours.

Afterward, they motored toward the new pier on the north side of Isla X'lak. A research boat was tied up on the windward side of the wooden pier. Three small lanchas were tied along the pier on the leeward side. Loco found space between the two lanchas closest to the beach and nudged the bow against the pier. Arlan jumped out with the bow line and tied it off. Flaco threw him the stern line, and he pulled the lancha parallel with the pier. Flaco jumped out and took the line from Arlan. He tied it off to a metal cleat. Fiona had already jumped onto the pier. Flaco and Loco stayed with the boat while Fiona and Arlan walked up the pier toward the beach. At the end of the pier was a large sign that read, "Welcome to the Isla X'lak Wildlife Preserve," in both Spanish and English.

Fiona and Arlan looked at each other and smiled.

When they reached the end of the pier, they followed a raised wooden boardwalk to a building not visible from the sea. Above the large entry was a sign that read, "Mauricio Sanchez Research Station and Interpretive Center." Both looked at it with watering eyes.

***

An hour later, after visiting the staff of the interpretive center and the volunteers from Fiona's environmental organization, and taking a short walk on the nature trails carved out of the jungle behind the center, they returned to the lancha. Flaco and Loco had prepared fresh ceviche with the fish Flaco had caught with a hand-held line from the pier. They lounged under the shade of the lancha's tarp and enjoyed their freshly caught, lime-marinated meal.

The rocking motion from the quiet surf, coupled with the day's events, made all of them tired. Conversation was minimal. Loco fell asleep on the hard plastic bench near the engine.

Arlan was first to notice the smoke coming from the jungle a couple of kilometers up the beach.

"What's that?"

Flaco sat up and looked in the direction Arlan pointed. He said, "It's the colonel."

"What's he doing?"

"He's clearing land."

Arlan and Fiona looked at each other.

"Can you take us closer?" Fiona asked.

Arlan and Flaco untied the boat and jumped in. Loco motored at a fast clip just off the beach and toward the smoke. He slowed and put his lancha in neutral when they reached it. The smoke was inland one hundred meters or so.

"Do you want to go to ashore?" Flaco asked.

"Let's stay out here for now. The jungle is thick with thorns and poisonwood trees. We're not dressed for it. I think we can see over the dune."

The boat bounced up and down lightly in the waves. The upswings were enough so that they could see over the dune and into a natural clearing, a savannah, in the middle of the jungle behind the beach. Several locals with machetes were cutting mangroves from the periphery of the savannah and throwing the branches on a fire. The flames danced above the tall grass. White smoke billowed above the flames and dispersed in the gentle breeze off the ocean. Some of it hung near the ground. The colonel's white sailor's suit was unmistakable through the smoky haze.

Fiona sat down on the plastic bench she had stood on to witness the destruction.

"Why is the colonel doing this?" Arlan asked Flaco. "This is a federal preserve."

"The colonel brings a crew out to the jungle several times a week. They've been doing it for a year. They've cleared many hectares."

Fiona put her elbows on her knees and placed her head in her hands. "Why?"

"Because he claims that the land is theirs."

"But it's not. Why don't the people in the village stop him?"

"Most know he's doing it. They join the clearing crew when they're not fishing."

"But why?"

Flaco looked over at the flames and said, "Because they have been promised that their island would be the next Cancun."

By now Loco had shut off the engine. They had drifted closer to the beach. Over the sound of light surf on the beach they heard the colonel shout, "Corte mas... rapido," as he pointed to another cluster of mangroves.

The End

www.ingramcontent.com/pod-product-compliance
Lightning Source LLC
Chambersburg PA
CBHW031951060726
47497CB00016B/1193